The Collected Supernatural and Weird Fiction of Amelia B. Edwards

The Collected
Supernatural and Weird
Fiction of
Amelia B. Edwards

Contains two novelettes 'Monsieur Maurice'
and 'The Discovery of the Treasure Isles',
onc ballad 'A Legend of Boisguilbert' and
seventeen short stories to chill the blood

Amelia B. Edwards

LEONAUR

The Collected
Supernatural and Weird
Fiction of
Amelia B. Edwards
Contains two novelettes 'Monsieur Maurice'
and 'The Discovery of the Treasure Isles',
one ballad 'A Legend of Boisguilbert' and
seventeen short stories to chill the blood
by *Amelia B. Edwards*

FIRST EDITION

Leonaur is an imprint
of Oakpast Ltd

Copyright in this form © 2009 Oakpast Ltd

ISBN: 978-1-84677-854-4 (hardcover)
ISBN: 978-1-84677-853-7 (softcover)

http://www.leonaur.com

Contents

Introduction

Amelia Ann Blandford Edwards was much more than a fine author of ghost stories; she was a remarkable woman in her own lifetime, a woman ahead of her time who possessed a fine intellect and an independence of spirit which would have guaranteed her fame even today.

This special Leonaur book has concentrated upon her extensive writings in the field of supernatural and strange fiction, and as such it represents her literary activities in the first part of her fascinating career.

Born in 1831, Amelia revealed her literary talents at a very early age, publishing her first poetry when she was only seven years old and her first story at the age of twelve. Thereafter, her career as writer seemed ordained and she wrote a rapidly expanding collection of poetry, stories and articles for a number of popular magazines including *Chamber's Journal, Household Words* and *All Year Round*. This put her in contact with a notable literary figure, a ghost story writer and enthusiast, who would influence her writing in the most positive and intriguing way. This was, of course, none other than the publisher of *Household Words*, Charles Dickens.

Although outside the scope of this volume Edwards developed her writing talent to the point where her novels were both published and well received. From 1855, when *My Brother's Wife* was published, she went on to pen a series of well crafted and researched novels culminating in *Lord Brackenbury* in 1880—a runaway success with her public that ran to fifteen editions and which is widely regarded as being her magnum fictional opus.

Edwards' association with Charles Dickens is particularly important for this present volume of her ghostly tales, since it is clear her style—either by design or accident—could be sufficiently close to Dickens' own to convince the reader that he, rather than Amelia—was the actual author.

So it was that one of her short ghost stories, perhaps confusingly titled, *Four Ghost Stories*, was attributed to Dickens until well into the twentieth century when in was finally discovered that Edwards was the author. The potential for this kind of error was, of course, established at the time of original publication because it was commonplace for stories in Victorian magazines to be published without an author's 'by-line'. So convincing was Edwards' version of the Dickens style that her story went on to appear in collections of Dickens' stories until quite recently.

The confusion was exacerbated because, unusually, *Four Ghost Stories* had a sequel titled, *The Portrait Painter's Story*. This, there seems little doubt, was the work of Dickens' pen and so, given the familiarity of his style, it was an error that is easy to understand. The Leonaur editors have taken the liberty of including Dickens' story in this Amelia Edwards collection—in its rightful place immediately following her own—for readers' interest and enjoyment.

1873 was a year of epiphany for Edwards when, in the company of close friends, she undertook a journey of exploration to Egypt. She became smitten with the world of Ancient Egypt and her new found fascination brought an end to her career as a writer of fiction. She became instead a successful and highly regarded writer on Egypt, famed for her books, including chronicles of her travels, most notably *A Thousand Miles Up the Nile,* and contributions to the *Encyclopaedia Britannica* on Egyptology. Edwards dedicated herself to the preservation of ancient Egyptian monuments and artefacts and her work in this sphere, at a time when uncontrolled tourism could have potentially destroyed the history of millennia, cannot, even today, be under estimated.

Amelia Edwards died in 1892

The Leonaur Editors

Monsieur Maurice

1

The events I am about to relate took place more than fifty years ago. I am a white-haired old woman now, and I was then a little girl scarce ten years of age; but those times, and the places and people associated with them, seem, in truth, to lie nearer my memory than the times and people of today. Trivial incidents which, if they had happened yesterday, would be forgotten, come back upon me sometimes with all the vivid detail of a photograph; and words unheeded many a year ago start out, like the handwriting on the wall, in sudden characters of fire.

But this is no new experience. As age creeps on, we all have the same tale to tell. The days of our youth are those we remember best and most fondly, and even the sorrows of that bygone time become pleasures in the retrospect. Of my own solitary childhood I retain the keenest recollection, as the following pages will show.

My father's name was Bernhard—Johann Ludwig Bernhard; and he was a native of Coblentz on the Rhine. Having grown grey in the Prussian service, fought his way slowly and laboriously from the ranks upward, been seven times wounded and twice promoted on the field, he was made colonel of his regiment in 1814, when the Allies entered Paris. In 1819, being no longer fit for active service, he retired on a pension, and was appointed King's steward of the *château* of Augustenburg at Bruehl—a sort of military curatorship to which few duties and certain contingent emoluments were attached. Of these last, a suite of rooms in the *château*, a couple of acres of private garden, and the revenue accruing from a small local impost, formed the most important part.

It was towards the latter half of this year (1819) that, having now for the first time in his life a settled home in which to receive me, my father fetched me from Nuremberg where I was living with my aunt, Martha Baur, and took me to reside with him at Bruehl.

Now my aunt, Martha Baur, was an exemplary person in her way; a rigid Lutheran, a strict disciplinarian, and the widow of a wealthy wool-stapler. She lived in a gloomy old house near the Frauen-Kirche, where she received no society, and led a life as varied and lively on the whole as that of a Trappist. Every Wednesday afternoon we paid a visit to the grave of her "blessed man" in the Protestant cemetery outside the walls, and on Sundays we went three times to church. These were the only breaks in the long monotony of our daily life. On market-days we never went out of doors at all; and when the great annual fair-time came round, we drew down all the front blinds and inhabited the rooms at the back.

As for the pleasures of childhood, I cannot say that I knew many of them in those old Nuremberg days. Still I was not unhappy, nor even very dull. It may be that, knowing nothing pleasanter, I was not even conscious of the dreariness of the atmosphere I breathed. There was, at all events, a big old-fashioned garden full of vegetables and cottage-flowers, at the back of the house, in which I almost lived in Spring and Summer-time, and from which I managed to extract a great deal of enjoyment; while for companions and playmates I had old Karl, my aunt's gardener, a pigeon-house full of pigeons, three staid elderly cats, and a tortoise. In the way of education I fared scantily enough, learning just as little as it pleased my aunt to teach me, and having that little presented to me under its driest and most unattractive aspect.

Such was my life till I went away with my father in the Autumn of 1819. I was then between nine and ten years of age-having lost my mother in earliest infancy, and lived with aunt Martha Baur ever since I could remember. The change from Nuremberg to Bruehl was for me like the transition from Purgatory to Paradise. I enjoyed for the first time all the delights of liberty. I had no lessons to learn; no stern aunt to obey; but, which was infinitely pleasanter, a kind-hearted Rhenish Maedchen, with a silver arrow in her hair, to wait upon me; and an indulgent father whose only orders were that I should be allowed to have my own way in everything.

And my way was to revel in the air and the sunshine; to roam about the park and pleasure-grounds; to watch the soldiers at drill, and hear the band play every day, and wander at will about the deserted state-apartments of the great empty *château*.

Looking back upon it from this distance of time, I should pronounce the Electoral Residenz at Bruehl to be a miracle of bad taste; but not Aladdin's palace if planted amid the gardens of Armida could then have seemed lovelier in my eyes. The building, a heavy many-windowed pile in the worst style of the worst Renaissance period, stood, and still stands, in a fat, flat country about ten miles from Cologne, to which city it bears much the same relation that Hampton Court bears to London, or Versailles to Paris. Stucco and whitewash had been lavished upon it inside and out, and pallid scagliola did duty everywhere for marble.

A grand staircase supported by agonised *colossi*, grinning and writhing in vain efforts to look as if they didn't mind the weight, led from the great hall to the state apartments; and in these rooms the bad taste of the building may be said to have culminated. Here were mirrors framed in meaningless arabesques, cornices painted to represent bas-reliefs, consoles and pilasters of mock marble, and long generations of Electors in the tawdriest style of portraiture, all at full length, all in their robes of office, and all too evidently by one and the same hand. To me, however, they were all majestic and beautiful. I believed in themselves, their wigs, their armour, their ermine, their high-heeled shoes and their stereotyped smirk, from the earliest to the latest.

But the gardens and grounds were my chief delight, as indeed

11

they were the main attraction of the place, making it the focus of a holiday resort for the townsfolk of Cologne and Bonn, and a point of interest for travellers. First came a great gravelled terrace upon which the ground-floor windows opened—a terrace where the sun shone more fiercely than elsewhere, and orange-trees in tubs bore golden fruit, and great green, yellow, and striped pumpkins, alternating with beds of brilliant white and scarlet geraniums, lay lazily sprawling in the sunshine as if they enjoyed it.

Beyond this terrace came vast flats of rich green sward laid out in formal walks, flower-beds and fountains; and beyond these again stretched some two or three miles of finely wooded park, pierced by long avenues that radiated from a common centre and framed in exquisite little far-off views of Falkenlust and the blue hills of the Vorgebirge.

We were lodged at the back, where the private gardens and offices abutted on the village. Our own rooms looked upon our own garden, and upon the church and Franciscan convent beyond. In the warm dusk, when all was still, and my father used to sit smoking his *meerschaum* by the open window, we could hear the low pealing of the chapel-organ, and the monks chanting their evening litanies.

A happy time—a pleasant, peaceful place! Ah me! how long ago!

2

A whole delightful Summer and Autumn went by thus, and my new home seemed more charming with every change of season. First came the gathering of the golden harvest; then the joyous vintage-time, when the wine-press creaked all day in every open cellar along the village street, and long files of country carts came down from the hills in the dusk evenings, laden with baskets and barrels full of white and purple grapes. And then the long avenues and all the woods of Bruehl put on their Autumn robes of crimson, and flame-colour, and golden brown; and the berries reddened in the hedges; and the Autumn burned itself away like a gorgeous sunset; and November came in grey and cold, like the night-time of the year.

I was so happy, however, that I enjoyed even the dull November. I loved the bare avenues carpeted with dead and rustling leaves—the solitary gardens—the long, silent afternoons and evenings when the big logs crackled on the hearth, and my father smoked his pipe in the chimney corner. We had no such wood-fires at Aunt Martha Baur's in those dreary old Nuremberg days, now almost forgotten; but then, to be sure, Aunt Martha Baur, who was a sparing woman and looked after every *groschen*, had to pay for her own logs, whereas ours were cut from the Crown Woods, and cost not a *pfennig*.

It was, as well as I can remember, just about this time, when the days were almost at their briefest, that my father received an official communication from Berlin desiring him to make ready a couple of rooms for the immediate reception of a state-prisoner, for whose safe-keeping he would be held responsible till further notice. The letter—(I have it in my desk now)—was folded square, sealed with five seals, and signed in the King's name by the Minister of War; and it was brought, as I well remember, by a mounted orderly from Cologne.

So a couple of empty rooms were chosen on the second story, just over one of the State apartments at the end of the east wing; and my father, who was by no means well pleased with his office, set to work to ransack the *château* for furniture.

"Since it is the King's pleasure to make a gaoler of me," said he, "I'll try to give my poor devil of a prisoner all the comforts I can. Come with me, my little Gretchen, and let's see what chairs and tables we can find up in the garrets."

Now I had been longing to explore the top rooms ever since I came to live at Bruehl—those top rooms under the roof, of which the shutters were always closed, and the doors always locked, and where not even the housemaids were admitted oftener than twice a year. So at this welcome invitation I sprang up, joyfully enough, and ran before my father all the way. But when he unlocked the first door, and all beyond was dark, and the air that met us on the threshold had a faint and dead odour, like the atmosphere of a tomb, I shrank back trembling, and dared not venture in.

Nor did my courage altogether come back when the shutters were thrown open, and the wintry sunlight streamed in upon dusty floors, and cobwebbed ceilings, and piles of mysterious objects covered in a ghostly way with large white sheets, looking like heaps of slain upon a funeral pyre.

The slain, however, turned out to be the very things of which we were in search; old-fashioned furniture in all kinds of in-congruous styles, and of all epochs—Louis Quatorze cabinets in cracked tortoise-shell and blackened *buhl*—antique carved chairs emblazoned elaborately with coats of arms, as old as the time of Albert Duerer—slender-legged tables in battered mar-queterie—time-pieces in lack-lustre *ormolu*, still pointing to the hour at which they had stopped, who could tell how many years ago? Bundles of moth-eaten tapestries and faded silken hangings—exquisite oval mirrors framed in chipped wreaths of delicate Dresden china—mouldering old portraits of dead-and-gone court beauties in powder and patches, warriors in wigs, and prelates in point-lace—whole suites of furniture in old stamped leather and worm-eaten *Utrecht* velvet; broken *toilette* services in pink and blue Sevres; screens, wardrobes, cornices—in short, all kinds of luxurious lumber going fast to dust, like those who once upon a time enjoyed and owned it.

And now, going from room to room, we chose a chair here, a table there, and so on, till we had enough to furnish a bedroom and sitting-room.

"He must have a writing-table," said my father, thoughtfully, "and a book-case."

Saying which, he stopped in front of a ricketty-looking gild-ed cabinet with empty red-velvet shelves, and tapped it with his cane.

"But supposing he has no books!" suggested I, with the pre-cocious wisdom of nine years of age.

"Then we must beg some, or borrow some, my little *Maed-*

chen," replied my father, gravely; "for books are the main solace of the captive, and he who hath them not lies in a twofold prison."

"He shall have my picture-book of Hartz legends!" said I, in a sudden impulse of compassion. Whereupon my father took me up in his arms, kissed me on both cheeks, and bade me choose some knicknacks for the prisoner's sitting-room.

"For though we have gotten together all the necessaries for comfort, we have taken nothing for adornment," said he, "and 'twere pity the prison were duller than it need be. Choose thou a pretty face or two from among these old pictures, my little Gretchen, and an ornament for his mantelshelf. Young as thou art, thou hast the woman's wit in thee."

So I picked out a couple of Sevres candlesticks; a painted Chinese screen, all pagodas and parrots; two portraits of patched and powdered beauties in the Watteau style; and a queer old clock surmounted by a gilt Cupid in a chariot drawn by doves. If these failed to make him happy, thought I, he must indeed be hard to please.

That afternoon, the things having been well dusted, and the rooms thoroughly cleaned, we set to work to arrange the furniture, and so quickly was this done that before we sat down to supper the place was ready for occupation, even to the logs upon the hearth and the oil-lamp upon the table.

All night my dreams were of the prisoner. I was seeking him in the gloom of the upper rooms, or amid the dusky mazes of the leafless plantations—always seeing him afar off, never overtaking him, and trying in vain to catch a glimpse of his features. But his face was always turned from me. My first words on waking, were to ask if he had yet come. All day long I was waiting, and watching, and listening for him, starting up at every sound, and continually running to the window. Would he be young and handsome? Or would he be old, and white-haired, and world-forgotten, like some of those Bastille prisoners I had heard my father speak of?

Would his chains rattle when he walked about? I asked myself these questions, and answered them as my childish imagination prompted, a hundred times a day; and still he came not. So another twenty-four hours went by, and my impatience was almost beginning to wear itself out, when at last, about five o'clock in the afternoon of the third day, it being already quite dark, there came a sudden clanging of the gates, followed by a rattle of wheels in the courtyard, and a hurrying to and fro of feet upon the stairs.

Then, listening with a beating heart, but seeing nothing, I knew that he was come. I had to sleep that night with my curiosity ungratified; for my father had hurried away at the first sounds from without, nor came back till long after I had been carried off to bed by my Rhenish handmaiden.

3

He was neither old nor white-haired. He was, as well as I, in my childish way could judge, about thirty-five years of age, pale, slight, dark-eyed, delicate-looking. His chains did not rattle as he walked, for the simple reason that, being a prisoner on parole, he suffered no kind of restraint, but was as free as myself of the *château* and grounds. He wore his hair long, tied behind with a narrow black ribbon, and very slightly powdered; and he dressed always in deep mourning—black, all black, from head to foot, even to his shoe-buckles. He was a Frenchman, and he went by the name of Monsieur Maurice.

I cannot tell how I knew that this was only his Christian name; but so it was, and I knew him by no other, neither did my father. I have, indeed, evidence among our private papers to show that neither by those in authority at Berlin, nor by the prisoner himself, was he at any time informed either of the family name of Monsieur Maurice, or of the nature of the offence, whether military or political, for which that gentleman was consigned to his keeping at Bruehl.

"Of one thing at least I am certain," said my father, holding out his pipe for me to fill it. "He is a soldier." It was just after dinner, the second day following our prisoner's arrival, and I was

16

sitting on my father's knee before the fire, as was our pleasant custom of an afternoon.

"I see it in his eye," my father went on to say. "I see it in his walk. I see it in the way he arranges his papers on the table. Everything in order. Everything put away into the smallest possible compass. All this bespeaketh the camp."

"I don't believe he is a soldier, for all that," said I, thoughtfully. "He is too gentle."

"The bravest soldiers, my little Gretchen, are oft-times the gentlest," replied my father. "The great French hero, Bayard, and the great English hero, Sir Philip Sidney, about whom thou wert reading 'tother day, were both as tender and gentle as women."

"But he neither smokes, nor swears, nor talks loud," said I, persisting in my opinion.

My father smiled, and pinched my ear. "Nay, little one," said he, "Monsieur Maurice is not like thy father—a rough German Dragoon risen from the ranks. He is a gentleman, and a Frenchman; and he hath all the polish of what the Frenchman calls the *vieille ecole*. And there again he puzzles me with his court-manners and his powdered hair! He's no Bonapartist, I'll be sworn—yet if he be o' the King's side, what doth he here, with the usurper at Saint Helena, and Louis the Eighteenth come to his own again?"

"But he *is* a Bonapartist, father," said I, "for he carries the Emperor's portrait on his snuff-box."

My father laid down his pipe, and drew a long breath expressive of astonishment. "He showed thee his snuff-box!" exclaimed he.

"Ay—and told me it was the Emperor's own gift."

"Thunder and Mars! And when was this, my little Gretchen?"

"Yesterday morning, on the terrace. And he asked my name; and told me I should go up some day to his room and see his sketches; and he kissed me when he said goodbye; and—and I like Monsieur Maurice very much, father, and I'm sure it's very wicked of the King to keep him here in prison!"

17

My father looked at me, shook his head, and twirled his long grey moustache. "Bonapartist or Legitimist, again I say what doth he here?" muttered he presently, more to himself than to me. "If Legitimist, why not with his King? If Bonapartist—then he is his King's prisoner; not ours. It passeth my comprehension how we should hold him at Bruehl."

"Let him run away, father dear, and don't run after him!" whispered I, putting my arms coaxingly about his neck.

"But 'tis some cursed mess of politics at bottom, depend on't!" continued my father, still talking to himself. "Ah, you don't know what politics are, my little Gretchen!—so much the better for you!"

"I do know what politics are," replied I, with great dignity. "They are the *chef-d'oeuvre* of Satan. I heard you say so the other day."

My father burst into a Titanic roar of laughter. "Said I so?" shouted he. "Thunder and Mars! I did not remember that I had ever said anything half so epigrammatic!"

Now from this it will be seen that the prisoner and I were already acquainted. We had, indeed, taken to each other from the first, and our mutual liking ripened so rapidly that before a week was gone by we had become the fastest friends in the world. Our first meeting, as I have already said, took place upon the terrace. Our second, which befell on the afternoon of the same day when my father and I had held the conversation just recorded, happened on the stairs. Monsieur Maurice was coming up with his hat on; I was running down.

He stopped, and held out both his hands. "*Bonjour, petite,*" he said, smiling. "Whither away so fast?" The hoar frost was clinging to his coat, where he had brushed against the trees in his walk, and he looked pale and tired.

"I am going home," I replied.

"Home? Did you not tell me you lived in the *château*?"

"So I do, *Monsieur,* but at the other side, up the other staircase. This is the side of the state-apartments."

Then, seeing in his face a look half of surprise, half of curiosity, I added:—"I often go there in the afternoon, when it is too cold, or too late for out-of-doors. They are such beautiful rooms, and full of such beautiful pictures! Would you like to see them?"

He smiled, and shook his head. "Thanks, *petite*," he said, "I am too cold now, and too tired; but you shall show them to me some other day. Meanwhile, suppose you come up and pay me that promised visit?"

I assented joyfully, and slipping my hand into his with the ready confidence of childhood, turned back at once and went with him to his rooms on the second floor. Here, finding the fire in the salon nearly out, we went down upon our knees and blew the embers with our breath, and laughed so merrily over our work that by the time the new logs had caught, I was as much at home as if I had known Monsieur Maurice all my life.

"*Tiens!*" he said, taking me presently upon his knee and brushing the specks of white ash from my clothes and hair, "what a little Cinderella I have made of my guest! This must not happen again, Gretchen. Did you not tell me yesterday that your name was Gretchen?"

"Yes, but Gretchen, you know, is not my real name," said I, "my real name is Marguerite. Gretchen is only my pet name."

"Then you will always be Gretchen for me," said Monsieur Maurice, with the sweetest smile in the world. There were books upon the table; there was a thing like a telescope on a brass stand in the window; there was a guitar lying on the couch. The fire, too, was burning brightly now, and the room altogether wore a cheerful air of habitation.

"It looks more like a lady's *boudoir* than a prison," said Monsieur Maurice, reading my thoughts. "I wonder whose rooms they were before I came here!"

"They were nobody's rooms," said I. "They were quite empty." And then I told him where we had found the furniture, and how the ornamental part thereof had been of my choosing.

"I don't know who the ladies are," I said, referring to the portraits. "I only chose them for their pretty faces."

19

"Their lovers probably did the same, petite, a hundred years ago," replied Monsieur Maurice. "And the clock—did you choose that also?"

"Yes; but the clock doesn't go."

"So much the better. I would that time might stand still also—till I am free! till I am free!" The tears rushed to my eyes. It was the tone more than the words that touched my heart.

He stooped and kissed me on the forehead. "Come to the window, little one," said he, "and I will show you something very beautiful. Do you know what this is?"

"A telescope!"

"No; a solar microscope. Now look down into this tube, and tell me what you see. A piece of Persian carpet? No—a butterfly's wing magnified hundreds and hundreds of times. And this which looks like an *aigrette* of jewels? Will you believe that it is just the tiny plume which waves on the head of every little gnat that buzzes round you on a Summer's evening?"

I uttered exclamation after exclamation of delight. Every fresh object seemed more wonderful and beautiful than the last, and I felt as if I could go on looking down that magic tube forever. Meanwhile Monsieur Maurice, whose good-nature was at least as inexhaustible as my curiosity, went on changing the slides till we had gone through a whole box-full. By this time it was getting rapidly dusk, and I could see no longer.

"You will show me some more another day?" said I, giving up reluctantly.

"That I will, *petite*, I have at least a dozen more boxes full of slides."

"And—and you said I should see your sketches, Monsieur Maurice."

"All in good time, little Gretchen," he said, smiling. "All in good time. See—those are the sketches, in yonder folio; that mahogany case under the couch contains a collection of gems in glass and paste; those red books in the bookcase are full of pictures. You shall see them all by degrees; but only by degrees. For if I did not keep something back to tempt my little guest, she would not care to visit the solitary prisoner."

I felt myself colour crimson. "But—but indeed I would care to come, Monsieur Maurice, if you had nothing at all to show me," I said, half hurt, half angry.

He gave me a strange look that I could not understand, and stroked my hair caressingly. "Come often, then, little one," he said. "Come very often; and when we are tired of pictures and microscopes, we will sit upon the floor, and tell sad stories of the deaths of kings."

Then, seeing my look puzzled, he laughed and added:—"'Tis a great English poet says that, Gretchen, in one of his plays."

Here a shrill trumpet-call in the courtyard, followed by the prolonged roll of many drums, warned me that evening parade was called, and that as soon as it was over my father would be home and looking for me. So I started up, and put out my hand to say goodbye.

Monsieur Maurice took it between both his own. "I don't like parting from you so soon, little *Maedchen*," he said. "Will you come again tomorrow?"

"Every day, if you like!" I replied eagerly. "Then every day it shall be; and—let me see—you shall improve my bad German, and I will teach you French." I could have clapped my hands for joy. I was longing to learn French, and I knew how much it would also please my father; so I thanked Monsieur Maurice again and again, and ran home with a light heart to tell of all the wonders I had seen.

4

From this time forth, I saw him always once, and sometimes twice a day—in the afternoons, when he regularly gave me the promised French lesson; and occasionally in the mornings, provided the weather was neither too cold nor too damp for him to join me in the grounds. For Monsieur Maurice was not strong. He could not with impunity face snow, and rain, and our keen Rhenish north-east winds; and it was only when the wintry sun shone out at noon and the air came tempered from the south, that he dared venture from his own fireside.

When, however, there shone a sunny day, with what delight I used to summon him for a walk, take him to my favourite points of view, and show him the woodland nooks that had been my chosen haunts in summer! Then, too, the unwonted colour would come back to his pale cheek, and the smile to his lips, and while the ramble and the sunshine lasted he would be all jest and gaiety, pelting me with dead leaves, chasing me in and out of the plantations, and telling me strange stories, half pathetic, half grotesque, of Dryads, and Fauns, and Satyrs—of Bacchus, and Pan, and Polyphemus—of nymphs who became trees, and shepherds who were transformed to fountains, and all kinds of beautiful wild myths of antique Greece—far more beautiful and far more wild than all the tales of gnomes and witches in my book of Hartz legends.

At other times, when the weather was cold or rainy, he would take down his *Musee Napoleon*, a noble work in eight or ten volumes, and show me engravings after pictures by great masters in the Louvre, explaining them to me as we went along, painting in words the glow and glory of the absent colour, and steeping my childish imagination in golden dreams of Raphael and Titian, and Paulo Veronese.

And sometimes, too, as the dusk came on and the firelight brightened in the gathering gloom, he would take up his guitar, and to the accompaniment of a few slight chords sing me a quaint old French *chanson* of the feudal times; or an Arab chant picked up in the tent or the Nile boat; or a Spanish ballad, half love-song, half litany, learned from the lips of a muleteer on the Pyrenean border.

For Monsieur Maurice, whatever his present adversities, had travelled far and wide at some foregone period of his life—in Syria, and Persia; in northernmost Tartary and the Siberian steppes; in Egypt and the Nubian desert, and among the perilous wilds of central Arabia. He spoke and wrote with facility some ten or twelve languages. He drew admirably, and had a profound knowledge of the Italian schools of art; and his memory was a rich storehouse of adventure and anecdote, legend and song.

I am an old woman now, and Monsieur Maurice must have passed away many a year ago upon his last long journey; but even at this distance of time, my eyes are dimmed with tears when I remember how he used to unlock that storehouse for my pleasure, and ransack his memory for stories either of his own personal perils by flood and field, or of the hairbreadth 'scapes of earlier travellers. For it was his amusement to amuse me; his happiness to make me happy.

And I in return loved him with all my childish heart. Nay, with something deeper and more romantic than a childish love—say rather with that kind of passionate hero-worship which is an attribute more of youth than of childhood, and, like the quality of mercy, blesseth him that gives even more than him that takes.

"What dreadful places you have travelled in, Monsieur Maurice!" I exclaimed one day. "What dangers you have seen!"

He had been showing me a little sketchbook full of Eastern jottings, and had just explained how a certain boat therein depicted had upset with him on a part of the Upper Nile so swarming with alligators that he had to swim for his life, and even so, barely scrambled up the slimy bank in time.

"He who travels far courts many kinds of death," replied Monsieur Maurice; "but he escapes that which is worst—death from *ennui*."

"Suppose they had dragged you back, when you were half way up the bank!" said I, shuddering. And as I spoke, I felt myself turn pale; for I could see the brown monsters crowding to shore, and the red glitter of their cruel eyes and the hot breath steaming from their open jaws.

"Then they would have eaten me up as easily as you might swallow an oyster," laughed Monsieur Maurice. "Nay, my child, why that serious face? I should have escaped a world of trouble, and been missed by no one—except poor Ali."

"Who was Ali?" I asked quickly.

"Ali was my Nubian servant—my only friend, then; as you, little Gretchen, are my only friend, now," replied Monsieur

Maurice, sadly. "Aye, my only little friend in the wide world-and I think a true one."

I did not know what to say; but I nestled closer to his side; and pressed my cheek up fondly against his shoulder. "Tell me more about him, Monsieur Maurice," I whispered. "I am so glad he loved you dearly."

"He loved me very dearly," said Monsieur Maurice "so dearly that he gave his life for me."

"But is Ali dead?"

"Ay—Ali is dead. Nay, his story is brief enough, petite. I bought him in the slave market at Cairo—a poor, sickly, soulless lad, half stupid from ill-treatment. I gave him good food, good clothes, and liberty. I taught him to read. I made him my own servant; and his soul and his strength came back to him as if by a miracle. He became stalwart and intelligent, and so faithful that he was ten times more my slave than if I had held him to his bondage. I took him with me through all my Eastern pilgrimage. He was my bodyguard; my cook; my dragoman; everything. He slept on a mat at the foot of my bed every night, like a dog. So he lived with me for nearly four years—till I lost him."

He paused. I did not dare to ask, "what more?" but waited breathlessly. "The rest is soon told," he said presently; but in an altered voice. "It happened in Ceylon. Our way lay along a bridle-path overhanging a steep gorge on the one hand and skirting the jungle on the other. Do you know what the jungle is, little Gretchen? Fancy an untrodden wilderness where huge trees, matted together by trailing creepers of gigantic size, shut out the sun and make a green roof of inextricable shade—where the very grass grows taller than the tallest man—where apes chatter, and parrots scream, and deadly reptiles swarm; and where nature has run wild since ever the world began.

"Well, so we went—I on my horse; Ali at my bridle; two porters following with food and baggage; the precipice below; the forest above; the morning sun just risen over all. On a sudden, Ali held his breath and listened. His practised ear had caught a sound that mine could not detect. He seized my rein—forced my horse back upon his haunches—drew his hunting knife, and ran forward to reconnoitre. The turn of the road hid him for a moment from my sight. The next instant, I had sprung from the saddle, pistol in hand, and run after him to share the sport or the danger. My little Gretchen—he was gone."

"Gone!" I echoed.

Monsieur Maurice shook his head, and turned his face away. "I heard a crashing and crackling of the underwood," he said; "a faint moan dying on the sultry air. I saw a space of dusty road trampled over with prints of an enormous paw—a tiny trail of blood—a shred of silken fringe—and nothing more. He was gone."

"What was it?" I asked presently, in an awestruck whisper.

Monsieur Maurice, instead of answering my question, opened the sketch-book at a page full of little outlines of animals and birds, and laid his finger silently on the figure of a sleeping tiger. I shuddered. "*Pauvre petite!*" he said, shutting up the book, "it is too terrible a story. I ought not to have told it to you. Try to forget it."

"Ah, no!" I said. "I shall never forget it, Monsieur Maurice. Poor Ali! Have you still the piece of fringe you found lying in the road?"

He unlocked his desk and touched a secret spring; whereupon a small drawer flew out from a recess just under the lock. "Here it is," he said, taking out a piece of folded paper. It contained the thing he had described—a scrap of fringe composed of crimson and yellow twist, about two inches in length.

"And those other things?" I said, peering into the secret drawer with a child's inquisitiveness. "Have they a history, too?"

Monsieur Maurice hesitated—took them out—sighed—and said, somewhat reluctantly:— "You may see them, little Gretchen, if you will. Yes; they, too, have their history—but let it be. We have had enough sad stories for today." Those other things, as I had called them, were a withered rose in a little cardboard box, and a miniature of a lady in a purple morocco case.

5

It so happened that the Winter this year was unusually severe, not only at Bruehl and the parts about Cologne, but throughout all the Rhine country. Heavy snows fell at Christmas and lay unmelted for weeks upon the ground. Long forgotten sleighs were dragged out from their hiding places and put upon the road, not only for the transport of goods, but for the conveyance of passengers. The ponds in every direction and all the smaller streams were fast frozen.

Great masses of dirty ice, too, came floating down the Rhine, and there were rumours of the great river being quite frozen over somewhere up in Switzerland, many hundred miles nearer its source. For myself, I enjoyed it all—the bitter cold, the short days, the rapid exercise, the blazing fires within, and the glittering snow without. I made snow-men and snow-castles to my heart's content. I learned to skate with my father on the frozen ponds. I was never weary of admiring the wintry landscape— the wide plains sheeted with silver; the purple mountains peeping through brown *vistas* of bare forest; the nearer trees standing out in featherlike tracery against the blue-green sky.

To me it was all beautiful; even more beautiful than in the radiant summertime. Not so, however, was it with Monsieur Maurice. Racked by a severe cough and unable to leave the house for weeks together, he suffered intensely all the winter through. He suffered in body, and he suffered also in mind. I could see that he was very sad, and that there were times when the burden of life was almost more than he knew how to bear.

He had brought with him, as I have shown, certain things wherewith to alleviate the weariness of captivity—books, music, drawing materials, and the like; but I soon discovered that the books were his only solace, and that he never took up pencil or guitar, unless for my amusement. He wrote a great deal, however, and so consumed many a weary hour of the twenty-four. He used a thick yellowish paper cut quite square, and wrote a very small, neat, upright hand, as clear and legible as print.

Every time I found him at his desk and saw those closely

covered pages multiplying under his hand, I used to wonder what he could have to write about, and for whose eyes that elaborate manuscript was intended.

"How cold you are, Monsieur Maurice!" I used to say. "You are as cold as my snowman in the courtyard! Won't you come out today for half-an-hour?" And his hands, in truth, were always ice-like, even though the hearth was heaped with blazing logs.

"Not today, *petite*," he would reply. "It is too bleak for me—and besides, you see, I am writing."

It was his invariable reply. He was always writing—or if not writing, reading; or brooding listlessly over the fire. And so he grew paler every day.

"But the writing can wait, Monsieur Maurice," I urged one morning, "and you can't always be reading the same old books over and over again!"

"Some books never grow old, little Gretchen," he replied. "This, for instance, is quite new; and yet it was written by one Horatius Flaccus somewhere about eighteen hundred years ago."

"But the sun is really shining this morning, Monsieur Maurice!"

"*Comment!*" he said, smiling. "Do you think to persuade me that yonder is the sun—the great, golden, glorious, bountiful sun? No, no, my child! Where I come from, we have the only true sun, and believe in no other!"

"But you come from France, don't you, Monsieur Maurice?" I asked quickly. "From the South of France, *petite*—from the France of palms, and orange-groves, and olives; where the myrtle flowers at Christmas, and the roses bloom all the year round!"

"But that must be where Paradise was, Monsieur Maurice!" I exclaimed.

"Ay; it was Paradise once—for me," he said, with a sigh. Thus, after a moment's pause, he went on:—"The house in which I was born stands on a low cliff above the sea. It is an old, old house, with all kinds of quaint little turrets, and gable ends, and picturesque nooks and corners about it—such as one sees in most French *châteaux* of that period; and it lies back somewhat, with a great rambling garden stretching out between it and the edge of the cliff. Three *berceaux* of orange-trees lead straight away from the paved terrace on which the salon windows open, to another terrace overhanging the beach and the sea.

"The cliff is overgrown from top to bottom with shrubs and wild flowers, and a flight of steps cut in the living rock leads down to a little cove and a strip of yellow sand a hundred feet below. Ah, *petite*, I fancy I can see myself scrambling up and down those steps—a child younger than yourself; watching the sun go down into that purple sea; counting the sails in the offing at early morn; and building castles with that yellow sand, just as you build castles out yonder with the snow!"

I clasped my hands and listened breathlessly. "Oh, Monsieur Maurice," I said, "I did not think there was such a beautiful place in the world! It sounds like a fairy tale."

He smiled, sighed, and—being seated at his desk with the pen in his hand—took up a blank sheet of paper, and began sketching the *château* and the cliff.

"Tell me more about it, Monsieur Maurice," I pleaded coaxingly.

"What more can I tell you, little one? See—this window in the turret to the left was my bed-room window, and here, just below, was my study, where as a boy I prepared my lessons for my tutor. That large Gothic window under the gable was the window of the library."

"And is it all just like that still?" I asked.

"I don't know," he said dreamily. "I suppose so." He was now putting in the rocks, and the rough steps leading down to the beach.

"Had you any little brothers and sisters, Monsieur Maurice?" I asked next; for my interest and curiosity were unbounded.

He shook his head. "None," he said, "none whatever. I was an only child; and I am the last of my name."

I longed to question him further, but did not dare to do so. "You will go back there someday, Monsieur Maurice," I said hesitatingly, "when—when—"

"When I am free, little Gretchen? Ah! who can tell? Besides the old place is no longer mine. They have taken it from me, and given it to a stranger."

"Taken it from you, Monsieur Maurice!" I exclaimed indignantly.

"Ay; but—who knows? We see strange changes. Where a king reigns today, an emperor, or a mob, may rule tomorrow." He spoke more to himself than to me, but I had some dim understanding, nevertheless, of what he meant. He had by this time drawn the cliff, and the strip of sand, and the waste of sea beyond; and now he was blotting in some boats and figures-figures of men wading through the surf and dragging the boats in shore; and other figures making for the steps.

Last of all, close under the cliff, in advance of all the rest, he drew a tiny man standing alone—a tiny man scarce an eighth of an inch in height, struck out with three or four touches of the pen, and yet so full of character that one knew at a glance he was the leader of the others. I saw the outstretched arm in act of command—I recognised the well-known cocked hat—the general outline of a figure already familiar to me in a hundred prints, and I exclaimed, almost involuntarily:—"Bonaparte!"

Monsieur Maurice started; shot a quick, half apprehensive glance at me; crumpled the drawing up in his hand, and flung it into the fire.

"Oh, Monsieur Maurice!" I cried, "what have you done?"

"It was a mere scrawl," he said impatiently.

"No, no—it was beautiful. I would have given anything for it!"

Monsieur Maurice laughed, and patted me on the cheek. "Nonsense, *petite*, nonsense!" he said. "It was only fit for the fire. I will make you a better drawing, if you remind me of it, tomorrow."

When I told this to my father—and I used to prattle to him a good deal about Monsieur Maurice at supper, in those days—he tugged at his moustache, and shook his head, and looked very grave indeed. "The South of France!" he muttered, "the South of France! *Sacre coeur d'une bombe!* Why, the usurper, when he came from Elba, landed on that coast somewhere near Cannes!"

"And went to Monsieur Maurice's house, father!" I cried, "and that is why the King of France has taken Monsieur Maurice's house away from him, and given it to a stranger! I am sure that's it! I see it all now!"

But my father only shook his head again, and looked still more grave. "No, no, no," he said, "neither all—nor half—nor a quarter! There's more behind. I don't understand it—I don't understand it. Thunder and Mars! Why don't we hand him over to the French Government? That's what puzzles me."

6

The severity of the Winter had, I think, in some degree abated, and the snowdrops were already above ground, when again a mounted orderly rode in from Cologne, bringing another official letter for the Governor of Bruehl. Now my father's duties as Governor of Bruehl were very light—so light that he had not found it necessary to set apart any special room, or bureau, for the transaction of such business as might be connected therewith.

When, therefore, letters had to be written or accounts made up, he wrote those letters and made up those accounts at a certain large writing-table, fitted with drawers, pigeon-holes, and a shelf for account-books, that stood in a corner of our sitting-room. Here also, if any persons had to be received, he received them. To this day, whenever I go back in imagination to those bygone times, I seem to see my father sitting at that writing-table nibbling the end of his pen, and one of the sergeants off guard perched on the edge of a chair close against the door, with his hat on his knees, waiting for orders.

There being, as I have said, no especial room set apart for business purposes, the orderly was shown straight to our own room, and there delivered his despatch. It was about a quarter past one. We had dined, and my father had just brought out his pipe. The door leading into our little dining-room was, indeed, standing wide open, and the dishes were still upon the table.

My father took the despatch, turned it over, broke the seals one by one (there were five of them, as before), and read it slowly through. As he read, a dark cloud seemed to settle on his brow. Then he looked up frowning—seemed about to speak—checked himself—and read the despatch over again.

"From whose hands did you receive this?" he said abruptly.

"From General Berndorf, Excellency," stammered the orderly, carrying his hand to his cap.

"Is his Excellency the Baron von Bulow at Cologne?"

"I have not heard so, Excellency."

"Then this despatch came direct from Berlin, and has been forwarded from Cologne?"

"Yes, Excellency."

"How did it come from Berlin? By mail, or by special messenger?"

"By special messenger, Excellency."

Now General Berndorf was the officer in command of the garrison at Cologne, and the Baron von Bulow, as I well knew, was His Majesty's Minister of War at Berlin. Having received these answers, my father stood silent, as if revolving some difficult matter in his thoughts. Then, his mind being made up, he turned again to the orderly and said:—"Dine—feed your horse—and come back in an hour for the answer."

Thankful to be dismissed, the man saluted and vanished. My father had a rapid, stern way of speaking to subordinates, that had in general the effect of making them glad to get out of his presence as quickly as possible. Then he read the despatch for the third time; turned to his writing-table; dropped into his chair; and prepared to write. But the task, apparently, was not easy. Watching him from the fireside corner where I was sitting on a low stool with an open story-book upon my lap, I saw him begin and tear up three separate attempts. The fourth, however, seemed to be more successful.

Once written, he read it over, copied it carefully, called to me for a light, sealed his letter, and addressed it to "His Excellency the Baron von Bulow."

This done, he enclosed it under cover to "General Berndorf, Cologne"; and had just sealed the outer cover when the orderly came back. My father gave it to him with scarcely a word, and two minutes after, we heard him clattering out of the courtyard at a hand-gallop. Then my father came back to his chair by the fireside, lit his pipe, and sat thinking silently. I looked up in his face, but felt, somehow, that I must not speak to him; for the cloud was still there, and his thoughts were far away. Presently his pipe went out; but he held it still, unconscious and absorbed.

In all the months we had been living at Bruehl I had never seen him look so troubled. So he sat, and so he looked for a long time—for perhaps the greater part of an hour—during which I could think of nothing but the despatch, and Monsieur Maurice, and the Minister of War; for that it all had to do with Monsieur Maurice I never doubted for an instant. By just such another despatch, sealed and sent in precisely the same way, and from the same person, his coming hither had been heralded. How, then, should not this one concern him? And in what way would he be affected by it?

Seeing that dark look in my father's face, I knew not what to think or what to fear. At length, after what had seemed to me an interval of interminable silence, the time-piece in the corner struck half-past three—the hour at which Monsieur Maurice was accustomed to give me the daily French lesson; so I got up quietly and stole towards the door, knowing that I was expected upstairs.

"Where are you going, Gretchen?" said my father, sharply. It was the first time he had opened his lips since the orderly had clattered out of the courtyard.

"I am going up to Monsieur Maurice," I replied. My father shook his head. "Not today, my child," he said, "not today. I have business with Monsieur Maurice this afternoon. Stay here till I come back." And with this he got up, took his hat and went quickly out of the room.

So I waited and waited—as it seemed to me for hours. The waning daylight faded and became dusk; the dusk thickened into dark; the fire burned red and dull; and still I crouched there in the chimney-corner. I had no heart to read, work, or fan the logs into a blaze. I just watched the clock, and waited. When the room became so dark that I could see the hands no longer, I counted the strokes of the pendulum, and told the quarters off upon my fingers. When at length my father came back, it was past five o'clock, and dark as midnight.

"Quick, quick, little Gretchen," he said, pulling off his hat and gloves, and unbuckling his sword. "A glass of *kirsch*, and more logs on the fire! I am cold through and through, and wet into the bargain."

"But—but, father, have you not been with Monsieur Maurice?" I said, anxiously.

"Yes, of course; but that was an hour ago, and more. I have been over to Kierberg since then, in the rain."

He had left Monsieur Maurice an hour ago—a whole, wretched, dismal hour, during which I might have been so happy! "You told me to stay here till you came back," I said, scarce able to keep down the tears that started to my eyes.

"Well, my little *Maedchen*?"

"And—and I might have gone up to Monsieur Maurice, after all?"

My father looked at me gravely—poured out a second glass of *kirsch*—drew his chair to the front of the fire, and said:—"I don't know about that, Gretchen." I had felt all along that there was something wrong, and now I was certain of it.

"What do you mean, father?" I said, my heart beating so that I could scarcely speak. "What is the matter?"

"May the devil make broth of my bones, if I know!" said my father, tugging savagely at his moustache.

"But there is something!"

He nodded, grimly. "Monsieur Maurice, it seems, is not to have so much liberty," he said, after a moment. "He is not to walk in the grounds oftener than twice a week; and then only

33

with a soldier at his heels. And he is not to go beyond half a mile from the *château* in any direction. And he is to hold no communication whatever with any person, or persons, either in-doors or out-of-doors, except such as are in direct charge of his rooms or his person. And—and heaven knows what other confounded regulations besides! I wish the Baron von Bulow had been in Spitzbergen before he put it into the King's head to send him here at all!"

"But—but he is not to be locked up?" I faltered, almost in a whisper.

"Well, no—not exactly that; but I am to post a sentry in the corridor, outside his door."

"Then the King is afraid that Monsieur Maurice will run away!"

"I don't know—I suppose so," groaned my father.

I sat silent for a moment, and then burst into a flood of tears. "Poor Monsieur Maurice!" I cried. "He has coughed so all the Winter; and he was longing for the Spring! We were to have gathered primroses in the woods when the warm days came back again—and—and—and I suppose the King doesn't mean that I am not to speak to him anymore!" My sobs choked me, and I could say no more.

My father took me on his knee, and tried to comfort me. "Don't cry, my little Gretchen," he said tenderly; "don't cry! Tears can help neither the prisoner nor thee."

"But I may go to him all the same, father?" I pleaded.

"By my sword, I don't know," stammered my father. "If it were a breach of orders ... and yet for a baby like thee ... thou'rt no more than a mouse about the room, after all!"

"I have read of a poor prisoner who broke his heart because the gaoler killed a spider he loved," said I, through my tears.

My father's features relaxed into a smile. "But do you flatter yourself that Monsieur Maurice loves my little *Maedchen* as much as that poor prisoner loved his spider?" he said, taking me by the ear.

"Of course he does—and a hundred thousand times better!"

I exclaimed, not without a touch of indignation.

My father laughed outright. "Thunder and Mars!" said he, "is the case so serious? Then Monsieur Maurice, I suppose, must be allowed sometimes to see his little pet spider." He took me up himself next morning to the prisoner's room, and then for the first time I found a sentry in occupation of the corridor. He grounded his musket and saluted as we passed.

"I bring you a visitor, Monsieur Maurice," said my father. He was leaning over the fire in a moody attitude when we went in, with his arms on the chimney-piece, but turned at the first sound of my father's voice.

"Colonel Bernhard," he said, with a look of glad surprise, "this is kind, I—I had scarcely dared to hope". . . . He said no more, but took me by both hands, and kissed me on the forehead.

"I trust I'm not doing wrong," said my father gruffly. "I hope it's not a breach of orders."

"I am sure it is not," replied Monsieur Maurice, still holding my hands. "Were your instructions twice as strict, they could not be supposed to apply to this little maiden."

"They are strict enough, Monsieur Maurice," said my father, drily.

A faint flush rose to the prisoner's cheek. "I know it," he said. "And they are as unnecessary as they are strict. I had given you my parole, Colonel Bernhard."

My father pulled at his moustache, and looked uncomfortable. "I'm sure you would have kept it, Monsieur Maurice," he said.

Monsieur Maurice bowed. "I wish it, however, to be distinctly understood," he said, "that I withdrew that parole from the moment when a sentry was stationed at my door."

"Naturally—naturally."

"And, for my papers". . . .

"I wish to heaven they had said nothing about them!" interrupted my father, impatiently.

"Thanks. 'Tis a petty tyranny; but it cannot be helped. Since,

35

however, you are instructed to seize them, here they are. They contain neither political nor private matter—as you will see."

"I shall see nothing of the kind, Monsieur Maurice," said my father. "I would not read a line of them for a marshal's baton. The King must make a gaoler of me, if it so pleases him; but not a spy. I shall seal up the papers and send them to Berlin."

"And I shall never see my manuscript again!" said Monsieur Maurice, with a sigh. "Well—it was my first attempt at author-ship—perhaps, my last—and there is an end to it!"

My father ground some new and tremendous oath between his teeth. "I hate to take it, Monsieur Maurice," he said. "'Tis an odious office."

"The office alone is yours, Colonel Bernhard," said the pris-oner, with all a Frenchman's grace. "The odium rests with those who impose it on you." Hereupon they exchanged formal salu-tations; and my father, having warned me not to be late for our midday meal, put the papers in his pocket, and left me to take my daily French lesson.

7

The Winter lingered long, but the Spring came at last in a burst of sunshine. The grey mists were rent away, as if by magic. The cold hues vanished from the landscape. The earth became all freshness; the air all warmth; the sky all light. The hedgerows caught a tint of tender green. The crocuses came up in a single night. The woods which till now had remained bare and brown, flushed suddenly, as if the coming Summer were imprisoned in their glowing buds. The birds began to try their little voices here and there.

Never once, in all the years that have gone by since then, have I seen so startling a transition. It was as if the Prince in the dear old fairy tale had just kissed the Sleeping Beauty, and all that enchanted world had sprung into life at the meeting of their lips. But the Spring, with its sudden beauty and brightness, seems to have no charm for Monsieur Maurice. He has permission to walk in the grounds twice a week—with a sentry at his heels;

but of that permission he sternly refuses to take advantage.

It was not wonderful that he preferred his fireside and his books, while the sleet, and snow, and bitter east winds lasted; but it seems too cruel that he should stay there now, cutting himself off from all the warmth and sweetness of the opening season. In vain I come to him with my hands full of dewy crocuses. In vain I hang about him, pleading for just a turn or two on the terrace where the sunshine falls hottest. He shakes his head, and is immoveable.

"No, *petite*," he says. "Not today."

"That is just what you said yesterday, Monsieur Maurice."

"And it is just what I shall say tomorrow, Gretchen, if you ask me again."

"But you won't stay in forever, Monsieur Maurice!"

"Nay—'forever' is a big word, little Gretchen."

"I don't believe you know how brightly the sun is shining!" I say coaxingly. "Just come to the window, and see."

Unwillingly enough, he lets himself be dragged across the room—unwillingly he looks out upon the glittering slopes and budding avenues beyond. "Yes, yes—I see it," he replies with an impatient sigh; "but the shadow of that fellow in the corridor would hide the brightest sun that ever shone! I am not a galley-slave, that I should walk about with a *garde-chiourme* behind me."

"What do you mean, Monsieur Maurice?" I ask, startled by his unusual vehemence.

"I mean that I go free, *petite*—or not at all."

"Then—then you will fall ill!" I falter, amid fast-gathering tears.

"No, no—not I, Gretchen. What can have put that idea into your wise little head?"

"It was papa, Monsieur Maurice . . . he said you were". . . . Then, thinking suddenly how pale and wasted he had become of late, I hesitated.

"He said I was—What?"

"I—I don't like to tell!"

"But if I insist on being told? Come, Gretchen, I must know what Colonel Bernhard said."

"He said it was wrong to stay in like this week after week, and month after month. He—he said you were killing yourself by inches, Monsieur Maurice."

Monsieur Maurice laughed a short bitter laugh. "Killing myself!" he repeated. "Well, I hope not; for weary as I am of it, I would sooner go on bearing the burden of life than do my enemies the favour of dying out of their way."

The words, the look, the accent made me tremble. I never forgot them. How could I forget that Monsieur Maurice had enemies—enemies who longed for his death? So the first blush of early Spring went by; and the crocuses lived their little life and passed away, and the primroses came in their turn, yellowing every shady nook in the scented woods; and the larches put on their crimson tassels, and the laburnum its mantle of golden fringe, and the almond-tree burst into a leafless bloom of pink- and still Monsieur Maurice, adhering to his resolve, refused to stir one step beyond the threshold of his rooms.

Sad and monotonous now to the last degree, his life dragged heavily on. He wrote no more. He read, or seemed to read, nearly the whole day through; but I often observed that his eyes ceased travelling along the lines, and that sometimes, for an hour and more together, he never turned a page.

"My little Gretchen," he said to me one day, "you are too much in these close rooms with me, and too little in the open air and sunshine."

"I had rather be here, Monsieur Maurice," I replied.

"But it is not good for you. You are losing all your roses."

"I don't think it is good for me to be out when you are always indoors," I said, simply. "I don't care to run about, and- and I don't enjoy it." He looked at me—opened his lips as if about to speak—then checked himself; walked to the window; and looked out silently.

The next morning, as soon as I made my appearance, he said:—"The French lesson can wait awhile, *petite*. Shall we go out for a walk instead?"

I clapped my hands for joy. "Oh, Monsieur Maurice!" I cried, "are you in earnest?" For in truth it seemed almost too good to be true. But Monsieur Maurice was in earnest, and we went-closely followed by the sentry.

It was a beautiful, sunny April day. We went down the terraces and slopes; and in and out of the flower-beds, now gaudy with Spring flowers; and on to the great central point whence the three avenues diverged. Here we rested on a bench under a lime-tree, not far from the huge stone basin where the fountain played every Sunday throughout the Summer, and the sleepy water-lilies rocked to and fro in the sunshine.

All was very quiet. A gardener went by now and then, with his wheelbarrow, or a gamekeeper followed by his dogs; a black-bird whistled low in the bushes; a cow-bell tinkled in the far distance; the wood-pigeons murmured softly in the plantations. Other passers-by, other sounds there were none—save when a noisy party of flaxen-haired, bare-footed children came whooping and racing along, but turned suddenly shy and silent at sight of Monsieur Maurice sitting under the lime-tree.

The sentry, meanwhile, took up his position against the pedestal of a mutilated statue close by, and leaned upon his musket. Monsieur Maurice was at first very silent. Once or twice he closed his eyes, as if listening to the gentle sounds upon the air-once or twice he cast an uneasy glance in the direction of the sentry; but for a long time he scarcely moved or spoke.

At length, as if following up a train of previous thought, he said suddenly:—"There is no liberty. There are comparative degrees of captivity, and comparative degrees of slavery; but of liberty, our social system knows nothing but the name. That sentry, if you asked him, would tell you that he is free. He pities me, perhaps, for being a prisoner. Yet he is even less free than myself. He is the slave of discipline. He must walk, hold up his head, wear his hair, dress, eat, and sleep according to the will of his superiors. If he disobeys, he is flogged. If he runs away, he is shot.

"At the present moment, he dares not lose sight of me for his life. I have done him no wrong; yet if I try to escape, it is his duty to shoot me. What is there in my captivity to equal the slavery of his condition? I cannot, it is true, go where I please; but, at least, I am not obliged to walk up and down a certain corridor, or in front of a certain sentry-box, for so many hours a day; and no power on earth could compel me to kill an innocent man who had never harmed me in his life."

In an instant I had the whole scene before my eyes—Monsieur Maurice flying—pursued—shot down—brought back to die! "But—but you won't try to run away, Monsieur Maurice!" I cried, terrified at the picture my own fancy had drawn.

He darted a scrutinising glance at me, and said, after a moment's hesitation:—"If I intended to do so, *petite*, I should hardly tell Colonel Bernhard's little daughter beforehand. Besides, why should I care now for liberty? What should I do with it? Have I not lost all that made it worth possessing—the Hero I worshipped, the Cause I honoured, the home I loved, the woman I adored? What better place for me than a prison . . . unless the grave?"

He roused himself. He had been thinking aloud, unconscious of my presence; but seeing my startled eyes fixed full upon his face, he smiled, and said with a sudden change of voice and manner:—"Go pluck me that namesake of yours over yonder-the big white Marguerite on the edge of the grass *plat*. Thanks, *petite*. Now I'll be sworn you guess what I am going to do with it! No? Well, I am going to question these little sibylline leaves, and make the Marguerite tell me whether I am destined to a prison all the days of my life. What! you never heard of the old flower sortilege? Why, Gretchen, I thought every little German maiden learned it in the cradle with her mother tongue!"

"But how can the Marguerite answer you, Monsieur Maurice?" I exclaimed.

"You shall see—but I must tell you first that the flower is not used to pronounce upon such serious matters. She is the oracle of village lads and lasses—not of grave prisoners like myself."

And with this, half sadly, half playfully, he began stripping the leaves off one by one, and repeating over and over again:—"Tell me, sweet Marguerite, shall I be free? Soon—in time—perhaps —never! Soon—in time—perhaps—never! Soon—in time-perhaps—" It was the last leaf. "Pshaw!" he said, tossing away the stalk with an impatient laugh. "You could have given me as good an answer as that, little Gretchen. Let us go in."

8

It was about a week after this when I was startled out of my deepest midnight sleep by a rush of many feet, and a fierce and sudden knocking at my father's bedroom door—the door opposite my own. I sat up, trembling. A bright blaze gleamed along the threshold, and high above the clamour of tongues outside, I recognised my father's voice, quick, sharp, imperative. Then a door was opened and banged. Then came the rush of feet again—then silence. It was a strange, wild hubbub; and it had all come, and gone, and was over in less than a minute. But what was it? Seeing that fiery line along the threshold, I had thought for a moment that the *château* was on fire; but the light vanished with those who brought it, and all was darkness again.

"Bertha!" I cried tremulously, "Bertha!" Now Bertha was my Rhenish hand-maiden, and she slept in a closet opening off my room; but Bertha was as deaf to my voice as one of the Seven Sleepers.

Suddenly a shrill trumpet-call rang out in the courtyard. I sprang out of bed, flew to Bertha, and shook her with all my strength till she woke. "Bertha! Bertha!" I cried. "Wake up-strike a light—dress me quickly! I must know what is the matter!"

In vain Bertha yawns, rubs her eyes, protests that I have had a bad dream, and that nothing is the matter. Get up she must; dress herself and me in the twinkling of an eye; and go upon whatsoever dance I choose to lead her. My father is gone, and his door stands wide open. We turn to the stairs, and a cold wind rushes up in our faces. We go down, and find the side-door that leads to the courtyard unfastened and ajar. There is not a soul in the courtyard.

There is not the faintest glimmer of light from the guard-house windows. The sentry who walks perpetually to and fro in front of the gate is not at his post; and the gate is wide open! Even Bertha sees by this time that something strange is afoot, and stares at me with a face of foolish wonder.

"*Ach, Herr Gott!*" she cries, clapping her hands together, "what's that?" It is very faint, very distant; but quite audible in the dead silence of the night.

In an instant I know what it is that has happened! "It is the report of a musket!" I exclaim, seizing her by the hand, and dragging her across the courtyard. "Quick! quick! Oh, Monsieur Maurice! Monsieur Maurice!"

The night is very dark. There is no moon, and the stars, glimmering through a veil of haze, give little light. But we run as recklessly as if it were bright day, past the barracks, past the parade-ground, and round to the great gates on the garden side of the *château*. These, however, are closed, and the sentry, standing watchful and motionless, with his musket made ready, refuses to let us through.

In vain I remind him that I am privileged, and that none of these gates are ever closed against me. The man is inexorable. "No, Fraeulein Gretchen," he says, "I dare not. This is not a fit hour for you to be out. Pray go home."

"But Gaspar, good Gaspar," I plead, clinging to the gate with both hands, "tell me if he has escaped! Hark; oh, hark! there it is again!" And another, and another shot rings through the still night-air. The sentry almost stamps with impatience.

"Go home, dear little *Fraeulein*! Go home at once," he says. "There is danger abroad tonight. I cannot leave my post, or I would take you home myself. . . . Holy Saint Christopher! they are coming this way! Go—go—what would his Excellency the Governor say, if he found you here?"

I see quick gleams of wandering lights among the trees—I hear a distant shout! Then, seized by a sudden panic, I turn and fly, with Bertha at my heels—fly back the way I came, never pausing till I find myself once more at the courtyard gate. Here—breathless, trembling, panting—I stop to listen and look back. All is silent;—as silent as before.

"But, *liebe* Gretchen," says Bertha, as breathless as myself, "what is to do tonight?" There is a coming murmur on the air. There is a red glow reflected on the barrack windows . . . they are coming! I turn suddenly cold and giddy.

"Hush, Bertha!" I whisper, "we must not stay here. Papa will be angry! Let us go up to the corridor window."

So we go back into the house, upstairs the way we came, and station ourselves at the corridor window, which looks into the courtyard. Slowly the glow broadens; slowly the sound resolves itself into an irregular tramp of many feet and a murmur of many voices. Then suddenly the courtyard is filled with soldiers and lighted torches, and . . . and I clasp my hands over my eyes in an agony of terror, lest the picture I drew a few days since should be coming true.

"What do you see, Bertha?" I falter. "Do you—do you see Monsieur Maurice?"

"No, but I see Gottlieb Kolb, and Corporal Fritz, and . . . yes—here is Monsieur Maurice between two soldiers, and his Excellency the Colonel walking beside them!"

I looked up, and my heart gave a leap of gladness. He was not dead—he was not even wounded! He had been pursued and captured; but at least he was safe! They stopped just under the corridor window. The torchlight fell full upon their faces. Monsieur Maurice looked pale and composed; perhaps just a shade haughtier than usual. My father had his drawn sword in his hand.

"Corporal Fritz," he said, turning to a soldier near him, "conduct the prisoner to his room, and post two sentries at his door, and one under his windows."

Then turning to Monsieur Maurice, "I thank God, Sir," he said gravely, "that you have not paid for your imprudence with your life. I have the honour to wish you goodnight."

Monsieur Maurice ceremoniously took off his hat. "Good

night, Colonel Bernhard," he said. "I beg you, however, to remember that I had withdrawn my parole."

"I remember it, Monsieur Maurice," replied my father, drawing himself up, and returning the salutation. Monsieur Maurice then crossed the courtyard with his guards, and entered the *château* by the door leading to the state apartments. My father, after standing for a moment as if lost in thought, turned away and went over to the guard-house. The soldiers then dispersed, or gathered into little knots of twos and threes, and talked in low voices of the events of the night.

"Accomplices!" said one, just close against the window where Bertha and I still lingered. "*Liebe Mutter*! I'll take my oath he had one! Why, it was I who first caught sight of the prisoner gliding through the trees—I saw him as plainly as I see you now—I covered him with my musket—I wouldn't have given a copper *pfennig* for his life, when paff! at the very moment I pulled the trigger, out steps a fellow from behind my shoulder, knocks up my musket, and disappears like a flash of lightning—Heaven only knows where, for I never laid eyes on him again!"

"What was he like?" asks another soldier, incredulously.

"Like? How should I know? It was as dark as pitch. I just caught a glimpse of him in the flash of the powder—an ugly, brown-looking devil he seemed! but he was gone in a breath, and I had no time to look for him."

The soldiers round about burst out laughing. "Hold, Karl!" says one, slapping him boisterously on the shoulder. "You are a good shot, but you missed aim for once. No need to conjure up a brown devil to account for that, old comrade!"

Karl, finding his story discredited, retorted angrily; and a quarrel was fast brewing, when the sergeant on guard came up and ordered the men to their several quarters.

"Holy Saint Bridget!" said Bertha, shivering, "how cold it is! and there, I declare, is the Convent clock striking half after one! *Liebe* Gretchen, you really must go to bed—what would your father say?"

So we both crept back to bed. Bertha was asleep again almost before she had laid her head upon her pillow; but I lay awake till dawn of day.

<h1 style="text-align:center">9</h1>

It was in my father's disposition to be both strict and indulgent—that is to say, as a father he was all tenderness, and as a soldier all discipline. His men both loved and feared him; but I, who never had cause to fear him in my life, loved him with all my heart, and never thought of him except as the fondest of parents. Chiefly, perhaps, for my sake, he had up to this time been extremely indulgent in all that regarded Monsieur Maurice.

Now, however, he conceived that it was his duty to be indulgent no longer. He was responsible for the person of Monsieur Maurice, and Monsieur Maurice had attempted to escape; from this moment, therefore, Monsieur Maurice must be guarded, hedged in, isolated, like any other prisoner under similar circumstances—at all events until further instructions should arrive from Berlin. So my father, as it was his duty to do, wrote straightway to the Minister of War, doubled all previous precautions, and forbade me to go near the prisoner's rooms on any pretext whatever. I neither coaxed nor pleaded.

I had an instinctive feeling that the thing was inevitable, and that I had nothing to do but to suffer and obey. And I did suffer bitterly. Day after day, I hung about the terraces under his windows, watching for the glimpse that hardly ever came. Night after night I sobbed till I was tired, and fell asleep with his name upon my lips. It was a childish grief; but not therefore the less poignant. It was a childish love, too; necessarily transient and irrational, as such childish passions are; but not therefore the less real. The dull web of my later life has not been without its one golden thread of romance (alas! how long since tarnished!), but not even that dream has left a deeper scar upon my memory than did the hero-worship of my first youth.

It was something more than love; it was adoration. To be with him was measureless content—to be banished from him was something akin to despair. So Monsieur Maurice and his little Gretchen were parted. No more happy French lessons—no more walks—no more stories told by the firelight in the gloaming! All was over; all was blank. But for how long? Surely not forever!

"Perhaps the king will think fit to hand him over to some other gaoler," said my father one day; "and, by Heaven! I'd thank him more heartily for that boon than for the order of the Red Eagle!"

My heart sank at the thought. Many and many a time had I pictured to myself what it would be if he were set at liberty, and with what mingled joy and grief I should bid him goodbye; but it had never occurred to me as a possibility that he might be transferred to another prison-house. Thus a week—ten days—a fortnight went by, and still there came nothing from Berlin. I began to hope at last that nothing would come, and that matters would settle down in time, and be as they were before. But of such vain hopes I was speedily and roughly disabused; and in this wise.

It was a gloomy afternoon—one of those dun-coloured afternoons that seem all the more dismal for coming in the midst of Spring. I had been out of the way somewhere (wandering to and fro, I believe, like a dreary little ghost, among the grim galleries of the state apartments), and was going home at dusk to be in readiness for my father, who always came in after the afternoon parade. Coming up the passage out of which our rooms opened, I heard voices—my father's and another. Concluding that he had Corporal Fritz with him, I went in unhesitatingly. To my surprise, I found the lamp lighted, and a strange officer sitting face to face with my father at the table.

The stranger was in the act of speaking; my father listening, with a grave, intent look upon his face. . . ."and if he had been shot, Colonel Bernhard, the State would have been well rid of a troublesome burden."

My father saw me in the doorway, put up his hand with a warning gesture, and said hastily:—"You here, Gretchen! Go into the dining-room, my child, till I send for you."

The dining-room, as I have said elsewhere, opened out of the sitting-room which also served for my father's bureau. I had therefore to cross the room, and so caught a full view of the stranger's face. He was a sallow, dark man, with iron grey hair cut close to his head, a hard mouth, a cold grey eye, and a deep furrow between his brows. He wore a blue military frock buttoned to the chin; and a plain cocked hat lay beside his gloves upon the table. I went into the dining-room and closed the door. It was half-door, half-window, the upper panels being made of ground glass, so as to let in a borrowed light; for the little room was at all times somewhat of the darkest.

Such as it was, this borrowed light was now all I had; for the dining-room fire had gone out hours ago, and though there were candles on the chimney-piece, I had no means of lighting them. So I groped my way to the first chair I could find, and waited my father's summons. "And if he had been shot, Colonel Bernhard, the State would have been well rid of a troublesome burden." It was all I had heard; but it was enough to set me thinking.

"If he had been shot".... If who had been shot? My fears answered that question but too readily. Who, then, was this newcomer? Was he from Berlin? And if from Berlin, what orders did he bring? A vague terror of coming evil fell upon me. I trembled—I held my breath. I tried to hear what was being said, but in vain.

The voices in the next room went on in a low incessant murmur; but of that murmur I could not distinguish a word. Then the sounds swelled a little, as if the speakers were becoming more earnest. And then, forgetting all I had ever heard or been taught about the heinousness of eavesdropping, I got up very softly and crept close against the door.

"That is to say, you dislike the responsibility, Colonel Bernhard." These were the first words I heard.

"I dislike the office," said my father, bluntly. "I'd almost as soon be a hangman as a gaoler."

The stranger here said something that my ear failed to

catch.

Then my father spoke again. "To tell you the truth, Herr Count, I only wish it would please His Excellency to transfer him elsewhere."

The stranger paused a moment, and then said in a low but very distinct voice:—"Supposing, Colonel Bernhard, that you were yourself transferred—shall we say to Koenigsberg? Would you prefer it to Bruehl?"

"Koenigsberg!" exclaimed my father in a tone of profound amazement. "The appointment, I believe, is worth six hundred *thalers* a year more than Bruehl," said the stranger.

"But it has never been offered to me," said my father, in his simple straightforward way. "Of course I should prefer it—but what of that? And what has Koenigsberg to do with Monsieur Maurice?"

"Ah, true—Monsieur Maurice! Well, to return then to Monsieur Maurice—how would it be, do you think, somewhat to relax the present vigilance?"

"To relax it?" "To leave a door or a window unguarded now and then, for instance In short, to—to provide certain facilities . . . you understand?"

"Facilities?" exclaimed my father, incredulously. "Facilities for escape?"

"Well—yes; if you think fit to put it so plainly," replied the other, with a short little cough, followed by a snap like the opening and shutting of a snuff-box.

"But—but in the name of the Eleven Thousand Virgins, why wait for the man to run away? Why not give him his liberty, and get rid of him pleasantly?"

"Because—ahem!—because, you see, Colonel Bernhard, it would not then be possible to pursue him," said the stranger, drily.

"To pursue him?"

"Just so—and to shoot him." I heard the sound of a chair pushed violently back; and my father's shadow, vague and menacing, started up with him, and fell across the door.

"What?" he shouted, in a terrible voice. "Are you taking me at my word? Are you offering me the hangman's office?"

Then, with a sudden change of tone and manner, he added:— "But—I must have misunderstood you. It is impossible."

"We have both altogether misunderstood each other, Colonel Bernhard," said the stranger, stiffly. "I had supposed you would be willing to serve the State, even at the cost of some violence to your prejudices."

"Great God! then you did mean it!" said my father, with a strange horror in his voice.

"I meant—to serve the King. I also hoped to advance the interests of Colonel Bernhard," replied the other, haughtily.

"My sword is the King's—my blood is the King's, to the last drop," said my father in great agitation; "but my honour—my honour is my own!"

"Enough, Colonel Bernhard; enough. We will drop the subject." And again I heard the little dry cough, and the snap of the snuff-box. A long silence followed, my father walking to and fro with a quick, heavy step; the stranger, apparently, still sitting in his place at the table.

"Should you, on reflection, see cause to take a different view of your duty, Colonel Bernhard," he said at last, "you have but to say so before. . . ."

"I can never take a different view of it, Herr Count!" interrupted my father, vehemently.

"—before I take my departure in the morning," continued the other, with studied composure; "in the meanwhile, be pleased to remember that you are answerable for the person of your prisoner. Either he must not escape, or he must not escape with life." My father's shadow bent its head. "And now, with your permission, I will go to my room."

My father rang the bell, and when Bertha came, bade her light the Count von Rettel to his chamber. Hearing them leave the room, I opened the door very softly and hesitatingly, scarce knowing whether to come out or not. I saw my father standing with his back towards me and his face still turned in the direction

49

by which they had gone out. I saw him throw up his clenched hands, and shake them wildly above his head. "And it was for this!—for this!" he said fiercely. "A bribe! God of Heaven! He offered me Koenigsberg as a bribe! Oh, that I should have lived to be treated as an assassin!" His voice broke into hoarse sobs. He dropped into a chair—he covered his face with his hands.

He had forgotten that I was in the next room, and now I dared not remind him of my presence. His emotion terrified me. It was the first time I had seen a man shed tears; and this alone, let the man be whom he might, would have seemed terrible to me at any time. How much more terrible when those tears were tears of outraged honour, and when the man who shed them was my father! I trembled from head to foot. I had an instinctive feeling that I ought not to look upon his agony. I shrank back-closed the door—held my breath, and waited.

Presently the sound of sobbing ceased. Then he sighed heavily twice or thrice—got up abruptly—threw a couple of logs on the fire, and left the room. The next moment I heard him unlock the door under the stairs, and go into the cellar. I seized the opportunity to escape, and stole up to my own room as rapidly and noiselessly as my trembling knees would carry me.

I had my supper with Bertha that evening, and the Count ate at my father's table; but I afterwards learned that, though the Governor of Bruehl himself waited ceremoniously upon his guest and served him with his best, he neither broke bread nor drank wine with him. I saw that unwelcome guest no more. I heard his voice under the window, and the clatter of his horse's hoofs as he rode away in the early morning; but that was long enough before Bertha came to call me.

10

Weeks went by. Spring warmed, and ripened, and blossomed into Summer. Gardens and terraces were ablaze once more with many-coloured flowers; fountains played and sparkled in the sunshine; and travellers bound for Cologne or Bonn put up again at Bruehl in the midst of the day's journey, to bait their horses and see the *château* on their way. For in these years just following the Peace of Paris, the Continent was overrun by travellers, two thirds of whom were English. The diligence—the great, top-heavy, lumbering diligence of fifty years ago—used then to come lurching and thundering down the main street five times a week throughout the Summer season; and as many as three and four travelling carriages a day would pass through in fine weather.

The landlord of the "Lion d'Or" kept fifty horses in his stables in those days, and drove a thriving trade. So the Summer came, and brought the stir of outer life into the precincts of our sleepy *château*; but brought no better change in the fortunes of Monsieur Maurice. Ever since that fatal night, the terms of his imprisonment had been more rigorous than ever.

Till then, he might, if he would, walk twice a week in the grounds with a soldier at his heels; but now he was placed in strict confinement in his own two rooms, with one sentry always pacing the corridor outside his door, and another under his windows. And across each of those windows might now be seen a couple of bright new iron bars, thick as a man's wrist, forged and fixed there by the village blacksmith. I have no words to tell how the sight of those bars revolted me. If instead of being a little helpless girl, I had been a man like my father, and a servant of the State, I think they would have made a rebel of me.

Worse, however, than iron bars, locked doors, and guarded corridors, was Hartmann—Herr Ludwig Hartmann, as he was styled in the despatch that announced his coming—a pale, slight, silent man, with colourless grey eyes and white eyelashes, who came direct from Berlin about a month later, to act as Monsieur Maurice's "personal attendant."

Stealthy, watchful, secret, civil, he established himself in a room adjoining the prisoner's apartment, and was as much at home in the course of a couple of hours as if he had been settled there from the first. He brought with him a paper of instructions, and, having on his arrival submitted these instructions to my father, he at once took up a certain routine of duties that never varied.

He brushed Monsieur Maurice's clothes, waited upon him at table, attended him in his bedroom, was always within hearing, always on the alert, and haunted the prisoner like his shadow.

Not even a housemaid could go in to sweep but he was present. Now the man's perpetual presence was intolerable to Monsieur Maurice. He had borne all else with patience, but this last tyranny was more than he could endure without murmuring. He appealed to my father; but my father, though Governor of Bruehl, was powerless to help him. Hartmann had presented his instructions as a minister presents his credentials, and those instructions emanated from Berlin.

So the newcomer, valet, gaoler, spy as he was, became an established fact, and was detested throughout the *château*—by no one more heartily than myself. I still, however, saw Monsieur Maurice now and then.

My father often took me with him in his rounds, and always when he visited his prisoner. Sometimes, too, he would leave me for an hour with my friend, and call for me again on his way back; so that we were not wholly parted even now. But Hartmann took care never to leave us alone. Before my father's footsteps were out of hearing, he would be in the room; silent, unobtrusive, perfectly civil, but watchful as a lynx. We could not talk before him freely. Nothing was as it used to be. It was better than total banishments; it was better than never hearing his voice; but the constraint was hard to bear, and the pain of these meetings was almost greater than the pleasure.

And now, as I approach that part of my narrative which possesses the deepest interest for myself, I hesitate—hesitate and draw back before the great mystery in which it is involved. I ask myself what interpretation the world will put upon facts for which I can vouch; upon events which I myself witnessed? I cannot prove those events. They happened over fifty years ago; but they are as vividly present to my memory as if they had taken place yesterday. I can only relate them in their order, knowing them to be true, and leaving each reader to judge of them according to his convictions.

It was about the middle of the second week in June. Hartmann had been about six weeks at Bruehl, and all was going on in the usual dull routine, when that routine was suddenly broken by the arrival of three mounted dragoons—an officer and two privates—whose errand, whatever it might be, had the effect of throwing the whole establishment into sudden and unwonted confusion.

I was out in the grounds when they arrived, and came back at midday to find no dinner on the table, no cook in the kitchen; but a full-dress parade going on in the courtyard, and all the interior of the *château* in a state of wild commotion. Here were peasants bringing in wood, gardeners laden with vegetables and flowers, women running to and fro with baskets full of linen, and all to the accompaniment of such a hammering, bell-ringing, and clattering of tongues as I had never heard before. I stood bewildered, not knowing what to do, or where to go.

"What is the matter? What has happened? What are you doing?" I asked, first of one and then of another; but they were all too busy to answer.

"*Ach, lieber Gott!*" said one, "I've no time for talking!"

"Don't ask me, little *Fraeulein*," said another. "I have eight windows to clean up yonder, and only one pair of hands to do them with!"

"If you want to know what is to do," said a third impatiently, "you had better come and see."

The head-gardener's son came by with two pots of magnificent geraniums, one under each arm.

"Where are you going with those flowers, Wilhelm?" I asked, running after him. "They are for the state salon, Fraeulein Gretchen," he replied, and hurried on.

For the state salon! I ran round to the side of the grand entrance. There were soldiers putting up banners in the hall; others helping to carry furniture up stairs; carpenters with ladders; women with brooms and brushes; and Corporal Fritz bustling hither and thither, giving orders, and seeing after everything.

"But Corporal Fritz!" I exclaimed, "what are all these people about?"

"We are preparing the state apartments, dear little *Fraeulein*," replied Corporal Fritz, rubbing his hands with an air of great enjoyment.

"But why? For whom?"

"For whom? Why, for the King, to be sure"; and Corporal Fritz clapped his hand to the side of his hat like a loyal soldier. "Don't you know, dear little *Fraeulein*, that His Majesty sleeps here tonight, on his way to Ehrenbreitstein?"

This was news indeed! I ran upstairs—I was all excitement—I got in everybody's way—I tormented everybody with questions. I saw the table being laid in the grand salon where the King was to sup, and the bedstead being put up in the little salon where he was to sleep, and the ante-room being prepared for his officers. All was being made ready as rapidly, and decorated as tastefully, as the scanty resources of the *château* would permit. I recognised much of the furniture from the attics above, and this, faded though it was, being helped out with flowers, flags, and greenery, made the great echoing rooms look gay and habitable.

By and by, my father came round to see how the work was going on, and finding me in the midst of it, took me by the hand and led me away. "You are not wanted here, my little Gretchen," he said; "and, indeed, all the world is so busy today that I scarcely know what to do with thee."

"Take me to Monsieur Maurice!" I said, coaxingly.

"Ay—so I will," said my father; "with him, at all events, you will be out of the way."

So he took me round to Monsieur Maurice's rooms, and told me as we went along that the King had only given him six hours' notice, and that in order to furnish his Majesty's bed and his Majesty's supper, he had bought up all the poultry and eggs, and borrowed well-nigh all the silver, glass, and linen in the town. By this time we were almost at Monsieur Maurice's door. A sudden thought flashed upon me. I pulled him back, out of the sentry's hearing.

"Oh, father!" I cried eagerly, "will you not ask the King to let

Monsieur Maurice free?"

My father shook his head. "Nay," he said, "I must not do that, my little *Maedchen*. And look you—not a word that the King is coming here tonight. It would only make the prisoner restless, and could avail nothing. Promise me to be silent."

So I promised, and he left me at the door without going in. I spent all the afternoon with Monsieur Maurice. He divided his luncheon with me; he gave me a French lesson, he told me stories. I had not had such a happy day for months. Hartmann, it is true, was constantly in and out of the room, but even Hartmann was less in the way than usual. He seemed absent and preoccupied, and was therefore not so watchful as at other times. In the meanwhile I could still hear, though faintly, the noises in the rooms below; but all became quiet about five o'clock in the evening, and Monsieur Maurice, who had been told they were only cleaning the state apartments, asked no questions.

Meanwhile the afternoon waned, and the sun bent westward, and still no one came to fetch me away. My father knew where I was; Bertha was probably too busy to think about me; and I was only too glad to stay as long as Monsieur Maurice was willing to keep me. By and by, about half-past six o'clock, the sky became over-clouded, and we heard a low muttering of very distant thunder. At seven, it rained heavily.

Now it was Monsieur Maurice's custom to dine late, and ours to dine early; but then, as his luncheon hour corresponded with our dinner-hour, and his dinner fell only a little later than our supper, it came to much the same thing, and did not therefore seem strange. So it happened that just as the storm came up, Hartmann began to prepare the table.

Then, in the midst of the rain and the wind, my quick ear caught a sound of drums and bugles, and I knew the King was come. Monsieur Maurice evidently heard nothing; but I could see by Hartmann's face (he was laying the cloth and making a noise with the glasses) that he knew all, and was listening. After this I heard no more. The wind raved; the rain pattered; the gloom thickened; and at half-past seven, when the soup was brought to table, it was so dark that Monsieur Maurice called for lights. He would not, however, allow the curtains to be drawn. He liked, he said, to sit and watch the storm.

A cover was laid for me at his right hand; but my supper hour was past, and what with the storm without, the heaviness in the air, and the excitement of the day, I was no longer hungry. So, having eaten a little soup and sipped some wine from Monsieur Maurice's glass, I went and curled myself up in an easy chair close to the window, and watched the driving mists as they swept across the park, and the tossing of the treetops against the sky.

It was a wild evening, lit by lurid gleams and openings in the clouds; and it seemed all the wilder by contrast with the quiet room and the dim radiance of the wax lights on the table. There was a soft halo round each little flame, and a dreamy haze in the atmosphere, from the midst of which Monsieur Maurice's pale face stood out against the shadowy background, like a head in a Dutch painting.

We were both very silent; partly because Hartmann was waiting, and partly, perhaps, because we had been talking all the afternoon. Monsieur Maurice ate slowly, and there were long intervals between the courses, during which he leaned his elbow on the table and his chin on his hand, looking across towards the window and the storm. Hartmann, meanwhile, seemed to be always listening. I could see that he was holding his breath, and trying to catch every faint echo from below. It was a long, long dinner, and probably seemed all the longer to me because I did not partake of it.

As for Monsieur Maurice, he tasted some dishes, and sent more away untouched. "I think it is getting lighter," he said by and by. "Does it still rain?"

"Yes," I replied; "it is coming down steadily."

"We must open the window presently," he said. "I love the fresh smell that comes with the rain."

Here the conversation dropped again, and Hartmann, having been gone for a moment, came back with a dish of stewed fruit.

Then, for the first time, I observed there was a second attendant in the room.

"Will you not have some raspberries, Gretchen?" said Monsieur Maurice. I shook my head. I was too much startled by the sight of the strange man, to answer him in words. Who could he be? Where had he come from? He was standing behind Monsieur Maurice, far back in the gloom, near the door—a small, dark man, apparently; but so placed with regard to the table and the lights, that it was impossible to make out his features with distinctness.

Monsieur Maurice just tasted the raspberries and sent his plate away. "How heavy the air of the room is!" he said. "Give me some Seltzer-water, and open that farthest window."

Hartmann reversed the order. He opened the window first; and as he did so, I saw that his hand shook upon the hasp, and that his face was deadly pale. He then turned to the sideboard and opened a stone bottle that had been standing there since the beginning of dinner. He filled a tumbler with the sparkling water.

At the moment when he placed this tumbler on the salver-at the moment when he handed it to Monsieur Maurice—the other man glided quickly forward. I saw his bright eyes and his brown face in the full light. I saw *two hands* put out to take the glass; a brown hand and a white—his hand, and the hand of Monsieur Maurice. I saw—yes, before Heaven! as I live to remember and record it, I saw the brown hand grasp the tumbler and dash it to the ground!

"Pshaw!" said Monsieur Maurice, brushing the Seltzer-water impatiently from his sleeve, "how came you to upset it?"

But Hartmann, livid and trembling, stood speechless, staring at the door.

"It was the other man!" said I, starting up with a strange kind of breathless terror upon me. "He threw it on the ground—I saw him do it—where is he gone? what has become of him?"

"The other man! What other man?" said Monsieur Maurice. "My little Gretchen, you are dreaming."

"No, no, I am not dreaming. There was another man—a brown man! Hartmann saw him—"

"A brown man!" echoed Monsieur Maurice.

Then catching sight of Hartmann's face, he pushed his chair back, looked at him steadily and sternly; and said, with a sudden change of voice and manner:—"There is something wrong here. What does it mean? You saw a man—both of you? What was he like?"

"A brown man," I said again. "A brown man with bright eyes."

"And you?" said Monsieur Maurice, turning to Hartmann.

"I—I thought I saw something," stammered the attendant, with a violent effort at composure. "But it was nothing."

Monsieur Maurice looked at him as if he would look him through; got up, still looking at him; went to the sideboard, and, still looking at him, filled another tumbler with Seltzer-water. "Drink that," he said, very quietly. The man's lips moved, but he uttered never a word.

"Drink that," said Monsieur Maurice for the second time, and more sternly. But Hartmann, instead of drinking it, instead of answering, threw up his hands in a wild way, and rushed out of the room. Monsieur Maurice stood for a moment absorbed in thought; then wrote some words upon a card, and gave the card into my hand.

"For thy father, little one," he said. "Give it to no one but himself, and give it to him the first moment thou seest him. There's matter of life and death in it."

11

How the King supped, how the King slept, and what he thought of his *château* of Augustenburg which he now saw for the first time, are matters respecting which I have no information. I only know that I had fallen asleep on Monsieur Maurice's sofa when Bertha came at ten o'clock that night to fetch me home; that I was very drowsy and unwilling to be moved; and that I woke in the morning dreaming of a brown man with bright eyes, and calling upon Monsieur Maurice to make haste and come before he should again have time to vanish away. It was a lovely morning; bright and fresh, and sunshiny after the night's storm. My first thought was of Monsieur Maurice, and the card he had entrusted to my keeping. I had it still.

My father was not at home when I came back last night. He was in attendance on the King, and did not return till long after I was asleep in my own little bed. This morning, early as I awoke, he was gone again, on the same duty. I jumped up. I bade Bertha dress me quickly.

"I must go to papa," I said. "I have a card for him from Monsieur Maurice."

"Nay, *liebe* Gretchen," said Bertha, "he is with the King."

But I told myself that I would find him, and see him, and give the card into his own hands, though a dozen kings were in the way. I could not read what was written on the card. I could read print easily and rapidly, but handwriting not at all. I knew, however, that it was urgent. Had he not said that it was matter of life or death? I hurried to dress; I hurried to get out. I could not rest, I could not eat till I had given up the card.

As good fortune would have it, the first person I met was Corporal Fritz. I asked him where I could find my father. "Dear little *Fraeulein*," said Corporal Fritz, "you cannot see him just yet. He is with the King."

"But I must see him," I said. "I must—indeed, I must. Go to him for me—please go to him, dear, good Corporal Fritz, and tell him his little Gretchen must speak to him, if only for one moment!"

"But dear little *Fraeulein*". . . .

"Is the King at breakfast?" I interrupted.

"At breakfast! Eh, then, our gallant King hath a soldier's habits. His Majesty breakfasted at six this morning, and is gone out betimes to visit his hunting-lodge at Falkenlust."

"And my father?"

"His Excellency the Governor is in attendance upon the King."

"Then I will go to Falkenlust."

Corporal Fritz shook his head; shrugged his shoulders; took a pinch of snuff. "'Tis a long road to Falkenlust, dear little *Fraeulein*," said he; "and His Excellency, methinks, would be better pleased". . . . I stayed to hear no more, but ran off at full speed down the terraces, straight to the Round Point and the fountain, and along the great avenue that led to Falkenlust.

I ran till I was out of breath—then rested—then ran again, on, and on, and on, till the road lengthened and narrowed behind me, and the *château* of Augustenburg looked almost as small in the distance at one end as the Falkenlust Lodge at the other. Then all at once, far, far away, I saw a moving group of figures. They grew larger and more distinct—they were coming towards me! I had run till I could run no farther.

Panting and breathless, I leaned against a tree, and waited. And now, as they drew nearer, I saw that the group consisted of some eight or ten officers, two of whom were walking somewhat in advance of the rest. One of the two wore a plain cocked hat and an undress military frock; the other was in full uniform, and wore two or three glittering medals on his breast.

This other was my father. I scarcely looked at the first. I never even asked myself whether he was, or was not the King. I had no eyes, no thought for any but my father. So I stood, eager and breathless, on the verge of the gravel. So they every moment drew nearer the spot where I was standing. As they came close, my father's eyes met mine. He shook his head, and frowned. He thought I had come there to stare at the King. Nothing daunted, I took two steps forward. I had Monsieur Maurice's card in my hand. I held it out to him.

"Read it," I said. "It is from Monsieur Maurice." But he crushed it in his hand without looking at it, and waved me back authoritatively.

"At once!" I cried; "at once!"

The gentleman in the blue frock stopped and smiled. "Is this your little girl, Colonel Bernhard?" he asked.

My father replied by a low bow. The strange gentleman beckoned me to draw nearer. "A golden-haired little *Maedchen!*" said he. "Come hither, pretty one, and tell me your name."

I knew then that he was the King. I trembled and blushed. "My name is Gretchen," I said.

"And you have brought a letter for your father?"

"It is not a letter," I said. "It is a card. It is from Monsieur Maurice."

"And who is Monsieur Maurice?" asked the King.

"So please your Majesty," said my father, answering the question for me, "Monsieur Maurice is the prisoner I hold in charge."

The smile went out of the King's face. "The prisoner!" he repeated, inquiringly. "What prisoner?"

"The state-prisoner whom I received, according to your Majesty's command, eight months ago—Monsieur Maurice."

"Monsieur Maurice!" echoed the King.

"I know the gentleman by no other name, please your Majesty," said my father.

The King looked grave. "I never heard of Monsieur Maurice," he said, "I know of no state-prisoner here."

"The prisoner was consigned to my keeping by your Majesty's Minister of War," said my father.

"By von Bulow?" My father bowed.

"Upon whose authority?"

"In your Majesty's name."

The King frowned. "What papers did you receive with your prisoner, Colonel Bernhard?" he said.

"None, your Majesty—except a despatch from your Majesty's Minister of War, delivered a day or two before the prisoner arrived at Bruehl."

"How did he come? and where did he come from?"

"He came in a close carriage, your Majesty, attended by two officers who left Bruehl the same night and whose names and persons are unknown to me. I do not know where he came from. I only know that they had taken the last relay of horses from Cologne."

"You were not told his offence?"

"I was told nothing, your Majesty, except that Monsieur Maurice was an enemy to the state, and—"

"And what?"

My father's hand went up to his moustache, as it was wont to do in perplexity. "I—so please your Majesty, I think there is some foul mystery in it at bottom," he said, bluntly. "There hath been that thing proposed to me that I am ashamed to repeat. I do beseech your Majesty that some investigation . . . ."

His eyes happened for a moment to rest upon the card. He stammered—changed colour—stopped short in his sentence-took off his hat—laid the card upon it—and so handed it to the King. His Majesty Frederick William the Third of Prussia was, like most of the princes of his house, tanned, soldierly, and fresh-complexioned; but florid as he was, there came a darker flush into his face as he read what Monsieur Maurice had written.

"An attempt upon his life!" he exclaimed. "The thing is not possible."

My father was silent. The king looked at him keenly. "*Is* it possible, Colonel Bernhard?" he said.

"I think it may be possible, your Majesty," replied my father in a low voice.

The King frowned. "Colonel Bernhard," he said, "how can that be? You are responsible for the safety as well as the person of any prisoner committed to your charge."

"So long as the prisoner is left wholly to my charge I can answer for his safety with my head, so please your Majesty," said my father, reddening; "but not when he is provided with a special attendant over whom I have no control."

"What special attendant? Where did he come from? Who sent him?"

"I believe he came from Berlin, your Majesty. He was sent by your Majesty's Minister of War. His name is Hartmann."

The King stood thinking. His officers had fallen out of ear-shot, and were talking together in a little knot some four yards behind. I was still standing on the spot to which the King had called me. He looked round, and saw my anxious face. "What, still there, little one?" he said. "You have not heard what we were saying?"

"Yes," I said; "I heard it."

"The child may have heard, your Majesty," interposed my father, hastily; "but she did not understand. Run home, Gretchen. Make thy obeisance to his Majesty, and run home quickly."

But I had understood every word. I knew that Monsieur Maurice's life had been in danger. I knew the King was all-powerful. Terrified at my own boldness—terrified at the thought of my father's anger—trembling—sobbing—scarcely conscious of what I was saying, I fell at the King's feet, and cried:—"Save him—save him, Sire! Don't let them kill poor Monsieur Maurice! Forgive him—please forgive him, and let him go home again!"

My father seized me by the hand, forced me to rise, and dragged me back more roughly than he had ever touched me in his life. "I beseech your Majesty's pardon for the child," he said. "She knows no better."

But the King smiled, and called me back to him. "Nay, nay," he said, laying his hand upon my head, "do not be vexed with her. So, little one, you and Monsieur Maurice are friends?"

I nodded; for I was still crying, and too frightened at what I had done to be able to speak.

"And you love him dearly?"

"Better than anyone—in the world—except Papa," I faltered, through my tears.

"Not better than your brothers and sisters?"

"I have no brothers and sisters," I replied, my courage coming back again by degrees. "I have no one but Papa, and Monsieur Maurice, and Aunt Martha Baur—and I love Monsieur Maurice a thousand, thousand times more than Aunt Martha Baur!"

There came a merry sparkle into the King's eyes, and my father turned his face away to conceal a smile. "But if Monsieur Maurice was free, he would go away and you would never see him again. What would you do then?"

"I—should be very sorry," I faltered; "but". . . .

"But what?"

"I would rather he went away, and was happy."

The King stooped down and kissed me on the brow. "That, my little *Maedchen*, is the answer of a true friend," he said, gravely and kindly. "If your Monsieur Maurice deserves to go free, he shall have his liberty. You have our royal word for it. Colonel Bernhard, we will investigate this matter without the delay of an hour."

Saying thus, he turned from me to my father, and, followed by his officers, passed on in the direction of the *château*. I stood there speechless, his gracious words yet ringing in my ears. He had left me no time for thanks, if even I could have framed any. But he had kissed me—he had promised me that Monsieur Maurice should go free, "if he deserved it!" and who better than I knew how impossible it was that he should not deserve it? It was all true. It was not a dream. I had the King's royal word for it. I had the King's royal word for it—and yet I could hardly believe it!

12

I have told my story up to this point from my own personal experience, relating in their order, quite simply and faithfully, the things I myself heard and saw. I can do this, however, no longer. Respecting those matters that happened when I was not present, I can only repeat what was told me by others; and as regards certain foregone events in the life of Monsieur Maurice, I have but vague rumour; and still more vague conjecture upon which to base my conclusions.

The King had said that Monsieur Maurice's case should be investigated without the delay of an hour, and, so far as it could then and there be done, it was investigated immediately on his return to the *château*. He first examined Baron von Bulow's original despatch, and all my father's minutes of matters relating to the prisoner, including a statement written immediately after the departure of a stranger calling himself the Count von Rettel, and detailing from memory, very circumstantially and fully, the substance of a certain conversation to which I had been accidentally a witness, and which I have myself recorded elsewhere.

The King, on reading this statement, was observed to be greatly disturbed. He questioned my father minutely as to the age, complexion, height, and general appearance of the said Count von Rettel, and with his own hand noted down my father's replies on the back of my father's manuscript. This done, His Majesty desired that the man Hartmann should be brought before him.

But Hartmann was nowhere to be found. His room was empty. His bed had not been slept in. He had disappeared, in short, as completely as if he had never dwelt within the precincts of the *château*. It was found, on more particular inquiry being made, that he had not been seen since the previous evening. Overwhelmed with terror, and perhaps with remorse, he had rushed out of Monsieur Maurice's presence, never to return. It was supposed that he had then immediately gathered together all that belonged to him, and had taken advantage of the bustle and confusion consequent on the King's arrival, to leave Bruehl in one of the return carriages or *fourgons* that had brought the royal party from Cologne.

I am not aware that anything more was ever seen or heard of him; or that any active search for him was judicially instituted either then, or at any other time. But he might easily have been pursued, and taken, and dealt with according to the law, without our being any the wiser at Bruehl. Hartmann being gone, the King then sent for the prisoner, and Monsieur Maurice, for the first time in many weeks, left his own rooms, and was brought round to the state-apartments. Seeing so many persons about; seeing also the flowers and flags upon the walls, he seemed surprised, but said nothing.

Being brought into the royal presence, however, he appeared at once to recognise the King. He bowed profoundly, and a faint flush was seen to come into his face. He then cast a rapid glance round the room, as if to see who else was present; bowed also (but less profoundly) to my father, who was standing behind the King's chair; and waited to be spoken to. "*Vous etes Francais, Monsieur?*" said the King, addressing him in French, of which language my father understood only a few words.

"*Je suis Francais, votre Majeste,*" replied Monsieur Maurice.

"*Comment!*" said the King, still in French. "Our person, then, is not unknown to you?"

"I have repeatedly enjoyed the honour of being in your Majesty's presence," replied Monsieur Maurice, respectfully. Being then asked where, and on what occasion, my father understood him to say that he had seen his Majesty at Erfurt during the great meeting of the Sovereigns under Napoleon the First, and again at the Congress of Vienna; and also that he had, at that time, occupied some important office, such, perhaps, as military secretary, about the person of the Emperor.

The King then proceeded to question him on matters relating to his imprisonment and his previous history, to all of which Monsieur Maurice seemed to reply at some length, and with great earnestness of manner.

Of these explanations, however, my father's imperfect knowledge of the language enabled him to catch only a few words here and there. Presently, in the midst of a somewhat lengthy statement, Monsieur Maurice pronounced the name of Baron von Bulow. Hereupon the King checked him by a gesture; desired all present to withdraw; caused the door to be closed; and carried on the rest of the examination in private. By and by, after the lapse of nearly three quarters of an hour, my father was recalled, and an officer in waiting was despatched to Monsieur Maurice's rooms to fetch what was left of the bottle of Seltzer-water, which Monsieur Maurice had himself locked up in the sideboard the night before.

The King then asked if there was any scientific man in Bruehl capable of analysing the liquid; to which my father replied that no such person could be found nearer than Cologne or Bonn. Hereupon a dog was brought in from the stables, and, having been made to swallow about a quarter of a pint of the Seltzer-water, was presently taken with convulsions, and died on the spot. The King then desired that the body of the dog, and all that yet remained in the bottle should be despatched to the Professor of Chemistry at Bonn, for immediate examination.

This done, he turned to Monsieur Maurice, and said in German, so that all present might hear and understand:—"*Monsieur*, so far as we have the present means of judging, you have suffered an illegal and unjust imprisonment, and a base attempt has been made upon your life. You appear to be the victim of a foul conspiracy, and it will be our first care to sift that conspiracy to the bottom. In the meanwhile, we restore your liberty, requiring only your *parole d'honneur*, as a gentleman, a soldier, and a Frenchman, to present yourself at Berlin, if summoned, at any time required within the next three months."

Monsieur Maurice bowed, laid his hand upon his heart, and said:—"I promise it, your Majesty, on my word of honour as a gentleman, a soldier, and a Frenchman."

"You are probably in need of present funds," the King then said; "and if so, our Secretary shall make you out an order on the Treasury for five hundred *thalers*."

"Believing myself to be beggared of all I once possessed, I gratefully accept your Majesty's bounty," replied Monsieur Maurice.

The King then held out his hand for Monsieur Maurice to kiss, which he did on bended knee, and so went out from the royal presence, a free man. Half an hour later, he and I were strolling hand in hand under the trees. His step was slow, and the hand that held mine had grown sadly thin and transparent.

"Let us sit here awhile, and rest," he said, as we came to the bench by the fountain. I reminded him that we had sat and rested in the same spot the very last time we walked together.

"Ay," he replied, with a sigh. "I was stronger then."

"You will get strong again, now that you are free," I said.

"Perhaps—if liberty, like most earthly blessings, has not come too late."

"Too late for what?"

"For enjoyment—for use—for everything. My friends believe me dead; my place in the life of the world is filled up; my very name is by this time forgotten. I am as one shipwrecked on the great ocean, and cast upon a foreign shore."

"Are you—are you going away soon?" I said, almost in a whisper.

"Yes," he said, "I go tomorrow."

"And you will—never—come back again?" I faltered.

"Heaven forbid!" he said quickly. Then, remembering how that answer would grieve me, he added; "but I will never forget thee, *petite*. Never, while I live."

"But—but if I never see you any more".... Monsieur Maurice drew my head to his shoulder, and kissed my wet eyes.

"Tush! that cannot, shall not be," he said, caressingly. "Someday, perhaps, I may win back that old home by the sea of which I have so often told thee, little one; and then thou shalt come and visit me."

"Shall I?" I said, wistfully. "Shall I indeed?"

And he said—"Ay, indeed." But I felt, somehow, that it would never come to pass. After this, we got up and walked on again, very silently; he thinking of the new life before him; I, of the sorrow of parting.

By-and-by, a sudden recollection flashed upon me. "But, Monsieur Maurice," I exclaimed, "who was the brown man that stood behind your chair last night, and what has become of him?"

Monsieur Maurice turned his face away. "My dear little Gretchen," he said, hastily, "there was no brown man. He existed in your imagination only."

"But I saw him!"

"You fancied you saw him. The room was dark. You were half asleep in the easy chair—half asleep, and half dreaming."

"But Hartmann saw him!"

"A wicked man fears his own shadow," said Monsieur Maurice, gravely. "Hartmann saw nothing but the reflection of his crime upon the mirror of his conscience." I was silenced, but not convinced.

Some minutes later, having thought it over, I returned to the charge. "But, Monsieur Maurice," I said, "it is not the first time he has been here."

"Who? The King?"

"No—the brown man." Monsieur Maurice frowned.

"Nay, nay," he said, impatiently, "prithee, no more of the brown man. 'Tis a folly, and I dislike it."

"But he was here in the park the night you tried to run away," I said, persistently. "He saved your life by knocking up the musket that was pointed at your head!"

Pale as he always was, Monsieur Maurice turned paler still at these words of mine. His very lips whitened. "What is that you say?" he asked, stopping short and laying his hand upon my shoulder. And then I repeated, word for word, all that I had heard the soldiers saying that night under the corridor window.

When I had done, he took off his hat and stood for a moment as if in prayer, silent and bare-headed. "If it be so," he said presently, "if such fidelity can indeed survive the grave—then not once, but thrice. . . . Who knows? Who can tell?" He was speaking to himself. I heard the words, and I remembered them; but I did not understand them till long after.

The King left Bruehl that same afternoon *en route* for Ehrenbreitstein, and Monsieur Maurice went away the next morning in a post-chaise and pair, bound for Paris. He gave me, for a farewell gift, his precious microscope and all his boxes of slides, and he parted from me with many kisses; but there was a smile on his face as he got into the carriage, and something of triumph in the very wave of his hand as he drove away.

Alas! how could it be otherwise? A prisoner freed, an exile returning to his country, how should he not be glad to go, even though one little heart should be left to ache or break in the land of the stranger? I never saw him again; never—never—never. He wrote now and then to my father, but only for a time; perhaps as many as six letters during three or four years—and then we heard from him no more.

To these letters he gave us no opportunity of replying, for they contained no address; and although we had reason to believe that he was a man of family and title, he never signed himself by any other name than that by which we had known him. We did hear, however, (I forget now through what channel) of the sudden disgrace and banishment of His Majesty's Minister of War, the Baron von Bulow. Respecting the causes of his fall there were many vague and contradictory rumours.

He had starved to death a prisoner of war and forced his widow into a marriage with himself. He had sold State secrets to the French. He had been over to Elba in disguise, and had there held treasonable intercourse with the exiled Emperor, before his return to France in 1815. He had attempted to murder, or caused to be murdered, the witnesses of his treachery. He had forged the King's signature. He had tampered with the King's servants. He had been guilty, in short, of every crime, social and political, that could be laid to the charge of a fallen favourite.

Knowing what we knew, it was not difficult to disentangle a thread of truth here and there, or to detect under the most extravagant of these fictions, a substratum of fact. Among other significant circumstances, my father, chancing one day to see a portrait of the late minister in a shop-window at Cologne, discovered that his former visitor, the Count von Rettel, and the Baron von Bulow were one and the same person. He then understood why the King had questioned him so minutely with regard to this man's appearance, and shuddered to think how deadly that enmity must have been which could bring him in person upon so infamous an errand. And here all ended.

The guilty and the innocent vanished alike from the scene, and we at least, in our remote home on the Rhenish border, heard of them no more. Monsieur Maurice never knew that I had been in any way instrumental in bringing his case before the King. He took his freedom as the fulfilment of a right, and dreamed not that his little Gretchen had pleaded for him. But that he should know it, mattered not at all. He had his liberty, and was not that enough? Enough for me, for I loved him. Ay,

child as I was, I loved him; loved him deeply and passionately-
to my cost—to my loss—to my sorrow.

An old, old wound; but I shall carry the scar to my grave!
And the brown man? Hush! a strange feeling of awe and wonder creeps upon me to this day, when I remember those bright
eyes glowing through the dusk, and the swift hand that seized
the poisoned draught and dashed it on the ground. What of that
faithful Ali, who went forward to meet the danger alone, and
was snatched away to die horribly in the jungle? I can but repeat his master's words. I can but ask myself "Docs such fidelity
indeed survive the grave? Who knows? Who can tell?"

A Night on the Borders
of the Black Forest

My story (if story it can be called, being an episode in my own early life) carries me back to a time when the world and I were better friends than we are likely, perhaps, ever to be again. I was young then. I had good health, good spirits, and tolerably good looks. I had lately come into a snug little patrimony, which I have long since dissipated; and I was in love, or fancied myself in love, with a charming *coquette*, who afterwards threw me over for a West-country baronet with seven thousand a year.

So much for myself. The subject is not one that I particularly care to dwell upon; but as I happen to be the hero of my own narrative, some sort of self-introduction is, I suppose, necessary.

To begin then—Time: seventeen years ago.

Hour:—three o'clock p.m., on a broiling, cloudless September afternoon.

Scene:—a long, straight, dusty road, bordered with young trees; a far-stretching, undulating plain, yellow for the most part with corn-stubble; singularly barren of wood and water; sprinkled here and there with vineyards, farmsteads, and hamlets; and bounded in the extreme distance by a low chain of purple hills.

Place—a certain dull, unfrequented district in the little kingdom of Würtemberg, about twelve miles north of Heilbronn, and six south-east of the Neckar.

Dramatis Personae:—myself, tall, sunburnt, dusty; in grey suit, straw hat, knapsack and gaiters. In the distance, a broad-backed pedestrian wielding a long stick like an old English quarter-staff.

Now, not being sure that I took the right turning at the cross-roads a mile or two back, and having plodded on alone all day, I resolved to overtake this same pedestrian, and increased my pace accordingly. He, meanwhile, unconscious of the vicinity of another traveller, kept on at an easy "sling-trot," his head well up, his staff swinging idly in his hand—a practised pedestrian, evidently, and one not easily out-walked through a long day.

I gained upon him, however, at every step, and could have passed him easily; but as I drew near he suddenly came to a halt, disencumbered himself of his wallet, and stretched himself at full length under a tree by the way-side.

I saw now that he was a fine, florid, handsome fellow of about twenty-eight or thirty years of age—a thorough German to look at; frank, smiling, blue-eyed; dressed in a light holland blouse and loose grey trousers, and wearing on his head a little crimson cap with a gold tassel, such as the students wear at Heidelberg university. He lifted it, with the customary "*Guten Abend*" as I came up, and when I stopped to speak, sprang to his feet with ready politeness, and remained standing.

"*Niedersdorf, mein Herr?*" said he, in answer to my inquiry. "About four miles farther on. You have but to keep straight forward."

"Many thanks," I said. "You were resting. I am sorry to have disturbed you."

He put up his hand with a deprecating gesture.

"It is nothing," he said. "I have walked far, and the day is warm."

"I have only walked from Heilbronn, and yet I am tired. Pray don't let me keep you standing."

"Will you also sit, *mein Herr?*" he asked with a pleasant smile. "There is shade for both."

So I sat down, and we fell into conversation. I began by offering him a cigar; but he pulled out his pipe—a great dangling German pipe, with a flexible tube and a painted china bowl like a small coffee-cup.

"A thousand thanks," he said; "but I prefer this old pipe to all the cigars that ever came out of Havannah. It was given to me eight years ago, when I was a student; and my friend who gave it to me is dead."

"You were at Heidelberg?" I said interrogatively.

"Yes; and Fritz (that was my friend) was at Heidelberg also. He was a wonderful fellow; a linguist, a mathematician, a botanist, a geologist. He was only five-and-twenty when the government appointed him naturalist to an African exploring party; and in Africa he died."

"Such a man," said I, "was a loss to the world."

"Ah, yes," he replied simply; "but a greater loss to me."

To this I could answer nothing; and for some minutes we smoked in silence.

"I was not clever like Fritz," he went on presently. "When I left Heidelberg, I went into business. I am a brewer, and I live at Stuttgart. My name is Gustav Bergheim—what is yours?"

"Hamilton," I replied; "Chandos Hamilton."

He repeated the name after me.

"You are an Englishman?" he said.

I nodded.

"Good. I like the English. There was an Englishman at Heidelberg—such a good fellow! his name was Smith. Do you know him?"

I explained that, in these fortunate islands, there were probably some thirty thousand persons named Smith, of whom, however, I did not know one.

"And are you a milord, and a Member of Parliament?"

I laughed, and shook my head.

"No, indeed," I replied; "neither. I read for the bar; but I do not practise. I am an idle man—of very little use to myself, and of none to my country."

"You are travelling for your amusement?"

"I am. I have just been through the Tyrol, and as far as the Italian lakes—on foot, as you see me.

But tell me about yourself. That is far more interesting."

"About myself?" he said smiling. "Ah, *mein Herr*, there is not much to tell. I have told you that I live at Stuttgart. Well, at this time of the year, I allow myself a few weeks' holiday, and I am now on my way to Frankfort, to see my *Mädchen*, who lives there with her parents."

"Then I may congratulate you on the certainty of a pleasant time."

"Indeed, yes. We love each other well, my *Mädchen* and I. Her name is Frederika, and her father is a rich banker and wine merchant. They live in the Neue Mainzer Strasse near the Taunus Gate; but the Herr Hamilton does not, perhaps, know Frankfort?"

I replied that I knew Frankfort very well, and that the Neue Mainzer Strasse was, to my thinking, the pleasantest situation in the city. And then I ventured to ask if the Fraulein Frederika was pretty.

"I think her so," he said with his boyish smile; "but then, you see, my eyes are in love. You shall judge, however, for yourself."

And with this, he disengaged a locket from his watch-chain, opened it, and showed me the portrait of a golden-haired girl, who, without being actually handsome, had a face as pleasant to look upon as his own.

"Well?" he said anxiously. "What do you say?"

"I say that she has a charming expression," I replied.

"But you do not think her pretty?"

"Nay, she is better than pretty. She has the beauty of real goodness."

His face glowed with pleasure.

"It is true," he said, kissing the portrait, and replacing it upon his chain. "She is an angel! We are to be married in the Spring."

Just at this moment, a sturdy peasant came trudging up from the direction of Niedersdorf, under the shade of a huge red cotton umbrella. He had taken his coat off, probably for coolness, or it might be for economy, and was carrying it, neatly folded up, in a large, new wooden bucket. He saluted us with the usual "*Guten Abend*" as he approached.

To which Bergheim laughingly replied by asking if the bucket was a love-token from his sweetheart.

"*Nein, nein,*" he answered stolidly; "I bought it at the *Kermess*[1] up yonder."

"So! there is a *Kermess* at Niedersdorf?"

"Ach, *Himmel!*—a famous *Kermess*. All the world is there to-day."

And with a nod, he passed on his way.

My new friend indulged in a long and dismal whistle.

"*Der Teufel!*" he said, "this is awkward. I'll be bound, now, there won't be a vacant room at any inn in the town. And I had intended to sleep at Niedersdorf tonight. Had you?"

"Well, I should have been guided by circumstances. I should perhaps have put up at Niedersdorf, if I had found myself tired and the place comfortable; or I might have dined there, and after dinner taken some kind of light vehicle as far as Rotheskirche."

"Rotheskirche!" he repeated. "Where is that?"

"It is a village on the Neckar. My guide-book mentions it as a good starting-point for pedestrians, and I am going to walk from there to Heidelberg."

"But have you not been coming out of your way?"

"No; I have only taken a short cut inland, and avoided the dull part of the river. You know the Neckar, of course?"

"Only as far as Neckargemund; but I have heard that higher up it is almost as fine as the Rhine."

"Hadn't you better join me?" I said, as we adjusted our knapsacks and prepared to resume our journey.

He shook his head, smiling.

"Nay," he replied, "my route leads me by Buchen and Darmstadt. I have no business to go round by Heidelberg."

"It would be worth the detour"

"Ah, yes; but it would throw me two days later."

"Not if you made up for lost time by taking the train from Heidelberg."

He hesitated.

---

1. *Kermess*—A fair.

"I should like it," he said.

"Then why not do it?"

"Well—yes—I will do it. I will go with you. There! let us shake hands on it, and be friends."

So we shook hands, and it was settled.

The shadows were now beginning to lengthen; but the sun still blazed in the heavens with unabated intensity. Bergheim, however, strode on as lightly, and chatted as gaily, as if his day's work was only just beginning. Never was there so simple, so openhearted a fellow. He wore his heart literally upon his sleeve, and, as we went along, told me all his little history; how, for instance, his elder sister, having been betrothed to his friend Fritz, had kept single ever since for his sake; how he was himself an only son, and the idol of his mother, now a widow; how he had resolved never to leave either her or his maiden sister; but intended when he married to take a larger house, and bring his wife into their common home; how Frederika's father had at first opposed their engagement for that reason; how Frederika (being, as he had already said, an angel) had won the father's consent last New Year's Day; and how happy he was now; and how happy they should be in the good time coming; together with much more to the same effect.

To all this I listened, and smiled, and assented, putting in a word here and there, as occasion offered, and encouraging him to talk on to his heart's content.

And now with every mile that brought us nearer to Niedersdorf, the signs of fair-time increased and multiplied. First came straggling groups of homeward-bound peasants—old men and women tottering under the burden of newly-purchased household goods; little children laden with gingerbread and toys; young men and women in their holiday-best—the latter with garlands of oak-leaves bound about their hats. Then came an open cart full of laughing girls; then more pedestrians; then an old man driving a particularly unwilling pig; then a roystering party of foot-soldiers; and so on, till not only the road, but the fields on either side and every path in sight, swarmed with a double stream of wayfarers—the one coming from the fair—the other setting towards it.

Presently, through the clouds of dust and tobacco-smoke that fouled the air, a steeple and cottages became visible; and then, quite suddenly, we found ourselves in the midst of the fair.

Here a compact, noisy, smoking, staring, laughing, steaming crowd circulated among the booths; some pushing one way, some another—some intent on buying—some on eating and drinking—some on love-making and dancing. In one place we came upon rows of little open stalls for the sale of every commodity under heaven. In another, we peeped into a great restaurant-booth full of country folks demolishing pyramids of German sausage and seas of Bairisch beer.

Yonder, on a raised stage in front of a temporary theatre, strutted a party of strolling players in their gaudy tinsels and ballet-dresses. The noise, the smells, the elbowing, the braying of brass bands, the insufferable heat and clamour, made us glad to push our way through as fast as possible, and take refuge in the village inn. But even here we could scarcely get a moment's attention. There were parties dining and drinking in every room in the house—even in the bedrooms; while the passages, the bar, and the little gardens, front and back, were all full of soldiers, free-shooters, and farmers.

Having with difficulty succeeded in capturing a couple of platters of bread and meat and a measure of beer, we went round to the stable-yard, which was crowded with *charrettes*, ein-*spänner*, and country carts of all kinds. The drivers of some of these were asleep in their vehicles; others were gambling for *kreutzers* on the ground; none were willing to put their horses to for the purpose of driving us to Rotheskirche-on-the-Neckar.

"Ach, *Herr Gott!*" said one, "I brought my folks from Frühlingsfeld—near upon ten *stunden*— and shall have to take them back by and by. That's as much as my beasts can do in one day, and they shouldn't do more for the king!"

"I've just refused five florins to go less than half that distance," said another.

At length one fellow, being somewhat less impracticable than the rest, consented to drive us as far as a certain point where four roads met, on condition that we shared his vehicle with two other travellers, and that the two other travellers consented to let us do so.

"And even so," he added, "I shall have to take them two miles out of their way—but, perhaps, being fair-time, they won't mind that."

As it happened, they were not in a condition to mind that or anything very much, being a couple of free-shooters from the Black Forest, wild with fun and frolic, and somewhat the worse for many potations of *Lager-bier*. One of them, it seemed, had won a prize at some shooting-match that same morning, and they had been celebrating this triumph all day. Having kept us waiting, with the horses in, for at least three-quarters of an hour, they came, escorted by a troop of their comrades, all laughing, talking, and wound up to the highest pitch of excitement. Then followed a scene of last health-drinkings, last hand-shakings, last embracements. Finally, we drove off just as it was getting dusk, followed by many huzzahs, and much waving of grey and green caps.

For the first quarter of an hour they were both very noisy, exchanging boisterous greetings with every passer-by, singing snatches of songs, and laughing incessantly. Then, as the dusk deepened and we left the last stragglers behind, they sank into a tipsy stupor, and ended by falling fast asleep.

Meanwhile, the driver lit his pipe and let his tired horses choose their own pace; the stars came out one by one overhead; and the road, leaving the dead level of the plain, wound upwards through a district that became more hilly with every mile.

Then I also fell asleep—I cannot tell for how long—to be waked by-and-by by the stopping of the *charrette*, and the voice of the driver, saying:—

"This is the nearest point to which I can take these *Herren*. Will they be pleased to alight?"

I sat up and rubbed my eyes. It was bright starlight. Bergheim was already leaning out, and opening the door. Our fellow-travellers were still sound asleep. We were in the midst of a wild, hilly country, black with bristling pine-woods; and had drawn up at an elevated point where four roads meet.

"Which of these are we to take?" asked Bergheim, as he pulled out his purse and counted the stipulated number of florins into the palm of the driver.

The man pointed with his whip in a direction at right angles to the road by which he was himself driving.

"And how far shall we have to walk?"

"To Rotheskirche?"

"Yes—to Rotheskirche."

He grunted doubtfully. "Ugh!" he said, "I can't be certain to a mile or so. It may be twelve or fourteen."

"A good road?"

"Yes—a good road; but hilly. These *Herren* have only to keep straight forward. They cannot miss the way."

And so he drives off, and leaves us standing in the road. The moon is now rising behind a slope of dark trees—the air is chill—an owl close by utters its tremulous, melancholy cry. Place and hour considered, the prospect of twelve or fourteen miles of a strange road, in a strange country, is anything but exhilarating. We push on, however, briskly; and Bergheim, whose good spirits are invincible, whistles and chatters, and laughs away as gaily as if we were just starting on a brilliant May morning.

"I wonder if you were ever tired in your life!" I exclaim by and by, half peevishly.

"Tired!" he echoes. "Why, I am as tired at this moment as a dog; and would gladly lie down by the roadside, curl myself up under a tree, and sleep till morning. I wonder, by the way, what o'clock it is."

I pulled out my fusee-box, struck a light, and looked at my watch. It was only ten o'clock.

"We have been walking," said Bergheim, "about half an hour, and I don't believe we have done two miles in the time. Well, it can't go on uphill like this all the way!"

"Impossible," I replied. "Rotheskirche is on the level of the river. We must sooner or later begin descending towards the valley of the Neckar."

"I wish it might be sooner, then," laughed my companion, "for I had done a good twenty miles today before you overtook me."

"Well, perhaps we may come upon some place half way. If so, I vote that we put up for the night, and leave Rotheskirche till the morning."

"Ay, that would be capital!" said he. "If it wasn't that I am as hungry as a wolf, I wouldn't say no to the hut of a charcoal-burner tonight."

And now, plodding on more and more silently as our fatigue increased, we found the pine-forests gradually drawing nearer, till by and by they enclosed us on every side, and our road lay through the midst of them. Here in the wood, all was dark—all was silent—not a breath stirred. The moon was rising fast; but the shadows of the pines lay long and dense upon the road, with only a sharp silvery patch breaking through here and there. By and by we came upon a broad space of clearing, dotted over with stacks of brushwood and great symmetrical piles of barked trunks. Then followed another tract of close forest. Then our road suddenly emerged into the full moonlight, and sometimes descending abruptly, sometimes keeping at a dead level for half a mile together, continued to skirt the forest on the left.

"I see a group of buildings down yonder," said Bergheim, pointing to a spot deep in the shadow of the hillside.

I could see nothing resembling buildings, but he stuck to his opinion.

"That they are buildings," he said, "I am positive. More I cannot tell by this uncertain light. It may be a mere cluster of cottages, or it may be a farmhouse, with stacks and sheds close by. I think it is the latter."

Animated by this hope, we now pushed on more rapidly. For some minutes our road carried us out of sight of the spot; but when we next saw it, a long, low, white-fronted house and some other smaller buildings were distinctly visible.

"A mountain farmstead, by all the gods of Olympus!" exclaimed Bergheim, joyously. "This is good fortune! And they are not gone to. bed yet, either."

"How do you know that?" I asked.

"Because I saw a light."

"But suppose they do not wish to take us in?" I suggested.

"Suppose an impossibility! Who ever heard of inhospitality among our Black Forest folk?"

"Black Forest!" I repeated. "Do you call this the Black Forest?"

"Undoubtedly. All these wooded hills south of Heidelberg and the Odenwald are outlying spurs and patches of the old legendary Schwarzwald—now dwindling year by year. Hark! the dogs have found us out already!"

As he spoke, a dog barked loudly in the direction of the farm; and then another, and another. Bergheim answered them with a shout. Suddenly a bright light flashed across the darkness— flitted vaguely for a moment to and fro, and then came steadily towards us; resolving itself presently into a lanthorn carried by a man.

We hurried eagerly to meet him—at all, square-built, heavy-browed peasant, about forty years of age.

"Who goes there?" he said, holding the lanthorn high above his head, and shading his eyes with his hand.

"Travellers," replied my companion. "Travellers wanting food and shelter for the night."

The man looked at us for a moment in silence.

"You travel late," he said, at length.

"Ay— and we must have gone on still later, if we had not come upon your house. We were bound for Rotheskirche. Can you take us in."

"Yes," he said sullenly. "I suppose so. This way."

And, swinging the lanthorn as he went, he turned on his heel abruptly, and led the way back to the house.

"A boorish fellow enough!" said I, as we followed.

"Nay—a mere peasant!" replied Bergheim. "A mere peasant—rough, but kindly."

As we drew near the house, two large mastiff pups came rushing out from a yard somewhere at the back, and a huge, tawny dog chained up in an open shed close by, strained at his collar and yelled savagely.

"Down, Caspar! Down, Schwartz!" growled our conductor, with an oath.

And immediately the pups slunk back into the yard, and the dog in the shed dropped into a low snarl, eyeing us fiercely as we passed.

The house-door opened straight upon a large, low, raftered kitchen, with a cavernous fireplace at the further end, flanked on each side by a high-backed settle. The settles, the long table in the middle of the room, the stools and chairs ranged round the walls, the heavy beams overhead, from which hung strings of dried herbs, ropes of onions, hams, and the like, were all of old, dark oak. The ceiling was black with the smoke of at least a century.

An oak dresser laden with rough blue and grey ware and rows of metal-lidded drinking mugs; an old blunderbuss and a horn-handled riding-whip over the chimney-piece; a couple of hatchets, a spade, and a fishing-rod behind the door; and a Swiss clock in the corner, completed the furniture of the room. A couple of half-charred logs smouldered on the hearth. An oil-lamp flared upon the middle of the table, at one corner of which sat two men with a stone jug and a couple of beer-mugs between them, playing at cards, and a third man looking on. The third man rose as we entered, and came forward. He was so like the one who had come out to meet us, that I saw at once they must be brothers.

"Two travellers," said our conductor, setting down his lanthorn, and shutting the door behind us.

The players laid down their greasy cards to stare at us. The second brother, a trifle more civil than the first, asked if we wished for anything before going to bed.

Bergheim unslung his wallet, flung himself wearily into a corner of the settle, and said:—

"Heavens and earth! yes. We are almost starving. We have been on the road all day, and have had no regular dinner. Is this a farmhouse or an inn?"

"Both."

"What have you in the house?"

"Ham—eggs—*voorst*—cheese—wine—beer—coffee."

"Then bring us the best you have, and plenty of it, and as fast as you can. We'll begin on the *voorst* and a bottle of your best wine, while the ham and eggs are frying; and we'll have the coffee to finish."

The man nodded; went to a door at the other end of the room—repeated the order to some one out of sight; and came back again, his hands in his pockets. The first brother, meanwhile, was lounging against the table, looking on at the players.

"It's a long game," he said.

"Ay—but it's just ended," replied one of the men, putting down his card with an air of triumph.

His adversary pondered, threw down his hand, and, with a round oath, owned himself beaten.

Then they divided the remaining contents of the stone jug, drained their mugs, and rose to go. The loser pulled out a handful of small coin, and paid the reckoning for both.

"We've sat late," said he, with a glance at the clock. "Good night, Karl—goodnight, Friedrich."

The first brother, whom I judged to be Karl, nodded sulkily. The second muttered a gruff sort of good night. The countrymen lit their pipes, took another long stare at Bergheim and myself, touched their hats, and went away.

The first brother, Karl, who was evidently the master, went out with them, shutting the door with a tremendous bang. The younger, Friedrich, cleared the board, opened a cupboard under the dresser, brought out a loaf of black bread, a lump of *voorst*, and part of a goat's milk cheese, and then went to fetch the wine. Meanwhile we each drew a chair to the table, and fell to vigorously. When Friedrich returned with the wine, a pleasant smell of broiling ham came in with him through the door.

"You are hungry," he said, looking down at us from under his black brows.

"Ay, and thirsty," replied Gustav, reaching out his hand for the bottle. "Is your wine good?"

The man shrugged his shoulders.

"Drink and judge for yourself," he answered. "It's the best we have."

"Then drink with us," said my companion, good-humouredly, filling a glass and pushing it towards him across the table.

But he shook his head with an ungracious "*Nein, nein*," and again left the room. The next moment we heard his heavy footfall going to and fro overhead.

"He is preparing our beds," I said. "Are there no women, I wonder, about the place?"

"Well, yes—this looks like one," laughed Bergheim, as the door leading to the inner kitchen again opened, and a big stolid-looking peasant girl came in with a smoking dish of ham and eggs, which she set down before us on the table. "Stop! stop!" he exclaimed, as she turned away. "Don't be in such a hurry, my girl. What is your name?"

She stopped with a bewildered look, but said nothing. Bergheim repeated the question.

"My—my name?" she stammered. "Annchen."

"Good. Then, Annchen" (filling a bumper and draining it at a draught), "I drink to thy health. Wilt thou drink to mine?" And he pointed to the glass poured out for the landlord's brother.

But she only looked at him in the same scared, stupid way, and kept edging away towards the door.

"Let her go," I said. "She is evidently half an idiot."

"She's no idiot to refuse that wine," replied Bergheim, as the door closed after her. "It's the most abominable mixture I ever put inside my lips. Have you tasted it?"

I had not tasted it as yet, and now I would not; so, the elder brother coming back just at that moment, we called for beer.

"Don't you like the wine?" he said, scowling.

"No," replied Bergheim. "Do you? If so, you're welcome to the rest of it."

The landlord took up the bottle and held it between his eyes and the lamp.

"Bad as it is," he said, "you've drunk half of it."

"Not I—only one glass, thanks be to Bacchus! There stands the other. Let us have a *schoppen* of your best beer—and I hope it will be better than your best wine."

The landlord looked from Bergheim to the glass—from the glass to the bottle. He seemed to be measuring with his eye how much had really been drunk. Then he went to the inner door; called to Friedrich to bring a *schoppen* of the Bairisch, and went away, shutting the door after him. From the sound of his footsteps, it seemed to us as if he also was gone upstairs, but into some more distant part of the house. Presently the younger brother reappeared with the beer, placed it before us in silence, and went away as before.

"The most forbidding, disagreeable, uncivil pair I ever saw in my life!" said I.

"They're not fascinating, I admit," said Bergheim, leaning back in his chair with the air of a man whose appetite is somewhat appeased. "I don't know which is the worst—their wine or their manners."

And then he yawned tremendously, and pushed out his plate, which I heaped afresh with ham and eggs. When he had swallowed a few mouthfuls, he leaned his head upon his hand, and declared he was too tired to eat more.

"And yet," he added, "I am still hungry."

"Nonsense!" I said; "eat enough now you are about it. How is the beer?"

He took a pull at the *schoppen*.

"Capital," he said. "Now I can go on again."

The next instant he was nodding over his plate.

"I am ashamed to be so stupid," he said, rousing himself presently; "but I am overpowered with fatigue. Let us have the coffee; it will wake me up a bit."

But he had no sooner said this than his chin dropped on his breast, and he was sound asleep.

I did not call for the coffee immediately. I let him sleep, and went on quietly with my supper. Just as I had done, however, the brothers came back together, Friedrich bringing the coffee—two large cups on a tray. The elder, standing by the table, looked down at Bergheim with his unfriendly frown.

"Your friend is tired," he said.

"Yes, he has walked far today—much farther than I have."

"Humph! you will be glad to go to bed."

"Indeed we shall. Are our rooms ready?"

"Yes."

I took one of the cups, and put the other beside Bergheim's plate.

"Here, Bergheim," I said, "wake up; the coffee is waiting."

But he slept on, and never heard me.

I then lifted my own cup to my lips—paused—set it down untasted. It had an odd, pungent smell that I did not like.

"What is the matter with it?" I said, "it does not smell like pure coffee."

The brothers exchanged a rapid glance.

"It is the *kirschenwasser*," said Karl. "We always put it in our black coffee."

I tasted it, but the flavour of the coffee was quite drowned in that of the coarse, fiery spirit.

"Do you not like it?" asked the younger brother.

"It is very strong," I said.

"But it is very good," replied he; "real Black Forest Kirsch—the best thing in the world, if one is tired after a journey. Drink it off, *mein Herr*, it is of no use to sip it. It will make you sleep."

This was the longest speech either of them had yet made.

"Thanks," I said, pulling out my cigar-case, "but this stuff is too powerful to be drunk at a draught. I shall make it last out a cigar or two."

"And your friend?"

"He is better without the *kirsch*, and may sleep till I am ready to go to bed."

Again they looked at each other.

"You need not sit up," I said impatiently; for it annoyed me, somehow, to have them standing there, one at each side of the table, alternately looking at me and at each other. "I will call the *Mädchen* to show us to our rooms when we are ready."

"Good," said the elder brother, after a moment's hesitation. "Come, Friedrich."

Friedrich turned at once to follow him, and they both left the room.

I listened. I heard them for awhile moving to and fro in the inner kitchen; then the sound of their double footsteps going up the stairs; then the murmur of their voices somewhere above, yet not exactly overhead; then silence.

I felt more comfortable, now that they were fairly gone, and not likely to return. I breathed more freely. I had disliked the brothers from the first. I had felt uneasy from the moment I crossed their threshold. Nothing, I told myself, should induce me at any time, or under any circumstances, to put up under their roof again.

Pondering thus, I smoked on, and took another sip of the coffee. It was not so hot now, and some of the strength of the spirit had gone off; but under the flavour of the *kirschenwasser* I could (or fancied I could) detect another flavour, pungent and bitter—a flavour, in short, just corresponding to the smell that I had at first noticed.

This startled me. I scarcely knew why, but it did startle me, and somewhat unpleasantly. At the same instant I observed that Bergheim, in the heaviness and helplessness of sleep, had swayed over on one side, and was hanging very uncomfortably across one arm of his chair.

"Come, come," I said, "wake up, *Herr* fellow-traveller. This sort of dozing will do you no good. Wake up, and come to bed."

And with this I took him by the arm, and tried to rouse

him. Then for the first time I observed that his face was deadly white—that his teeth were fast clenched—that his breathing was unnatural and laboured.

I sprang to my feet. I dragged him into an upright posture; I tore open his neck-cloth; I was on the point of rushing to the door to call for help, when a suspicion—one of those terrible suspicions which are suspicion and conviction in one—flashed suddenly upon me.

The rejected glass of wine was still standing on the table. I smelt it—tasted it. My dread was confirmed. It had the same pungent odour, the same bitter flavour as the coffee.

In a moment I measured all the horror of my position; alone—unarmed—my unconscious fellow-traveller drugged and help-less on my hands—the murderers overhead, biding their time—the silence and darkness of night—the unfrequented road—the solitary house—the improbability of help from without—the imminence of the danger from within. . . . I saw it all! What could I do? Was there any way, any chance, any hope?

I turned cold and dizzy. I leaned against the table for support. Was I also drugged, and was my turn coming? I looked round for water, but there was none upon the table. I did not dare to touch the beer, lest it also should be doctored.

At that instant I heard a faint sound outside, like the creak-ing of a stair. My presence of mind had not as yet for a mo-ment deserted me, and now my strength came back at the ap-proach of danger. I cast a rapid glance round the room. There was the blunderbuss over the chimney-piece—there were the two hatchets in the corner. I moved a chair loudly, and hummed some snatches of songs.

They should know that I was awake—this might at least keep them off a little longer. The scraps of songs covered the sound of my footsteps as I stole across the room and secured the hatchets. One of these I laid before me on the table; the other I hid among the wood in the wood-basket beside the hearth—singing, as it were to myself, all the time.

Then I listened breathlessly.

All was silent.

Then I clinked my tea-spoon in my cup—feigned a long yawn—under cover of the yawn took down the blunderbuss from its hook—and listened again.

Still all was silent—silent as death—save only the loud ticking of the clock in the corner, and the heavy beating of my heart.

Then, after a few seconds that dragged past like hours, I distinctly heard a muffled tread stealing softly across the floor overhead, and another very faint retreating creak or two upon the stairs.

To examine the blunderbuss, find it loaded with a heavy charge of slugs, test the dryness of the powder, cock it, and place it ready for use beside the hatchet on the table, was but the work of a moment.

And now my course was taken. My spirits rose with the possession of a certain means of defence, and I prepared to sell my own life, and the life of the poor fellow beside me, as dearly as might be.

I must turn the kitchen into a fortress, and defend my fortress as long as defence was possible. If I could hold it till daylight came to my aid, bringing with it the chances of traffic, of passers-by, of farm-labourers coming to their daily work—then I felt we should be comparatively safe. If, however, I could not keep the enemy out so long, then I had another resource But of this there was no time to think at present. First of all, I must barricade my fortress.

The windows were already shuttered-up and barred on the inside. The key of the house-door was in the lock, and only needed turning. The heavy iron bolt, in like manner, had only to be shot into its place. To do this, however, would make too much noise just now. First and most important was the door communicating with the inner kitchen and the stairs. This, above all, I must secure; and this, as I found to my dismay, had no bolts or locks whatever on the inside—nothing but a clumsy wooden latch!

To pile against it every moveable in the room was my obvious course; but then it was one that, by the mere noise it must make, would at once alarm the enemy. No! I must secure that door—but secure it silently—at all events for the next few minutes.

Inspired by dread necessity, I became fertile in expedients. With a couple of iron forks snatched from the table, I pinned the latch down, forcing the prongs by sheer strength of hand deep into the woodwork of the door. This done, I tore down one of the old rusty bits from its nail above the mantel-shelf, and, linking it firmly over the thump-piece of the latch on one side, and over the clumsy catch on the other, I improvised a door-chain that would at least act as a momentary check in case the door was forced from without. Lastly, by means of some half-charred splinters from the hearth, I contrived to wedge up the bottom of the door in such a manner that, the more it was pushed inwards, the more firmly fixed it must become.

So far my work had been noiseless; but now the time was come when it could be so no longer. The house-door must be secured at all costs; and I knew beforehand that I could not move those heavy fastenings unheard. Nor did I. The key, despite all my efforts, grated loudly in the lock, and the bolt resisted the rusty staples. I got it in, however, and the next moment heard rapid footsteps overhead.

I knew now that the crisis was coming, and from this moment prepared for open resistance.

Regardless of noise, I dragged out first one heavy oaken settle, and then the other—placed them against the inner door—piled them with chairs, stools, firewood, every heavy thing I could lay hands upon—raked the slumbering embers, and threw more wood upon the hearth, so as to bar that avenue, if any attempt was made by way of the chimney—and hastily ransacked every drawer in the dresser, in the hope of finding something in the shape of ammunition.

Meanwhile, the brothers had taken alarm, and having tried the inner door, had now gone round to the front, where I heard them try first the house-door and then the windows.

"Open! open, I say!" shouted the elder—(I knew him by his

voice). "What is the matter within?"

"The matter is that I choose to spend the night in this room," I shouted in reply.

"It is a public room—you have no right to shut the doors!" he said, with a thundering blow upon the lock.

"Right or no right," I answered, "I shoot dead the first man who forces his way in!"

There was a momentary silence, and I heard them muttering together outside.

I had by this time found, at the back of one of the drawers, a handful of small shot screwed up in a bit of newspaper, and a battered old powder-flask containing about three charges of powder. Little as it was, it helped to give me confidence.

Then the *parleying* began afresh.

"Once more, accursed Englishman will you open the door?"

"No."

A torrent of savage oaths—then a pause.

"Force us to break it open, and it will be the worse for you!"

"Try."

All this time I had been wrenching out the hooks from the dresser, and the nails, wherever I could find any, from the walls. Already I had enough to reload the blunderbuss three times, with my three charges of powder. If only Bergheim were himself now! . . . .

I still heard the murmuring of the brothers' voices outside—then the sound of their retreating footsteps—then an outburst of barking and yelping at the back, which showed they had let loose the dogs. Then all was silent.

Where were they gone? How would they begin the attack? In what way would it all end? I glanced at my watch. It was just twenty minutes past one. In two hours and a half, or three hours, it would be dawn. Three hours! Great Heavens! what an eternity!

I looked round to see if there was anything I could still do for defence; but it seemed to me that I had already done what little it was possible to do with the material at hand. I could only wait.

All at once I heard their footsteps in the house again. They were going rapidly to and fro overhead; then up and down the stairs; then overhead again; and presently I heard a couple of bolts shot, and apparently a heavy wooden bar put up, on the other side of the inner kitchen-door which I had just been at so much pains to barricade. This done, they seemed to go away. A distant door banged heavily; and again there was silence.

Five minutes, ten minutes, went by. Bergheim still slept heavily; but his breathing, I fancied, was less stertorous, and his countenance less rigid, than when I first discovered his condition. I had no water with which to bathe his head; but I rubbed his forehead and the palms of his hands with beer, and did what I could to keep his body upright.

Then I heard the enemy coming back to the front, slowly, and with heavy footfalls. They paused for a moment at the front door, seemed to set something down, and then retreated quickly. After an interval of about three minutes, they returned in the same way; stopped at the same place; and hurried off as before. This they did several times in succession. Listening with suspended breath and my ear against the keyhole, I distinctly heard them deposit some kind of burden each time—evidently a weighty burden, from the way in which they carried it; and yet, strange to say, one that, despite its weight, made scarcely any noise in the setting down.

Just at this moment, when all my senses were concentrated in the one act of listening, Bergheim stirred for the first time, and began muttering.

"The man!" he said, in a low, suppressed tone. "The man under the hearth!"

I flew to him at the first sound of his voice. He was recovering. Heaven be thanked, he was recovering! In a few minutes we should be two—two against two—right and might on our side—both ready for the defence of our lives!

"One man under the hearth," he went on, in the same unnatural tone. "Four men at the bottom of the pond—all murdered—foully murdered!"

I had scarcely heeded his first words; but now, as their sense broke upon me, that great rush of exultation and thankfulness was suddenly arrested. My heart stood still; I trembled; I turned cold with horror.

Then the veins swelled on his forehead; his face became purple; and he struck out blindly, as one oppressed with some horrible nightmare.

"Blood!" he gasped. "Everywhere blood—don't touch it. God's vengeance—help!" . . .

And so, struggling violently in my arms, he opened his eyes, stared wildly round, and made an effort to get upon his feet.

"What is the matter?" he said, sinking back again, and trembling from head to foot. "Was I asleep?"

I rubbed his hands and forehead again with beer. I tasted it, and finding no ill flavour upon it, put a tiny drop to his lips.

"You are all right now," I said. "You were very tired, and you fell asleep after supper. Don't you remember?"

He put his hand to his head. "Ah, yes," he said, "I remember. I have been dreaming" . . .

He looked round the room in a bewildered way; then, struck all at once by the strange disorder of the furniture, asked what was the matter.

I told him in the least alarming way, and with the fewest words I could muster, but before I could get to the end of my explanation he was up, ready for resistance, and apparently himself again.

"Where are they?" he said. "What are they doing now? Outside, do you say? Why, good heavens! man, they're blocking us in. Listen!—don't you hear?—it is the rustling of straw. Bring the blunderbuss! quick!—to the window . . . God grant we may not be too late!"

We both rushed to the window; Bergheim to undo the shutter, and I to shoot down the first man in sight.

"Look there!" he said, and pointed to the door.

A thin stream of smoke was oozing under the threshold and stealing upward in a filmy cloud that already dimmed the atmosphere of the room.

"They are going to burn us out!" I exclaimed.

"No, they are going to burn us alive," replied Bergheim, between his clenched teeth. "We know too much, and they are determined to silence us at all costs, though they burn the house down over our heads. Now hold your breath, for I am going to open the window, and the smoke will rush in like a torrent."

He opened it, but very little came in—for this reason, that the outside was densely blocked with straw, which had not yet ignited.

In a moment we had dragged the table under the window—put our weapons aside ready for use—and set to work to cut our way out.

Bergheim, standing on the table, wrenched away the straw in great armfuls. I caught it, and hurled it into the middle of the room. We laboured at the work like giants. In a few moments the pile had mounted to the height of the table. Then Bergheim cried out that the straw under his hands was taking fire, and that he dared throw it back into the room no longer!

I sprang to his aid with the two hatchets. I gave him one—I fell to work with the other. The smoke and flame rushed in our faces, as we hewed down the burning straw.

Meanwhile, the room behind us was full of smoke, and above the noise of our own frantic labour we heard a mighty crackling and hissing, as of a great conflagration.

"Take the blunderbuss—quick!" cried Bergheim, hoarsely. "There is nothing but smoke outside now, and burning straw below. Follow me! Jump as far out as you can, and shoot the first you see!"

And with this, he leaped out into the smoke, and was gone!

I only waited to grope out the blunderbuss; then, holding it high above my head, I shut my eyes and sprang after him, clearing the worst of the fire, and falling on my hands and knees among a heap of smouldering straw and ashes beyond. At the same instant that I touched the ground, I heard the sharp crack of a rifle, and saw two figures rush past me.

To dash out in pursuit without casting one backward glance at the burning house behind me—to see a tall figure vanishing among the trees, and two others in full chase—to cover the foremost of these two and bring him down as one would bring down a wolf in the open, was for me but the work of a second.

I saw him fall. I saw the other hesitate, look back, throw up his hands with a wild gesture, and fly towards the hills.

The rest of my story is soon told. The one I had shot was Friedrich, the younger brother. He died in about half an hour, and never spoke again. The elder escaped into the forest, and there succeeded in hiding himself for several weeks among the charcoal-burners. Being hunted down, however, at last, he was tried at Heilbronn, and there executed.

The pair, it seemed, were practised murderers. The pond, when dragged, was found to contain four of their victims; and when the crumbling ruins of the homestead were cleared for the purpose, the mortal remains of a fifth were discovered under the hearth, in that kitchen which had so nearly proved our grave. A store of money, clothes, and two or three watches, was also found secreted in a granary near the house; and these things served to identify three out of the five corpses thus providentially brought to light.

My friend, Gustav Bergheim (now the friend of seventeen years) is well and prosperous; married to his "*Mädchen*;" and the happy father of a numerous family. He often tells the tale of our terrible night on the borders of the Black Forest, and avers that in that awful dream in which his senses came back to him, he distinctly saw, as in a vision, the mouldering form beneath the hearth, and the others under the sluggish waters of the pond.

A Service of Danger

I, Frederick George Byng, who write this narrative with my own hand, without help of spectacles, am so old a man that I doubt if I now have a hundred living contemporaries in Europe. I was born in 1780, and I am eighty-nine years of age. My reminiscences date so far back that I almost feel, when I speak of them, as if I belonged to another world. I remember when news first reached England of the taking of the Bastille in 1789. I remember when people, meeting each other in the streets, talked of Danton and Robespierre, and the last victims of the guillotine. I remember how our whole household was put into black for the execution of Louis XVI., and how my mother who was a devout Roman Catholic, converted her oratory for several days into a *chapelle ardente*. That was in 1793, when I was just thirteen years of age.

Three years later, when the name of General Bonaparte was fast becoming a word of power in European history, I went abroad, and influenced by considerations which have nothing to do with my story, entered the Austrian army.

A younger son of a younger branch of an ancient and noble house, and distantly connected, moreover, with more than one great Austrian family, I presented myself at the Court of Vienna under peculiarly favourable auspices. The Archduke Charles, to whom I brought letters of recommendation, accorded me a gracious welcome, and presented me almost immediately upon my arrival with a commission in a cavalry corps commanded by a certain Colonel von Beust, than whom a more unpopular officer did not serve in the Imperial army.

Hence, I was glad to exchange, some months later, into Lichtenstein's Cuirassiers. In this famous corps which was commanded by his uncle the Prince of Lichtenstein, my far-off cousin, Gustav von Lichtenstein, had lately been promoted to a troop. Serving in the same corps, sharing the same hardships, incurring the same dangers, we soon became sworn friends and comrades. Together we went through the disastrous campaign of 1797, and together enjoyed the brief interval of peace that followed upon the treaty of Campo Formio and the cession of Venice. Having succeeded in getting our leave of absence at the same time, we then travelled through Styria and Hungary. Our tour ended, we came back together to winter quarters in Vienna.

When hostilities were renewed in 1800, we joyfully prepared to join the army of the Inn. In peace or war, at home or abroad, we two held fast by each other. Let the world go round as it might, we at least took life gaily, accepted events as they came, and went on becoming truer and stauncher friends with every passing day. Never were two men better suited. We understood each other perfectly. We were nearly of the same age; we enjoyed the same sports, read the same books, and liked the same people. Above all, we were both passionately desirous of military glory, and we both hated the French.

Gustav von Lichtenstein, however, was in many respects, both physically and mentally, my superior. He was taller than myself, a finer horseman, a swifter runner, a bolder swimmer, a more graceful dancer. He was unequivocally better-looking; and having to great natural gifts superadded a brilliant University career at both Göttingen and Leipzig, he was as unequivocally better educated. Fair-haired, blue-eyed, athletic—half dreamer and poet, half sportsman and soldier—now lost in mists of speculative philosophy—now given up with keen enthusiasm to military studies—the idol of his soldiers—the *beau sabreur* of his corps—Gustav von Lichtenstein was then, and has ever since remained, my ideal of a true and noble gentleman.

An orphan since his early childhood, he owned large estates

in Franconia, and was, moreover, his uncle's sole heir. He was just twenty when I first came to know him personally in Vienna in 1796; but his character was already formed, and he looked at least four years older than his age. When I say that he was even then, in accordance with a family arrangement of long standing, betrothed to his cousin, Constance von Adelheim, a rich and beautiful Franconian heiress, I think I shall have told all that need be told of my friend's private history.

I have said that we were rejoiced by the renewal of hostilities in 1800; and we had good reason to rejoice, he as an Austrian, I as an Englishman; for the French were our bitterest enemies, and we were burning to wipe out the memory of Marengo. It was in the month of November that Gustav and I received orders to join our regiment; and, commanded by Prince Lichtenstein in person, we at once proceeded, in great haste and very inclement weather, to fall in with the main body of the Imperial forces near Landshut on the Inn. The French, under Moreau, came up from the direction of Ampfing and Mühldorf; while the Austrians, sixty thousand strong, under the Archduke John, advanced upon them from Dorfen.

Coming upon the French by surprise in the close neighbourhood of Ampfing on the 30th, we fell upon them while in line of march, threw them into confusion, and put them to the rout. The next day they fell back upon that large plateau which lies between the Isar and the Inn, and took up their position in the forest of Hohenlinden. We ought never to have let them so fall back. We ought never to have let them entrench themselves in the natural fastnesses of that immense forest which has been truly described as "a great natural stockade between six and seven leagues long, and from a league to a league and a half broad."

We had already achieved a brilliant *coup*, and had our General known how to follow up his success, the whole fortune of the campaign would in all probability have been changed. But the Archduke John, though a young man of ability and sound military training, wanted that boldness which comes of experience, and erred on the side of over-caution.

All that day (the 2nd of December) it rained and sleeted in torrents. An icy wind chilled us to the bone. We could not keep our camp-fires alight. Our soldiers, however, despite the dreadful state of the weather, were in high spirits, full of yesterday's triumph, and longing for active work. Officers and men alike, we all confidently expected to be on the heels of the enemy soon after daybreak, and waited impatiently for the word of command. But we waited in vain. At midday the Archduke summoned a council of his generals. But the council by-and-by broke up; the afternoon wore on; the early Winter dusk closed in; and nothing was done.

That night there was discontent in the camp. The officers looked grave. The men murmured loudly, as they gathered round the sputtering embers and tried in vain to fence off the wind and rain. By-and-by the wind ceased blowing and the rain ceased falling, and it began to snow.

At midnight, my friend and I were sitting together in our little tent, trying to kindle some damp logs, and talking over the day's disappointment.

"It is a brilliant opportunity lost," said Gustav, bitterly. "We had separated them and thrown them into confusion; but what of that, when we have left them this whole day to reassemble their scattered forces and reform their broken battalions? The Archduke Charles would never have been guilty of such an oversight. He would have gone on forcing them back, column upon column, till soon they would have been unable to fly before us. They would have trampled upon each other, thrown down their arms, and been all cut to pieces or taken prisoners."

"Perhaps it is not yet too late," said I.

"Not yet too late!" he repeated. "*Gott im Himmel!* Not too late, perhaps to fight hard and get the worst of the fight; but too late to destroy the whole French army, as we should have destroyed it this morning. But, there! of what use is it to talk? They are all safe now in the woods of Hohenlinden."

"Well, then, we must rout them out of the woods of Hohenlinden, as we routed the wild boars last Winter in Franconia," I said, smiling.

But my friend shook his head.

"Look here," he said, tearing a leaf from his pocket-book, and, with a few bold strokes, sketching a rough plan of the plateau and the two rivers. "The forest is pierced by only two great roads—the road from Munich to Wasserburg, and the road from Munich to Mühldorf. Between the roads, some running transversely, some in parallel lines, are numbers of narrow footways, known only to the peasants, and impassable in Winter. If the French have had recourse to the great thoroughfares, they have passed through ere this, and taken up their position on some good ground beyond; but if they have thrown themselves into the forest on either side, they are either taking refuge in thickets whence it will be impossible to dislodge them, or they are lying in wait to fall upon our columns when we attempt to march through."

I was struck by the clearness of his insight and his perfect mastery of the situation.

"What a general you will make by-and-by, Lichtenstein!" I exclaimed.

"I shall never live to be a general, my dear fellow," he replied gloomily. "Have I not told you before now that I shall die young?"

"Pshaw!—a mere *presentiment*!"

"Ay—a mere *presentiment*; but a *presentiment* of which you will someday see the fulfilment."

I shook my head and smiled incredulously; but Lichtenstein, stooping over the fire, and absorbed in his own thoughts, went on, more, as it were, to himself than to me.

"Yes," he said, "I shall die before I have done anything for which it might be worthwhile to have lived. I am conscious of power—I feel there is the making of a commander in me—but what chance have I? The times are rich in great soldiers .... Ah, if I could but once distinguish myself—if I could but achieve one glorious deed before I die!.... My uncle could help me if he would. He could so easily appoint me to some service of danger; but he will not—it is in vain to ask him. There was last year's expedition—you remember how I implored him to let me lead the assaulting party at Mannheim. He refused me. Von Ranke got it, and covered himself with glory! Now if we do have a battle tomorrow".....

"Do you really think we shall have a battle tomorrow?" I said eagerly.

"I fancy so; but who can answer for what the Archduke may do? Were we not confident of fighting today?"

"Yes—but the Prince of Lichtenstein was at the council."

"My uncle tells me nothing," replied Gustav, drily.

And then he went to the door of the tent and looked out. The snow was still coming down in a dense drifting cloud, and notwithstanding the heavy rains of the last few days, was already beginning to lie upon the ground.

"Pleasant weather for a campaign!" said Gustav. "I vote we get a few hours' sleep while we can."

And with this he wrapped himself up in his cloak and lay down before the fire. I followed his example, and in a few moments we were both fast asleep.

Next day—the memorable 3rd of December *a.d.*1800—was fought the famous battle of Hohenlinden; a day great and glorious in the annals of French military history, yet not inglorious for those who bravely suffered defeat and disaster.

I will not attempt to describe the conflict in detail—that has been done by abler pens than mine. It will be enough if I briefly tell what share we Lichtensteiners bore in the fray. The bugles sounded to arms before daylight, and by grey dawn the whole army was in motion. The snow was still falling heavily; but the men were in high spirits and confident of victory.

Divided into three great columns—the centre commanded by the Archduke, the right wing under Latour, and the left under Riesch—we plunged into the forest. The infantry marched first, followed by the artillery and *caissons*, and the cavalry brought up the rear. The morning, consequently, had far advanced, and our comrades in the van had already reached the farther extremity of the forest, when we, with the rest of the cavalry, crossed, if I may so express it, the threshold of those fatal woods.

The snow was now some fourteen inches deep upon the ground, and still falling in such thick flakes as made it impossible to see twenty yards ahead. The gloomy pine-trees closed round our steps in every direction, thick-set, uniform, endless. Except the broad *chaussée,* down which the artillery was lumbering slowly and noiselessly, no paths or side-tracks were distinguishable. Below, all was white and dazzling; above, where the wide-spreading pine-branches roofed out the leaden sky, all was dark and oppressive. Presently the Prince of Lichtenstein rode up, and bade us turn aside under the trees on either side of the road till Kollowrath's reserves had passed on. We did so; dismounted; lit our pipes; and waited till our turn should come to follow the rest.

Suddenly, without a moment's warning, as if they had sprung from the earth, an immense body of the enemy's foot poured in upon us from the very direction in which our left wing, under Riesch, had lately passed along. In an instant the air was filled with shouts, and smoke, and shots, and gleaming sabres-the snow was red with blood—men, horses, and artillery were massed together in inextricable confusion, and hundreds of our brave fellows were cut down before they could even draw their swords to strike a single blow.

"Call up the Bavarian reserve!" shouted the Prince, sitting his horse like a statue and pointing up the road with his sword.

The next instant I was rolling under my own horse's feet, with a murderous grip upon my throat, a pistol at my head, and in my ears a sound like the rushing of a mighty sea. After this I remember nothing more, till by-and-by I came to my senses, and found myself, with some five or six wounded *cuirassiers,* lying in an open cart, and being transported along a country road apparently skirting the forest. I thought at first that I also was wounded and that we were all prisoners, and so closed my eyes in despair.

But as the tide of consciousness continued to flow back, I discovered that we were in the care of our own people, and in the midst of a long string of ambulances bringing up the rear of the Imperial army. And I also found that, more fortunate than my companions, I had been stunned and badly bruised, but was otherwise unhurt.

Presently Gustav came riding up, and with a cry of joy exclaimed:—

"How now, *lieber Freund!* No broken bones? All well and safe this time?"

"All well and safe," I replied; "but sore from head to foot, and jolted almost to death. Where's my horse, I wonder?"

"Dead, no doubt; but if you can ride, take mine, and I'll secure the first I can get."

"Is the battle over?"

He shook his head.

"Ay," he said, gloomily. "The battle is over—and lost."

"Lost!—utterly?"

"Utterly."

And then, still riding beside the cart and bending towards me as he rode, he told, in a few bitter sentences, all he knew of the day's disaster.

Moreau, the Generals Groucy and Grandjean, had, it seemed, lain in wait with the main body of his army at the farther end of the forest, where the great Munich and Wasserburg road debouches upon the open plain, in order to drive our forces back as soon as the heads of the first columns should emerge on that side; while Ney, prepared to execute a similar manoeuvre with his division, was stationed for the same purpose at the mouth of the other great *chaussée*.

Richepanse, meanwhile, separated by an accident from half his brigade, instead of retreating, advanced with great intrepidity, and fell upon us flank and rear, as I have said, when we least expected danger. Thus it was that the Imperial army was attacked and driven back upon itself from three points, and defeated with great slaughter.

"As for our losses," said Lichtenstein, "Heaven only knows what they are! It seems to me that we have scarcely a gun or a baggage-wagon left; while our men, herded together, trampled, cut down by thousands—*Herr Gott!* I cannot bear to think of it."

That night we retired across the Inn and halted upon the Tyrolean side, making some show of defence along the line of the river, in the direction of Saltzburg. Our men, however, had none of the spirit of resistance left in them. They seemed as if crushed by the magnitude of their defeat. Hundreds deserted daily. The rest clamoured impatiently for a retreat. The whole camp was in dismay and disorder.

Suddenly, none could exactly tell how, a rumour went about that Moreau was about to attempt the passage of the Lower Inn.

This rumour soon became more definite.

The point chosen was distant some three or four marches from that where we were now posted.

All the boats upon the Isar had been seized and sent down the river as far as Munich.

From Munich they were about to be transported overland to the nearest point upon the Inn.

Two bridges of boats were then to be thrown across the river, and the French battalions were to march over to our attack.

Such was the information which the peasantry brought to our camp, and which was confirmed by the scouts whom we sent out in every direction. The enemy's movements were open and undisguised. Confident of success and secure in our weakness, he disdained even the semblance of strategy.

On the 4th of December the Archduke called another council of war; and some hours before daybreak on the morning of the 5th, our whole right wing was despatched to the point at which we anticipated an attack.

At dawn, Gustav, who had been out all night on duty, came in wet and weary, and found me still asleep.

"Rouse up dreamer!" he said. "Our comrades are gone, and

now we can sing *'De Profundis'* for ourselves."

"Why for ourselves?" I asked, raising myself upon my elbow.

"Because Riesch is gone; and, if I am not very much mistaken, we shall have to fight the French without him."

"What do you mean? Riesch is gone to repulse the threatened attack down the river?"

"I mean that my mind misgives me about that attack. Moreau is not wont to show his cards so plainly. I have been thinking about it all night; and the more I think of it, the more I suspect that the French have laid a trap, and the Archduke has walked into it."

And then, while we lit our fire and breakfasted together off our modest rations of black bread and soup, my friend showed me, in a few words, how unlikely it was that Moreau should conduct any important operation in so ostentatious a fashion. His object, argued Lichtenstein, was either to mislead us with false rumours, and then, in the absence of Riesch's division, to pour across the river and attack us unexpectedly, or, more probably still, it was his design to force the passage of the Upper Inn and descend upon us from the hills to our rear.

I felt a sudden conviction that he was right.

"It is so—it must be so!" I exclaimed. "What is to be done?"

"Nothing—unless to die hard when the time comes."

"Will you not lay your suspicions before the Archduke?"

"The Archduke would not thank me, perhaps, for seeing farther than himself. Besides, suspicions are nothing. If I had proof—proof positive . . . . if my uncle would but grant me a party of reconnoissance . . . . By Heaven! I will ask him."

"Then ask him one thing more—get leave for me to go with you!"

At this moment three or four drums struck up the *rappel*—were answered by others—and again by others far and near, and in a few seconds the whole camp was alive and stirring. In the meanwhile, Lichtenstein snatched up his cap and rushed away, eager to catch the Prince before he left his tent.

In about half an hour he came back, radiant with success. His uncle had granted him a troop of twenty men, with permission to cross the Inn and reconnoitre the enemy's movements.

"But he will not consent to let thee join, *mein Bruder*," said Gustav, regretfully.

"Why not?"

"Because it is a service of danger, and he will not risk the life of a second officer when one is enough."

"Pshaw! as if my life were worth anything! But there—it's just my luck. I might have been certain he would refuse. When do you go?"

"At midday. We are to keep on this side following the road to Neubevern till we find some point narrow enough to swim our horses over. After that, we shall go round by any unfrequented ways and bridle-paths we can find; get near the French camp as soon as it is dusk; and find out all we can."

"I'd have given my black mustang to be allowed to go with you."

"I don't half forgive the Prince for refusing," said Gustav. "But then, you see, not a man of us may come back; and after all, it's more satisfactory to get one's bullet on the open battlefield than to be caught and shot for a spy."

"I should prefer to take my chance of that."

"I am not quite sure that I should prefer it for you," said my friend. "I have gained my point—I am glad to go: but I have an impression of coming disaster."

"Ah! you know I don't believe in *presentiments*."

"I do know it, of old. But the sons of the house of Lichtenstein have reason to believe in them. I could tell you many a strange story if I had time..... But it is already ten, and I must write some letters and put my papers in order before I start."

With this he sat down to his desk, and I went out, in order to leave him alone while he wrote. When I came back, his charger was waiting outside in care of an orderly; the troop had already assembled in an open space behind the tent; and the men were busy tightening their horses' girths, looking to the locks of their pistols, and gaily preparing to be gone.

I found Lichtenstein booted and spurred and ready. A letter and a sealed packet lay upon the table, and he had just opened a locker to take a slice of bread and a glass of *kirschwasser* before starting.

"Thank heaven you are come!" he said. "In three minutes more I should have been gone. You see this letter and packet?—I entrust them to you. The packet contains my watch, which was my father's, given to him by the Empress Catherine of Russia; my hereditary star and badge as a Count of the early Roman Empire; my will; my commission; and my signet ring. If I fall today, the packet is to be given to my uncle. The letter is for Constance, bidding her farewell. I have enclosed in it my mother's portrait and a piece of my hair. You will forward it, *lieber Freund....*"

"I will."

He took a locket from his bosom, opened it, kissed it, and gave it to me with a sigh.

"I would not have her portrait fall into rude and sacrilegious hands," he said; "if I never come back, destroy it. And now for a parting glass, and goodbye!"

We then chinked our glasses together, drank to each other in silence, clasped hands, and parted.

Away they rode through the heavy mire and beating rain, twenty picked men, two and two, with their Captain at their head. I watched them as they trotted leisurely down the long line of tents, and when the last man had disappeared, I went in with a heavy heart, telling myself that I should perhaps never see Gustav von Lichtenstein again.

Throughout the rest of the day it continued to rain incessantly. It was my turn that night to be on duty for five hours; to go the round of the camp, and to visit all the outposts. I therefore made up the best fire I could, stopped indoors, and, following my friend's example, wrote letters all the afternoon.

About six in the evening the rain ceased, and it began to snow. It was just the Hohenlinden weather over again.

At eight, having cooked and eaten my solitary supper, I

wrapped myself in my rug, lay down before the fire, and slept till midnight, when the orderly came, as usual, to wake me and accompany me on my rounds.

"Dreadful weather, I suppose, Fritz?" I said, getting up unwillingly, and preparing to face the storm.

"No, *mein Herr*, it is a beautiful night."

I could hardly believe him.

But so it was. The camp lay around us, one sheet of smooth dazzling snow; the clouds had parted, and were clearing off rapidly in every direction; and just over the Archduke's tent where the Imperial banner hung drooping and heavy, the full moon was rising in splendour.

A magnificent night—cold, but not piercing—pleasant to ride in—pleasant to smoke in as one rode. A superb night for trotting leisurely round about a peaceful camp; but a bad night for a reconnoitring party on hostile ground,—a fatal night for Austrian white-coats in danger of being seen by vigilant French sentries.

Where now were Gustav and his troop? What had they done? What had happened since they left? How soon would they come back? I asked myself these questions incessantly.

I could think of nothing else. I looked at my watch every few minutes. As the time wore on, the hours appeared to grow longer. At two o'clock, before I had gone half my round, it seemed to me that I had been all night in the saddle. From two to three, from three to four, the hours dragged by as if every minute were weighted with lead.

"The Graf von Lichtenstein will be coming back this way, *mein Herr*," said the orderly, spurring his horse up beside mine, and saluting with his hand to the side of his helmet as he spoke.

"Which way? Over the hill, or down in the hollow?"

"Through the hollow, *mein Herr*. That is the road by which the Herr Graf rode out; and the river is too wide for them to cross anywhere but upstream."

"Then they must come this way?"

"Yes, *mein Herr*."

We were riding along the ridge of a long hill, one side of which sloped down towards the river, while on the other side it terminated in an abrupt precipice overhanging a narrow road or ravine, some forty feet below. The opposite bank was also steep, though less steep than that on our side; and beyond it the eye travelled over a wide expanse of dusky pine-woods, now white and heavy with snow.

I reined in my horse the better to observe the scene. Yonder flowed the Inn, dark and silent, a river of ink winding through meadow flats of dazzling silver. Far away upon the horizon rose the mystic outlines of the Franconian Alps. A single sentry, pacing to and fro some four hundred yards ahead, was distinctly visible in the moonlight; and such was the perfect stillness of the night that, although the camp lay at least two miles and a half away, I could hear the neighing of the horses and the barking of the dogs.

Again I looked at my watch, again calculated how long my friend had been absent. It was now a quarter past four a.m., and he had left the camp at midday.

If he had not yet returned—and of course he might have done so at any moment since I had been out on duty—he had now been gone sixteen hours and a quarter.

Sixteen hours and quarter! Time enough to have ridden to Munich and back!

The orderly again brought his horse up abreast with mine.

"Pardon, *mein Herr*," he said, pointing up the ravine with his sabre; "but do you see nothing yonder—beyond the turn of the road—just where there is a gap in the trees?"

I looked; but I saw nothing.

"What do you think you see?" I asked him.

"I scarcely know, *mein Herr*;—something moving close against the trees, beyond the hollow way."

"Where the road emerges upon the plain and skirts the pine-woods?"

"Yes, *mein Herr*; several dark objects—Ah! they are horsemen!"

"It is the Graf von Lichtenstein and his troop!" I exclaimed.

"Nay, *mein Herr;* see how slowly they ride, and how they keep close under the shade of the woods! The Graf von Lichtenstein would not steal back so quietly."

I stood up in my stirrups, shaded my eyes with my hand, and stared eagerly at the approaching cavalcade.

They were perhaps half-a-mile away as the crow flies, and would not have been visible from this point but for a long gap in the trees on this side of the hill. I could see that they were soldiers. They might be French; but, somehow, I did not think they were. I fancied, I hoped, they were our own Lichtensteiners come back again.

"They are making for the hollow way, *mein Herr*," said the orderly.

They were evidently making for the hollow way. I watched them past the gap till the last man had gone by, and it seemed to me they were about twenty in number.

I dismounted, flung my reins to the orderly, and went to where the edge of the precipice overhung the road below. Hence, by means of such bushes and tree-stumps as were rooted in the bank, I clambered down a few feet lower, and there lay concealed till they should pass through.

It now seemed to me that they would never come. I do not know how long I waited. It might have been ten minutes—it might have been half an hour; but the time that elapsed between the moment when I dismounted and the moment when the first helmet came in sight seemed interminable.

The road, as I have already said, lay between a steep declivity on the one side and a less abrupt height, covered with pine-trees, on the other—a picturesque winding gorge or ravine, half dark as night, half bright as day; here deep in shadow, there flooded with moonlight; and carpeted a foot deep with fresh-fallen snow. After I had waited and watched till my eyes ached with staring in the gloom, I at last saw a single horseman coming round the turn of the road, about a hundred yards from the spot where I was lying. Slowly, and as it seemed to me, dejectedly, he rode in advance of his comrades. The rest followed, two and two.

At the first glance, while they were yet in deep shadow, and, as I have said, a hundred yards distant, I recognised the white cloaks and plumes and the black chargers of my own corps. I knew at once that it was Lichtenstein and his troop.

Then a sudden terror fell upon me. Why were they coming back so slowly? What evil tidings did they bring? How many were returning? How many were missing? I knew well, if there had been a skirmish, who was sure to have been foremost in the fight. I knew well, if but three or four had fallen, who was sure to be one of the fallen.

These thoughts flashed upon me in the first instant when I recognised the Lichtenstein uniform. I could not have uttered a word, or have done anything to attract the men's attention, if it had been to save my life. Dread paralyzed me.

Slowly, dejectedly, noiselessly, the first *cuirassier* emerged into the moonlight, passed on again into the gloom, and vanished in the next turn of the road. It was but for a moment that the moonlight streamed full upon him; yet in that moment I saw there had been a fray, and that the man had been badly wounded.

As slowly, as dejectedly, as noiselessly, with broken plumes and battered helmets, and cloaks torn and blood-stained, the rest came after, two and two; each pair, as they passed, shining out momentarily, distinctly, like the images projected for an instant upon the disc of a magic-lantern.

I held my breath and counted them as they went by—first one alone; then two and two, till I had counted eighteen riding in pairs. Then one alone, bringing up the rear. Then . . . .

I waited—I watched—I refused to believe that this could be all. I refused to believe that Gustav must not presently come galloping up to overtake them. At last, long after I knew it was in vain to wait and watch longer, I clambered up again—cramped, and cold, and sick at heart—and found the orderly walking the horses up and down on the brow of the hill. The man looked me in the face, as if he would fain have asked me what I had seen.

"It was the Graf von Lichtenstein's troop," I said, by an effort; "but—but the Graf von Lichtenstein is not with them."

And with this I sprang into the saddle, clapped spurs to my horse, and said no more.

I had still two outposts to visit before finishing my round; but from that moment to this I have never been able to remember any one incident of my homeward ride. I visited those outposts, without doubt; but I was an unconscious of the performance of my duty as a sleeper is unconscious of the act of breathing.

Gustav was the only man missing. Gustav was dead. I repeated it to myself over and over again. I felt that it was true. I had no hope that he was taken prisoner. No—he was dead. He had fallen, fighting to the last. He had died like a hero. But—he was dead.

At a few minutes after five, I returned to camp. The first person I met was von Blumenthal, the Prince of Lichtenstein's secretary. He was walking up and down outside my tent, waiting for me. He ran to me as I dismounted.

"Thank heaven you are come!" he said. "Go at once to the prince—the Graf von Lichtenstein is dying. He has fought a troop of French lancers three times as many as his own, and carried off a bundle of despatches. But he has paid for them with his life, and with the lives of all his men. He rode in, covered with wounds, a couple of hours ago, and had just breath enough left to tell the tale."

"His own life, and the lives of all his men!" I repeated hoarsely.

"Yes, he left every man on the field—himself the only survivor. He cut his way out with the captured despatches in one hand and his sword in the other—and there he lies in the Prince's tent—dying."

He was unconscious—had been unconscious ever since he was laid upon his uncle's bed—and he died without again opening his eyes or uttering a word. I saw him breathe his last, and that was all. Even now, old man as I am, I cannot dwell upon that scene. He was my first friend, and I may say my best friend.

I have known other friendships since then; but none so intimate—none so precious.

But now comes a question which I yet ask myself "many a time and oft," and which, throughout all the years that have gone by since that night, I have never yet been able to answer. Gustav von Lichtenstein met and fought a troop of French Lancers; saw his own twenty *cuirassiers* cut to pieces before his eyes; left them all for dead upon a certain hillside on the opposite bank of the Inn; and rode back into camp, covered with wounds—the only survivor!

What, then, was that silent cavalcade that I saw riding through the hollow way—twenty men without their leader? Were those the dead whom I met, and was it the one living man who was absent?

An Engineer's Story

a.k.a. No. 5 Branch Line—the Engineer

His name, sir, was Matthew Price; mine is Benjamin Hardy. We were born within a few days of each other; bred up in the same village; taught at the same school. I cannot remember the time when we were not close friends. Even as boys, we never knew what it was to quarrel. We had not a thought, we had not a possession, that was not in common. We would have stood by each other, fearlessly, to the death. It was such a friendship as one reads about sometimes in books: fast and firm as the great Tors upon our native moorlands, true as the sun in the heavens.

The name of our village was Chadleigh. Lifted high above the pasture flats which stretched away at our feet like a measure-less green lake and melted into mist on the furthest horizon, it nestled, a tiny stone-built hamlet, in a sheltered hollow about midway between the plain and the plateau. Above us, rising ridge beyond ridge, slope beyond slope, spread the mountain-ous moor-country, bare and bleak for the most part, with here and there a patch of cultivated field or hardy plantation, and crowned highest of all with masses of huge grey crag, abrupt, isolated, hoary, and older than the deluge.

These were the Tors—Druids' Tor, King's Tor, Castle Tor, and the like; sacred places, as I have heard, in the ancient time, where crownings, burnings, human sacrifices, and all kinds of bloody heathen rites were performed. Bones, too, had been found there, and arrow-heads, and ornaments of gold and glass. I had a vague awe of the Tors in those boyish days, and would not have gone near them after dark for the heaviest bribe.

I have said that we were born in the same village. He was the son of a small farmer, named William Price, and the eldest of a family of seven; I was the only child of Ephraim Hardy, the Chadleigh blacksmith—a well-known man in those parts, whose memory is not forgotten to this day. Just so far as a farmer is supposed to be a bigger man than a blacksmith, Mat's father might be said to have a better standing than mine; but William Price with his small holding and his seven boys, was, in fact, as poor as many a day-labourer; whilst, the blacksmith, well-to-do, bustling, popular, and open-handed, was a person of some importance in the place.

All this, however, had nothing to do with Mat and myself. It never occurred to either of us that his jacket was out at elbows, or that our mutual funds came altogether from my pocket. It was enough for us that we sat on the same school-bench, conned our tasks from the same primer, fought each other's battles, screened each other's faults, fished, nutted, played truant, robbed orchards and birds' nests together, and spent every half-hour, authorised or stolen, in each other's society.

It was a happy time; but it could not go on forever. My father, being prosperous, resolved to put me forward in the world. I must know more, and do better, than himself. The forge was not good enough, the little world of Chadleigh not wide enough, for me. Thus it happened that I was still swinging the satchel when Mat was whistling at the plough, and that at last, when my future course was shaped out, we were separated, as it then seemed to us, for life.

For, blacksmith's son as I was, furnace and forge, in some form or other, pleased me best, and I chose to be a working engineer. So my father by-and-by apprenticed me to a Birmingham iron-master; and, having bidden farewell to Mat, and Chadleigh, and the grey old Tors in the shadow of which I had spent all the days of my life, I turned my face northward, and went over into "the Black Country."

I am not going to dwell on this part of my story. How I

116

worked out the term of my apprenticeship; how, when I had served my full time and become a skilled workman, I took Mat from the plough and brought him over to the Black Country, sharing with him lodging, wages, experience—all, in short, that I had to give; how he, naturally quick to learn and brimful of quiet energy, worked his way up a step at a time, and came by-and-by to be a "first hand" in his own department; how, during all these years of change, and trial, and effort, the old boyish affection never wavered or weakened, but went on, growing with our growth and strengthening with our strength—are facts which I need do no more than outline in this place.

About this time—it will be remembered that I speak of the days when Mat and I were on the bright side of thirty—it happened that our firm contracted to supply six first-class locomotives to run on the new line, then in process of construction, between Turin and Genoa. It was the first Italian order we had taken. We had had dealings with France, Holland, Belgium, Germany; but never with Italy. The connection, therefore, was new and valuable—all the more valuable because our Transalpine neighbours had but lately begun to lay down the iron roads, and would be safe to need more of our good English work as they went on.

So the Birmingham firm set themselves to the contract with a will, lengthened our working hours, increased our wages, took on fresh hands, and determined, if energy and promptitude could do it, to place themselves at the head of the Italian labour-market, and stay there. They deserved and achieved success. The six locomotives were not only turned out to time, but were shipped, despatched, and delivered with a promptitude that fairly amazed our Piedmontese consignee. I was not a little proud, you may be sure, when I found myself appointed to superintend the transport of the engines. Being allowed a couple of assistants, I contrived that Mat should be one of them; and thus we enjoyed together the first great holiday of our lives.

It was a wonderful change for two Birmingham operatives fresh from the Black Country. The fairy city, with its crescent background of Alps; the port crowded with strange shipping; the marvellous blue sky and the bluer sea; the painted houses on the quays; the quaint cathedral, faced with black and white marble; the street of jewellers, like an Arabian Nights' bazaar; the street of palaces, with its Moorish courtyards, its fountains and orange-trees; the women veiled like brides; the galley-slaves chained two and two; the processions of priests and friars; the everlasting clangour of bells; the babble of a strange tongue; the singular lightness and brightness of the climate—made, altogether, such a combination of wonders that we wandered about, the first day, in a kind of bewildered dream, like children at a fair. Before that week was ended, being tempted by the beauty of the place and the liberality of the pay, we had agreed to take service with the Turin and Genoa Railway Company, and to turn our backs upon Birmingham forever.

Then began a new life—a life so active and healthy, so steeped in fresh air and sunshine, that we sometimes marvelled how we could have endured the gloom of the Black Country. We were constantly up and down the line: now at Genoa, now at Turin, taking trial trips with the locomotives, and placing our old experiences at the service of our new employers.

In the meanwhile we made Genoa our headquarters, and hired a couple of rooms over a small shop in a bystreet sloping down to the quays. Such a busy little street—so steep and winding that no vehicles could pass through it, and so narrow that the sky looked like a mere strip of deep-blue ribbon overhead! Every house in it, however, was a shop, where the goods encroached on the footway, or were piled about the door, or hung like tapestry from the balconies; and all day long, from dawn to dusk, an incessant stream of passersby poured up and down between the port and the upper quarter of the city.

Our landlady was the widow of a silver-worker, and lived by the sale of filigree ornaments, cheap jewellery, combs, fans, and toys in ivory and jet. She had an only daughter named Gianetta, who served in the shop, and was simply the most beautiful woman I ever beheld. Looking back across this weary chasm of years, and bringing her image before me (as I can and do) with all the vividness of life, I am unable, even now, to detect a flaw in her beauty.

I do not attempt to describe her. I do not believe there is a poet living who could find the words to do it; but I once saw a picture that was somewhat like her (not half so lovely, but still like her), and, for aught I know, that picture is still hanging where I last looked at it—upon the walls of the Louvre. It represented a woman with brown eyes and golden hair, looking over her shoulder into a circular mirror held by a bearded man in the background. In this man, as I then understood, the artist had painted his own portrait; in her, the portrait of the woman he loved. No picture that I ever saw was half so beautiful, and yet it was not worthy to be named in the same breath with Gianetta Coneglia.

You may be certain the widow's shop did not want for customers. All Genoa knew how fair a face was to be seen behind that dingy little counter; and Gianetta, flirt as she was, had more lovers than she cared to remember, even by name. Gentle and simple, rich and poor, from the red-capped sailor buying his earrings or his amulet, to the nobleman carelessly purchasing half the filigrees in the window, she treated them all alike—encouraged them, laughed at them, led them on and turned them off at her pleasure. She had no more heart than a marble statue; as Mat and I discovered by-and-by, to our bitter cost.

I cannot tell to this day how it came about, or what first led me to suspect how things were going with us both; but long before the waning of that autumn a coldness had sprung up between my friend and myself. It was nothing that could have been put into words. It was nothing that either of us could have explained or justified, to save his life.

We lodged together, ate together, worked together, exactly as before; we even took our long evening's walk together, when the day's labour was ended; and except, perhaps, that we were more silent than of old, no mere looker-on could have detected a shadow of change. Yet there it was, silent and subtle, widening the gulf between us every day.

It was not his fault. He was too true and gentle-hearted to have willingly brought about such a state of things between us. Neither do I believe—fiery as my nature is—that it was mine. It was all hers—hers from first to last—the sin, and the shame, and the sorrow.

If she had shown a fair and open preference for either of us, no real harm could have come of it. I would have put any constraint upon myself, and, Heaven knows! have borne any suffering, to see Mat really happy. I know that he would have done the same, and more if he could, for me. But Gianetta cared not one sou for either. She never meant to choose between us. It gratified her vanity to divide us; it amused her to play with us. It would pass my power to tell how, by a thousand imperceptible shades of *coquetry*—by the lingering of a glance, the substitution of a word, the flitting of a smile—she contrived to turn our heads, and torture our hearts, and lead us on to love her.

She deceived us both. She buoyed us both up with hope; she maddened us with jealousy; she crushed us with despair. For my part, when I seemed to wake to a sudden sense of the ruin that was about our path and I saw how the truest friendship that ever bound two lives together was drifting on to wreck and ruin, I asked myself whether any woman in the world was worth what Mat had been to me and I to him. But this was not often. I was readier to shut my eyes upon the truth than to face it; and so lived on, wilfully, in a dream.

Thus the autumn passed away, and winter came—the strange, treacherous Genoese winter, green with olive and ilex, brilliant with sunshine, and bitter with storm. Still, rivals at heart and friends on the surface, Mat and I lingered on in our lodging in the Vicolo Balba. Still Gianetta held us with her fatal wiles and her still more fatal beauty. At length there came a day when I felt I could bear the horrible misery and suspense of it no longer.

The sun, I vowed, should not go down before I knew my sentence. She must choose between us. She must either take me or let me go. I was reckless. I was desperate. I was determined to know the worst, or the best. If the worst, I would at once turn my back upon Genoa, upon her, upon all the pursuits and purposes of my past life, and begin the world anew. This I told her, passionately and sternly, standing before her in the little parlour at the back of the shop, one bleak December morning.

"If it's Mat whom you care for most," I said, "tell me so in one word, and I will never trouble you again. He is better worth your love. I am jealous and exacting; he is as trusting and unselfish as a woman. Speak, Gianetta; am I to bid you goodbye forever and ever, or am I to write home to my mother in England, bidding her pray to God to bless the woman who has promised to be my wife?"

"You plead your friend's cause well," she replied, haughtily. "Matteo ought to be grateful. This is more than he ever did for you."

"Give me my answer, for pity's sake," I exclaimed, "and let me go!"

"You are free to go or stay, Signor Inglese," she replied. "I am not your jailor."

"Do you bid me leave you?"

"Beata Madre! not I."

"Will you marry me, if I stay?"

She laughed aloud—such a merry, mocking, musical laugh, like a chime of silver bells!

"You ask too much," she said.

"Only what you have led me to hope these five or six months past!"

"That is just what Matteo says. How tiresome you both are!"

"O, Gianetta," I said, passionately, "be serious for one moment! I am a rough fellow, it is true—not half good enough or clever enough for you; but I love you with my whole heart, and an Emperor could do no more."

"I am glad of it," she replied; "I do not want you to love me less."

"Then you cannot wish to make me wretched! Will you

promise me?"

"I promise nothing," said she, with another burst of laughter; "except that I will not marry Matteo!"

Except that she would not marry Matteo! Only that. Not a word of hope for myself. Nothing but my friend's condemnation. I might get comfort, and selfish triumph, and some sort of base assurance out of that, if I could. And so, to my shame, I did. I grasped at the vain encouragement, and, fool that I was! let her put me off again unanswered. From that day, I gave up all effort at self-control, and let myself drift blindly on—to destruction.

At length things became so bad between Mat and myself that it seemed as if an open rupture must be at hand. We avoided each other, scarcely exchanged a dozen sentences in a day, and fell away from all our old familiar habits. At this time—I shudder to remember it!—there were moments when I felt that I hated him.

Thus, with the trouble deepening and widening between us day by day, another month or five weeks went by; and February came; and, with February, the Carnival. They said in Genoa that it was a particularly dull carnival; and so it must have been; for, save a flag or two hung out in some of the principal streets, and a sort of festa look about the women, there were no special indications of the season. It was, I think, the second day when, having been on the line all the morning, I returned to Genoa at dusk, and, to my surprise, found Mat Price on the platform. He came up to me, and laid his hand on my arm.

"You are in late," he said. "I have been waiting for you three-quarters of an hour. Shall we dine together today?"

Impulsive as I am, this evidence of returning goodwill at once called up my better feelings.

"With all my heart, Mat," I replied; "shall we go to Gozzoli's?"

"No, no," he said, hurriedly. "Some quieter place—some place where we can talk. I have something to say to you."

I noticed now that he looked pale and agitated, and an uneasy sense of apprehension stole upon me. We decided on the

"Pescatore," a little out-of-the-way *trattoria*, down near the Molo Vecchio. There, in a dingy *salon*, frequented chiefly by seamen, and redolent of tobacco, we ordered our simple dinner. Mat scarcely swallowed a morsel; but, calling presently for a bottle of Sicilian wine, drank eagerly.

"Well, Mat," I said, as the last dish was placed on the table, "what news have you?"

"Bad."

"I guessed that from your face."

"Bad for you—bad for me. Gianetta."

"What of Gianetta?"

He passed his hand nervously across his lips.

"Gianetta is false—worse than false," he said, in a hoarse voice. "She values an honest man's heart just as she values a flower for her hair—wears it for a day, then throws it aside for ever. She has cruelly wronged us both."

"In what way? Good Heavens, speak out!"

"In the worst way that a woman can wrong those who love her. She has sold herself to the Marchese Loredano."

The blood rushed to my head and face in a burning torrent. I could scarcely see, and dared not trust myself to speak.

"I saw her going towards the cathedral," he went on, hurriedly. "It was about three hours ago. I thought she might be going to confession, so I hung back and followed her at a distance. When she got inside, however, she went straight to the back of the pulpit, where this man was waiting for her. You remember him—an old man who used to haunt the shop a month or two back. Well, seeing how deep in conversation they were, and how they stood close under the pulpit with their backs towards the church, I fell into a passion of anger and went straight up the aisle, intending to say or do something: I scarcely knew what; but, at all events, to draw her arm through mine, and take her home. When I came within a few feet, however, and found only a big pillar between myself and them, I paused. They could not see me, nor I them; but I could hear their voices distinctly, and—and I listened."

"Well, and you heard——"

"The terms of a shameful bargain—beauty on the one side, gold on the other; so many thousand *francs* a year; a villa near Naples——Pah! it makes me sick to repeat it."

And, with a shudder, he poured out another glass of wine and drank it at a draught.

"After that," he said, presently, "I made no effort to bring her away. The whole thing was so cold-blooded, so deliberate, so shameful, that I felt I had only to wipe her out of my memory, and leave her to her fate. I stole out of the cathedral, and walked about here by the sea for ever so long, trying to get my thoughts straight. Then I remembered you, Ben; and the recollection of how this wanton had come between us and broken up our lives drove me wild. So I went up to the station and waited for you. I felt you ought to know it all; and—and I thought, perhaps, that we might go back to England together."

"The Marchese Loredano!"

It was all that I could say; all that I could think. As Mat had just said of himself, I felt "like one stunned."

"There is one other thing I may as well tell you," he added, reluctantly, "if only to show you how false a woman can be. We—we were to have been married next month."

"*We?* Who? What do you mean?"

"I mean that we were to have been married—Gianetta and I."

A sudden storm of rage, of scorn, of incredulity, swept over me at this, and seemed to carry my senses away.

"*You!*" I cried. "Gianetta marry you! I don't believe it."

"I wish I had not believed it," he replied, looking up as if puzzled by my vehemence. "But she promised me; and I thought, when she promised it, she meant it."

"She told me, weeks ago, that she would never be your wife!"

His colour rose, his brow darkened; but when his answer came, it was as calm as the last.

"Indeed!" he said. "Then it is only one baseness more. She

told me that she had refused you; and that was why we kept our engagement secret."

"Tell the truth, Mat Price," I said, well-nigh beside myself with suspicion. "Confess that every word of this is false! Confess that Gianetta will not listen to you, and that you are afraid I may succeed where you have failed. As perhaps I shall—as perhaps I shall, after all!"

"Are you mad?" he exclaimed. "What do you mean?"

"That I believe it's just a trick to get me away to England-that I don't credit a syllable of your story. You're a liar, and I hate you!"

He rose, and, laying one hand on the back of his chair, looked me sternly in the face.

"If you were not Benjamin Hardy," he said, deliberately, "I would thrash you within an inch of your life."

The words had no sooner passed his lips than I sprang at him. I have never been able distinctly to remember what followed. A curse—a blow—a struggle—a moment of blind fury—a cry—a confusion of tongues—a circle of strange faces. Then I see Mat lying back in the arms of a bystander; myself trembling and bewildered—the knife dropping from my grasp; blood upon the floor; blood upon my hands; blood upon his shirt. And then I hear those dreadful words:

"O, Ben, you have murdered me!"

He did not die—at least, not there and then. He was carried to the nearest hospital, and lay for some weeks between life and death. His case, they said, was difficult and dangerous. The knife had gone in just below the collar-bone, and pierced down into the lungs. He was not allowed to speak or turn—scarcely to breathe with freedom. He might not even lift his head to drink. I sat by him day and night all through that sorrowful time. I gave up my situation on the railway; I quitted my lodging in the Vicolo Balba; I tried to forget that such a woman as Gianetta Coneglia had ever drawn breath.

I lived only for Mat; and he tried to live more, I believe, for my sake than his own. Thus, in the bitter silent hours of pain and penitence, when no hand but mine approached his lips or smoothed his pillow, the old friendship came back with even more than its old trust and faithfulness. He forgave me, fully and freely; and I would thankfully have given my life for him.

At length there came one bright spring morning, when, dismissed as convalescent, he tottered out through the hospital gates, leaning on my arm, and feeble as an infant. He was not cured; neither, as I then learned to my horror and anguish, was it possible that he ever could be cured. He might live, with care, for some years; but the lungs were injured beyond hope of remedy, and a strong or healthy man he could never be again. These, spoken aside to me, were the parting words of the chief physician, who advised me to take him further south without delay.

I took him to a little coast-town called Rocca, some thirty miles beyond Genoa—a sheltered lonely place along the Riviera, where the sea was even bluer than the sky, and the cliffs were green with strange tropical plants, cacti, and aloes, and Egyptian palms. Here we lodged in the house of a small tradesman; and Mat, to use his own words, "set to work at getting well in good earnest." But, alas! it was a work which no earnestness could forward.

Day after day he went down to the beach, and sat for hours drinking the sea air and watching the sails that came and went in the offing. By-and-by he could go no further than the garden of the house in which we lived. A little later, and he spent his days on a couch beside the open window, waiting patiently for the end. Ay, for the end! It had come to that. He was fading fast, waning with the waning summer, and conscious that the Reaper was at hand. His whole aim now was to soften the agony of my remorse, and prepare me for what must shortly come.

"I would not live longer, if I could," he said, lying on his couch one summer evening. and looking up to the stars. "If I had my choice at this moment, I would ask to go. I should like Gianetta to know that I forgave her."

"She shall know it," I said, trembling suddenly from head to foot.

He pressed my hand.

"And you'll write to father?"

"I will."

I had drawn a little back, that he might not see the tears raining down my cheeks; but he raised himself on his elbow, and looked round.

"Don't fret, Ben," he whispered; laid his head back wearily upon the pillow—and so died.

And this was the end of it. This was the end of all that made life life to me. I buried him there, in hearing of the wash of a strange sea on a strange shore. I stayed by the grave till the priest and the bystanders were gone. I saw the earth filled in to the last sod, and the gravedigger stamped it down with his feet. Then, and not till then, I felt that I had lost him forever—the friend I had loved, and hated, and slain. Then, and not till then, I knew that all rest, and joy, and hope were over for me.

From that moment my heart hardened within me, and my life was filled with loathing. Day and night, land and sea, labour and rest, food and sleep, were alike hateful to me. It was the curse of Cain, and that my brother had pardoned me made it lie none the lighter. Peace on earth was for me no more, and goodwill towards men was dead in my heart for ever. Remorse softens some natures; but it poisoned mine. I hated all mankind; but above all mankind I hated the woman who had come between us two, and ruined both our lives.

He had bidden me seek her out, and be the messenger of his forgiveness. I had sooner have gone down to the port of Genoa and taken upon me the serge cap and shotted chain of any galley-slave at his toil in the public works; but for all that I did my best to obey him. I went back, alone and on foot. I went back, intending to say to her, "Gianetta Coneglia, he forgave you; but God never will." But she was gone.

The little shop was let to a fresh occupant; and the neighbours only knew that mother and daughter had left the place quite suddenly, and that Gianetta was supposed to be under the "protection" of the Marchese Loredano. How I made inquiries here and there—how I heard that they had gone to Naples—and how, being restless and reckless of my time, I worked my passage in a French steamer, and followed her—how, having found the sumptuous villa that was now hers, I learned that she had left there some ten days and gone to Paris, where the Marchese was ambassador for the Two Sicilies—how, working my passage back again to Marseilles, and thence, in part by the river and in part by the rail, I made my way to Paris—how, day after day, I paced the streets and the parks, watched at the ambassador's gates, followed his carriage, and at last, after weeks of waiting, discovered her address—how, having written to request an interview, her servants spurned me from her door and flung my letter in my face—how, looking up at her windows, I then, instead of forgiving, solemnly cursed her with the bitterest curses my tongue could devise—and how, this done, I shook the dust of Paris from my feet, and became a wanderer upon the face of the earth, are facts which I have now no space to tell.

The next six or eight years of my life were shifting and unsettled enough. A morose and restless man, I took employment here and there, as opportunity offered, turning my hand to many things, and caring little what I earned, so long as the work was hard and the change incessant. First of all I engaged myself as chief engineer in one of the French steamers plying between Marseilles and Constantinople.

At Constantinople I changed to one of the Austrian Lloyd's boats, and worked for some time to and from Alexandria, Jaffa, and those parts After that, I fell in with a party of Mr. Layard's men at Cairo, and so went up the Nile and took a turn at the excavations of the mound of Nimroud. Then I became a working engineer on the new desert line between Alexandria and Suez; and by-and-by I worked my passage out to Bombay, and took service as an engine fitter on one of the great Indian railways. I stayed a long time in India; that is to say, I stayed nearly two years, which was a long time for me; and I might not even have left so soon, but for the war that was declared just then with Russia.

That tempted me. For I loved danger and hardship as other men love safety and ease; and as for my life, I had sooner have parted from it than kept it, any day. So I came straight back to England; betook myself to Portsmouth, where my testimonials at once procured me the sort of berth I wanted. I went out to the Crimea in the engine-room of one of her Majesty's war steamers.

I served with the fleet, of course, while the war lasted; and when it was over, went wandering off again, rejoicing in my liberty. This time I went to Canada, and after working on a railway then in progress near the American frontier. I presently passed over into the States; journeyed from north to south; crossed the Rocky Mountains; tried a month or two of life in the gold country; and then, being seized with a sudden, aching, unaccountable longing to revisit that solitary grave so far away on the Italian coast, I turned my face once more towards Europe.

Poor little grave! I found it rank with weeds, the cross half shattered, the inscription half effaced. It was as if no one had loved him, or remembered him. I went back to the house in which we had lodged together. The same people were still living there, and made me kindly welcome. I stayed with them for some weeks. I weeded, and planted, and trimmed the grave with my own hands, and set up a fresh cross in pure white marble. It was the first season of rest that I had known since I laid him there; and when at last I shouldered my knapsack and set forth again to battle with the world, I promised myself that, God willing, I would creep back to Rocca, when my days drew near to ending, and be buried by his side.

From hence, being, perhaps, a little less inclined than formerly for very distant parts, and willing to keep within reach of that grave, I went no further than Mantua, where I engaged myself as an engine-driver on the line, then not long completed, between that city and Venice. Somehow, although I had been trained to the working engineering, I preferred in these days to earn my bread by driving. I liked the excitement of it, the sense of power, the rush of the air, the roar of the fire, the flitting of the landscape.

Above all, I enjoyed to drive a night express. The worse the weather, the better it suited with my sullen temper. For I was as hard, and harder than ever. The years had done nothing to soften me. They had only confirmed all that was blackest and bitterest in my heart.

I continued pretty faithful to the Mantua line, and had been working on it steadily for more than seven months when that which I am now about to relate took place.

It was in the month of March. The weather had been unsettled for some days past, and the nights stormy; and at one point along the line, near Ponte di Brenta, the waters had risen and swept away some seventy yards of embankment. Since this accident, the trains had all been obliged to stop at a certain spot between Padua and Ponte di Brenta, and the passengers, with their luggage, had thence to be transported in all kinds of vehicles, by a circuitous country road, to the nearest station on the other side of the gap, where another train and engine awaited them.

This, of course, caused great confusion and annoyance, put all our timetables wrong, and subjected the public to a large amount of inconvenience. In the mean while an army of navvies was drafted to the spot, and worked day and night to repair the damage. At this time I was driving two through trains each day; namely, one from Mantua to Venice in the early morning, and a return train from Venice to Mantua in the afternoon—a tolerably full days' work, covering about one hundred and ninety miles of ground, and occupying between ten and eleven hours.

I was therefore not best pleased when, on the third or fourth day after the accident, I was informed that, in addition to my regular allowance of work, I should that evening be required to drive a special train to Venice. This special train, consisting of an engine, a single carriage, and a break-van, was to leave the Mantua platform at eleven; at Padua the passengers were to alight and find post-chaises waiting to convey them to Ponte di Brenta; at Ponte di Brenta another engine, carriage, and break-van were to be in readiness, I was charged to accompany them throughout.

"Corpo di Bacco," said the clerk who gave me my orders, "you need not look so black, man. You are certain of a handsome gratuity. Do you know who goes with you?"

"Not I."

"Not you, indeed! Why, it's the Duca Loredano, the Neapolitan ambassador."

"Loredano!" I stammered. "What Loredano? There was a Marchese——"

"Certo. He was the Marchese Loredano some years ago; but he has come into his dukedom since then."

"He must be a very old man by this time."

"Yes, he is old; but what of that? He is as hale, and bright, and stately as ever. You have seen him before?"

"Yes," I said, turning away; "I have seen him—years ago."

"You have heard of his marriage?"

I shook my head.

The clerk chuckled, rubbed his hands, and shrugged his shoulders.

"An extraordinary affair," he said. "Made a tremendous esclandre at the time. He married his mistress—quite a common, vulgar girl—a Genoese—very handsome; but not received, of course. Nobody visits her."

"Married her!" I exclaimed. "Impossible."

"True, I assure you."

I put my hand to my head. I felt as if I had had a fall or a blow.

"Does she—does she go tonight?" I faltered.

"O dear, yes—goes everywhere with him—never lets him out of her sight. You'll see her—*la bella Duchessa!*"

With this my informant laughed, and rubbed his hands again, and went back to his office.

The day went by, I scarcely know how, except that my whole soul was in a tumult of rage and bitterness. I returned from my afternoon's work about 7.25, and at 10.30 I was once again at the station. I had examined the engine; given instructions to the

Fochista, or stoker, about the fire; seen to the supply of oil; and got all in readiness, when, just as I was about to compare my watch with the clock in the ticket-office, a hand was laid upon my arm, and a voice in my ear said:

"Are you the engine-driver who is going on with this special train?"

I had never seen the speaker before. He was a small, dark man, muffled up about the throat, with blue glasses, a large black beard, and his hat drawn low upon his eyes.

"You are a poor man, I suppose," he said, in a quick, eager whisper, "and, like other poor men, would not object to be better off. Would you like to earn a couple of thousand florins?"

"In what way?"

"Hush! You are to stop at Padua, are you not, and to go on again at Ponte di Brenta?"

I nodded.

"Suppose you did nothing of the kind. Suppose, instead of turning off the steam, you jump off the engine, and let the train run on?"

"Impossible. There are seventy yards of embankment gone, and——"

"*Basta*! I know that. Save yourself, and let the train run on. It would be nothing but an accident."

I turned hot and cold; I trembled; my heart beat fast, and my breath failed.

"Why do you tempt me?" I faltered.

"For Italy's sake," he whispered; "for liberty's sake. I know you are no Italian; but, for all that, you may be a friend. This Loredano is one of his country's bitterest enemies. Stay, here are the two thousand florins."

I thrust his hand back fiercely.

"No—no," I said. "No blood-money. If I do it, I do it neither for Italy nor for money; but for vengeance."

"For vengeance!" he repeated.

At this moment the signal was given for backing up to the platform. I sprang to my place upon the engine without another word. When I again looked towards the spot where he had been standing, the stranger was gone.

I saw them take their places—Duke and Duchess, secretary and priest, valet and maid. I saw the station-master bow them into the carriage, and stand, bareheaded, beside the door. I could not distinguish their faces; the platform was too dusk, and the glare from the engine fire too strong; but I recognised her stately figure, and the poise of her head. Had I not been told who she was, I should have known her by those traits alone. Then the guard's whistle shrilled out, and the station-master made his last bow; I turned the steam on; and we started.

My blood was on fire. I no longer trembled or hesitated. I felt as if every nerve was iron, and every pulse instinct with deadly purpose. She was in my power, and I would be avenged. She should die—she, for whom I had stained my soul with my friend's blood! She should die, in the plenitude of her wealth and her beauty, and no power upon earth should save her!

The stations flew past. I put on more steam; I bade the fireman heap in the coke, and stir the blazing mass. I would have outstripped the wind, had it been possible. Faster and faster—hedges and trees, bridges, and stations, flashing past—villages no sooner seen than gone—telegraph wires twisting, and dipping, and twining themselves in one, with the awful swiftness of our pace! Faster and faster, till the fireman at my side looks white and scared, and refuses to add more fuel to the furnace. Faster and faster, till the wind rushes in our faces and drives the breath back upon our lips.

I would have scorned to save myself. I meant to die with the rest. Mad as I was—and I believe from my very soul that I was utterly mad for the time—I felt a passing pang of pity for the old man and his suite. I would have spared the poor fellow at my side, too, if I could; but the pace at which we were going made escape impossible.

Vicenza was passed—a mere confused vision of lights. Pojana flew by. At Padua, but nine miles distant, our passengers were to alight. I saw the fireman's face turned upon me in remonstrance;

I saw his lips move, though I could not hear a word; I saw his expression change suddenly from remonstrance to a deadly terror, and then—merciful Heaven! then, for the first time, I saw that he and I were no longer alone upon the engine.

There was a third man—a third man standing on my right hand, as the fireman was standing on my left—a tall, stalwart man, with short curling hair, and a flat Scotch cap upon his head. As I fell back in the first shock of surprise, he stepped nearer; took my place at the engine, and turned the steam off. I opened my lips to speak to him; he turned his head slowly, and looked me in the face.

Matthew Price!

I uttered one long wild cry, flung my arms wildly up above my head, and fell as if I had been smitten with an axe.

I am prepared for the objections that may be made to my story. I expect, as a matter of course, to be told that this was an optical illusion, or that I was suffering from pressure on the brain, or even that I laboured under an attack of temporary insanity. I have heard all these arguments before, and, if I may be forgiven for saying so, I have no desire to hear them again. My own mind has been made up upon this subject for many a year. All that I can say—all that I *know* is—that Matthew Price came back from the dead, to save my soul and the lives of those whom I, in my guilty rage, would have hurried to destruction. I believe this as I believe in the mercy of Heaven and the forgiveness of repentant sinners.

Cain

I had already made some way in my profession, when I went over to France about sixteen years ago, to study under Paul Delaroche. The great master was absent from Paris at the time of my arrival, and for some weeks I wandered from church to church, from gallery to gallery, dreaming, hoping, worshipping. I spent long days in the Louvre. To me the place was sacred; and I well remember how I often stood gazing into the golden glooms of a Rembrandt, or the airy distances of a Claude, till tears of boyish enthusiasm shut away the pictures from my sight.

While I was yet revelling in this delicious liberty, I visited the Luxembourg gallery for the first time. It was on a superb morning in June. There had been a shower, and the rain-drops were yet glittering on the acacias. The clouds had cleared off; white statues gleamed here and there among the trees; and the great glass dome of the *Observatoire* looked all glad and golden in the sunshine.

I turned away reluctantly from the brilliant gardens, and passed through the little sidedoor leading to the upper rooms of the palace. I was devoted, at this time, to the elder schools of art, and felt but little interest in the works of my contemporaries; so I strolled on listlessly from room to room, pausing now and then before a Flandrin or a Paul Delaroche, but caring little for the collection as a whole.

At last, in the obscurest corner of a small, ill-lighted room, I came upon a picture that riveted my attention the moment I beheld it. The subject was *Cain after the murder of Abel*: the artist's name, Camille Prévost.

Never, while I live, shall I forget the thrill with which I first beheld that fearful painting; never that ghastly landscape, and that still more ghastly face! The murderer stood on a bleak precipice, his head half turned, as if looking over his shoulder towards the spectator. The red sun was setting behind a gloomy forest on the far horizon. The sky and stagnant ocean were bathed in a copper-coloured glow. A snake glided through a foreground of loathsome weeds; and a distant vulture hovered in the air, as if scenting the first drops of human blood.

Powerful as it was, however, the design had less to do with the effect of this strange picture than the marvellous poetry of the execution. There was a dramatic unity about it which I find it impossible to describe—an atmosphere of death and horror that seemed to foul the very air around it. The face of Cain was instinct with unearthly meaning. The cold sweat stood in visible beads upon his brow, and his eyes were fixed as if upon some fearful vision. The very sea beyond looked thick and lifeless. The very trees were like funereal plumes.

When I went out, the sunshine of the summer afternoon offended my eyes. I chose a shady avenue, and there paced to and fro, thinking of the picture. Evening came, and it still haunted me. I strove to shake off the weird influence. I stepped into one of the theatres—but the laughter, the music, the lights were alike insupportable to me. Then I went home to my books, but could not read—to bed, but sleep forsook my pillow.

Thus the night wore past, and morning found me again at the Luxembourg. I had come too early; and I rambled about with feverish impatience till the gallery was opened. I spent the whole of that clay before the painting. I resolved to copy it. The next day I had taken up my position *en permanence*, and begun my task.

From this moment the picture began to exercise a strange, mysterious influence upon my whole being. I dreaded it, yet could not tear myself from it. My health suffered; my nerves were painfully overwrought; my sleep and appetite failed. I started at the merest sound; I trembled as I crossed the public streets. Unless when in the very act of painting, my hand lost its steadiness and my eye its certainty. I could not endure the light of an unshaded candle—nor pour out a glass of water without spilling it.

This was but the first stage of my disease. The second was still more distressing.

A morbid fascination now seemed to bind me to the picture, and the picture to me. I felt as if I could not live away from it. Cain became for me as a living man, or something more than man, having possession of my will, and transfixing me with the bright horror of his eyes. At night, when the gallery was closed, I used to linger in the neighbourhood for hours, unable to break the spell that chained me to my task; and when at last, worn out with fatigue, I went home and flung myself upon my bed, I lay awake half the night, or slept to dream of that which haunted me when waking.

Let it not be supposed that I yielded myself a willing victim to this monomania. Far from it, I wrestled with my torment—I reasoned, struggled, combated—but all in vain. It was too strong for me; and I had no one to help me in the fight. I felt at last that I might die or go mad, and there would be none to weep for me. I asked myself over and over again whither I was tending? What I should do? To whom appeal for aid and sympathy? Should I write to my friends in England? Should I leave Paris? Alas! my volition was gone. I was the slave of the picture, and though at the price of life or reason, I felt I must remain.

Matters were at this crisis (and I believe my senses were fast abandoning me) when a young man, somewhat older than myself, took up his position in the same room, and began copying a picture distant only a few yards from that on which I was employed. His presence irritated me. I felt that I was no longer alone, and I dreaded interruption.

He was a very quiet fellow, however, and so fully respected my taciturnity, that I soon ceased to remember I was no longer alone. His name, I should observe, was Achille Désiré Leroy.

It were both useless and painful to enter upon a more minute analysis of my mental condition. It became each day less and less endurable; as I became each day less capable of resistance. The whole thing wears now in my memory, the aspect of a dream—long, vivid, terrible; but still a dream.

At last the time came when body and mind could bear their bondage no longer. The afternoon was dark and oppressive, as if a tempest were brewing. Not a breath of air found its way to the gloomy corner in which I sat at work. The bright, cruel eyes of Cain seemed to pierce my very brain. I felt as if I were being suffocated. My head swam—my heart throbbed—my brush fell from my fingers. All at once I fell back in my chair, uttered a despairing cry, and covered my face with my hands.

"You are ill," said a voice close by.

I turned, and found Achille Leroy standing beside me.

"It is nothing," I faltered.

He shook his head.

"I have been observing you," he said, "for some days past. You are ill; and need not only change of air and scene, but change of occupation. This picture of Prévost's is not good for you."

"I must finish it," I replied with a shudder.

"We will discuss that question presently," said M. Leroy. "In the meanwhile, a breath of fresh air will do you more service than advice. Lean upon my arm, and come out with me for half an hour into the gardens."

I was passive as a child, and obeyed him without a word. He led me out among the trees, and sought a bench in a retired spot, where we sat down. For some time we were both silent. When at length my companion spoke, it was to urge upon me the abandonment of my undertaking.

"You are wrong," he said, "to set yourself so frightful a task. Let me recommend you to give it up from this moment."

"Alas!" I said, "I cannot."

"Why not? If the copy be a commission, it is already admirable, and needs not another touch."

"It is not that," I replied gloomily. "I have copied the picture for my own satisfaction—or rather for my own torment—and it has taken a hold upon me that I cannot shake off."

He looked at me with compassionate incredulity.

"If—if you will promise not to regard me as a madman," I added, "I will explain my words."

He promised, and I told him all that I have here recorded. When I had brought my narrative to an end, he rose, walked thoughtfully to and fro under the trees, and then, returning to his seat beside me, said:—

"As a stranger, I have no right to offer you counsel; but, as a brother artist and fellow-student, I feel as if it were my duty to make one more effort. If you will entrust me with the sale of your copy, I will undertake to find you a purchaser. But I implore you never again to look upon original or copy while you live. In urging this course upon you, I am actuated by no ordinary motive. I know the picture to be a fatal picture. I know its history, and the history of him who painted it. If you are strong enough to listen to me for a quarter of an hour, I will relate the circumstances to you as briefly as I can."

I expressed my eagerness to hear them; and M. Leroy thus began:

"Camille Prévost was the younger of two brothers. I knew them both intimately. Their father was a *négociant* of moderate fortune, residing a few miles north of Paris. He died about ten years since, leaving the bulk of his property to Hippolyte Prévost, his elder son. Camille was a painter; Hippolyte a *négociant*, like his father. The brothers were both unamiable men. Hippolyte was prudent, cold, and crafty; Camille was sullen, vindictive, and reserved. I seldom visited Hippolyte after the death of his father; and had I not met Camille daily at the Ecole des Beaux Arts, I have little doubt that our acquaintance would have ceased altogether.

"Camille Prévost was an unlovable man; but, like many unlovable men, he could love, and love passionately. As lovers, these reserved men are exacting; as husbands, jealous; as fathers, harsh; as friends, suspicious. But their attachments, however unpromising, are profound, and, like their enmities, lifelong. Camille loved his cousin. Mademoiselle Dumesnil. She was young, rich, and tolerably handsome, and resided in the Faubourg St. Grermain. Camille Prévost was a proud man, and could not endure to owe his social position to any woman, however beloved; so, having made his declaration, and obtained the consent of the lady and her family, he went for three years to Italy, to study the works of the Italian masters, and achieve some fame, if not some fortune. By the help of great natural talent, an iron will, and a dauntless ambition, he rose rapidly in his profession. In the course of the first two years he carried off several prizes at the Academies of St. Luca in Rome and the Belle Arti of Venice; and towards the close of the third sent home a painting of such remarkable merit that it obtained him the rank of Chevalier of the Legion of Honour.

"On receiving intelligence of this great success, he returned to France, radiant with gratified ambition, and elate with hope. But these three years, which had been so fortunate in one way, had proved fatal in another.

"Mademoiselle Dumesnil was married to his brother.

"Wholly unprepared for the blow that awaited him, he had hastened to her hotel immediately upon his arrival. He asked for Mademoiselle Dumesnil, and was told that Madame Prévost was at home. He found her at breakfast, and his brother, in his dressing-gown and slippers, sipping his coffee at the opposite corner of the table. Hippolyte had played his cards well; and while Camille was toiling fourteen hours a day in his Roman *atelier*, the unscrupulous elder brother had stepped in, and borne away the bride with her twenty thousand *livres* of dowry.

"The lady received her former lover as coolly and calmly as if they had never been betrothed. Hippolyte affected cordiality, and pressed his brother to make the Hotel Prévost his home whenever he might be in Paris. Camille disguised his fury under a mask of stern politeness. He neither wept nor stormed. Outwardly cold and cynical as ever, he betrayed by neither look nor word the passions that raged at his heart. When he took his leave. Monsieur and Madame Prévost flattered themselves that the wanderer had forgotten all about his early love.

"'Three years in Italy, *ma chère*,' said the husband, as he drew on his gloves, and prepared to take his daily ride in the Bois, 'make wonderful havoc in a lover's memory. Depend on it, he is as glad to have regained his liberty as I am to have relinquished mine.'

"About a week after this, the body of M. Hippolyte Prévost was found in one of the *contre allées* of the Bois de Boulogne, with a bullet in his brain, and his horse feeding quietly beside him.

"There was a long and tedious investigation, the details of which have long since escaped my recollection. Several persons were in turn suspected; but the murder could be brought home to none, and the event was in time forgotten. Camille, having inherited the greater part of his brother's fortune, continued to follow his profession with unabated industry. It was rumoured at first that he would marry his brother's widow; but, on the contrary, he avoided her by every means in his power; and at last those who had prophesied of his marriage were heard to whisper that he had taken a solemn oath never to see, or speak with her again.

"About this time he began his last and best painting—*Cain after the Murder of Abel*. I need say nothing to you of the merits of this extraordinary work. You have studied it more closely than I, and know it only too well.

"Always misanthropic, Camille Prévost had sunk, ever since his return from Rome, into a dark and sullen melancholy. He shut himself up in his rooms; saw no one; and worked without intermission upon this fatal picture. Day by day, and week by week, he wasted away, beneath the burthen of a fascination which, like yourself, he could neither resist nor control. As the painting progressed, his sufferings became more acute, and his strength diminished. A profound despondency was succeeded by paroxysms of nervous terror. There were times when he would shriek aloud, as if unable to endure the sight of his own handiwork; and once or twice he was found insensible at the foot of his easel. On one of these occasions his servants called in the nearest medical man, who in vain strove to persuade his patient to lay the picture aside, and try change of air and scene. Camille refused to listen to him, and the doctor's visit was never repeated.

"At last the painting was finished, exhibited, and purchased by the Government.

"As one of our modern masterpieces, it occupies its present position on the walls of the Luxembourg. Doubtless a day will come when, to use the language of the catalogue, 'it will receive a last and honourable asylum in the galleries of the Louvre, where it will take a place beside its illustrious predecessors, and continue the history of French Art.'"

"But the artist?" I exclaimed, when Leroy had brought his story to an end. "What became of Camille Prévost?"

We had risen from our quiet seat under the acacias some minutes back, and were now strolling down the shady side of an old-fashioned street adjoining the gardens. As I spoke, we arrived in front of a large private mansion approached by a pair of ponderous wooden gates thickly studded with bosses of iron. To my surprise, Monsieur Leroy, instead of replying to my question, rang the bell, nodded to the *conçierge*, and requested me to follow him.

We passed through a spacious courtyard, up a flight of steps, and into a large hall paved with alternate squares of black and white marble. Here we were met by an elderly man of mild and benevolent aspect, who shook hands with my companion, and pointed to the staircase.

"You know your way. Monsieur Leroy," he said. "You will find François in the corridor."

To which my fellow-student replied by a word of acknowledgment, and preceded me up the stairs. At the first landing, we were met by an attendant in a sombre livery of grey and black, who saluted us in silence, and led the way through a long corridor in which were some ten or twelve doors, thickly clamped with iron. Before the last of these he paused, took a key from his pocket, unlocked the door, and stood aside to let us pass.

I found myself in a small sitting-room, neatly but plainly furnished. Close under the window stood an easel, and on the easel an incoherent fantastic daub in oil, more like a paint-smeared palette than a picture. The window, like the door, was closely barred, and looked out into a dreary yard surrounded by high walls. I shuddered. There was a heavy, unnatural silence about the house, a kind of palpable gloom, that chilled me like an evil presence.

"What place is this?" I said. "Why have you brought me here?"

Monsieur Leroy pointed to a door at the farther end of the room, which the attendant proceeded to unlock like the first.

At this moment a frightful scream rang through the rooms—a scream so shrill, so agonized, so dissonant, that I involuntarily covered my face with my hands, as if some awful sight must follow it.

"There is the painter," said Leroy. "There is Camille Prévost."

I looked in. One glance was enough—one glance at a wild, pale, savage face, from which all light of human reason had faded. In Camille Prévost I saw a raging madman, strapped down upon a wooden pallet, laughing, screaming, blaspheming, and crying aloud that he was Cain—Cain, the slayer of Abel!

"And is he really the murderer of his brother ?" I asked, as I turned away, cold and horror-stricken.

"God only knows," replied my fellow-student. "This is one of his violent days, and he always accuses himself when the paroxysm is upon him. At all events, you now know why I have brought you hither. That fatal picture has driven one painter mad, and I was determined it should not do the same by another."

In the Confessional

The things of which I write befell—let me see, some fifteen or eighteen years ago. I was not young then; I am not old now. Perhaps I was about thirty-two; but I do not know my age very exactly, and I cannot be certain to a year or two one way or the other.

My manner of life at that time was desultory and unsettled. I had a sorrow—no matter of what kind—and I took to rambling about Europe; not certainly in the hope of forgetting it, for I had no wish to forget, but because of the restlessness that made one place after another *triste* and intolerable to me.

It was change of place, however, and not excitement, that I sought. I kept almost entirely aloof from great cities, Spas, and beaten tracks, and preferred for the most part to explore districts where travellers and foreigners rarely penetrated.

Such a district at that time was the Upper Rhine. I was traversing it that particular Summer for the first time, and on foot; and I had set myself to trace the course of the river from its source in the great Rhine glacier to its fall at Schaffhausen. Having done this, however, I was unwilling to part company with the noble river; so I decided to follow it yet a few miles farther—perhaps as far as Mayence, but at all events as far as Basle.

And now began, if not the finest, certainly not the least charming part of my journey. Here, it is true, were neither Alps, nor glaciers, nor ruined castles perched on inaccessible crags; but my way lay through a smiling country, studded with picturesque hamlets, and beside a bright river, hurrying along over swirling rapids, and under the dark arches of antique covered bridges, and between hillsides garlanded with vines.

It was towards the middle of a long day's walk among such scenes as these that I came to Rheinfelden, a small place on the left bank of the river, about fourteen miles above Basle.

As I came down the white road in the blinding sunshine, with the vines on either hand, I saw the town lying low on the opposite bank of the Rhine. It was an old walled town, enclosed on the land side and open to the liver, the houses going sheer down to the water's edge, with flights of slimy steps worn smooth by the wash of the current, and overhanging eaves, and little built-out rooms with penthouse roofs, supported from below by jutting piles black with age and tapestried with water-weeds. The stunted towers of a couple of churches stood up from amid the brown and tawny roofs within the walls.

Beyond the town, height above height, stretched a distance of wooded hills. The old covered bridge, divided by a bit of rocky island in the middle of the stream, led from bank to bank—from Germany to Switzerland. The town was in Switzerland; I, looking towards it from the road, stood on Baden territory; the river ran sparkling and foaming between.

I crossed, and found the place all alive in anticipation of a *Kermess*, or fair, that was to be held there the next day but one. The townsfolk were all out in the streets or standing about their doors; and there were carpenters hard at work knocking up rows of wooden stands and stalls the whole length of the principal thoroughfare. Shop-signs in open-work of wrought iron hung over the doors. A runlet of sparkling water babbled down a stone channel in the middle of the street. At almost every other house (to judge by the rows of tarnished watches hanging in the dingy parlour windows), there lived a watchmaker; and presently I came to a fountain—a regular Swiss fountain, spouting water from four ornamental pipes, and surmounted by the usual armed knight in old grey stone.

As I rambled on thus (looking for an inn, but seeing none), I suddenly found that I had reached the end of the street, and with it the limit of the town on this side. Before me rose a lofty, picturesque old gate-tower, with a tiled roof and a little window over the archway; and there was a peep of green grass and golden sunshine beyond. The town walls (sixty or seventy feet in height, and curiously roofed with a sort of projecting shed on the inner side) curved away to right and left, unchanged since the Middle Ages. A rude wain, laden with clover and drawn by mild-eyed, cream-coloured oxen, stood close by in the shade.

I passed out through the gloom of the archway into the sunny space beyond. The moat outside the walls was bridged over and filled in—a green ravine of grasses and wild-flowers. A stork had built its nest on the roof of the gate-tower. The *cicalas* shrilled in the grass. The shadows lay sleeping under the trees, and a family of cocks and hens went plodding inquisitively to and fro among the cabbages in the adjacent field. Just beyond the moat, with only this field between, stood a little solitary church—a church with a wooden porch, and a quaint, bright-red steeple, and a churchyard like a rose-garden, full of colour and perfume, and scattered over with iron crosses wreathed with *immortelles*.

The churchyard gate and the church door stood open. I went in. All was clean, and simple, and very poor. The walls were whitewashed; the floor was laid with red bricks; the roof raftered. A tiny confessional like a sentry-box stood in one corner; the font was covered with a lid like a wooden steeple; and over the altar, upon which stood a pair of battered brass candlesticks and two vases of artificial flowers, hung a daub of the Holy Family, in oils.

All here was so cool, so quiet, that I sat down for a few moments and rested. Presently an old peasant woman trudged up the church-path with a basket of vegetables on her head. Having set this down in the porch, she came in, knelt before the altar, said her simple prayers, and went her way.

Was it not time for me also to go my way? I looked at my watch. It was past four o'clock, and I had not yet found a lodging for the night.

I got up, somewhat unwillingly; but, attracted by a tablet near the altar, crossed over to look at it before leaving the church. It was a very small slab, and bore a very brief German inscription to this effect:—

To the Sacred Memory
of
The Reverend Père Chessez,
For twenty years the beloved Pastor of this Parish.
Died April 16th, 1825. Aged 44.
He Lived a Saint ; He Died a Martyr.

I read it over twice, wondering idly what story was wrapped up in the concluding line. Then, prompted by a childish curiosity, I went up to examine the confessional.

It was, as I have said, about the size of a sentry-box, and was painted to imitate old dark oak. On the one side was a narrow door with a black handle, on the other a little opening like a ticket-taker's window, closed on the inside by a faded green curtain.

I know not what foolish fancy possessed me, but, almost without considering what I was doing, I turned the handle and opened the door. Opened it—peeped in—found the priest sitting in his place—started back as if I had been shot—and stammered an unintelligible apology.

"I—I beg a thousand pardons," I exclaimed. "I had no idea—seeing the church empty—"

He was sitting with averted face, and clasped hands lying idly in his lap— a tall, gaunt man, dressed in a black *soutane*. When I paused, and not till then, he slowly, very slowly, turned his head, and looked me in the face.

The light inside the confessional was so dim that I could not see his features very plainly. I only observed that his eyes were large, and bright, and wild-looking, like the eyes of some fierce animal, and that his face, with the reflection of the green curtain upon it, looked lividly pale.

For a moment we remained thus, gazing at each other, as if fascinated. Then, finding that he made no reply, but only stared at me with those strange eyes, I stepped hastily back, shut the door without another word, and hurried out of the church.

I was very much disturbed by this little incident; more disturbed, in truth, than seemed reasonable, for my nerves for the moment were shaken. Never, I told myself, never while I lived could I forget that fixed attitude and stony face, or the glare of those terrible eyes. What was the man's history? Of what secret despair, of what life-long remorse, of what wild unsatisfied longings was he the victim? I felt I could not rest till I had learned something of his past life.

Full of these thoughts, I went on quickly into the town, half running across the field, and never looking back. Once past the gateway and inside the walls, I breathed more freely. The wain was still standing in the shade, but the oxen were gone now, and two men were busy forking out the clover into a little yard close by. Having inquired of one of these regarding an inn, and being directed to the Krone, "over against the Frauenkirche," I made my way to the upper part of the town, and there, at one corner of a forlorn, weed-grown market-place, I found my hostelry.

The landlord, a sedate, bald man in spectacles, who, as I presently discovered, was not only an inn-keeper but a clock-maker, came out from an inner room to receive me. His wife, a plump, pleasant body, took my orders for dinner. His pretty daughter showed me to my room. It was a large, low, whitewashed room, with two lattice windows overlooking the market-place, two little beds, covered with puffy red eiderdowns at the farther end, and an army of clocks and ornamental timepieces arranged along every shelf, table, and chest of drawers in the room. Being left here to my meditations, I sat down and counted these companions of my solitude.

Taking little and big together, Dutch clocks, cuckoo clocks, *châlet* clocks, skeleton clocks, and *pendules* in ormolu, bronze, marble, ebony, and alabaster cases, there were exactly thirty-two. Twenty-eight were going merrily. As no two among them were of the same opinion as regarded the time, and as several struck the quarters as well as the hours, the consequence was that one or other gave tongue about every five minutes. Now, for a light and nervous sleeper such as I was at that time, here was a lively prospect for the night!

Going downstairs presently with the hope of getting my land-lady to assign me a quieter room, I passed two eight-day clocks on the landing, and a third at the foot of the stairs. The public room was equally well-stocked. It literally bristled with clocks, one of which played a spasmodic version of Gentle Zitella with variations every quarter of an hour. Here I found a little table prepared by the open window, and a dish of trout and a flask of country wine awaiting me. The pretty daughter waited upon me; her mother bustled to and fro with the dishes; the landlord stood by, and beamed upon me through his spectacles.

"The trout were caught this morning, about two miles from here," he said, complacently.

"They are excellent," I replied, filling him out a glass of wine, and helping myself to another. "Your health, Herr Wirth."

"Thanks, *mein Herr*—yours."

Just at this moment two clocks struck at opposite ends of the room—one twelve, and the other seven. I ventured to suggest that mine host was tolerably well reminded of the flight of time; whereupon he explained that his work lay chiefly in the repair-ing and regulating line, and that at that present moment he had no less than one hundred and eighteen clocks of various sorts and sizes on the premises.

"Perhaps the *Herr* Englander is a light sleeper," said his quick-witted wife, detecting my dismay. "If so, we can get him a bed-room elsewhere. Not, perhaps, in the town, for I know no place where he would be as comfortable as with ourselves; but just outside the Friedrich's Thor, not five minutes' walk from our door."

I accepted the offer gratefully.

"So long," I said, "as I ensure cleanliness and quiet, I do not care how homely my lodgings may be."

"Ah, you'll have both, *mein Herr*, if you go where my wife is thinking of," said the landlord. "It is at the house of our pastor—

the Père Chessez."

"The Père Chessez!" I exclaimed. "What, the pastor of the little church out yonder?"

"The same, *mein Herr.*"

"But—but surely the Pèe Chessez is dead! I saw a tablet to his memory in the chancel."

"Nay, that was our pastor's elder brother," replied the landlord, looking grave. "He has been gone these thirty years and more. His was a tragical ending."

But I was thinking too much of the younger brother just then to feel any curiosity about the elder; and I told myself that I would put up with the companionship of any number of clocks, rather than sleep under the same roof with that terrible face and those unearthly eyes.

"I saw your pastor just now in the church," I said, with apparent indifference. "He is a singular-looking man."

"He is too good for this world," said the landlady.

"He is a saint upon earth!" added the pretty *Fräulein.*

"He is one of the best of men," said, more soberly, the husband and father. "I only wish he was less of a saint. He fasts, and prays, and works beyond his strength. A little more beef and a little less devotion would be all the better for him."

"I should like to hear something more about the life of so good a man," said I, having by this time come to the end of my simple dinner. "Come, Herr Wirth, let us have a bottle of your best, and then sit down and tell me your pastor's history!"

The landlord sent his daughter for a bottle of the "green seal," and, taking a chair, said:—

"*Ach Himmel! mein Herr,* there is no history to tell. The good father has lived here all his life. He is one of us. His father, Johann Chessez, was a native of Rheinfelden and kept this' very inn. He was a wealthy farmer and vine-grower. He had only those two sons—Nicholas, who took to the church and became pastor of Feldkirche; and this one, Matthias, who was intended to inherit the business; but who also entered religion after the death of his elder brother, and is now pastor of the same parish."

"But why did he enter religion?" I asked. "Was he in any way to blame for the accident (if It was an accident) that caused the death of his elder brother?"

"Ah Heavens! no!" exclaimed the landlady, leaning on the back of her husband's chair. "It was the shock—the shock that told so terribly upon his poor nerves! He was but a lad at that time, and as sensitive as a girl—but the *Herr* Englander does not know the story. Go on, my husband."

So the landlord, after a sip of the "green seal," continued:—

"At the time my wife alludes to, *mein Herr*, Johann Chessez was still living. Nicholas, the elder son, was in holy orders and established in the parish of Feldkirche, outside the walls; and Matthias, the younger, was a lad of about fourteen years old, and lived with his father. He was an amiable good boy—pious and thoughtful—fonder of his books than of the business. The neighbour-folk used to say even then that Matthias was cut out for a priest, like his elder brother. As for Nicholas, he was neither more nor less than a saint. Well, *mein Herr*, at this time there lived on the other side of Rheinfelden, about a mile beyond the Basel Thor, a farmer named Caspar Rufenacht and his wife Margaret. Now Caspar Rufenacht was a jealous, quarrelsome fellow; and the Frau Margaret was pretty; and he led her a devil of a life. It was said that he used to beat her when he had been drinking, and that sometimes, when he went to fair or market, he would lock her up for the whole day in a room at the top of the house. Well, this poor, ill-used Frau Margaret—"

"Tut, tut, my man," interrupted the landlady. "The Frau Margaret was a light one!"

"Peace, wife! Shall we speak hard words of the dead? The Frau Margaret was young and pretty, and a flirt; and she had a bad husband, who left her too much alone."

The landlady pursed up her lips and shook her head, as the best of women will do when the character of another woman is under discussion. The innkeeper went on.

"Well, *mein Herr*, to cut a long story short, after having been jealous first of one and then of another, Caspar Rufenacht became furious about a certain German, a Badener named Schmidt, living on the opposite bank of the Rhine. I remember the man quite well—a handsome, merry fellow, and no saint; just the sort to make mischief between man and wife. Well, Caspar Rufenacht swore a great oath that, cost what it might, he would come at the truth about his wife and Schmidt; so he laid all manner of plots to surprise them—waylaid the Frau Margaret in her walks; followed her at a distance when she went to church; came home at unexpected hours; and played the spy as if he had been brought up to the trade. But his spying was all in vain. Either the Frau Margaret was too clever for him, or there was really nothing to discover; but still he was not satisfied. So he cast about for some way to attain his end, and, by the help of the Evil One, he found it.'

Here the innkeeper's wife and daughter, who had doubtless heard the story a hundred times over, drew near and listened breathlessly.

"What, think you," continued the landlord, "does this black-souled Caspar do? Does he punish the poor woman within an inch of her life, till she confesses? No. Does he charge Schmidt with having tempted her from her duty, and fight it out with him like a man? No. What else then? I will tell you. He waits till the vigil of St. Margaret—her saint's day—when he knows the poor sinful soul is going to confession; and he marches straight to the house of the Père Chessez—the very house where our own Père Chessez is now living—and he finds the good priest at his devotions in his little study, and he says to him:

"'Father Chessez, my wife is coming to the church this afternoon to make her confession to you.'

"'She is,' replies the priest.

"'I want you to tell me all she tells you,' says Caspar; 'and I will wait here till you come back from the church, that I may hear it. Will you do so?'

"'Certainly not,' replies the Père Chessez. 'You must surely know, Caspar, that we priests are forbidden to reveal the secrets of the confessional.'

152

"'That is nothing to me,' says Caspar, with an oath. 'I am resolved to know whether my wife is guilty or innocent; and know it I will, by fair means or foul.'

"'You shall never know it from me, Caspar,' says the Père Chessez, very quietly.

"'Then, by Heavens!' says Caspar, 'I'll learn it for myself.' And with that he pulls out a heavy horse-pistol from his pocket, and with the butt-end of it deals the Père Chessez a tremendous blow upon the head, and then another, and another, till the poor young man lay senseless at his feet. Then Caspar, thinking he had quite killed him, dressed himself in the priest's own *soutane* and hat; locked the door; put the key in his pocket; and stealing round the back way into the church, shut himself up in the confessional."

"Then the priest died!" I exclaimed, remembering the epitaph upon the tablet.

"Ay, *mein Herr*—the Père Chessez died; but not before he had told the story of his assassination, and identified his murderer."

"And Caspar Rufenacht, I hope, was hanged?"

"Wait a bit, *mein Herr*, we have not come to, that yet. We left Caspar in the confessional, waiting for his wife."

"And she came?"

"Yes, poor soul! she came."

"And made her confession?"

"And made her confession, *mein Herr*."

"What did she confess?"

The innkeeper shook his head.

"That no one ever knew, save the good God and her murderer."

"Her murderer!" I exclaimed.

"Ay, just that. Whatever it was that she confessed, she paid for it with her life. He heard her out, at all events, without discovering himself, and let her go home believing that she had received absolution for her sins. Those who met her that afternoon said she seemed unusually bright and happy. As she passed through the town, she went into the shop in the Mongarten Strasse, and bought some ribbons. About half an hour later, my own father met her outside the Basel Thor, walking briskly homewards. He was the last who saw her alive.

"That evening (it was in October, and the days were short), some travellers coming that way into the town heard shrill cries, as of a woman screaming, in the direction of Caspar's farm. But the night was very dark, and the house lay back a little way from the road; so they told themselves it was only some drunken peasant quarrelling with his wife, and passed on. Next morning Caspar Rufenacht came toRheinfelden, walked very quietly into the *Polizei*, and gave himself up to justice.

"'I have killed my wife,' said he. I have killed the Père Chessez. And I have committed sacrilege.'

"And so, indeed, it was. As for the Frau Margaret, they found her body in an upper chamber, well-nigh hacked to pieces, and the hatchet with which the murder was committed lying beside her on the floor. He had pursued her, apparently, from room to room; for there were pools of blood and handfuls of long light hair, and marks of bloody hands along the walls, all the way from the kitchen to the spot where she lay dead."

"And so he was hanged?" said I, coming back to my original question.

"Yes, yes," replied the innkeeper and his womankind in chorus. "He was hanged—of course he was hanged."

"And it was the shock of this double tragedy that drove the younger Chessez into the church?"

"Just so, *mein Herr.*"

"Well, he carries it in his face. He looks like a most unhappy man."

"Nay, he is not that, *mein Herr!*" exclaimed the landlady. "He is melancholy, but not unhappy."

"Well, then, austere."

"Nor is he austere, except towards himself."

"True, wife," said the innkeeper; "but, as I said, he carries that sort of thing too far. You understand, *mein Herr,*" he added, touching his forehead with his forefinger, "the good pastor has let his mind dwell too much upon the past. He is nervous—too nervous, and too low."

I saw it all now. That terrible light in his eyes was the light of insanity. That stony look in his face was the fixed, hopeless melancholy of a mind diseased.

"Does he know that he is mad?" I asked, as the landlord rose to go.

He shrugged his shoulders and looked doubtful.

"I have not said that the Père Chessez is mad, *mein Herr*," he replied. "He has strange fancies sometimes, and takes his fancies for facts—that is all. But I am quite sure that he does not believe himself to be less sane than his neighbours."

So the innkeeper left me, and I (my head full of the story I had just heard) put on my hat, went out into the market-place, asked my way to the Basel Thor, and set off to explore the scene of the Frau Margaret's murder.

I found it without difficulty—a long, low-fronted, beetle-browed farm-house, lying back a meadow's length from the road. There were children playing upon the threshold, a flock of turkeys gobbling about the barn-door, and a big dog sleeping outside his kennel close by. The chimneys, too, were smoking merrily. Seeing these signs of life and cheerfulness, I abandoned all idea of asking to go over the house. I felt that I had no right to carry my morbid curiosity into this peaceful home; so I turned away, and retraced my steps towards Rheinfelden.

It was not yet seven, and the sun had still an hour's course to run. I re-entered the town, strolled back through the street, and presently came again to the Friedrich's Thor and the path leading to the church. An irresistible impulse seemed to drag me back to the place.

Shudderingly, and with a sort of dread that was half longing, I pushed open the churchyard gate and went in. The doors were closed; a goat was browsing among the graves; and the rushing of the Rhine, some three hundred yards away, was distinctly audible in the silence. I looked round for the priest's house—the scene of the first murder; but from this side, at all events, no house was visible. Going round, however, to the back of the church, I saw a gate, a box-bordered path, and, peeping through some trees, a chimney and the roof of a little brown-tiled house.

This, then, was the path along which Caspar Rufenacht, with the priest's blood upon his hands and the priest's gown upon his shoulders, had taken his guilty way to the confessional ! How quiet it all looked in the golden evening light! How like the church-path of an English parsonage!

I wished I could have seen something more of the house than that bit of roof and that one chimney. There must, I told myself, be some other entrance—some way round by the road! Musing and lingering thus, I was startled by a quiet voice close against my shoulder, saying:—

"A pleasant evening, *mein Herr*!"

I turned, and found the priest at my elbow. He had come noiselessly across the grass, and was standing between me and the sunset, like a shadow.

"I—I beg your pardon," I stammered, moving away from the gate. "I was looking—"

I stopped in some surprise, and indeed with some sense of relief, for it was not the same priest that I had seen in the morning. No two, indeed, could well be more unlike, for this man was small, white-haired, gentle-looking, with a soft, sad smile inexpressibly sweet and winning.

"You were looking at my *arbutus*?" he said.

I had scarcely observed the *arbutus* till now, but I bowed and said something to the effect that it was an unusually fine tree.

"Yes," he replied; "but I have a rhododendron round at the front that is still finer. Will you come in and see it?"

I said I should be pleased to do so. He led the way, and I followed.

"I hope you like this part of our Rhine-country?" he said, as we took the path through the shrubbery.

"I like it so well," I replied, "that if I were to live anywhere on the banks of the Rhine, I should certainly choose some spot on the Upper Rhine between Schaffhausen and Basle."

"And you would be right," he said. "Nowhere is the river so beautiful. Nearer the glaciers it is milky and turbid—beyond Basle it soon becomes muddy. Here we have it blue as the sky—sparkling as champagne. Here is my rhododendron. It stands twelve feet high, and measures as many in diameter. I had more than two hundred blooms upon it last Spring."

When I had duly admired this giant shrub, he took me to a little arbour on a bit of steep green bank overlooking the river, where he invited me to sit down and rest. From hence I could see the porch and part of the front of his little house; but it was all so closely planted round with trees and shrubs that no clear view of it seemed obtainable in any direction. Here we sat for some time chatting about the weather, the approaching vintage, and so forth, and watching the sunset. Then I rose to take my leave.

"I heard of you this evening at the Krone, *mein Herr*," he said. "You were out, or I should have called upon you. I am glad that chance has made us acquainted. Do you remain over tomorrow?"

"No; I must go on tomorrow to Basle," I answered. And then, hesitating a little, I added:—"you heard of me, also, I fear, in the church."

"In the church?" he repeated.

"Seeing the door open, I went in—from curiosity—as a traveller; just to look round for a moment and rest."

"Naturally."

"I—I had no idea, however, that I was not alone there. I would not for the world have intruded—"

"I do not understand," he said, seeing me hesitate. "The church stands open all day long. It is free to everyone."

"Ah! I see he has not told you!"

The priest smiled but looked puzzled.

"He? Whom do you mean?"

"The other priest, *mon père*—your colleague. I regret to have broken in upon his meditations; but I had been so long in the church, and it was all so still and quiet, that it never occurred to me that there might be someone in the confessional."

The priest looked at me in a strange, startled way.

"In the confessional!" he repeated, with a catching of his breath. "You saw some one—in the confessional?"

"I am ashamed to say that, having thoughtlessly opened the door—"

"You saw—what did you see?"

"A priest, *mon père*."

"A priest! Can you describe him? Should you know him again? Was he pale, and tall, and gaunt, with long black hair?"

"The same, undoubtedly."

"And his eyes—did you observe anything particular about his eyes?"

"Yes; they were large, wild-looking, dark eyes, with a look in them—a look I cannot describe."

"A look of terror!" cried the pastor, now greatly agitated. "A look of terror—of remorse—of despair!"

"Yes, it was a look that might mean all that," I replied, my astonishment increasing at every word. "You seem troubled. Who is he?"

But instead of answering my question, the pastor took off his hat, looked up with a radiant, awestruck face, and said:—

"All-merciful God, I thank Thee! I thank Thee that I am not mad, and that Thou hast sent this stranger to be my assurance and my comfort!"

Having said these words, he bowed his head, and his lips moved in silent prayer. When he looked up again, his eyes were full of tears.

"My son," he said, laying his trembling hand upon my arm, "I owe you an explanation; but I cannot give it to you now. It must wait till I can speak more calmly—till tomorrow, when I must see you again. It involves a terrible story—a story peculiarly painful to myself—enough now if I tell you that I have seen the Thing you describe—seen It many times; and yet, because It has been visible to my eyes alone, I have doubted the evidence of my senses. The good people here believe that much sorrow and meditation have touched my brain. I have half believed it myself till now. But you—you have proved to me that I am the victim of no illusion."

"But in Heaven's name," I exclaimed, "what do you suppose I saw in the confessional?"

"You saw the likeness of one who, guilty also of a double murder, committed the deadly sin of sacrilege in that very spot, more than thirty years ago," replied the Père Chessez, solemnly.

"Caspar Rufenacht!"

"Ah! you have heard the story? Then I am spared the pain of telling it to you. That is well."

I bent my head in silence. We walked together without another word to the wicket, and thence round to the churchyard gate. It was now twilight, and the first stars were out.

"Goodnight, my son," said the pastor, giving me his hand. "Peace be with you."

As he spoke the words his grasp tightened—his eyes dilated—his whole countenance became rigid.

"Look!" he whispered. "Look where it goes!"

I followed the direction of his eyes, and there, with a freezing horror which I have no words to describe, I saw—distinctly saw through the deepening gloom—a tall, dark figure in a priest's *soutane* and broad-brimmed hat, moving slowly across the path leading from the parsonage to the church. For a moment it seemed to pause—then passed on to the deeper shade, and disappeared.

"You saw it?" said the pastor.

"Yes— plainly."

He drew a deep breath; crossed himself devoutly; and leaned upon the gate, as if exhausted.

"This is the third time I have seen it this year," he said. "Again I thank God for the certainty that I see a visible thing, and that His great gift of reason is mine unimpaired. But I would that He were graciously pleased to release me from the sight—the horror of it is sometimes more than I know how to bear. Goodnight."

With this he again touched my hand; and so, seeing that he wished to be alone, I silently left him. At the Friedrich's Thor I turned and looked back. He was still standing by the church-yard gate, just visible through the gloom of the fast deepening twilight.

I never saw the Père Chessez again. Save his own old servant, I was the last who spoke with him in this world. He died that night—died in his bed, where he was found next morning with his hands crossed upon his breast, and with a placid smile upon his lips, as if he had fallen asleep in the act of prayer.

As the news spread from house to house, the whole town rang with lamentations. The church-bells tolled; the carpenters left their work in the streets; the children, dismissed from school, went home weeping.

"'Twill be the saddest *Kermess* in Rheinfelden tomorrow, *mein Herr!*" said my good host of the Krone, as I shook hands with him at parting. "We have lost the best of pastors and of friends. He was a saint. If you had come but one day later, you would not have seen him!"

And with this he brushed his sleeve across his eyes, and turned away.

Every shutter was up, every blind down, every door closed, as I passed along the Friedrich's Strasse about midday on my way to Basle; and the few townsfolk I met looked grave and down-cast. Then I crossed the bridge and, having shown my passport to the German sentry on the Baden side, I took one long, last farewell look at the little walled town as it lay sleeping in the sunshine by the river—knowing that I should see it no more.

Love And Money

Ems is a charming place. It lies about twelve the south-east of Coblentz, in the valley of the Lahn,—that miniature Rhine, all bordered with orchards and vineyards, and steep wooded hills. The town consists of one irregular line of hotels and lodging-houses, with the mountains at the back, the front, and long double rows of acacias and planted at each side of the carriage-way. Swarms of donkeys with gay saddles, attended by drivers in blue blouses and scarlet-trimmed caps, loiter beneath the trees, soliciting hire.

The Duke of Nassau's band plays alternate selections from German, Italian, and French music in the public garden. Fashionable invalids are promenading. Gaming is going forward busily in the Conversation-Haus alike daily and nightly. Ladies are reading novels and eating ices within hearing of the band; or go by, with coloured-glass tumblers in their hands, towards the Kurhaus, where the hot springs came bubbling up from their nauseous sources down in the low vaulted galleries filled with bazaar-like shops, loungers, touters, and health-seekers. All is pleasure, indolence, and flirtation.

To Ems, therefore, came the Herr Graff von Steinberg—or, as we should say, the Count von Steinberg—to drink the waters, and while away a few weeks of the summer season. He was a tall, fair, handsome young man; an excellent specimen of the German dragoon. You would never have supposed, to look at him, that illness could have brought him to Ems; and yet he suffered from two very serious maladies, both of which, it was to be feared, were incurable by any springs, medicinal or otherwise. In a word he was hopelessly in love, and desperately poor.

The case was this:—His grandfather had left a large property, which his father, an irreclaimable gamester, had spent to the uttermost farthing. The youth had been placed in the army, through the interest of a friend. His father was now dead; the inheritance for ever gone; and he had absolutely nothing beyond his pay as a captain of dragoons, and the distant prospect of one day retiring with the title and half-pay of major. A sorry future for one who was disinterestedly and deeply in love with one of the richest heiresses in Germany!

"Who marries my daughter will receive with her a dowry of 200,000 florins, and I shall expect her husband to possess, at the least, an equal fortune."

So said the Baron von Hohendorf, in cold reply to the lover's timid declaration; and with these words still sounding in his ears, weighing on his spirits, and lying by day and night heavily upon his heart, came the Count von Steinberg to seek forgetfulness, or, at least, temporary amusement, at the Brunnen of Ems. But in vain. Pale and silent, he roamed restlessly to and fro upon the public promenades, or wandered away to hide his wretchedness in the forests and valleys round about.

Sometimes he would mingle with the gay crowd in the Kurhaus, and taste the bitter waters; sometimes linger mournfully round the tables of the gaming company, gazing enviously, yet with a kind of virtuous horror, at the glittering heaps of gold, and the packets of crisp yellow notes which there changed hands so swiftly and in such profusion.

But Albert von Steinberg was no gambler. He had seen and experienced the evil of that terrible vice too keenly already in his own father, to fall a prey to it himself. Years ago, he had vowed never to play; and kept his oath. Even now, when he found himself, as it might happen now and then, looking on with some little interest at the gains and losses of others, he would shudder, turn suddenly away, and not return again for days.

Nothing could be more regular than his mode of life. In the

morning he took the waters; at noon he walked, or read, or wrote; in the evening he strolled out again and heard the band, and by the time that all the society of the place was assembled in the ballroom or at the tables, he had returned to his quiet lodgings, and, perhaps, already gone to bed, in order that he might rise early the next morning to study some scientific work, or take a pedestrian excursion to the ruins of some old castle within the limits of a long walk.

It was a dull life for a young man—especially with that sweet, sad recollection of Emma von Hohendorf pervading every thought of the day. And all because he was poor! Was poverty a crime, he asked himself, that he should be punished for it thus? He had a great mind to throw himself off the rock where he was standing—or to precipitate himself into the river, if it were deep enough—or to go to the baron's own castle-gate, and shoot himself—or—or, in short, to do anything desperate, if it were only sufficiently romantic; for his hot young German head, full of sentiment and Schiller, would be content with nothing less than an imposing tragedy.

He thought all this, sitting in a little fantastic summer-house perched high up on a ledge of steep rock just in front of the gardens and public buildings. He looked down at the gay company far beneath, and he heard the faint music of the royal band. The sun was just setting—the landscape was lovely—life was still sweet, and he thought that he would not commit suicide that evening, at all events. So he went moodily down the winding pathway, across the bridge, and, quite by chance, wandered once more into the Conversation Haus. The gaming was going on, the glittering gold pieces were changing hands, the earnest players sitting round as usual. The sight only made him more unhappy.

"Two hundred thousand florins !" he thought to himself. "Two hundred thousand florins would make me the happiest man on earth, and I cannot get them. These men win and lose two hundred thousand florins ten times over in a week, and think nothing of the good, the happiness, the wealth that sum would be to numbers of their fellow-creatures. What a miserable dog I am!"

And he pulled his hat on fiercely, folded his arms, and strode out of the rooms, taking the road to his own lodging with so dismal an air that the people in the streets turned and looked after him, saying, "He has lost money—we saw him come out of the gaming- rooms."

"Lost money!" muttered he to himself, as he went into his garret and locked the door. " Lost money, indeed! I wish I had any to lose."

And poor Albert von Steinberg fell asleep, lamenting that the age of fairies and gnomes had passed away.

His sleep was long, sound, dreamless—for young men, in spite of love and poverty, sleep pleasantly. He woke somewhat later than he had intended, rubbed his eyes, yawned, looked hazily at his watch, lay down again, once more opened his eyes, and at last sprang valiantly out of bed.

Is he still dreaming? Is it an hallucination? Can he be mad? No, it is real, true, wonderful! There upon the table lies a brilliant heap of golden pieces—hard, ringing, real golden pieces, and he turns them over, weighs them in his hands, lets them drop through his fingers to test the evidence of his senses.

How did they come there? That is the important question. He rings the bell violently, once—twice—thrice. The servant runs up, thinking some dreadful accident has occurred.

"Someone has been here to call upon me this morning?"

"No, *Monsieur.*"

"Indeed! Somebody, then, has been upstairs since I have been asleep."

"No, *Monsieur.*"

"Are you sure?"

"Quite sure. *Monsieur.*"

"Now speak the truth, Bertha; someone has been here. You are paid to deny it. Only tell me who it was, and I will give you double for your information."

The servant looked both alarmed and astonished.

"Indeed there has not been a soul. Does *monsieur* miss anything from his apartment? Shall I send for the *gendarmes*?"

The count looked searchingly in the girl's face. She seemed wholly sincere and truthful. He tried every means yet left—adroit questions, insinuations, bribes, sudden accusations; but in vain. She had seen no one—heard no one. The door of the house was closed, and had not been left open. No one—absolutely no one—had been there.

Puzzled, troubled, bewildered, our young friend dismissed her, believing, in spite of his surprise, the truth of what she stated. He then locked the door and counted the money.

Ten thousand florins! not a *groschen* more or less!

Well, it was there; but whence it came remained a mystery.

"All mysteries clear themselves up in time," said he, as he locked the money up in his bureau. "I daresay I shall find it all out by-and-by. In the meantime I will not touch a single florin of it."

He tried not to think of it, but it was so strange a thing that he could not prevent it running in his head. It even kept him awake at night, and took away his appetite by day. At last he began to forget it; at all events, he became used to it, and at the end of a week it had ceased to trouble him.

About eight days from the date of this occurrence he woke, as before, thinking of Emma, and not at all of the money, when, on looking round, lo! there it was again. The table was once more covered with glittering gold!

His first impulse was to run to the bureau in which the first ten thousand florins were stored away. Surely he must have taken them out the night before, and forgotten to replace them. No, there they lay in the drawer where he had hidden them, and there upon the table was a second supply, larger, if anything, than the first!

Pale and trembling, he turned them over. This time there were some notes—Prussian and French—mingled with the gold. In all, twelve thousand florins.

He had locked his door—could it be opened from without

165

by a skeleton key? He had a bolt fixed within, that very day. Honest Albert von Steinberg! he took as much pains against fortune as others do against robbery!

Two days later, however, his invisible benefactor came again; and this time he found himself fourteen thousand florins the richer. It was an inexplicable prodigy! No one could have entered by the bolted door, or from the window; for he lived in a garret on the fourth story—or by the chimney, for the room was heated by a stove, the funnel of which was no thicker than his arm? Was it a plot to ruin him? or was he tempted by the powers of evil? He had a great mind to apply to the police, or to a priest (for he was a good Catholic),—still he thought he would wait a little longer. After all, there might be more unpleasant visitations!

He went out, greatly agitated, and walked about the entire day, pondering this strange problem. Then he resolved, if ever it recurred, to state his case to the *chef de police*, and to set a watch upon the house by night.

Full of this determination, he came home and went to bed. In the morning, when he woke, he found that Fortune had again visited him. The first wonder of the thing had now worn off; so he rose, dressed himself, and sat down leisurely to count the money over, before lodging his declaration at the *bureau de police*. While he was engaged in making up little *rouleaux* of gold, twenty in each *rouleau*, there came a sudden knocking at his door.

He had no friends in Ems. He started like a guilty man, and threw an overcoat hastily upon the table, so as to conceal the gold. Could it be that this summons had anything to do with the money? Was he suspected of something that———. The knock was repeated, this time more imperatively. He opened the door. It was the Baron von Hohendorf!

"How! The Baron von Hohendorf in Ems! I am rejoiced— this honour—I—pray be seated."

The poor young dragoon's heart beat so fast, and he trembled so with pleasure, hope, and astonishment, that he could scarcely speak.

The baron looked at him steadily, but sternly; thrust back the proffered chair; and took no notice of the extended hand.

"Yes, *Herr* Count," he said drily. "I arrived yesterday in this place. You did not expect to see me."

"Indeed, no. It is a pleasure—a—delight—a—"

He was so agitated that he forgot his visitor was standing, and sat down; but rose again directly.

"And yet I saw you, *Herr* Count, yesterday evening, as you came out of the Conversation-rooms."

"Me? Indeed, sir, I never visited the Conversation-rooms at all yesterday; but I am very sorry that I was not there, since I should have had the honour of meeting you."

"Pardon me, *Herr* Count, I saw you. It is useless to argue the point with me, for I stood close behind your chair for the greater part of an hour. Do you know why I am here this morning in your apartment?"

The young man blushed, faltered, turned pale. He knew but one reason that could have brought a visit from the baron. Had he relented? Could it be his generous design to make two lovers' hearts happy by granting that consent which he formerly refused? There were things more impossible. The baron was capable of such goodness! Something to this effect he stammered in broken sentences, his eyes fixed upon the ground, and his hands playing nervously with a pen.

The baron drew himself to his full height. If he had looked stern before, he looked furious now. For a few moments he could hardly speak for rage. At last his wrath broke forth.

"Impertinence such as this, *Herr* Count, I did not expect! I came here, sir, to give some words of advice to your father's son—to warn—to interpose, if possible, between you and your destruction. I did not come to be insulted!"

"Insulted, baron?" repeated the young man, somewhat haughtily. "I have said nothing to call for such a phrase at your lips, unless, indeed, my poverty insults you. The richest man in this land could do no more than love your daughter, and were she a queen, the homage of the poorest would not disgrace her."

"Permit me to ask you one question. What brings you to Ems?"

The young man hesitated, and the baron smiled ironically.

"I came, sir," he said at length, "in search of—I will confess it—in search of peace, of forgetfulness, of consolation."

His voice broke: he looked down, and remained silent.

The baron laughed aloud—a harsh mocking laugh that caused Albert to raise his head with a movement of sudden indignation.

"I have not deserved this treatment at your hands. Baron Hohendorf," he said, turning towards the window.

"A gambler deserves only the contempt of honourable men," replied the baron.

"A gambler!" repeated Albert. "Good heavens, sir! I have never touched a card in my life."

"What effrontery! You forget, then, that it is in my power to confront you with the proof of your vice; nay, at this instant to confound and convict you. What gold is this?"

And the old gentleman, whose eyes had already detected the glimmer of the coin beneath the coat, lifted the garment away upon the end of his walking-stick. The lover turned pale, and could not speak.

"*Der Teufel*! For a poor man you have, it seems, a well-filled travelling purse! Ah! you never play!"

"Never, sir."

"Indeed! Pray, then, if your gold be not the fruit of the gaming-table, whence comes it?"

"I know not. You will not believe me, I am aware; but I swear that I speak the truth. This gold comes here, I know not how. This is the fourth time I have found it upon my table. I know not why it is here, who brings it, or how it is brought. By my honour as a gentleman and a soldier—by all my hopes of happiness in this life or the next, I am utterly ignorant of everything about it!"

"This is too much !" cried the baron, furiously. "Do you take me for an idiot or a dotard? Good morning to you, sir, and I hope I may never see your face again!"

He slammed the door violently behind him, and went away down the stairs, leaving poor Von Steinberg utterly overwhelmed and broken-hearted.

"Cursed gold!" he exclaimed, dashing it upon the floor in his anger, "what brought thee here, and why dost thou torment me!"

Then the poor fellow thought of Emma, and of how his last chance was wrecked; and he was so miserable, that he threw himself upon his bed, and wept bitterly. All at once he remembered that the baron had a sister at Langenschwalbach; she, perhaps, would believe him, would intercede for him! He started up, resolved to go thither at once; hastily gathered together the scattered pieces of money; locked them up in the drawer with the rest; ran down to a neighbouring carriage-stand; hired a vehicle to convey him to the railway-station, and in less than half an hour was on his way.

In about three hours he arrived. He passed nearly the whole day in trying to discover the lady's address, and, when he had found it, was told that she had been for the last two months at Vienna. It was a foolish journey, with disappointment at the end of it! He came back quite late in the evening to Ems, and entered his own room, utterly broken down by anxiety and fatigue.

In the meantime the baron, crimson with rage, had returned to his hotel, and told all the circumstances to his daughter. She would not believe in the guilt of her lover.

"He a gambler!" she exclaimed. "It is impossible!"

"But I saw the gold upon his table!"

"He says he knows nothing of it, and he never told an untruth in his life. It will all be explained by-and-by."

"But I saw him playing at the tables!"

"It was some other who resembled him."

"Will you believe it, if you see him yourself?"

"I will, my father, and I will renounce him forever. But not till then."

"Then you shall be convinced this evening."

The evening came, and the rooms were more than usually crowded. There was a ball in the *salon de danse*; supper in the ante-room; gaming, as usual, in the third apartment. The Baron von Hohendorf was there with his daughter and some friends. They made their way to the tables, but he whom they sought was not there. Eager faces enough were there around the board—faces of old women, cunning and avaricious; faces of pale dissipated boys, scarce old enough, one would have thought, to care for any games save those of the school-ground; faces of hardened, cool, determined gamblers; faces of girls young and beautiful, and of men old and feeble. Strange table, around which youth and beauty, age, deformity, and vice, meet on equal ground!

Suddenly there was a movement at the farther end of the room; a whisper went round; the spectators made way, and the players drew aside for one who now approached and took his place amongst them. This deference is shown only to those who play high and play frequently. Who is this noted gambler? Albert von Steinberg.

A cry of agony breaks from the pale lips of a young girl at the other end of the room. Alas! it is too surely he! He neither hears nor heeds anything around him. He does not even look towards her. He seats himself very quietly, as a matter of course; takes some *rouleaux* of gold and a packet of notes from his pocket; stakes a large sum; and begins to play with all the cool audacity of one whose faith in his own luck is unshakeable, and who is perfect master of the game.

Besides this, he carried his self-command to that point which is only attained by years of practice. It was splendid to see him so impassive. His features were fixed and inexpressive as those of a statue; the steady earnestness of his gaze had something terrible in it; his very movements were scarcely those of a man liable to human frailties and human emotions; and the right hand with which he staked and swept up the gold, was stiff and passionless as that of the commandant in *Don Giovanni*.

The baron could contain his indignation no longer. Leaving

his daughter with her friends, he made his way round the tables, and approached the young man's chair. He extended his hand to seize the player's arm, when his own was forcibly caught and held back. He turned, and saw a celebrated Prussian physician standing beside him.

"Stop, for heaven's sake!" he exclaimed. "Do not speak to him. You know not the injury you might do him!"

"That is exactly my object. I'll spoil his game for him, the unprincipled hypocrite!"

"You will kill him,"

"Absurd!"

"I am perfectly serious. Look at him. He sleeps! A sudden shock might be his death. You cannot see this, but I can. I have studied this thing narrowly, and I never beheld a more remarkable case of somnambulism."

The physician continued for some time conversing with the baron in an under tone. Presently the bank gave the signal; the players rose; the tables closed for that evening; and the Count von Steinberg, gathering up his enormous winnings, pushed back his chair and left the rooms, passing close before the baron without seeing him.

They followed him down the street to his own door. He entered by means of his latchkey, and closed it behind him without a sound. There was no light in his window—no one stirring in the house. None but those two had seen him enter.

The next morning, when he awoke, he found a larger pile of gold than ever on his table. He counted it with a shudder, and told over 44,000 florins.

Again there came a knock at his chamber-door. This time he did not even attempt to conceal the money; and when the baron and physician entered, he was too unhappy even to feel surprise at the sight of a stranger.

"You have again come to tell me that I am a gambler!" he exclaimed, despairingly, as he pointed to the gold, and leaned his head listlessly upon his hands.

"I say it, Count, because I saw it," replied the baron; "but at the same time I come to entreat your pardon for what passed at our last interview. You have gambled; but you are no gambler."

"Yes," interrupted the physician; "for somnambulists often perform the very actions which they would most abhor, if in a waking condition. But you are not a confirmed somnambulist. Yours is a mere functional derangement, and I can easily cure you. But, perhaps," he added, smiling, "you do not wish to lose so profitable a malady. You may become a *millionaire.*"

"Nay, doctor!" cried the count, "I place myself in your hands. Cure me, I entreat you I"

"Well, well, there is time enough for that," said the baron. "First of all, let us shake hands, and be friends."

"I have so great a horror of play," replied the involuntary gambler, "that I shall instantly restore this money to the bank. See, here are, altogether, 130,000 florins!"

"Take my advice, Albert," said the baron, "and do no such thing. Suppose that in your sleep you had lost 130,000 florins, do you think the bank would have restored it to you? No, no; entertain no such scruples. Your father lost more than thrice that sum at those very tables,—it is but a restitution in part. Keep your florins, and return with me to my hotel, where Emma is waiting to receive you. You have 130,000 there. I will excuse the other 70,000 upon which I formerly insisted, and you can make it up in love. Are you content; or must you restore the money to the bank?"

History has not recorded the lover's reply; at all events, he quitted Ems that same day in company with the Baron von Hohendorf and his pretty daughter. The prescriptions of the learned physician have, it is said, already affected a cure, and the *Frankfort Journal* announces the approaching marriage of Fraulein von Hohendorf with Albert, Count Steinberg.

My Brother's Ghost Story

The events which I am about to relate happened to my only brother. I have heard him tell the story many and many a time, never varying in the minutest particular. It happened about thirty years ago, more or less, while he was wandering, sketch-book in hand, among the High Alps, picking up subjects for an illustrated work on Switzerland. Having entered the Oberland by the Brunig Pass, and filled his portfolio with what he used to call "bits" from the neighbourhood of Meyringen, he went over the great Scheideck to Grindlewald, where he arrived one dusky September evening, about three quarters of an hour after sunset.

There had been a fair that day and the place was crowded. In the best inn there was not an inch of space to spare—there were only two inns at Grindlewald thirty years ago—so my brother went to the one other, at the end of the covered bridge next the church, and there, with some difficulty, obtained the promise of a pile of rugs and a mattress, in a room which was already occupied by three other travellers.

The "Adler" was a primitive hostelry, half farm, half inn, with great rambling galleries outside, and a huge general room, like a barn, At the upper end of this room stood long Stores, like metal counters, laden with steaming pans, and glowing underneath like furnaces. At the lower end, smoking, supping, and chatting, were congregated some thirty or forty guests, chiefly mountaineers, *char*-drivers, and guides.

Among these my brother took his seat; and was served, like

the rest, with a bowl of soup, a platter of beef, a flagon of country wine, and a loaf made of Indian corn. Presently, a huge St. Bernard dog came and laid his nose upon my brother's arm. In the meantime he fell into conversation with two Italian youths, bronzed and dark-eyed, near whom he happened to be seated.

They were Florentines. Their names, they told him, were Stefano and Battisto. They had been travelling for some months on commission, selling cameos, mosaics, sulphur casts, and the like pretty Italian trifles, and were now on their way to Interlaken and Geneva. Weary of the cold North, they longed, like children, for the moment which should take them back to their own blue hills and grey-green olives; to their Workshop on the Ponte Vecchio, and their home down by the Arno.

It was quite a relief to my brother, on going up to bed, to find that these youths were to be two of his fellow-lodgers. The third was already there, and sound asleep, with his face to the wall. They scarcely looked at this third. They were all tired, and all anxious to rise at daybreak, having agreed to walk together over the Wengern Alp as far as Lauterbrunnen. So, my brother and the two youths exchanged a brief goodnight, and, before many minutes, were all as far away in the land of dreams as their unknown companion.

My brother slept profoundly—so profoundly that, being roused in the morning by a glamour of merry voices, he sat up dreamily in his rugs, and wondered where he was.

"Good day, *signor*," cried Battisto. "Here is a fellow-traveller going the same way as ourselves."

"Christien Baumann, native of Kandersteg, musical-box maker by trade, Stands five feet eleven in his shoes, and is at monsieur's Service to command," said the sleeper of the night before.

He was as fine a young fellow as one would wish to see. Light, and strong, and well proportioned, with curling brown hair, and bright, honest eyes that seemed to dance at every Word he uttered.

"Good morning," said my brother. "You were asleep last

174

night when we came up."

"Asleep! I should think so, after being all day in the fair, and Walking from Meyringen the evening before. What a capital fair it was!"

"Capital, indeed," said Battisto. "We sold cameos and mosaics yesterday for nearly fifty *francs.*"

"Oh, you sell cameos and mosaics, you two! Show me your cameos, and I will show you my musical-boxes. I have such pretty ones, with coloured views of Geneva and Chillon on the lids, playing two, four, six, and even eight tunes. Bah! I will give you a concert!"

And with this he unstrapped his pack, displayed his little boxes on the table, and wound them up, one after the other, to the delight of the Italians.

"I helped to make them myself, everyone," said he, proudly. "Is it not pretty music? I sometimes set one of them when I go to bed at night, and fall asleep listening to it. I am sure, then, to have pleasant dreams! But let us see your cameos. Perhaps I may buy one for Marie if they are not too dear. Marie is my sweetheart, and we are to be married next week."

"Next week!" exclaimed Stefano. "That is very soon. Battisto has a sweetheart also, up at Impruneta; but they will have to wait a long time before they can buy the ring."

Battisto blushed like a girl.

"Hush, brother!" said he. "Show the cameos to Christien, and give your tongue a holiday."

But Christien was not so to be put off.

"What is her name?" said he. "Tush! Battisto, you must tell me her name! Is she pretty? Is she dark or fair ? Do you often see her when you are at home? Is she very fond of you? Is she as fond of you as Marie is of me?"

"Nay, how should I know that?" asked the soberer Battisto. "She loves me, and I love her—that is all."

"And her name?"

"Margherita."

"A charming name! And she is herself as pretty as her name,

I'll engage. Did you say she was fair?"

"I said nothing about it one way or the other," said Battisto, unlocking a green box clamped with iron, and taking out tray after tray of his pretty wares. "There! Those pictures all inlaid in little bits are Roman mosaics—these flowers on a black ground are Florentine. The ground is of hard dark stone, and the flowers are made of thin slices of Jasper, onyx, cornelian, and so forth. Those forget-me-notes, for instance, are bits of turquoise, and that poppy is cut from a piece of coral."

"I like the Roman ones best," said Christien. "What place is that with all the arches?"

"This is the Coliseum, and the one next to it is St. Peter's. But we Florentines care little for the Roman work. It is not half so fine, or so valuable as ours. The Romans make their mosaics of composition."

"Composition or no, I like the little landscapes best," said Christien. "There is a lovely one, with a pointed building, and a tree, and mountains at the back. How I should like that one for Marie!"

"You may have it for eight *francs*," replied Battisto; "we sold two of them yesterday for ten each. It represents the tomb of Caius Cestius, near Rome."

"A tomb echoed Christien, considerably dismayed. "*Diable!* That would be a dismal present to one's bride."

"She would never guess that it was a tomb, if you did not tell her," suggested Stefano.

Christien shook his head.

"That would be next door to deceiving her," Said he.

"Nay," interposed my brother, "the owner of that tomb has been dead these eighteen or nineteen hundred years. One almost forgets that he was ever buried in it."

"Eighteen or nineteen hundred years! Then he was a heathen?"

"Undoubtedly, if by that you mean that he lived before Christ."

Christien's face lighted up immediately.

"Oh! that settles the question," said he, pulling out his little canvas purse, and paying his money down at once. "A heathen's tomb is as good as no tomb at all. I'll have it made into a brooch for her, at Interlaken. Tell me, Battisto, what shall you take home to Italy for your Margherita?"

Battisto laughed, and chinked his eight *francs*.

"That depends on trade," said he; "if we make good profits between this and Christmas, I may take her a Swiss muslin from Berne; but we have already been away seven months, and we have hardly made a hundred *francs* over and above our expenses."

And with this, the talk turned upon general matters, the Florentines locked away their treasures, Christien restrapped his pack, and my brother and all went down together, and breakfasted in the open air outside the inn.

It was a magnificent morning, cloudless and sunny, with a cool breeze that rustled in the vine upon the porch, and flecked the table with shifting shadows of green leaves. All around and about them stood the great mountains, with their blue-white glaciers bristling down to the verge of the pastures, and the pine-woods creeping darkly up their sides. To the left, the Wetterhorn; to the right, the Eigher; straight before them, dazzling and imperishable, like peaks of frosted silver the Vischer-hörner clustered on the verge of an icy precipice.

Breakfast over, they bade farewell to their hostess, and, mountain-staff in band, took the path to the Wengern Alp. Half in light, half in shadow, lay the quiet Valley, dotted over with farms, and traversed by a torrent that rushed, milk-white, from its prison in the glacier. The three lads walked briskly in advance, their voices chiming together every now and then in chorus of laughter. Somehow, my brother felt sad. He lingered behind, and, plucking a little red flower from the bank, watched it hurry away with the torrent, like a life on the stream of time. Why was his heart so heavy, and why were their hearts so light?

As the day went on, my brother's melancholy, and the mirth of the young men, seemed to increase. Full of youth and hope, they talked of the joyous future, and built up pleasant Castles in the air. Battisto, grown more communicative, admitted that to marry Margherita, and become a master mosaicist, would fulfil the dearest wish of his life. Stefano, not being in love, preferred to travel.

Christien, who seemed to be the most prosperous, declared that it was his darling ambition to rent a farm in his native Kander Valley, and lead the patriarchal life of his fathers. As for the musical-box trade, he said, one must live in Geneva to make it answer; but, for his part, he loved the pine-forests and the snow-peaks better than all the towns in Europe.

Marie, too, had been born among the mountains, and it would break her heart if she thought she were to live in Geneva all her life, and never see the Kander Thai again. Chatting thus, the morning wore on to noon, and the party rested awhile in the shade of a clump of gigantic firs festooned with trailing banners of grey-green moss.

Here they ate their luncheon, to the silvery music of one of Christien's little boxes, and by-and-by heard the sullen echo of an avalanche far away on the Shoulder of the Jungfrau.

Then they went on again in the burning afternoon, to heights where the Alp-rose falls from the sterile steep, and the brown lichen grows more and more scantily among the stone. Here, only the bleached and barren skeletons of a forest of dead pines varied the desolate monotony; and high on the summit of the pass stood a little solitary inn, between them and the sky.

At this inn they rested again, and drank to the health of Christien and his bride, in a jug of country wine. He was in uncontrollable spirits, and shook hands with all of them over and over again.

"By nightfall tomorrow," said he, "I shall hold her once more in my arms ! It is now nearly two years since I came home to see her, at the end of my apprenticeship. Now I am foreman, with a salary of thirty *francs* a week, and well able to marry."

"Thirty *francs* a week !" echoed Battisto. "*Corpo di Bacco*! that is a little fortune."

Christien's face beamed.

"Yes," said he, "we shall be very happy; and, by and-by—who knows?—we may end our days in the Kander Thal, and bring up our children to succeed us. Ah! if Marie know that I should be there tomorrow night, how delighted she would be!"

"How so?" Said my brother. "Does she not expect you?"

"Not a bit of it. She has no idea that I can be there till the day after tomorrow—nor could I, if I took the road all round by Unterseen and Frütigen. I mean to sleep tonight at Lauterbrunnen, and tomorrow morning shall strike across the Tschlingel glacier to Kandersteg. If I rise a little before daybreak, I shall be at home by sunset."

At this moment the path took a sudden turn, and began to descend in sight of an immense perspective of very distant Valleys. Christien flung his cap into the air, and uttered a great shout.

"Look!" said he, stretching out his arms; as if to embrace the dear familiar scene; "oh, look! There are the hills and woods of Interlaken, and here, below the precipices on which we stand, lies Lauterbrunnen! God be praised, who has made our native land so beautiful!"

The Italians smiled at each other, thinking their own Arno valley far more fair; but my brother's heart warmed to the boy, and echoed his thanksgiving in that spirit which accepts all beauty as a birthright and an inheritance. And now their course lay across an immense plateau, all rich with cornfields and meadows, and studded with substantial homesteads built of old brown wood, with huge sheltering eaves, and strings of Indian corn hanging like golden ingots along the carven balconies.

Blue whortleberries grew beside the footway, and now and then they came upon a wild gentian or a star-shaped Immortelle. Then the path became a mere zigzag on the face of the precipice, and in less than half an hour they reached the lowest level of the Valley. The glowing afternoon had not yet faded from the uppermost pines, when they were all dining together in the parlour of a little inn looking to the Jungfrau. In the evening my brother wrote letters, while the three lads strolled about the village. At nine o'clock they bade each other goodnight, and went to their several rooms.

Weary as he was, my brother found it impossible to sleep. The same unaccountable melancholy still possessed him, and when at last he dropped into an uneasy slumber, it was but to Start over and over and over again from frightful dreams, faint with a nameless terror. Towards morning he fell into a profound sleep, and never woke until the day was fast advancing towards noon. He then found, to his regret, that Christien had long since gone. He had risen before daybreak, breakfasted by candlelight, and started off in the grey dawn—"as merry," said the host, "as a fiddler at a fair."

Stefano and Battisto were still waiting to see my brother; being charged by Christien with a friendly farewell message to him, and an invitation to the wedding. They, too, were asked, and meant to go; so my brother agreed to meet them at Interlaken on the following Tuesday, whence they might walk to Kandersteg by easy stages, reaching their destination on the Thursday morning, in time to go to church with the bridal party. My brother then bought some of the little Florentine cameos, wished the two boys every good fortune, and watched them down the road till he could see them no longer.

Left now to himself, he wandered out with his sketch-book, and spent the day in the Upper Valley. At sunset, he dined alone in his Chamber, by the light of a single lamp. This meal despatched, he drew nearer to the fire, took out a pocket edition of *Goethe's Essays on Art,* and promised himself some hours of pleasant reading.

Ah, how well I know that very book, in its faded cover, and how often I have heard him describe that lonely evening!

The night had by this time set in cold and wet. The damp logs spluttered on the hearth, and a wailing wind swept down the Valley, bearing the rain in sudden gusts against the panes. My brother soon found that to read was impossible. His attention wandered incessantly. He read the same sentence over and over again, unconscious of its meaning, and fell into long trains of thought leading far into the dim past.

Thus the hours went by, and at eleven o'clock he heard the doors closing below, and the household retiring to rest. He determined to yield no longer to this dreaming apathy.

He threw on fresh logs, trimmed the lamp, and took several turns about the room. Then he opened the casement, and suffered the rain to beat against his face, and the wind to ruffle his hair, as it ruffled the acacia leaves in the garden below. Some minutes passed thus, and when, at length, he closed the window and came back into the room, his face and hair and all the front of his shirt were thoroughly saturated. To unstrap his knapsack and take out a dry shirt was, of course, his first impulse— to drop the garment, listen eagerly, and start to his feet, breathless and bewildered, was the next.

For, borne fitfully upon the outer breeze—now sweeping past the window, now dying in the distance—he heard a well-remembered strain of melody, subtle and silvery as the "sweet airs" of Prospero's isle, and proceeding unmistakably from the musical-box which had, the day before, accompanied the luncheon under the fir-trees of the Wengern Alp!

Had Christien come back, and was it thus that he announced his return? If so, where was he? Under the window? Outside in the corridor? Sheltering in the porch, and waiting for admittance? My brother threw open the casement again, and called him by his name.

"Christien! Is that you?"

All without was intensely silent. He could hear the last gust of wind and rain moaning farther and farther away upon its wild course down the Valley, and the pine trees shivering, like living things.

"Christien!" he said again, and his own voice seemed to echo strangely on his ear. "Speak! Is it you?"

Still no one answered. He leaned out into the dark night; but could see nothing—not even the outline of the porch below. He began to think that his imagination had deceived him, when suddenly the strain burst forth again;—this time, apparently in his own chamber.

As he turned, expecting to find Christien at his elbow, the sounds broke off abruptly, and a sensation of intensest cold seized him in every limb—not the mere chill of nervous terror; not the mere physical result of exposure to wind and rain; but a deadly freezing of every vein, a paralysis of every nerve, an appalling consciousness that in a few moments more the lungs must cease to play, and the heart to beat! Powerless to speak or stir, he closed his eyes, and believed that he was dying,

This strange faintness lasted but a few seconds. Gradually the vital warmth returned, and, with it, strength to close the window, and stagger to a chair. As he did so, he found the breast of his shirt all stiff and frozen, and the rain clinging in solid icicles upon his hair.

He looked at his watch. It had stopped at twenty minutes before twelve. He took his thermometer from the chimney-piece, and found the mercury at seventy. Heavenly powers! How were these things possible in a temperature of seventy degrees, and with a large fire blazing on the hearth?

He poured out half a tumbler of cognac, and drank it at a draught. Going to bed was out of the question. He felt that he dared not sleep—that he scarcely dared to think. All he could do was to change his linen, pile on more logs, wrap himself in his blankets, and sit all night in an easy-chair before the fire.

My brother had not long sat thus, however, before the warmth, and probably the nervous reaction, drew him off to sleep. In the morning he found himself lying on the bed, without being able to remember in the least how or when he reached it.

It was again a glorious day. The rain and wind were gone, and the Silberhorn at the end of the Valley lifted its head into an unclouded sky. Looking out upon the sunshine, he almost doubted the events of the night, and, but for the evidence of his watch, which still pointed to twenty minutes before twelve, would have been disposed to treat the whole matter as a dream. As it was, he attributed more than half his terrors to the prompting of an over-active and over-wearied brain. For all this, he still felt depressed and uneasy, and so very unwilling to pass another night at Lauterbrunnen that he made up his mind to proceed that morning to Interlaken. While he was yet loitering over his breakfast, and considering whether he should walk the seven miles of road, or hire a vehicle, a *char* came rapidly to the inn door, and a young man jumped out.

"Why, Battisto!" exclaimed my brother in astonishment, as he came into the room, "what brings you here today? Where is Stefano?"

"I have left him at Interlaken, *signor*," replied the Italian.

Something there was in his voice, something in his face, both strange and startling.

"What is the matter?" asked my brother, breathlessly. "He is not ill? No accident has happened?"

Battisto shook his head, glanced furtively up and down the passage, and closed the door.

"Stefano is well, *signor*; but—but a circumstance has occurred—a circumstance so strange! . . . .*Signor*, do you believe in spirits?"

"In spirits, Battisto?"

"Ay, *signor*; for if ever the spirit of any man, dead or living, appealed to human ears, the spirit of Christien came to me last night at twenty minutes before twelve o'clock."

"At twenty minutes before twelve o'clock!" repeated my brother.

"I was in bed, *signor*, and Stefano was sleeping in the same room. I had gone up quite warm, and had fallen asleep, full of pleasant thoughts. By-and-by, although I had plenty of bed-clothes, and a rug over me as well, I woke, frozen with cold and scarcely able to breathe. I tried to call to Stefano; but I had no power to utter the slightest sound. I thought my last moment was come. All at once, I heard a sound under the window—a sound which I knew to be Christien's musical box; and it played as it played when we lunched under the fir-trees, except that it was more wild, and strange, and melancholy,—solemn to hear—

183

awful to hear!

"Then, *signor*, it grew fainter and fainter—and then it seemed to float past upon the wind, and die away. When it had ceased, my frozen blood grew warm again, and I cried out to Stefano. When I told him what had happened, he declared I had been only dreaming. I made him strike a light, that I might look at my watch. It pointed to twenty minutes before twelve, and had stopped there; and, stranger still, Stefano's watch had done the very same. Now tell me, *signor*, do you believe that there is any meaning in this, or do you think, as Stefano persists in thinking, that it was all a dream?"

"What is your own conclusion, Battisto?"

"My conclusion, *signor*, is that some harm has happened to poor Christien on the glacier, and that his spirit came to me last night."

"Battisto, he shall have help if living, or rescue for his poor corpse if dead; for I, too, believe that all is not well."

And with this, my brother told him briefly what had occurred to himself in the night; despatched messengers for the three best guides in Lauterbrunnen; and prepared ropes, ice-hatchets, Alpenstocks, and all such matters necessary for a glacier expedition. Hasten as he would, however, it was nearly mid-day before the party started.

Arriving in about half an hour at a place called Stechelberg, they left the *char*, in which they had travelled so far, at a *châlet*, and ascended a steep path in full view of the Breithorn glacier, which rose up to the left like a battlemented wall of solid ice. The way now lay for some time among pastures and pine-forests. Then they came to a little colony of *châlets*, called Steinberg, where they filled their water-bottles, got their ropes in readiness, and prepared for the Tschlingel glacier. A few minutes more, and they were on the ice.

At this point the guides called a halt, and consulted together. One was for striking across the lower glacier towards the left, and reaching the upper glacier by the rocks which bound it on the south. The other two preferred the north, or right side; and this my brother finally took. The sun was now pouring down with almost tropical intensity, and the surface of the ice, which was broken into long treacherous fissures, smooth as glass and blue as the summer sky, was both difficult and dangerous.

Silently and cautiously they went, tied together at intervals of about three yards each, with two guides in front, and the third bringing up the rear. Turning presently to the right, they found themselves at the foot of a steep rock, some forty feet in height, up which they must climb to reach the Upper glacier.

The only way in which Battisto or my brother could hope to do this, was by the help of a rope steadied from below and above. Two of the guides accordingly clambered up the face of the crag by notches in the surface, and one remained below. The rope was then let down, and my brother prepared to go first. As he planted his foot in the first notch, a smothered cry from Battisto arrested him. "*Santa Maria! Signor*, look yonder!" My brother looked, and there (he ever afterwards declared), as surely as there is a heaven above us all, he saw Christien Baumann

Standing in the full sunlight, not a hundred yards distant ! Almost in the same moment that my brother recognized him, he was gone. He neither faded, nor sank down, nor moved away; but was simply gone, as if he had never been. Pale as death, Battisto fell upon his knees, and covered his face with his hands. My brother, awe-stricken and speechless, leaned against the rock, and felt that the object of his journey was but too fatally accomplished. As for the guides, they could not conceive what had happened.

"Did you see nothing?" asked my brother and Battisto, both together. But the men had seen nothing, and the one who had remained below, said:—

"What should I see, but the ice and the sunlight?"

To this my brother made no other reply than by announcing his intention to have a certain crevasse, from which he had not once removed his eyes since he saw the figure Standing on the brink, thoroughly explored before he went a step farther; whereupon the two men came down from the top of the crag, resumed the ropes, and followed him, incredulously. At the narrow end of the fissure, he paused, and drove his Alpenstock firmly into the ice. It was an unusually long crevasse—at first a mere crack, but widening gradually as it went, and reaching down to unknown depths of dark deep blue, fringed with long pendent icicles, like diamond stalactites. Before they had followed the course of this crevasse for more than ten minutes, the youngest of the guides uttered a hasty exclamation.

"I see something!" cried he. "Something dark, wedged in the teeth of the crevasse, a great way down!"

They all saw it:—a mere indistinguishable mass, almost closed over by the ice-walls at their feet. My brother offered a hundred *francs* to the man who would go down and bring it up. They all hesitated.

"We don't know what it is," said one.

"Perhaps it is only a dead chamois," suggested another.

Their apathy enraged him.

"It is no chamois," he said, angrily, "It is the body of Christien Baumann, native of Kandersteg. And, by Heaven, if you are all too cowardly to make the attempt, I will go down myself!"

The youngest guide threw off his hat and coat, tied a rope about his waist, and took a hatchet in his hand.

"I will go, *monsieur*," said he; and without another word, suffered himself to be lowered in.

My brother turned away. A sickening anxiety came upon him, and presently he heard the dull echo of the hatchet far down in the ice. Then there was a call for another rope, and then—the men all drew aside in silence, and my brother saw the youngest guide Standing once more beside the chasm, flushed and trembling, with the body of Christien lying at his feet.

Poor Christien! They made a rough bier with their ropes and Alpenstocks, and carried him, with great difficulty, back to Steinberg. There, they got additional help as far as Stechelberg, where they laid him in the *char*, and so brought him on to Lauterbrunnen. The next day, my brother made it his sad business to precede the body to Kandersteg, and prepare his friends for its arrival. To this day, though all these things happened thirty years ago, he cannot bear to recall Marie's despair, or all the mourning that he innocently brought upon that peaceful valley. Poor Marie has been dead this many a year; and when my brother last passed through the Kander Thal on his way to the Ghemmi, he saw her grave, beside the grave of Christien Baumann, in the village burial-ground.

This is my brother's Ghost Story.

Number Three

Aka: How the Third Floor Knew the Potteries

I am a plain man, Major, and you may not dislike to hear a plain statement of facts from me. Some of those facts lie beyond my understanding. I do not pretend to explain them. I only know that they happened as I relate them, and that I pledge myself for the truth of every word of them.

I began life roughly enough, down among the Potteries. I was an orphan; and my earliest recollections are of a great porcelain manufactory in the country of the Potteries, where I helped about the yard, picked up what halfpence fell in my way, and slept in a harness-loft over the stable. Those were hard times; but things bettered themselves as I grew older and stronger, especially after George Barnard had come to be foreman of the yard.

George Barnard was a Wesleyan—we were mostly dissenters in the Potteries—sober, clear-headed, somewhat sulky and silent, but a good fellow every inch of him, and my best friend at the time when I most needed a good friend. He took me out of the yard, and set me to the furnace-work. He entered me on the books at a fixed rate of wages. He helped me to pay for a little cheap schooling four nights a week; and he led me to go with him on Sundays to the chapel down by the riverside, where I first saw Leah Payne.

She was his sweetheart, and so pretty that I used to forget the preacher and everybody else, when I looked at her. When she joined in the singing, I heard no voice but hers. If she asked me for the hymn-book, I used to blush and tremble. I believe I worshipped her, in my stupid ignorant way; and I think I worshipped Barnard almost as blindly, though after a different fashion. I felt I owed him everything. I knew that he had saved me, body and mind; and I looked up to him as a savage might look up to a missionary.

Leah was the daughter of a plumber, who lived close by the chapel. She was twenty, and George about seven or eight-and-thirty. Some captious folks said there was too much difference in their ages; but she was so serious-minded, and they loved each other so earnestly and quietly, that, if nothing had come between them during their courtship, I don't believe the question of disparity would ever have troubled the happiness of their married lives.

Something did come, however; and that something was a Frenchman, called Louis Laroche. He was a painter on porcelain, from the famous works at Sèvres; and our master, it was said, had engaged him for three years certain, at such wages as none of our own people, however skilful, could hope to command. It was about the beginning or middle of September when he first came among us. He looked very young; was small, dark, and well made; had little white soft hands, and a silky moustache; and spoke English nearly as well as I do.

None of us liked him; but that was only natural, seeing how he was put over the head of every Englishman in the place. Besides, though he was always smiling and civil, we couldn't help seeing that he thought himself ever so much better than the rest of us; and that was not pleasant. Neither was it pleasant to see him strolling about the town, dressed just like a gentleman, when working hours over; smoking good cigars, when we were forced to be content with a pipe of common tobacco; hiring a horse on Sunday afternoons, when we were trudging a-foot; and taking his pleasure as if the world was made for him to enjoy, and us to work in.

"Ben, boy," said George, "there's something wrong about that Frenchman."

It was on a Saturday afternoon, and we were sitting on a pile of empty seggars against the door of my furnace-room, waiting till the men should all have cleared out of the yard. Seggars are deep earthen boxes in which the pottery is put, while being fired in the kiln.

I looked up, inquiringly.

"About the Count?" said I, for that was the nickname by which he went in the pottery.

George nodded, and paused for a moment with his chin resting on his palms.

"He has an evil eye," said he; "and a false smile. Something wrong about him."

I drew nearer, and listened to George as if he had been an oracle.

"Besides," added he, in his slow quiet way, with his eyes fixed straight before him as if he was thinking aloud, "there's a young look about him that isn't natural. Take him just at sight, and you'd think he was almost a boy; but look close at him—see the little fine wrinkles under his eyes, and the hard lines about his mouth, and then tell me his age, if you can! Why, Ben boy, he's as old as I am, pretty near; ay, and as strong, too. You stare; but I tell you that, slight as he looks, he could fling you over his shoulder as if you were a feather. And as for his hands, little and white as they are, there are muscles of iron inside them, take my word for it."

"But, George, how can you know?"

"Because I have a warning against him," replied George, very gravely. "Because, whenever he is by, I feel as if my eyes saw clearer, and my ears heard keener, than at other times. Maybe it's presumption, but I sometimes feel as if I had a call to guard myself and others against him. Look at the children, Ben, how they shrink away from him; and see there, now! Ask Captain what he thinks of him! Ben, that dog likes him no better than I do."

I looked, and saw Captain crouching by his kennel with his ears laid back, growling audibly, as the Frenchman came slowly down the steps leading from his own workshop at the upper end of the yard. On the last step he paused; lighted a cigar; glanced round, as if to see whether anyone was by; and then walked straight over to within a couple of yards of the kennel. Captain gave a short angry snarl, and laid his muzzle close down upon his paws, ready for a spring.

The Frenchman folded his arms deliberately, fixed his eyes on the dog, and stood calmly smoking. He knew exactly how far he dared go, and kept just that one foot out of harm's way. All at once he stooped, puffed a mouthful of smoke in the dog's eyes, burst into a mocking laugh, turned lightly on his heel, and walked away; leaving Captain straining at his chain, and barking after him like a mad creature.

Days went by, and I, at work in my own department, saw no more of the Count. Sunday came—the third, I think, after I had talked with George in the yard. Going with George to chapel, as usual, in the morning, I noticed that there was something strange and anxious in his face, and that he scarcely opened his lips to me on the way. Still I said nothing. It was not my place to question him; and I remember thinking to myself that the cloud would all clear off as soon as he found himself by Leah's side, holding the same book, and joining in the same hymn.

It did not, however, for no Leah was there. I looked every moment to the door, expecting to see her sweet face coming in; but George never lifted his eyes from his book, or seemed to notice that her place was empty. Thus the whole service went by, and my thoughts wandered continually from the words of the preacher. As soon as the last blessing was spoken, and we were fairly across the threshold, I turned to George, and asked if Leah was ill?

"No," said he, gloomily. "She's not ill."

"Then why wasn't she ——?"

"I'll tell you why," he interrupted, impatiently. "Because you've seen her here for the last time. She's never coming to chapel again."

"Never coming to the chapel again?" I faltered, laying my hand on his sleeve in the earnestness of my surprise. "Why, George, what is the matter?"

But he shook my hand off, and stamped with his iron heel till the pavement rang again.

"Don't ask me," said he, roughly. "Let me alone. You'll know soon enough."

And with this he turned off down a by-lane leading towards the hills, and left me without another word.

I had had plenty of hard treatment in my time; but never, until that moment, an angry look or syllable from George. I did not know how to bear it. That day my dinner seemed as if it would choke me; and in the afternoon I went out and wandered restlessly about the fields till the hour for evening prayers came round. I then returned to the chapel, and sat down on a tomb outside, waiting for George. I saw the congregation go in by twos and threes; I heard the first psalm-tune echo solemnly through the evening stillness; but no George came. Then the service began, and I knew that, punctual as his habits were, it was of no use to expect him any longer. Where could he be? What could have happened? Why should Leah Payne never come to chapel again? Had she gone over to some other sect, and was that why George seemed so unhappy?

Sitting there in the little dreary churchyard with the darkness fast gathering around me, I asked myself these questions over and over again, till my brain ached; for I was not much used to thinking about anything in those times. At last, I could bear to sit quiet no longer. The sudden thought struck me that I would go to Leah, and learn what the matter was, from her own lips. I sprang to my feet, and set off at once towards her home.

It was quite dark, and a light rain was beginning to fall. I found the garden-gate open, and a quick hope flashed across me that George might be there. I drew back for a moment, hesitating whether to knock or ring, when a sound of voices in the passage, and the sudden gleaming of a bright line of light under the door, warned me that someone was coming out. Taken by surprise, and quite unprepared for the moment with anything to say, I shrank back behind the porch, and waited until those within should have passed out. The door opened, and the light streamed suddenly upon the roses and the wet gravel.

"It rains," said Leah, bending forward and shading the candle with her hand.

"And is as cold as Siberia," added another voice, which was not George's, and yet sounded strangely familiar. "Ugh! what a climate for such a flower as my darling to bloom in!"

"Is it so much finer in France?" asked Leah, softly.

"As much finer as blue skies and sunshine can make it. Why, my angel, even your bright eyes will be ten times brighter, and your rosy cheeks ten times rosier, when they are transplanted to Paris. Ah! I can give you no idea of the wonders of Paris— the broad streets planted with trees, the palaces, the shops, the gardens!—it is a city of enchantment."

"It must be, indeed!" said Leah. "And you will really take me to see all those beautiful shops?"

"Every Sunday, my darling—Bah! don't look so shocked. The shops in Paris are always open on Sunday, and everybody makes holiday. You will soon get over these prejudices."

"I fear it is very wrong to take so much pleasure in the things of this world," sighed Leah.

The Frenchman laughed, and answered her with a kiss.

"Good night, my sweet little saint!" and he ran lightly down the path, and disappeared in the darkness. Leah sighed again, lingered a moment, and then closed the door.

Stupefied and bewildered, I stood for some seconds like a stone statue, unable to move; scarcely able to think. At length, I roused myself, as it were mechanically, and went towards the gate. At that instant a heavy hand was laid upon my shoulder, and a hoarse voice close beside my ear, said:

"Who are you? What are you doing here?"

It was George. I knew him at once, in spite of the darkness, and stammered his name. He took his hand quickly from my shoulder.

"How long have you been here?" said he, fiercely. "What right have you to lurk about, like a spy in the dark? God help me, Ben—I'm half mad. I don't mean to be harsh to you."

"I'm sure you don't," I cried, earnestly.

"It's that cursed Frenchman," he went on, in a voice that sounded like the groan of one in pain. "He's a villain. I know he's a villain; and I've had a warning against him ever since the first moment he came among us. He'll make her miserable, and break her heart some day—my pretty Leah—and I loved her so! But I'll be revenged—as sure as there's a sun in heaven, I'll be revenged!"

His vehemence terrified me. I tried to persuade him to go home; but he would not listen to me.

"No, no," he said. "Go home yourself, boy, and let me be. My blood is on fire: this rain is good for me, and I am better alone."

"If I could only do something to help you ——"

"You can't," interrupted he. "Nobody can help me. I'm a ruined man, and I don't care what becomes of me. The Lord forgive me! my heart is full of wickedness, and my thoughts are the promptings of Satan. There go—for Heaven's sake, go. I don't know what I say, or what I do!"

I went, for I did not dare refuse any longer; but I lingered a while at the corner of the street, and watched him pacing to and fro, to and fro in the driving rain. At length I turned reluctantly away, and went home.

I lay awake that night for hours, thinking over the events of the day, and hating the Frenchman from my very soul. I could not hate Leah. I had worshipped her too long and too faithfully for that; but I looked upon her as a creature given over to de-struction. I fell asleep towards morning, and woke again short-ly after daybreak. When I reached the pottery, I found George there before me, looking very pale, but quite himself, and setting the men to their work the same as usual. I said nothing about what had happened the day before.

Something in his face silenced me; but seeing him so steady and composed, I took heart, and began to hope he had fought through the worst of his trouble. By-and-by the Frenchman came through the yard, gay and off-hand, with his cigar in his mouth, and his hands in his pockets. George turned sharply away into one of the workshops, and shut the door. I drew a deep breath of relief. My dread was to see them come to an open quarrel; and I felt that as long as they kept clear of that, all would be well.

Thus the Monday went by, and the Tuesday; and still George kept aloof from me. I had sense enough not to be hurt by this. I felt he had a good right to be silent, if silence helped him to bear his trial better; and I made up my mind never to breathe another syllable on the subject, unless he began.

Wednesday came. I had overslept myself that morning, and came to work a quarter after the hour, expecting to be fined; for George was very strict as foreman of the yard, and treated friends and enemies just the same. Instead of blaming me, however, he called me up, and said:

"Ben, whose turn is it this week to sit up?"

"Mine, sir," I replied. (I always called him "Sir" in working hours.)

"Well, then, you may go home today, and the same on Thursday and Friday; for there's a large batch of work for the ovens tonight, and there'll be the same tomorrow night and the night after."

"All right, sir," said I. "Then I'll be here by seven this evening."

"No, half-past nine will be soon enough. I've some accounts to make up, and I shall be here myself till then. Mind you are true to time, though."

"I'll be as true as the clock, sir," I replied, and was turning away when he called me back again.

"You're a good lad, Ben," said he. "Shake hands."

I seized his hand, and pressed it warmly.

"If I'm good for anything, George," I answered with all my heart, "it's you who have made me so. God bless you for it!"

"Amen!" said he, in a troubled voice, putting his hand to his hat.

And so we parted.

In general, I went to bed by day when I was attending to the firing by night; but this morning I had already slept longer than usual, and wanted exercise more than rest. So I ran home; put a bit of bread and meat in my pocket; snatched up my big thorn stick; and started off for a long day in the country. When I came home, it was quite dark and beginning to rain, just as it had begun to rain at about the same time that wretched Sunday evening: so I changed my wet boots, had an early supper and a nap in the chimney-corner, and went down to the works at a few minutes before half-past nine.

Arriving at the factory-gate, I found it ajar, and so walked in and closed it after me. I remember thinking at the time that it was unlike George's usual caution to leave it so; but it passed from my mind next moment. Having slipped in the bolt, I then went straight over to George's little counting-house, where the gas was shining cheerfully in the window.

Here also, somewhat to my surprise, I found the door open, and the room empty. I went in. The threshold and part of the floor was wetted by the driving rain. The wages-book was open on the desk, George's pen stood in the ink, and his hat hung on its usual peg in the corner. I concluded, of course, that he had gone round to the ovens; so, following him, I took down his hat and carried it with me, for it was now raining fast.

The baking-houses lay just opposite, on the other side of the yard. There were three of them, opening one out of the other; and in each, the great furnace filled all the middle of the room. These furnaces are, in fact, large kilns built of brick, with an oven closed in by an iron door in the centre of each, and a chimney going up through the roof. The pottery, enclosed in seggars, stands round inside on shelves, and has to be turned from time to time while the firing is going on. To turn these seggars, test the heat, and keep the fires up, was my work at the period of which I am now telling you, Major.

Well! I went through the baking-houses one after the other, and found all empty alike. Then a strange, vague, uneasy feeling came over me, and I began to wonder what could have become of George. It was possible that he might be in one of the work-shops; so I ran over to the counting-house, lighted a lantern, and made a thorough survey of the yards.

I tried the doors; they were all locked as usual. I peeped into the open sheds; they were all vacant. I called "George! George!" in every part of the outer premises; but the wind and rain drove back my voice, and no other voice replied to it. Forced at last to believe that he was really gone, I took his hat back to the counting-house, put away the wages-book, extinguished the gas, and prepared for my solitary watch.

The night was mild, and the heat in the baking-rooms intense. I knew, by experience, that the ovens had been overheated, and that none of the porcelain must go in at least for the next two hours; so I carried my stool to the door, settled myself in a sheltered corner where the air could reach me, but not the rain, and fell to wondering where George could have gone, and why he should not have waited till the time appointed. That he had left in haste was clear—not because his hat remained behind, for he might have had a cap with him—but because he had left the book open, and the gas lighted.

Perhaps one of the workmen had met with some accident, and he had been summoned away so urgently that he had no time to think of anything; perhaps he would even now come back presently to see that all was right before he went home to his lodgings. Turning these things over in my mind, I grew drowsy, my thoughts wandered, and I fell asleep.

I cannot tell how long my nap lasted. I had walked a great distance that day, and I slept heavily but I awoke all in a moment, with a sort of terror upon me, and, looking up, saw George Barnard sitting on a stool before the oven door, with the firelight full upon his face.

Ashamed to be found sleeping, I started to my feet. At the same instant, he rose, turned away without even looking towards me, and went out into the next room.

"Don't be angry, George!" I cried, following him. "None of the seggars are in. I knew the fires were too strong, and ——"

The words died on my lips. I had followed him from the first room to the second, from the second to the third, and in the third—I lost him!

I could not believe my eyes. I opened the end door leading into the yard, and looked out; but he was nowhere in sight. I went round to the back of the baking-house, looked behind the furnaces, ran over to the counting-house, called him by his name over and over again; but all was dark, silent, lonely, as ever.

Then I remembered how I had bolted the outer gate, and how impossible it was that he should have come in without ringing. Then, too, I began again to doubt the evidence of my own senses, and to think I must have been dreaming.

I went back to my old post by the door of the first baking-house, and sat down for a moment to collect my thoughts.

"In the first place," said I to myself, "there is but one outer gate. That outer gate I bolted on the inside, and it is bolted still. In the next place, I searched the premises, and found all the sheds empty, and the workshop-doors padlocked as usual on the outside. I proved that George was nowhere about, when I came, and I know he could not have come in since, without my knowledge. Therefore it is a dream. It is certainly a dream, and there's an end of it."

And with this I trimmed my lantern and proceeded to test the temperature of the furnaces. We used to do this, I should tell you, by the introduction of little roughly-moulded lumps of common fire-clay. If the heat is too great, they crack; if too little, they remain damp and moist; if just right, they become firm and smooth all over, and pass into the biscuit stage.

Well! I took my three little lumps of clay, put one in each oven, waited while I counted five hundred, and then went round again to see the results. The two first were in capital condition, the third had flown into a dozen pieces. This proved that the seggars might at once go into ovens One and Two, but that number Three had been overheated, and must be allowed to go on cooling for an hour or two longer.

I therefore stocked One and Two with nine rows of seggars, three deep on each shelf; left the rest waiting till number Three was in a condition to be trusted; and, fearful of falling asleep again, now that the firing was in progress, walked up and down the rooms to keep myself awake. This was hot work, however, and I could not stand it very long; so I went back presently to my stool by the door, and fell to thinking about my dream.

The more I thought of it, the more strangely real it seemed, and the more I felt convinced that I was actually on my feet, when I saw George get up and walk into the adjoining room. I was also certain that I had still continued to see him as he passed out of the second room into the third, and that at that time I was even following his very footsteps. Was it possible, I asked myself, that I could have been up and moving, and yet not quite awake? I had heard of people walking in their sleep.

Could it be that I was walking in mine, and never waked till I reached the cool air of the yard? All this seemed likely enough, so I dismissed the matter from my mind, and passed the rest of the night in attending to the seggars, adding fresh fuel from time to time to the furnaces of the first and second ovens, and now and then taking a turn through the yards. As for number Three, it kept up its heat to such a degree that it was almost day before I dared trust the seggars to go in it.

Thus the hours went by; and at half-past seven on Thursday morning, the men came to their work. It was now my turn to go off duty, but I wanted to see George before I left, and so waited for him in the counting-house, while a lad named Steve Storr took my place at the ovens. But the clock went on from half-past seven to a quarter to eight; then to eight o'clock; then to a quarter-past eight—and still George never made his appearance. At length, when the hand got round to half-past eight, I grew weary of waiting, took up my hat, ran home, went to bed, and slept profoundly until past four in the afternoon.

That evening I went down to the factory quite early; for I had a restlessness upon me, and I wanted to see George before he left for the night. This time, I found the gate bolted, and I rang for admittance.

"How early you are, Ben!" said Steve Storr, as he let me in.

"Mr. Barnard's not gone?" I asked, quickly; for I saw at the first glance that the gas was out in the counting-house.

"He's not gone," said Steve, "because he's never been."

"Never been?"

"No: and what's stranger still, he's not been home either, since dinner yesterday."

"But he was here last night."

"Oh yes, he was here last night, making up the books. John Parker was with him till past six; and you found him here, didn't you, at half-past nine?"

I shook my head.

"Well, he's gone, anyhow. Good night!"

"Good night!"

I took the lantern from his hand, bolted him out mechanically, and made my way to the baking-houses like one in a stupor. George gone? Gone without a word of warning to his employer, or of farewell to his fellow-workmen? I could not understand it. I could not believe it. I sat down bewildered, incredulous, stunned. Then came hot tears, doubts, terrifying suspicions. I remembered the wild words he had spoken a few nights back; the strange calm by which they were followed; my dream of the evening before. I had heard of men who drowned themselves for love; and the turbid Severn ran close by—so close, that one might pitch a stone into it from some of the workshop windows.

These thoughts were too horrible. I dared not dwell upon them. I turned to work, to free myself from them, if I could; and began by examining the ovens. The temperature of all was much higher than on the previous night, the heat having been gradually increased during the last twelve hours. It was now my business to keep the heat on the increase for twelve more; after which it would be allowed, as gradually, to subside, until the pottery was cool enough for removal. To turn the seggars, and add fuel to the two first furnaces, was my first work.

As before, I found number Three in advance of the others, and so left it for half an hour, or an hour. I then went round the yard; tried the doors; let the dog loose; and brought him back with me to the baking-houses, for company. After that, I set my lantern on a shelf beside the door, took a book from my pocket, and began to read.

I remember the title of the book as well as possible. It was called *Bowlker's Art of Angling*, and contained little rude cuts of all kinds of artificial flies, hooks, and other tackle. But I could not keep my mind to it for two minutes together; and at last I gave it up in despair, covered my face with my hands, and fell into a long absorbing painful train of thought. A considerable time had gone by thus—maybe an hour—when I was roused by a low whimpering howl from Captain, who was lying at my feet. I looked up with a start, just as I had started from sleep the night before, and with the same vague terror; and saw, exactly in the same place and in the same attitude, with the firelight full upon him—George Barnard!

At this sight, a fear heavier than the fear of death fell upon me, and my tongue seemed paralysed in my mouth. Then, just as last night, he rose, or seemed to rise, and went slowly out into the next room. A power stronger than myself appeared to compel me, reluctantly, to follow him. I saw him pass through the second room—cross the threshold of the third room—walk straight up to the oven—and there pause.

He then turned, for the first time, with the glare of the red firelight pouring out upon him from the open door of the furnace, and looked at me, face to face. In the same instant, his whole frame and countenance seemed to glow and become transparent, as if the fire were all within him and around him—and in that glow he became, as it were, absorbed into the furnace, and disappeared!

I uttered a wild cry, tried to stagger from the room, and fell insensible before I reached the door.

When I next opened my eyes, the grey dawn was in the sky; the furnace-doors were all closed as I had left them when I last went round; the dog was quietly sleeping not far from my side; and the men were ringing at the gate, to be let in.

I told my tale from beginning to end, and was laughed at,

as a matter of course, by all who heard it. When it was found, however, that my statements never varied, and, above all, that George Barnard continued absent, some few began to talk it over seriously, and among those few, the master of the works. He forbade the furnace to be cleared out, called in the aid of a celebrated naturalist, and had the ashes submitted to a scientific examination. The result was as follows:

The ashes were found to have been largely saturated with some kind of fatty animal matter. A considerable portion of those ashes consisted of charred bone. A semi-circular piece of iron, which evidently had once been the heel of a workman's heavy boot, was found, half fused, at one corner of the furnace. Near it, a tibia bone, which still retained sufficient of its original form and texture to render identification possible. This bone, however, was so much charred, that it fell into powder on being handled.

After this, not many doubted that George Barnard had been foully murdered, and that his body had been thrust into the furnace. Suspicion fell upon Louis Laroche. He was arrested, a coroner's inquest was held, and every circumstance connected with the night of the murder was as thoroughly sifted and in-vestigated as possible. All the sifting in the world, however, failed either to clear or to condemn Louis Laroche.

On the very night of his release, he left the place by the mail-train, and was never seen or heard of there, again. As for Leah, I know not what became of her. I went away myself before many weeks were over, and never have set foot among the Potteries from that hour to this.

Sister Johanna's Story

If you have ever heard of the Grödner Thal, then you will also have heard of the village of St.Ulrich, of which I, Johanna Roederer, am a native. And if, as is more likely, you have never heard of either, then still, though without knowing it, many of you have, even from your earliest childhood, been familiar with the work by which, for many generations, we have lived and prospered. Your rocking-horse, your Noah's ark, your first doll, came from St. Ulrich— for the Grödner Thai is the children's paradise, and supplies the little ones of all Europe with toys.

In every house throughout the village—I might almost say in every house throughout the valley—you will find wood-carving, painting, or gilding perpetually going on; except only in the hay-making and harvest-time, when all the world goes up to the hills to mow and reap, and breathe the mountain air. Nor do our carvers carve only grotesque toys. All the crucifixes that you see by the wayside, all the carved stalls and tabernacles, all the painted and gilded saints decorating screens and side altars in our Tyrolean churches, are the work of their hands.

After what I have said, you will no doubt have guessed that ours was a family of wood-carvers. My father, who died when my sister and I were quite little children, was a wood-carver. My mother was also a wood-carver, as were her mother and grand-mother before her; and Katrine and I were of course brought up by her to the same calling. But, as it was necessary that one should look after the home duties, and as Katrine was always more delicate than myself, I gradually came to work less and less at the business; till at last, what with cooking, washing, mending, making, spinning, gardening, and so forth, I almost left it off altogether.

Nor did Katrine work very hard at it, either; for, being so delicate, and so pretty, and so much younger than myself, she came, of course, to be a great deal spoiled and to have her own way in everything. Besides, she grew tired, naturally, of cutting nothing but cocks, hens, dogs, cats, cows, and goats; which were all our mother had been taught to make, and, consequently, all she could teach to her children.

"If I could carve saints and angels, like Ulrich, next door," Katrine used sometimes to say; "or if might invent new beasts out of my own head, or if I might cut caricature nutcrackers of the Herr Pürger and Don Wian, I shouldn't care if I worked hard all day; but I hate the cocks and hens, and I hate the dogs and cats, and I hate all the birds and beasts that ever went into the ark—and I only wish they had all been drowned in the Deluge, and not one left for a pattern!"

And then she would fling her tools away, and dance about the room like a wild creature, and mimic the Herr Pürger, who was the great wholesale buyer of all our St. Ulrich ware, till even our mother, grave and sober woman as she was, could not help laughing, till the tears ran down her cheeks.

Now the Ulrich next door, of whom our little Katrine used to speak, was the elder of two brothers named Finazzer, and he lived in the house adjoining our own; for at St. Ulrich, as in some of the neighbouring villages, one frequently sees two houses built together under one roof, with gardens and orchards surrounded by a common fence. Such a house was the Finazzer's and ours; or I should rather say both houses were theirs, for they were our landlords, and we rented our cottage from them by the year.

Ulrich, named after the patron saint of our village, was a tall, brown, stalwart man, very grave, very reserved, very religious, and the finest wood-sculptor in all the Grödner Thai. No Madonnas, no angels, could compare with his for heavenly grace and tenderness; and as for his Christs, a great foreign critic who came to St. Ulrich some ten or twelve years ago said that no other modern artist with whose works he was acquainted could treat that subject with anything like the same dignity and pathos. But then, perhaps, no other modern artist went to his work in the same spirit, or threw into it, not only the whole force of a very noble and upright character, but all the loftiest aspirations of a profoundly religious nature.

His younger brother, Alois, was a painter—fair-haired, light-hearted, pleasure-loving; as unlike Ulrich, both in appearance and disposition, as it is possible to conceive. At the time of which I am telling you, he was a student in Venice and had already been three years away from home. I used to dream dreams, and weave foolish romances about Alois and my little Katrine, picturing to myself how he would someday come home, in the flush, per-haps, of his first success, and finding her so beautiful and a wom-an grown, fall in love with her at first sight, and she with him; and the thought of this possibility became at last such a happy certainty in my mind, that when things began to work round in quite the other way, I could not bring myself to believe it.

Yet so it was, and, much as I loved my darling, and quick-sighted as I had always been in everything that could possibly concern her, there was not a gossip in St. Ulrich who did not see what was coming before I even suspected it.

When, therefore, my little Katrine came to me one evening in the orchard and told me, half laughing, half crying, that Ul-rich Finazzer had that day asked her to be his wife, I was utterly taken by surprise.

"I never dreamed that he would think of me, dear," she said, with her head upon my bosom. "He is so much too good and too clever for such a foolish birdie as poor little Katrine."

"But—but my birdie loves him?" I said, kissing her bright hair.

She half lifted her head, half laughed through her tears, and said with some hesitation:—

"Oh, yes, I love him. I—I think I love him—and then I am

quite sure he loves me, and that is more than enough."

"But, Katrine "

She kissed me, to stop the words upon my lips.

"But you know quite well, dear, that I never could love any lover half as much as I love you and he knows it, too, for I told him so just now, and now please don't look grave, for I want to be very happy tonight, and I can't bear it."

And I also wanted her to be very happy, so I said all the loving things I could think of, and when we went in to supper we found Ulrich Finazzer waiting for us.

"Dear Johanna," he said, taking me by both hands, "you are to be my sister now."

And then he kissed me on the forehead. The words were few; but he had never spoken to me or looked at me so kindly before, and somehow my heart seemed to come into my throat, and I could not answer a word.

It was now the early summer time, and they were to be married in the autumn. Ulrich, mean-while, had his hands full of work, as usual, and there was, besides, one important task which he wanted to complete before his wedding. This task was a Christ, larger than life, which he designed as a gift to our parish church, then undergoing complete restoration. The committee of management had invited him in the first instance to undertake the work as an order, but Ulrich would not accept a price for it.

He preferred to give it as a freewill offering, and he meant it to be the best piece of wood-sculpture that had ever yet left his hand. He had made innumerable designs for it both in clay and on paper, and separate studies from life for the limbs, hands, and feet. In short, it was to be no ordinary piece of mere conventional Grödner Thai work, but a work of art in the true sense of the word. In the meanwhile, he allowed no one to see the figure in progress—not even Katrine;but worked upon it with closed doors, and kept it covered with a linen cloth whenever his workshop was open.

So the Summer time wore on, and the roses bloomed abundantly in our little garden, and the corn yellowed slowly on the hill-sides, and the wild white strawberry-blossoms turned to tiny strawberries, ruby-red, on every mossy bank among the fir-forests of the Seisser Alp. And still Ulrich laboured on a this great work, and sculptured many a gracious saint besides; and still the one object of his earthly worship was our little laughing Katrine.

Whether it was that, being so grave himself, and she so gay, he loved her the better for the contrast, I cannot tell; but his affection for her seemed to deepen daily. I watched it as one might watch the growth of some rare flower, and I wondered sometimes if she prized it as she ought. Yet I scarcely know how, child that she was, she should ever have risen to the heights or sounded the depths of such a nature as his.

That she could not appreciate him, however, would have mattered little, if she had loved him more. There was the pity of it. She had accepted him, as many a very young girl accepts her first lover, simply because he was her first. She was proud of his genius—proud of his preference—proud of the house, and the lands, and the worldly goods that were soon to be hers; but for that far greater wealth of love, she held it all too lightly.

Seeing this day after day, with the knowledge that nothing I could say would make things better, I fell, without being conscious of it, into a sad and silent way that arose solely out of my deep love for them both, and had no root of selfishness in it, as my own heart told me then, and tells me to this day.

In the midst of this time, so full of happiness for Ulrich, so full of anxiety for me, Alois Finazzer came home suddenly. We had been expecting him in a vague way ever since the Spring, but the surprise when he walked in unannounced was as great as if we had not expected him at all.

He kissed us all on both cheeks, and sat down as if he had not been away for a day.

"What a rich fellow I am!" he said, joyously. "I left only a grave elder brother behind when I went to Venice, and I come back finding two dear little sisters to welcome me home again."

And then he told us that he had just taken the gold medal at the Academy, that he had sold his prize-picture for two hundred florins, and that he had a pocketful of presents for us all—a necklace for Katrine, a spectacle-case for our mother, and a housewife for myself. When he put the necklace round my darling's neck he kissed her again, and praised her eyes, and said he should someday put his pretty little sister into one of his pictures.

He was greatly changed. He went away a curly-headed lad of eighteen; he came back a man, bearded and self-confident.

Three years, at certain turning-points on the road of life, work with us more powerfully, whether or better or worse, than would ten years at any other period. I thought I liked Alois Finazzer better when he was those three years younger.

Not so Katrine, however—not so our mother —not so the St. Ulrich folk, all of whom were loud in his praise. Handsome, successful, gay, generous, he treated the men, laughed with the girls, and carried all before him.

As for Ulrich, he put his work aside, and cleared his brow, and made holiday for two whole days, going round with his brother from house to house, and telling everyone how Alois had taken the great gold medal in Venice. Proud and happy as he was, however, he was prouder and happier still when, some three or four days later, at a meeting of the Church Committee of management, the Commune formally invited Alois to paint an altar-piece for the altar of San Marco at the price of three hundred florins.

That evening Ulrich invited us to supper, and we drank Alois's health in a bottle of good Barbera wine. He was to stay at home now, instead of going back to Venice, and he was to have a large room at the back of Ulrich's workshop for a studio.

"I'll bring your patron saint into my picture if you will sit for her portrait, Katrine," said Alois, laughingly.

And Katrine blushed and said, "Yes;" and Ulrich was delighted; and Alois pulled out his pocket-book, and began sketching her head on the spot.

"Only you must try to think of serious things, and not laugh when you are sitting for a saint, my little *Mädchen*," said Ulrich, tenderly; whereupon Katrine blushed still more deeply, and Alois, without looking up from his drawing, promised that they would both be as grave as judges whenever the sittings were going on.

And now there began for me a period of such misery that even at this distance of time I can scarcely bear to speak or think of it. There, day after day, was Alois painting in his new studio, and Katrine sitting to him for Santa Catarina, while Ulrich, unselfish, faithful, trustful, worked on in the next room, absorbed in his art, and not only unconscious of treachery, but incapable of conceiving it as a possibility.

How I tried to watch over her, and would fain have watched over her still more closely if I could, is known to myself alone. My object was to be with her throughout all those fatal sittings; Alois's object was to make the appointments for hours when my household duties compelled me to remain at home. He soon found out that my eyes were opened. From that moment it was a silent, unacknowledged fight between us, and we were always fighting it.

And now, as his work drew nearer to completion, Ulrich seemed every day to live less for the people and things about him, and more for his art. Always somewhat over-silent and reserved, he now seemed scarcely conscious, at times, of even the presence of others. He spoke and moved as in a dream; went to early mass every morning at four; fasted three days out of seven; and, having wrought himself up to a certain pitch of religious and artistic excitement, lived in a world of his own creation, from which even Katrine was for the time excluded.

Things being thus, what could I do but hold my peace? To speak to Ulrich would have been impossible at any time; to speak to my darling (she being, perhaps, wholly unconscious) might be to create the very peril I dreaded; to appeal to Alois, I felt beforehand, would be worse than useless. So I kept my trouble to myself, and prayed that the weeks might pass quickly, and bring their wedding-day.

Now, just about this time of which I am telling (that is towards the middle of August) came round the great annual fete, or *Sagro*, as we call it, at Botzen; and to this fete Katrine and I had for some years been in the habit of going—walking to Atzwang the first day by way of Castelruth; sleeping near Atzwang in the house of our aunt, Maria Bernhard, whose husband kept the *Gasthaus* called the Schwarze Adler; taking the railway next morning from Atzwang to Botzen, and there spending the day of the Sagro; and returning in the same order as we came.

This year, however, having the dread of Alois before my eyes, and knowing that Ulrich would not leave his work, I set my face against the Botzen expedition, and begged my little sister, since she could not have the protection of her betrothed husband, to give it up. And so I think she would have done at first, but that Alois was resolute to have us go; and at last even Ulrich urged it upon us, saying that he would not have his little *Mädchen* balked of her *festa* simply because he was too busy to take her there himself. Would not Johanna be there to take care of her, Alois to take care of them both? So my protest was silenced, and we went.

It is a long day's walk from St. Ulrich to Atzwang, and we did not reach our aunt's house till nearly supper-time; so that it was quite late before we went up to our room. And now my darling, after being in wild spirits all day, became suddenly silent, and instead of going to bed, stayed by the window, looking at the moon.

"What is my birdie thinking of?" I said, putting my arm about her waist.

"I am thinking," she said, softly, "how the moon is shining now at St. Ulrich on our mother's bedroom window, and on our father's grave."

And with this she laid her head down upon my shoulder, and cried as if her heart would break.

I have reproached myself since for letting that moment pass as I did. I believe I might have had her confidence if I had tried, and then what a world of sorrow might have been averted from us all!

We reached Botzen next morning in time for the six o'clock mass; went to high mass again at nine; and strolled among the booths between the services. Here Alois, as usual, was very free with his money, buying ribbons and trinkets for Katrine,and behaving in every way as if he, and not Ulrich, were her acknowledged lover.

At eleven, having met some of our St. Ulrich neighbours, we made a party and dined all together at a *Gasthaus* in theSilbergasse; and after dinner the young men proposed to take us to see an exhibition of rope-dancers and tumblers. Now I knew that Ulrich would not approve of this, and I entreated my darling for his sake, if not for mine, to stay away. But she would not listen to me.

"Ulrich, Ulrich!" she repeated, pettishly. "Don't tease me about Ulrich; I am tired of his very name!"

The next moment she had taken Alois's arm, and we were in the midst of the crowd.

Finding she would go, I of course went also, though sorely against my inclination; and one of our St. Ulrich friends gave me his arm, and got me through. The crowd, however, was so great that I lost sight somehow of Alois and Katrine, and found myself landed presently inside the booth and sitting on a front seat next to the orchestra, alone with the St. Ulrich people. We kept seats for them as long as we could, and stood upon the bench to look for them, till at last the curtain rose, and we had to sit down without them.

I saw nothing of the performance. To this day I have no idea how long it lasted, or what it consisted of. I remember nothing but the anxiety with which I kept looking towards the door, and the deadly sinking at my heart as the minutes dragged by. To go in search of them was impossible, for the entrance was choked, and there was no standing-room in any part of the booth, so that even when the curtain fell we were fully another ten minutes getting out.

You have guessed it, perhaps, before I tell you. They were not in the market-place; they were not at the *Gasthaus*; they were not in the Cathedral.

"The tall young man in a grey and green coat, and the pretty girl with a white rose in her hair ?"said a bystander. "Tush, my dear, don't be uneasy. They are gone home; I saw them running towards the station more than half an hour ago."

So we flew to the station, and there one of the porters, who was an Atzwang man and knew us both, confirmed the dreadful truth. They were gone indeed, but they were not gone home. Just in time to catch the Express, they had taken their tickets through to Venice, and were at this moment speeding southwards.

How I got home—not stopping at all at Atzwang, but going straight away on foot in the broiling afternoon sun—never resting till I reached Castelruth, a little after dusk—lying down outside my bed and sobbing all the night—getting up at the first glimmer of grey dawn and going on again before the sun was up—how I did all this, faint for want of food, yet unable to eat; weary for want of rest, yet unable to sleep—I know not. But I did it, and was home again at St. Ulrich, kneeling beside our mother's chair, and comforting her as best I could, by seven.

"How is Ulrich to be told?"

It was her first question. It was the question I had been asking myself all the way home. I knew well, however, that I must be the one to break it to him. It was a terrible task, and I put it from me as long as possible.

When at last I did go, it was past midday. The workshop door stood open—the Christ, just showing a vague outline through the folds, was covered with a sheet, and standing up against the wall—and Ulrich was working on the drapery of a St. Francis, the splinters from which were flying off rapidly in every direction.

Seeing me on the threshold, he looked up and smiled.

"So soon back, *liebe* Johanna?" he said. "We did not expect you till evening."

Then, finding I made no answer, he paused in his work, and

said, quickly:—

"What is the matter? Is she ill?"

I shook my head.

"No," I said, "she is not ill."

"Where is she, then?"

"She is not ill," I said, again, "but—she is not here."

And then I told him.

He heard me out in dead silence, never moving so much as a finger, only growing whiter as I went on. Then, when I had done, he went over to the window, and remained standing with his back towards me for some minutes.

"And you?" he said, presently, still without turning his head. "And you—through all these weeks— you never saw or suspected anything?"

"I feared—I was not sure—"

He turned upon me with a terrible pale anger in his face.

"You feared—you were not sure!" he said, slowly. "That is to say, you saw it going on, and let it go on, and would not put out your hand to save us all! False! false! false!—all false together—false love, false brother, false friend!"

"You are not just to me, Ulrich," I said; for to be called false by him was more than I could bear.

"Am I not just? Then I pray that God will be more just to you, and to them, than I can ever be; and that His justice may be the justice of vengeance— swift, and terrible, and without mercy."

And saying this he laid his hand on the veiled Christ, and cursed us all three with a terrible, passionate curse, like the curse of a prophet of old.

For one moment my heart stood still, and I felt as if there was nothing left for me but to die—but it was only for that one moment; for I knew, even before he had done speaking, that no words of his could harm either my poor little erring Katrine or myself. And then, having said so as gently as I could, I formally forgave him in her name and mine, and went away.

That night Ulrich Finazzer shut up his house and disappeared, no one knew whither. When questioned the old woman who lived with him as servant, she said that he had paid and dismissed her a little before dusk; that she then thought he was looking very ill, and that she had observed how, instead of being as usual hard at work all day in the workshop, he had fetched his gun out of the kitchen about two o'clock, and carried it up to his bedroom, where, she believed, he had spent nearly all the afternoon cleaning it. This was all she had to tell; but it was more than enough to add to the burden of my terrors.

Oh, the weary, weary time that followed—the long, sad, solitary days—the days that became weeks— the weeks that became months—the Autumn that chilled and paled as it wore on towards Winter —the changing wood—the withering leaves—the snow that whitened daily on the great peaks round about! Thus September and October passed away, and the last of the harvest was gathered in, and November came with bitter winds and rain; and save a few hurried lines from Katrine, posted in Perugia, I knew nothing of the fate of all whom I had loved and lost.

"We were married," she wrote, "in Venice, and Alois talks of spending the Winter in Rome. I should be perfectly happy if I knew that you and Ulrich had forgiven us."

This was all. She gave me no address; but I wrote to her at the Poste Restante Perugia, and again to the Poste Restante, Rome; both of which letters, I presume, lay unclaimed till destroyed by the authorities, for she never replied to either.

And now the Winter came on in earnest, as Winter always comes in our high valleys, and Christmas-time drew round again; and on the eve of St. Thomas, Ulrich Finazzer returned to his house as suddenly and silently as he had left it.

Next door neighbours as we were, we should not have known of his return but for the trampled snow upon the path, and the smoke going up from the workshop chimney. No other sign of life or occupation was to be seen. The shutters remained unopened. The doors, both front and back, remained fast locked. If any neighbour knocked, he was left to knock unanswered. Even the old woman who used to be his servant, was turned away by a stern voice from within, bidding her be gone and leave him at peace.

That he was at work was certain; for we could hear him in the workshop by night as well as by day. But he could work there as in a tomb, for the room was lighted by a window in the roof.

Thus St. Thomas's Day, and the next day which was the fourth Sunday in Advent, went by; and still he who had ever been so constant at mass showed no sign of coming out amongst us. On Monday our good *curé* walked down, all through the fresh snow (for there had been a heavy fall in the night), on purpose to ask if we were sure that Ulrich was really in his house; if we had yet seen him; and if we knew what he did for food, being shut in there quite alone. But to these questions we could give no satisfactory reply.

That day when we had dined, I put some bread and meat in a basket and left it at his door; but it lay there untouched all through the day and night, and in the morning I fetched it back again, with the food still in it.

This was the fourth day since his return. It was very dreadful—I cannot tell you how dreadful— to know that he was so near, yet never even to see his shadow on a blind. As the day wore on my suspense became intolerable. Tonight, I told myself, would be Christmas Eve; tomorrow Christmas Day. Was it possible that his heart would not soften if he remembered our Happy Christmas of only last year, when he and Katrine were not yet betrothed; how he supped with us, and how we all roasted nuts upon the hearth and sang part-songs after supper? Then, again, it seemed incredible that he should not go to church on Christmas Day.

Thus the day went by, and the evening dusk came on, and the village choir came round singing carols from house to house, and still he made no sign.

Now what with the suspense of knowing him to be so near, and the thought of my little Katrine far away in Rome, and the remembrance of how he—he whom I had honoured and admired above all the world my whole life long—had called down curses on us both the very last time that he and I stood face to face—what with all this, I say, and what with the season and its associations, I had such a great restlessness and anguish upon me that I sat up trying to read my Bible long after mother had gone to bed. But my thoughts wandered continually from the text, and at last the restlessness so gained upon me that I could sit still no longer, and so got up and walked about the room.

And now suddenly, while I was pacing to and fro, I heard, or fancied I heard, a voice in the garden calling to me by name. I stopped—I listened— I trembled. My very heart stood still! Then, hearing no more, I opened the window and outer shutters, and instantly there rushed in a torrent of icy cold air and a flood of brilliant moonlight, and there, on the shining snow below, stood Ulrich Finazzer.

Himself, and yet so changed! Worn, haggard, grey.

I saw him, I tell you, as plainly as I see my own hand at this moment. He was standing close, quite close, under the window, with the moonlight full upon him.

"Ulrich!" I said, and my own voice sounded strange to me, somehow, in the dead waste and silence of the night—"Ulrich, are you come to tell me we are friends again?"

But instead of answering me he pointed to a mark on his forehead—a small dark mark, that looked at this distance and by this light like a bruise—cried aloud with a strange wild cry, less like a human voice than a far-off echo, "The brand of Cain! The brand of Cain!" and so flung up his arms with a despairing gesture, and fled away into the night.

The rest of my story may be told in a few words—the fewer the better. Insane with the desire of vengeance, Ulrich Finazzer had tracked the fugitives from place to place, and slain his brother at mid-day in the streets of Rome. He escaped unmolested, and was well nigh over the Austrian border before the authorities began to inquire into the particulars of the murder.

He then, as was proved by a comparison of dates, must have

come straight home by way of Mantua, Verona, and Botzen, with no other object, apparently, than to finish the statue that he had designed for an offering to the church. He worked upon it, accordingly, as I have said, for four days and nights incessantly, completed it to the last degree of finish, and then, being in who can tell how terrible a condition of remorse, and horror, and despair, sought to expiate his crime with his blood.

They found him shot through the head by his own hand, lying quite dead at the feet of the statue upon which he had been working, probably, up to the last moment; his tools lying close by; the pistol still fast in his clenched hand, and the divine pitying face of the Redeemer whose law he had outraged, bending over him as if in sorrow and forgiveness.

Our mother has now been dead some years; strangers occupy the house in which Ulrich Finazzer came to his dreadful death; and already the double tragedy is almost forgotten. In the sad, faded woman, prematurely grey, who lives with me, ever working silently, steadily, patiently, from morning till night at our hereditary trade, few who had known her in the freshness of her youth would now recognise my beautiful Katrine. Thus from day today, from year to year, we journey on together, nearing the end.

Did I indeed see Ulrich Finazzer that night of his self-murder? If I did so with my bodily eyes and it was no illusion of the senses, then most surely I saw him not in life, for that dark mark which looked to me in the moonlight like a bruise was the bullet-hole in his brow.

But did I see him? It is a question I ask myself again and again, and have asked myself for years. Ah! who can answer it?

217

The Discovery of the Treasure Isles

1

It was on the 26th of October, 1760, at twenty-seven minutes past ten o'clock, a.m., that I shook hands for the last time with those worthy merchants and shipowners, Messrs. Fisher, Clarke, and Fisher, of Bristol. I went at once on board the *Mary-Jane*, then lying alongside the drawbridge by St. Augustine's parade, in the very heart of the old city. It was my first command, so I stepped on deck with some little pride of heart, and bade the men weigh anchor. My exultation may be pardoned when it is recollected that I was only twenty-six years of age, and naturally thought it a fine thing to be captain of a tight little trading schooner like the *Mary-Jane*, with a valuable cargo on board, and a mate, three sailors, and a boy under my absolute authority.

The flags were flying from every masthead and steeple, and the bells were pealing clamorously, as we worked out of port that morning; for it was the very day of the king's[2] accession, and all Bristol was wild with loyalty. I remember as well as if it were yesterday, how the sailors cheered from the ships as we went down the Avon; and how my men threw up their hats in reply, and shouted, "Long live King George!"

The Avon, however, was soon left behind, and we entered the Bristol Channel with a favourable wind, all sail set, and a sky brilliant with sunshine above our heads. We were bound, I should observe, for Jamaica, and carried a cargo consisting chiefly

---

1. From a MS. found on a bookstall.
2. The writer alludes, evidently, to King George III., who was proclaimed throughout the kingdom on the 26th Oct., 1760; King George II. having died suddenly, at Kensington, on the 25th.

of printed goods, hardware, and cutlery, which it was my duty to deliver to the consignee at Kingston. This done, my instructions were to ship a return cargo of cotton, indigo, rum, and other West Indian products. Perhaps it may be as well to add that the *Mary-Jane* carried about a hundred tons burthen, that my name is William Burton, and my mate's name was Aaron Taylor.

The *Mary-Jane* was not a quick sailer, as I soon discovered; but she was a good, sound, steady little craft, and I consoled myself by remembering that safety was better than speed. It was dusk before we reached Lundy Island, and almost daylight next morning when we passed the Land's-End. This was slow work; but as the wind had shifted a point or two during the night, I made the best of matters, and tried to hope we should do better by-and-by. After tossing about somewhat roughly off the Bay of Biscay, we made Cape Finisterre on the 4th of November; and on the 18th put in at Terceira for water.

Having remained here for the best part of two days, we put to sea again on the evening of the 20th. The wind now began to set in more and more against us, and ended by blowing steadily from the South; so that, although we had glorious weather overhead, we made almost as little way as if we had had storms to contend against. At length, after a week of ineffectual beating about, just as I was going to turn the ship's head and run back to Terceira, the breeze shifted suddenly to the North. The N.W. would have suited us better; but if we could not get exactly the wind we most wanted, we were thankful, at all events, to tack about, and make such progress as was possible.

Thus we went forward slowly towards the tropics, attended by perpetual sunshine and cloudless skies, and enjoying a climate that grew milder and more delicious every day. The incidents of our voyage, up to this time, had been few and unimportant. A Dutch merchantman seen one morning in the offing—a porpoise caught by one of the crew—a flight of swallows on the wing—a shark following the ship. These, and similar trifles, were all the events that befell us for many a week; events which are nothing when related, and yet afford matter for vivid interest to those on shipboard.

At length, on the 15th of December, we entered the tropic of Cancer; and on the 19th sailed into a light sea-fog, which surprised us very much at such a season, and in such a latitude; but which was welcome, nevertheless, for the sun's heat was now becoming intense, and seemed as if it would burn the very deck beneath our feet. All that day the fog hung low upon the sea, the wind fell, and the waters were lulled almost to a calm. My mate predicted a hurricane; but no hurricane came. On the contrary, sea and air stagnated more and more; and the last breath of wind died away as the sun went down. Then the sudden tropical night closed in, and the heat grew more oppressive than before.

I went to my cabin to write, as was my custom in the evening; but, though I wore only a thin linen suit, and kept every porthole open, I felt as if the cabin was a coffin, and would suffocate me. Having borne it till I could bear it no longer, I threw the pen aside and went on deck again. There I found Aaron Taylor keeping the first watch; and our youngest seaman, Joshua Dunn, at the helm.

"Close night, mate," said I.

"Queerest night *I* ever saw, sir, in these latitudes," replied Aaron.

"What way do we make?"

"None, sir, hardly: scarce one knot an hour."

"Have the men all turned in?"

"All, sir, except Dunn and me."

"Then you may turn in too, mate," said I. "I'll keep this watch and the next myself."

The mate touched his hat, and with a glad "ay, ay, sir," disappeared down the companion-ladder. We were so small a crew that I always took my turn at the watch, and tonight, feeling it impossible to stay below, willingly charged myself with the double duty.

It was now about ten o'clock. There was something almost awful in the heavy stillness of the night, and in the thin, white, ghastly fog that folded round us on all sides, like a shroud. Pacing to and fro along the solitary deck, with no other sounds to break the silence than the murmuring of the water along the ship's side, and the creaking of the wheel in the hands of the steersman, I fell into a profound reverie.

I thought of my friends far away; of my old home among the Mendip hills; of Bessie Robinson, who had promised to become my wife when I went back after this voyage; of a thousand hopes and projects, far enough removed from the schooner *Mary-Jane*, or any soul on board. From these dreams I was suddenly roused by the voice of Joshua Dunn shouting in a quick, startled tone—
"Ship ahoy!"

I was alive in a moment at this cry, for we were at war with both France and Spain at the time, and it would have been no pleasant matter to fall in with an enemy; especially as there had been some fierce fights more than once in these very waters since the war began. So I pulled up in my walk, looked sharply round on all sides, and saw nothing but fog.

"Whereabouts, Josh?" I cried.

"Coming right up, sir, under our weather-bow," replied the steersman.

I stepped aft, and, staring steadily in the direction indicated, saw, sure enough, the faint glimmer of a couple of lanterns coming up through the fog. To dash down into my cabin, seize a brace of pistols and my speaking-trumpet, and spring up again on deck, just as the spectral outline of a large brig loomed up almost within a stone's throw of the ship's side, was the work of a moment. I then stood silent, and waited, ready to answer if hailed, and willing enough to slip along unobserved in the fog, if our formidable neighbour passed us by. I had scarcely waited a moment, however, before a loud voice, made louder by the use of the trumpet, rang through the thick air, crying:—

"Ship ahoy! What name? Where from? Whither bound?"

To which I replied:—

"Trading schooner *Mary-Jane*—from Bristol to Jamaica. What ship? Where from? Whither bound?"

There was a moment's silence. Then the same voice replied:—

"The *Adventure*. Homeward bound."

The reply was informal.

"Where from?" I repeated. "What cargo?"

Again there seemed some hesitation on the part of the stranger; and again, after an instant's pause, he answered:—

"From the Treasure Isles, with gold and jewels."

From the Treasure Isles, with gold and jewels! I could not credit my ears. I had never heard of the Treasure Isles in my life. I had never seen them on any chart. I did not believe that any such islands existed.

"What Isles?" I shouted, the question springing to my lips as the doubt flashed on my mind.

"The Treasure Isles."

"What bearings?"

"Latitude twenty-two, thirty. Longitude sixty-three, fifteen."

"Have you any chart?"

"Yes."

"Will you show it?"

"Ay, ay. Come aboard, and see."

I bade the steersman lay to. The stranger did the same. Presently her great hull towered up beside us like a huge rock; a rope was thrown; a chain ladder lowered; and I stepped on deck. I looked round for the captain. A tall, gaunt man stood before me, with his belt full of pistols, and a speaking-trumpet under his arm. Beside him stood a sailor with a torch, the light from which flickered redly through the thick air, and showed some twenty men, or more, gathered round the binnacle. All were as silent as ghosts, and, seen through the mist, looked as unsubstantial.

The captain put his hand to his hat, looked at me with eyes that glittered like live coals, and said:—

"You want to see the chart of the islands?"

"I do, sir."

"Follow me."

The sailor lighted us down, the captain vent first, and I followed. As I passed down the cabin-stairs I eased the pistols in my belt, ready for use if necessary; for there was something strange about the captain and his crew—something strange in the very build and aspect of the ship, that puzzled me, and put me on my guard.

The captain's cabin was large, low, and gloomy, lighted by an oil-lamp swinging from the roof, like a murderer swinging in chains; fitted with old carved furniture that might have been oak, but was as black as ebony; and plentifully garnished about the walls with curious weapons of all kinds of antique shapes and workmanship.

On the table lay a parchment chart, elaborately drawn in red ink, and yellow with age. The captain silently laid his finger on the very centre of the parchment, and kept his glittering eyes fixed full upon me.

I leaned over the chart, silent as himself, and saw two islands, a greater and a less, lying just in the latitude he had named, with a narrow strait between them. The larger was somewhat crescent shaped; the smaller inclined to a triangular form, and lay up to the N.W. of the other, just in this fashion—

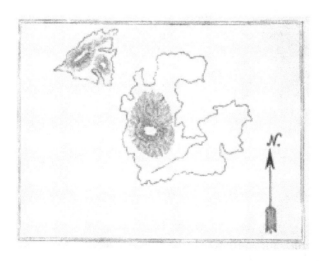

Both were very irregular in the outline. The little island seemed hilly throughout, the large one was scooped into a deep bay on the N. E. side, and was piled up into what appeared like a lofty mountain between the inner shore of the bay and the western coast. Not far from the southern side of this mountain, a small river was seen to take its rise, flow in a north-easterly direction, and empty itself into the bay.

"And these," said I, drawing along breath, "are the Treasure Isles?"

The captain nodded grimly.

"Are they under French or Spanish Government?"

"They are under no government," replied the captain.

"Unclaimed lands?"

"Wholly unclaimed."

"Are the natives friendly?"

"There are none."

"None? Then the islands are uninhabited!"

The captain nodded again. My amazement became more profound every moment.

"Why do you call them the Treasure Isles?" I asked, unable to keep my eyes from the map.

The captain of the *Adventure* stepped back, pulled aside a coarse canvas screen that had till now closed in the farther end of the cabin, and pointed to a symmetrical pile of golden ingots—solid golden ingots—about seven feet high and four deep, built row above row in transverse layers, as a builder might have laid the bricks in a wall.

I rubbed my eyes. I looked from the gold to the captain, from the captain to the map, from the map back to the gold.

The captain drew the screen to its place with a hollow laugh, and said:—

"There are two hundred and fifty-seven tons weight of silver in the hold, and six chests of precious stones."

I put my hand to my head, and leaned against the table. I was dazzled, bewildered, giddy.

"I must go back to my ship," said I, still staring covetously at the chart.

The captain took an odd-looking long-necked bottle, and a couple of quaint beakers with twisted stems from a locker close by; filled out a glassful of some kind of rich amber-coloured cordial, and handed it to me with a nod of invitation. Looking closely at the liquid, I saw that it was full of little sparkling fragments of gold ore.

"It is the genuine Golden Water," said the captain.

His fingers were like ice—the cordial like fire. It blistered my lips and mouth, and ran down my throat like a stream of liquid lava. The glass fell from my hand, and was shattered into a thousand fragments.

"Confound the liquor," gasped I, "how hot it is!"

The captain laughed his hollow laugh again, and the cabin echoed to it like a vault.

"Your health," said he; and emptied his own beaker as if it had been a glass of water.

I ran up the cabin stairs with my throat still on fire. The captain followed at a couple of strides.

"Goodnight," said I, with one foot already on the chain-ladder. "Did you not say latitude twenty-two, thirty?"

"Yes."

"And longitude sixty-three, fifteen?"

"Yes."

"Thanks, sir, and goodnight."

"Goodnight," replied the captain, his eyes glowing in his head like fiery carbuncles. "Good night, and a pleasant voyage to you."

With this he burst into a laugh louder and more hollow than ever—a laugh which was instantly taken up, echoed, and re-echoed by all the sailors aboard.

I sprang down upon my own deck in a towering passion, and swore at them pretty roundly, for a set of unmannerly lubbers; but this seemed only to redouble their infernal mirth. Then the *Adventure* hove off, faded again to a mere spectre, and disappeared in the mist just as the last peal of laughter died away, mockingly, in the distance.

The *Mary-Jane* now resumed her course, and I my watch. The same heavy silence brooded over the night. The same fog closed around our path. I alone was changed. My entire being seemed to have undergone a strange and sudden revolution. The whole current of my thoughts, the very hopes, aims, and purposes of my life, were turned into a new channel. I thought of nothing but the Treasure Isles and their untold wealth of gold and jewels. Why should not I seize upon my share of the spoil? Had I not as good a right to enrich myself as any other man that sailed the seas? I had but to turn the ship's course, and possess the wealth of kingdoms.

Who was to prevent me? Who should gainsay me? The schooner was not my own vessel, it was true; but would not her owners be more than satisfied if I brought them back double the value of her cargo in solid ingots? I might do this, and still have fabulous treasure for myself. It seemed like madness to delay even for a single hour; and yet I hesitated. I had no right to deviate from the route prescribed by my employers. I was bound to deliver my cargo at Jamaica within a given time, wind and weather permitting; and we had already lost weeks upon the way.

Beset by alternate doubts and desires, I went to my berth at the close of the second watch. I might as well have tried to sleep in the powder magazine of a burning ship. If I closed my eyes, the parchment chart lay before them as plainly as when I saw it on the captain's table. If I opened them, the two islands appeared as if traced upon the darkness in lines of fire. At length I felt I could lie there inactive no longer. I rose, dressed, lit my lamp, took out my own book of charts, and set myself to enter the Treasure Isles in their places on the map. Having drawn them in accurately with pencil, and then traced over the pencillings with ink, I felt a little calmer, and turned in again. This time I fell asleep from sheer exhaustion, and woke, dreaming of riches, just at dawn.

My first proceeding was to go on deck and take an observation of our position. The result of this observation was to show me, beyond all doubt, that we were then distant about seventy-two hours' sail from the coast of the larger island; whereupon, I yielded to a temptation stronger than my will or my reason, and changed the ship's course.

That decisive step once taken, I fell into a state of feverish eagerness, which allowed me no rest of body or mind. I could neither sleep, nor eat, nor sit still, nor remain in one spot for three minutes together. I went up to the masthead twenty times a day on the look-out for land, and raged against the fog. as if it were sent from heaven on purpose to torment me. My seamen thought I was mad; and so I was. Mad with the thirst of gain, as many a sane man has been before and since.

At length, on the morning of the third day, Aaron Taylor came to me in my cabin, and ventured on a respectful remonstrance. We had already deviated, he said, two degrees from our course, and were making straight for the Bahama islands, instead of for Jamaica. Had we kept steadily on our way, we should have shortly touched at Porto Rico for provisions and water; but both were running short, and could not possibly hold out for anything like the time it would take us to make land in the present direction. In reply to this statement, I showed my chart with the two islands sketched in according to their bearings.

He looked at them, shook his head, and said very earnestly:— "I have sailed in these latitudes for the last fifteen years, your honour, and I'll take my Bible oath there are no such lands."

Whereupon I flew into a violent fit of anger, as if the mate had presumed to doubt my word, and forbade him ever to speak to me on the subject again. My temper, in short, was as much impaired as my peace of mind, or, indeed, as my sense of duty; and gold, accursed gold, was at the bottom of it all!

Thus the third day passed on, and still the fog hung round and seemed to follow us. The seamen did their work sullenly, and whispered together when my back was turned. The mate looked pale and grave, like a man whose mind was full of anxious thoughts. For my part, I was more resolute than ever, and silently vowed to shoot the first sailor who showed a sign of mutiny. To this end I cleaned and primed my pistols, and hid a Spanish dagger between my waistcoat and my belt. Thus the long, monotonous hours went on, and the sun sank, and yet no hind, nor indication of land, had appeared on any side.

Sixty-five hours out of the seventy-two had now gone by, and it seemed as if the remaining seven would never expire. To sleep was impossible; so I paced the deck all night, and watched as eagerly for the first gleam of dawn as if my life depended on it. As the morning drew nearer, my excitement became almost more than I could bear. I even felt as if I would gladly have put off the moment which I had been so passionately awaiting.

At length the eastward grey grew visibly lighter, and was followed by a broad crimson flush all across the heavens. I went up aloft, trembling in every limb. As I reached the top-gallant-mast, the sun rose. I closed my eyes, and for a moment dared not look around me.

When I opened them again, I saw the fog lying all over the calm surface of the sea in fleecy tracts of vapour, like half-transparent snow; and straight ahead, distant some ten miles or so in a direct line, a pale blue peak rising above the level of the mist. At the sight of that peak my heart gave a great leap, and my head turned giddy; for I recognized it instantly as the mountain mapped out between the bay and western coast of the larger island.

As soon as I could command my agitation sufficiently, I pulled out a pocket-glass, and surveyed it narrowly. The glass only confirmed the evidence of my eyes. I then came down, intoxicated with success, and triumphantly bade Taylor go aloft and report all that he should see. The mate obeyed, but declared that there was nothing visible but sky and fog.

I was enraged. I would not believe him. I sent the boy up, and then one of the seamen, and both returned with the same story. At last I went up again myself, and found that they were right. The fog had risen with the rising of the sun, and the peak had utterly disappeared. All this, however, made no real difference. The land was there; I had seen it; and we were sailing for it, right before the wind. In the meantime, I caused the ship's boat to be got ready, directed that a bag of biscuit, a keg of brandy, a couple of cutlasses, a couple of muskets, a couple of sacks, and a good store of ammunition should be thrown into it; and provided myself with a pocket-compass, tinder-box, hatchet, and small telescope.

I then took a slip of parchment, and having written upon it the name and destination of the *Mary-Jane*, together with the date of the year and month, and my own signature as her captain, enclosed the whole in a stout glass bottle, sealed it down with my own seal, and stowed it away in the boat with the rest of the stores. This bottle, and a small union-jack which I tied round my waist like a sash, were destined to be hoisted on the mountain top as soon as we succeeded in climbing up to it.

My preparations for landing were but just completed, when the mate sung out, "Breakers ahead!" I ran at once on deck. The fog had grown denser than ever. There was no land in sight, though I knew we must be within a mile of the shore. Not even the breakers were visible, but we could hear the roaring of them quite distinctly. I gave orders to lay to immediately; and, taking Taylor aside, told him that it was my intention to go ashore in the boat without a moment's delay. He flung up his hands and implored me not to venture.

"I swear to you, sir," said he, emphatically, "that's there's no land within four hundred miles of us on any side. These are coral reefs; and to take a boat amongst them in this fog is to rush on certain destruction. For Heaven's sake, sir, stay aboard, at least, till the fog clears off!"

But I only laughed, and refused to listen to him.

"There's land, mate," said I, "within a mile. I saw it with my own eyes not two hours ago; and it's a land, let me tell you, that will make the fortune of every man on board. As for the breakers, I'll risk them. If the boat is swamped, it will be no great hardship to swim to shore."

"It will be death, sir," groaned the mate.

Of this, however, I took no notice, but proceeded to give my instructions. I left the command of the *Mary-Jane* in his hands during my absence, and desired him, if the fog cleared, to anchor in the large bay off which I knew we were lying. I then added that I expected to get back to the vessel before nightfall, but ordered that an exploring party should be sent ashore to search for me, if I had not returned by the end of eight-and forty hours. To all this the honest fellow assented reluctantly enough, and bade me farewell with as sorrowful an air as if he were attending me to the scaffold.

The boat was then lowered; I took Josh Dunn for my rower, laid my own hands to the helm, and gave the word to put off. The men on board uttered a feeble cheer as we parted company, and, in less time than it takes to tell, the *Mary-Jane* was hidden from us by the fog.

"Josh," said I, as the sound of the breakers grew more and more audible, "if the boat ships water, we shall have to swim for it."

"Ay, ay, sir," replied Josh, briskly.

"Straight ahead," I continued, "lies dry land; behind us the *Mary-Jane*. But a small schooner is more easily missed in a fog, Josh, than an island as big as Malta or Madeira."

"Ay, ay, sir," replied Josh, as before.

"If you're wise," said I, "you'll strike out for the shore, as I shall. In the meanwhile, we had better fill our pockets with biscuit, for fear of accidents."

I then divided the contents of the biscuit-bag, and we stuffed our pockets as full as they could hold. By this time, the noise had so increased that we could scarcely hear each other's voices, and the white foam was already visible through the mist.

"Steady, Josh," cried I, "there are rough seas before us."

The words were scarcely past my lips when we were tossing in the midst of the surf, drenched with spray, and well-nigh deafened by the roaring of the waters. I saw directly that no boat could live in such a whirlpool—ours did not hold out for five minutes. Flung from billow to billow like a mere cockleshell, she laboured onwards for something like a hundred yards, filled, heeled over, and disappeared suddenly from beneath our feet!

Prepared for this catastrophe, I rose like a cork, glued my arms to my sides, kept my mouth and eyes shut, and suffered the waves to carry me along. Finding, however, that instead of bearing me towards the shore, they only dashed me hither and thither among the breakers.

I presently gave up all hope of floating in, and, being an excellent swimmer, struck out for land. Blinded, buffeted, breathless, now carried to the summit of a mighty wave, now buried in the very heart of a mountain of green sea, now fighting forward again, in spite of wind and spray, I struggled on with a superhuman energy that only the love of life and riches could have inspired. Suddenly, my feet touched land—lost it—touched again. I threw all my strength into one last, desperate effort, precipitated myself through the raging foam that broke like a vast barrier all along the shore, and fell, face downwards, on the pebbly beach beyond.

I lay there for some minutes, just within reach of the spray, and beyond the line of the breakers, so utterly spent and stupefied as to be scarcely conscious of the danger from which I had escaped. Recovering, however, by degrees, I rose, looked around, and found myself on a shelving belt of shingle that reached far away on either side till lost in the fog.

Beyond the shingle ran a line of low cliffs, along the summits of which, looking dim and distant in the misty air, rose the feathery tops of a far-stretching forest of cocoanut palms. Here, then, was the island, palpable, undeniable, actual! I took up a handful of loose pebbles—stamped on the shingle—ran along the beach. In all this there was no illusion. I was awake, sober, in full possession of my senses. All was as it seemed—all tried, and proved, and real.

Passing instantaneously from a state of wonder, half confused, half incredulous, to a wild, unbounded joy, I ran about for some minutes like a maniac—shouting, leaping, clapping my hands, and giving way to the most extravagant demonstrations of triumph. In the midst of this folly, the thought of Josh Dunn flashed across my mind. I grew sober in a moment. What had become of the poor fellow? I had never seen him from the instant when the boat capsized. Had he swum for the ship or the shore? Was he saved or lost? I went backwards and forwards along the beach, dreading to see his corpse washed up by every coming wave, but found no trace of him in any direction. Convinced, at length, that further search was hopeless, I gave it up, and turned my face and footsteps towards the cliffs.

It was now, as nearly as I could calculate, about ten o'clock in the day. The heat was tempered by the fog and the sea-breeze, and I promised myself to reach the mountain-top before sunset. Making straight across the beach to a point where the cliffs looked somewhat lower and more broken than elsewhere, I succeeded in climbing up the face of the rock without much difficulty, and in gaining the skirts of the palm-forest above.

Here I flung myself down in the shade, and proceeded to examine the contents of my pockets. The rum, ammunition, and other loose stores were lost with the boat; but I found that I was still in possession of all that I had stowed about my person. One by one, I brought out my tinder-box, telescope, pocket-compass, clasp-knife, and other trifles; all of which (except the compass, which was enclosed in a tight tin case) were more or less damaged by the sea-water. As for the biscuit, it was reduced to a nauseous pulp, which I flung away in disgust, preferring to trust to the cocoanuts for my subsistence.

Of these I saw hundreds clustered overhead; and, being by this time quite ready for breakfast, I climbed the tree against which I had been lying, brought down three or four nuts, and made a delicious meal. I then unscrewed and cleaned the glasses of my telescope, consulted my compass, and prepared to continue my journey. Finding by the position of the needle that the north lay to the right, following the line of shore below, I concluded that I must have swum to land at some point of the eastern extremity of the bay where I had hoped to anchor. This being the case, I had but to march due west in order to arrive at the foot of the mountain, which I proposed to myself as the object of my first day's exploration.

Due west I turned accordingly, and, compass in hand, took my way through the green shade of the forest. Here the coolness, the silence, the solitude, were perfect. I could not hear my own footsteps for the moss that carpeted the ground; and though I saw several birds of brilliant plumage, they uttered no kind of note, but sat like painted creatures on the boughs, and looked at me without any sign of fear.

Once or twice, I saw a small long-tailed monkey flitting like a squirrel through the uppermost tree-tops; but it was gone in a moment, and seemed only to make the place more wild and solitary. On every side, like graceful columns supporting the roof of some vast temple, rose hundreds of slender palm-stems, ringed with the natural record of their yearly growth; whilst here and there, through openings in the boughs, came glimpses of blue sky and shafts of golden sunlight.

When I had walked thus for about a mile and a half, finding the atmosphere growing clearer and brighter at every step, I suddenly emerged upon a grassy plain studded with trees like an English park, and traversed by a small winding river that glittered like moving silver in the open sunshine. Beyond this plain, at the distance of about another mile and a half, lay a second forest, more extensive apparently, than the first; and beyond that again, defined so clearly against the deep blue sky that I could almost have believed I might touch it with my hand, rose a steep and rugged peak, clothed half-way up with trees, and surmounted by some kind of building, with a beacon on the top.

The height of this peak I calculated at something less than two thousand feet. I recognized it at once as the same which I had sighted from the masthead of the *Mary-Jane* at sunrise that morning. I also recognized the plain and river, each lying in its proper geographical position, according to the chart.

Finding my every hope becoming corroborated as I went on, I now made no question as to the result of my undertaking, but pushed gaily forward, and amused myself by speculating about the treasure. Where should I find it? In what form? Perhaps we should have to mine for it; and in that case I made up my mind to seek all round the island, if necessary, for some safe harbour in which to anchor the *Mary-Jane*. I should then land all my crew, build a few temporary huts, and set the men hard to work at digging and smelting, till our little ship would hold not another ingot.

This done, I would sail straight for Jamaica, lodge my treasure in some colonial bank, purchase a large vessel, engage a numerous crew, and return at once for a fresh cargo of riches. What was to prevent me, indeed, from coming again and again, and carrying hence such wealth as no king or *kaiser* in all the world could boast?

Absorbed in dreams of untold grandeur and power, I felt neither fatigue nor heat, nor was conscious of the miles I traversed. There was now no fog, nor sign of fog, and the atmosphere was magically clear and bright. A soft air blew from the west. The rich grass of the savannah was thick with flowers. Even the mossy glades of the second forest were radiant with purple and scarlet berries, which I dared not taste, although they gave out a delicious odour. This forest proved more extensive than the first, and was more closely planted. All at once, just as I began to wonder how much farther it would lead me, I found myself upon the inner verge of the woods, with a strange and startling panorama before my eyes.

The forest terminated abruptly, about half a mile from the foot of the mountain, and lay round it in one vast circular sweep, a zone of living green. Between these woods and the mountain lay the domes, obelisks, and ivy-mantled walls of a noble city, all deserted and in ruins. In the midst of these ruins rose the great solitary mountain towards which I had been journeying so long. More ruins were clustered about the base of it, and for some way up the lower slopes and buttresses of its sides. Above these came trees and under-wood, and, towering higher still against the sky, a lofty peak of rock and rugged precipice.

Examining this peak by the aid of my telescope, I saw some

kind of small white edifice upon the very summit, surmounted, apparently, by a pyramidal ornament supporting a glittering beacon. This beacon was the same that I had seen scintillating in the morning light.

On reaching the inner verge of the first forest, I observed it long and earnestly. Was it made of glass, or of some reflecting metal? Did it revolve? Or were these brilliant flashes, which seemed almost as if emanating from its very substance, mere refractions of the sunlight? These were questions which I found it impossible to solve without nearer observation. I could only turn my eyes away, dazzled and half blinded, and then press forward, more eagerly than ever, on my way.

A few yards brought me to a huge mound of shattered masonry, which, as far as I could see, ran all round the ruins like a line of fortification, in some places higher, in some lower, and overgrown in every part with trees and creeping plants. Having scrambled over this first obstacle, I found myself close against the remains of a lofty circular building, with a domed roof. The portals of this building were carved with strange hieroglyphics, and the dome yet showed traces of faded gold and colours.

Finding the entrance choked with fallen rubbish, I passed on as quickly as the uneven nature of the ground would permit, and came next upon a small quadrangular edifice, built, as it seemed, of the purest white marble, and engraved all over with arabesques, and mythologic birds and beasts. Being unable to distinguish any kind of entrance, I concluded that it was a tomb.

Then came another domed temple, the roof of which was plated with what looked like sheets of solid gold; then a vast number of tombs all together, some of white, some of red, and some of green marble; then a hillocky space of undistinguishable debris; then an obelisk inlaid with various kinds of jasper and onyx; and then, partly built up against, and partly excavated in, the rocky base of the central peak, close beneath which I was now standing, a building of grander dimensions than any I had yet seen.

The front, defaced as it was, rose to a clear height of at least three hundred feet. The great entrance was supported on either side by a colossal stone image, half man, half eagle, which, though buried in rubbish half way to the knees, yet stood full fifty feet clear in sight. From the middle of the roof rose a kind of low, broad pyramid, fantastically ornamented in gold and colours.

In this temple, I felt sure I should find treasure. My only difficulty would be to force an entrance. The great portals were literally blocked up by a mass of broken sculpture that seemed to have fallen from the facade immediately above the entrance. Over and among the rubbish and debris had grown a tangled mass of under-wood, trailing plants, and huge prickly growths of the cactus tribe.

The hand of man could scarcely have barricaded the approach to the sanctuary of his gods more effectually than time and decay had done.

With only a pocket-knife, I knew that it would be hopeless to attempt to cut my way through such a jungle; I therefore left the front, and made a survey of the temple from the sides where it projected from the face of the rock. Even this was no easy matter, for the area all about it was strewn with great mounds of bush-grown rubbish, over which I had to climb as I best could, without heeding how my hands and face were wounded in the effort. All this time I could see no sign of any openings or windows, by which the building could have been lighted, or any other doorway than the great entrance on the other side.

At length it occurred to me that I might find some means of penetrating to the interior of the building by climbing that part of the mountain against which it was reared, and finding some way of dropping down upon the roof. So I went on a little farther, to a point where the ascent looked somewhat less difficult than elsewhere, and succeeded in clambering up to a ledge that commanded the roof of the temple. It lay before me like a vast terrace, with the pyramid in the midst.

Comparatively free from the rubble that strewed every foot of the ground below, it was only grass-grown and mossy, with a few young trees and bushes springing up here and there where the dust of ages had deposited sufficient nourishment for their roots. I sprang down upon it, and proceeded to reconnoitre the surface from end to end, taking good care, all the while, lest I should step on some weak spot, and be precipitated into the chasm below. It was well that I did so.

Having gone half-way along from the back towards the front, and left the pyramid a few feet behind me, I came suddenly upon what seemed like a great pit, over the edges of which the bushes clung suspended, and linked their tangled boughs together, as if they feared to fall. I drew back startled, for another step would have carried me over. I peered in—all below was dark and unfathomable. I traced the boundaries of the pit, and found that it was an oblong parallelogram, constructed evidently for the purpose of giving light to the interior. Here, then, was an unobstructed opening into the building, but one of which it would be impossible to avail myself without the aid of a ladder.

I tore away a bush that grew at the verge of the chasm, and, flinging myself down at full length, shaded my eyes with one hand, and looked into the abyss below. For some minutes I could see nothing—all seemed intensely dark, like the crater of an extinct volcano. At length, one dim outline after another became faintly visible.

I distinguished mounds of stones and rubbish, which had probably fallen from the inside of the ceiling, and the lower limbs of another colossal figure, the upper part of which I could only have seen by descending into the building. It was in vain that I leaned over till another inch would have caused me to lose my balance. It was in vain that I tested the strength of every bush and creeper all round the opening. This was all that I had gained, or could hope to gain, in return for my labour in mounting there.

I rose at last, slowly and reluctantly, and paused to think what it was best for me next to do. The city lay at my feet—the mountain rose high above my head. At the level on which I now stood, and for some distance higher up the mountain side, were scattered several more of those small buildings which I had concluded must be places of sepulture. Should I examine these, in the hope of finding some access to the probable treasures buried with the dust of their inmates? Or should I pursue my first design of ascending the peak, planting the English flag on the summit, and beginning my explorations with a thorough observation of the whole city and surrounding country? I did not waste much time in hesitation. I felt as yet almost unwearied, despite my exertions and my long night's watch; and I decided for the ascent.

It was a difficult task, and needed all the energy and perseverance of which I was master.

The first two hundred yards or so, where the slope was less abrupt, and the terraces were covered with buildings, were comparatively easy; and here I could not resist turning aside for a few minutes to examine a tomb which seemed to be more dilapidated than any which I had yet encountered.

As I drew nearer, I found that it bore every mark of having been broken open at some not very distant time. It was a simple square building of white marble, with a dome-shaped roof. This roof had evidently received several blows from some sharp instrument, and was cracked and chipped in many places. A large portion of the masonry at one end had also been removed, and piled back against the spot where it had been broken open.

An irresistible curiosity impelled me to displace the stones again, and see the inside of the chamber. The blocks were ponderous, and I dragged them out with difficulty. As I did so, one rolled down the slope, and fell crashing through the bushes, a hundred and fifty feet below, whereupon a number of gorgeous birds rose screaming into the air, and flapped heavily away.

"What a fool I am!" I said aloud, as I wiped the perspiration from my brow, and paused to rest; "what a fool I am to exhaust myself thus, when others have been before me, and have, no doubt, rifled the place of anything that might have been valuable!

Well, never mind; those others have, at all events, done the worst of the work, and I may as well see whether it was really a tomb, and whether the rest of them are likely to be worth our trouble hereafter."

So I went on again with a will, and found, to my satisfaction, that when the three or four large marble blocks were fairly rolled away, only small stones and rubble remained. These were rapidly cleared out, and in about another quarter of an hour I had succeeded in making a space large enough to enable me to creep in. Having done so, and found that I could stand upright inside the building, I waited till my eyes had grown accustomed to the darkness. Gradually, as before, one object and then another became visible, and I found that the place was beyond all doubt a sepulchre.

The inner chamber measured about six feet by ten, and was closed in by a ceiling, about three inches above my head. The walls were lined with slabs of the purest alabaster, engraved all over with strange characters. The ceiling was rudely painted with representations of birds, fishes, plants, and beings half human and half brute. Some broken urns of dark blue pottery lay scattered about the floor, and at the farther end of the chamber, on a raised shelf of plain white marble, stood an alabaster coffer, the lid of which, shattered in a dozen fragments, lay close by. It was too dark for me to see to the bottom of this coffer, but I put my hand in, and found it, as I had expected, empty. Just as I was withdrawing my fingers, however, they encountered a small object that felt like a pea. I seized and brought it to light. It was a fine pearl, somewhat discoloured by the damp, but as large as an ordinary holy-berry.

This discovery made my heart leap for joy, and rewarded me for all the trouble I had given myself to break into this tomb. The pearl itself was probably of no great value, but it was an earnest of what I might hope to find in those tombs which as yet had never been disturbed by previous adventurers. I put it inside my tinder-box for safety, and promised myself the pleasure of displaying it to the crew of the *Mary-Jane*, in proof of the booty that awaited us.

"If there is treasure in the tombs," thought I, exultingly, "what may we not hope to find in the temples and palaces?"

My head swam with visions of wealth. I pictured to myself temples with costly altars, and sacrificial vessels of gold and silver—palaces with unexplored apartments, containing thrones, and royal furniture, and weapons studded with precious stones—tombs filled with gorgeous ornaments of buried kings. Aladdin's garden of jewels was not more lavish of wonder than became now to me the ruins of this forgotten city. Then came the bewildering thought that all the riches of this vanished race were mine.

The island was unclaimed, uninhabited, unpossessed. It was mine to explore, to ransack, to plunder at my pleasure.

I crept out of the tomb and exultingly breathed the fresh air again. I looked up at the great peak, which I could hardly be said to have even begun to ascend. The sun seemed as yet scarcely to have moved in the heavens, and the glorious day was still at its zenith. I sat down for a few moments to rest, and refreshed my parching throat with a few delicious purple berries that grew upon the bushes close beside me. Then I took out my pearl and examined it again in the open daylight. The sight seemed to stimulate me—I rose, replaced it in the box, and resumed my task.

In a few minutes, I had left the last terrace and the last tomb below my feet, and had entered upon that part of the ascent where the rock grew steeper and was overgrown with thorny under-wood, through which I had to force a passage as I could. I did force it, however, though my hands and face bled for it, and my clothes were well-nigh torn to pieces on my back. Panting and exhausted, I at length fought through the belt of brushwood and emerged upon the bare rock above.

Hence the barren peak rose, steep and sheer, some twelve hundred feet above my head. At the sight of these awful precipices, my heart sunk within me. There was no visible footing for even a goat, as far as I could see; and scarce a twig, or blade of grass, for the climber to hold by. Thinking that it might possibly be less steep elsewhere, I contrived to work my way round more to the westward, and there, sure enough, found the commencement of what seemed like a gigantic staircase, hewn roughly out from the very substance of the rock.

Each step of this ascent was from three to four feet in height. Some were cut in deep shelves, on which three or four persons could have lain down at length; others were so narrow as scarcely to afford space for the foot; and many were quite broken away, which tenfold increased the difficulty of climbing. By the help, however, of perseverance, great natural agility, a cool head, and a resolute will, I sprang, clambered, and swung myself, somehow or another, from shelf to shelf of this perilous staircase, only pausing now and then to rest, and look down at the widening landscape. At length I found my feet on the last step, and the summit, which had hitherto been hidden by the impending precipices, close above my head.

That summit was artificially heightened by a kind of shelving platform, like a pyramid with the apex cut away. On the top of this platform stood a massive square building of white marble, with a large open entrance looking east; and this building served in turn as the pedestal to a gigantic idol, which sat, cross-legged and hideous, with its face to the setting sun. Sitting as it was, the image measured at least twenty feet in height, and wore on its head a large ornament of some strange and dazzling substance, which almost blinded me, at first, by its intolerable splendour.

When I had somewhat recovered the command of my sight, I went nearer and examined it. To my amazement, I found this idol to be one incrustation of precious stones from head to foot. The body was carved in jasper; the legs and arms in red onyx; the hands, feet, and face in the purest alabaster. Round its neck, inlaid upon the surface of the jasper ground, ran a rich collar of turquoises and garnets; round its waist a belt of great emeralds; round its ankles, wrists, arms, and knees, elaborate bands of amethysts and opals.

Each eye was represented by a ruby as large as a crown piece. From its ears hung enormous pendants of the purest sapphires, each the size of an ordinary hen's egg, and richly mounted in gold. Across its knees lay a golden *scimitar*, the hilt of which was carved from a single beryl; while on its head . . . . I stared—rubbed my eyes, as if to be sure I was not dreaming—scaled the walls of the building—climbed the shoulders of the idol—examined it from every side—and came at last to the conclusion that this ornament, which I had taken for a beacon far away at sea, was no other thing than one pure, gigantic, inestimable diamond, such as the world had never seen before!

It was almost spherical in shape, though slightly flattened, like the globe, at the two poles; was cut all over in the smallest facets, each of which reflected every colour of the prism; and measured just twenty-two inches and a half in circumference.

When I had in some degree recovered from the state of excitement and wonder into which this great discovery had thrown me, and was cool enough to look down at the scene below, I saw the whole island at my feet, as if drawn out upon a map.

The smaller island lay close by, to the north-west, separated from this one by a strait of about two miles in width; and all around and about, from the verge of the beach below to the farthest limit of the horizon, stretched one rippling, sparkling, brilliant expanse of sapphire sea, unclouded by a breath of vapour, and unbroken by a single sail. I looked for the *Mary-Jane*; but she was hidden by the cliffs that bounded the eastward coast in the direction where I landed.

Then I took out my glass, and made a careful observation of both islands. Scattered up and down the hills of the farther one, I saw the remains of various domed and pyramidal buildings, most of which appeared to be plated on the roofs and sides with gold, and glittered to the sun. Beneath my feet, reaching over a much greater extent of ground than I had at first supposed, lay the ruins of a vast number of palaces, temples, tombs, and triumphal arches; many of which, especially to the west side of the island, which I had not before seen, were in a high state of preservation, and richly decorated with gilding, painting, sculpture, and precious metals. In all of them, no doubt, were idols made after the pattern of this on which I was perched so unceremoniously, and treasure of every imaginable description.

However, the present and actual were all that concerned me just then; so I left the investigation of the ruins till such time as I could bring my men to help me, and set to work with my clasp-knife, to secure as much as possible of the spoil within my grasp. My first attack was made of course upon the diamond, which I dislodged with infinite difficulty, it being "set" into the head of the idol with some kind of very hard cement, that I had to grate to powder as I went on.

When, at last, I had quite freed it, I tied it up in the Union-Jack which had been all this time about my waist, and let myself down upon the east side of the building, where I had seen an opening into the basement. Looking inside this opening, I found the whole interior filled with human skulls; which somewhat startled me. I made room among them, however, for my diamond, and then climbed up again to secure a few more stones.

This time I fell upon the idol's eyes and ear-rings, which I soon transferred to my own pockets; and, having knocked out some of the great emeralds from his belt, and one or two of the largest opals from his bangles and bracelets, and taken possession of his golden *scimitar* for my own use, I made up my mind to rest from my labours for this day, and go back by the way I had come. So I tied the loose stones up with the diamond, secured the bundle to my belt, buckled the *scimitar* to my side, and prepared to descend the mountain. Loaded as I was now, however, this proved no easy matter; but I got to the bottom at last, after some perilous falls and scrambles; took the same route through the ruins, scaled the outer line of wall as before, and plunged into the forest.

The sun was low in the heavens, and I was thoroughly exhausted by the mental and physical exertions of the day. I doubted whether it would be possible for me to reach the coast before sunset; and I stood in great need of food and rest. The shade and silence of the woods—the springy moss, offering a natural carpet to my feet—the cocoanuts and fragrant berries all around, were temptations not to be resisted: so I decided to spend the night in the forest, and proceeded to choose my lodging. A snug bank at the foot of a clump of banana and cocoa trees was soon found; and here, with a pile of cocoanuts by my side, my precious bundle at my feet, and my scimitar lying ready to my hand, I lay down, ate a hearty supper, and settled myself for the night.

The sun went down upon the silence of the forest. Not a bird twittered—not a monkey chattered—not an insect hummed near. Then came darkness and the southern stars; and I fell into a profound sleep.

I awoke next morning with the dawn; breakfasted on a cocoanut, drank the milk of two or three others; and set off, compass in hand, towards the coast. As I went along, I remembered all at once, with a sense of shame at having forgotten it till then, that it was the morning of Christmas-day, which, though summer-time out here in this tropical latitude, was a wintry epoch enough far away in England among those who loved me! Christmas-day, when the quiet grey-turreted church in my native village would be garlanded with holly; when many a true heart would ache for my absence; when many a prayer for my safety would be whispered as the Litany was read; and my health be drunk loudly at the Christmas-feast!

And I—what had I been doing all this time? Lost in ambitious dreams, had I given a single thought to those who gave so many thoughts to me? Had I longed for wealth, and dared danger and death, to share my riches with them and make them happy? My heart smote me at these questions, and I brushed away two or three remorseful tears. I saw how selfish had been my aims, and soothed my conscience with a number of good resolutions, all of which were to be carried out when I returned to England with a shipload of jewels and gold.

Absorbed in these wholesome reflections, I traversed the mazes of the forest, crossed the flowery savannah, and threaded the majestic glades of the cocoa-woods that lay nearest the shore. Emerging, by-and-by, in sight of the beach and the sea, I saw, to my surprise and satisfaction, the *Mary-Jane* lying close up against the cliffs, in a little rocky cove not half a mile away. The next instant, I had scrambled down the cliff as recklessly as if it had been a mere slope of smooth lawn, and was running towards the ship at my utmost speed, only pausing every now and then to shout and wave my hat, in case any of the crew were on the lookout for me.

No answering shout, however, bade me welcome. Not a head appeared above the ship's side. Not even a pennant fluttered from the mast-head. Had the crew deserted the *Mary-Jane*, and gone up the island in search of treasure for themselves?

At this thought I ran on again, breathless, but very angry. As I drew nearer, however, my anger gave place to a kind of terrified bewilderment. I hesitated—ran forward again—stood still—trembled—could not believe the evidence of my eyes; for at every step the aspect of the *Mary-Jane* grew more strange and startling.

She was lying high and dry upon the beach—a wreck! Her shrouds were hanging in shreds; her hull was clustered thick with barnacles; her sails were white with mould; her anchor, broken and covered with rust, lay some yards off, half buried in the sand. Could she be the same little schooner that I had left only yesterday, as trim and stout as when she was turned out of the builder's yard? Was that indeed her name still visible in letters half effaced? Was I mad or dreaming? I had now come up close under her bulwarks.

I walked slowly round and round her, three or four times, quite dumb and stupefied. It was impossible that she could be the same ship. Her build, her size, her name, it is true, seemed precisely those of my little schooner; but common sense, and the testimony of my own reason, forbade me to believe that twenty-four hours could have done the work of twenty-four years. Here was a vessel that had been deserted for perhaps a quarter of a century, and had rotted where it lay. It was a coincidence—a strange, dramatic, incredible coincidence—nothing more.

I looked round for some means of clambering on board this ruin, and succeeded in finding the end of a broken chain. It hung rather short, but I caught it by a leap, and hauled myself up, hand over hand. In another moment I stood upon her deck. The timbers of that deck were all gaping and rotten, and overgrown with rank fungi.

A sea-bird had built its nest in the binnacle. Some smaller nests, deserted and gone to wreck like the ship herself, clung to the rotten shrouds. One boat yet hung in its place, by ropes that looked as if a touch would break them to tinder. The other boat—just precisely the small one which would have been missing if this were indeed all that remained of the *Mary-Jane*—was gone from its moorings.

Curiosity, and something deeper than mere curiosity, took me down the crazy stairs, and into the captain's cabin. It was a foot deep in water, and all the furniture was rotting away. The table yet held together, though spotted all over with white mould; the chairs had fallen to pieces, and were lying in the water. The paper was hanging in black rags from the walls, and the presses looked ready to fall on the head of anyone who should venture to approach them.

I looked round, amazed, upon this scene of desolation. Strange! Dilapidated and disfigured as the place was, it yet bore a weird and unaccountable resemblance to my own cabin on board the *Mary-Jane*. My wardrobe stood in that corner of the cabin, just as this did. My berth occupied the recess beside the stove, just as this did. My table stood in the same spot, under the window, just as this did. I could not comprehend it!

I turned to the table and tried the drawers, but the locks were rusty, and the wood had swollen with the damp, and it was only with the utmost difficulty that I broke away the surrounding woodwork, and wrenched them out. They were filled with mildewed parchments, bundles of letters, pens, account-books, and such other trifles. In one corner lay a mouldy looking-glass in a sliding cover. I recognised the little thing at once—recognized it undeniably, positively. It had been given to me by my mother when I was a boy, and I had never parted with it. I snatched it up with a hand that trembled as if I had the ague. I caught sight

246

of my own face reflected upon its scarred surface.

To my terror, I saw that my beard and hair were no longer chestnut brown, but almost white.

The glass fell from my grasp, and was shattered to fragments upon the wet floor. Merciful Heaven! what spell was upon me? What had happened to me? What strange calamity had befallen my ship? Where were my crew? Grey—grey and old in one short day and night? My ship a ruin, my youth a dream, myself the sport of some mysterious destiny, the like of which no man had ever known before!

I gathered the papers together from the table drawers, and staggered up on deck with them like a drunken man. There I sat down, stupefied, not knowing what to think or do. A frightful gulf seemed to lie between me and the past. Yesterday I was young—yesterday I left my ship, with hope in my heart, and brown locks upon my head; today, I am a middle-aged man—today, I find my ship rotting on a desolate beach, the hair white upon my brow, and the future all a blank! Mechanically I untied one of the packets of letters.

The outer ones were so discoloured that no writing remained visible upon them. They were mere folds of damp brown tinder, and fell to shreds as I unfolded them. Only two, which lay protected in the middle of the packet, were yet legible. I opened them. One was from my mother, the other from Bessie Robinson. I remembered so well when I read them last. It was the evening before that misty night when I met the *Adventure* with her cargo of gold and jewels. Fatal night! Accursed ship! Accursed, and thrice accursed wealth, that had tempted me from my duty, and dragged me to destruction!

I read the letters through—at least, all that was legible of them—and my tears fell fast the while. When I had read them a second time, I fell upon my knees and prayed to God to deliver me. After this, I felt somewhat calmer, and having laid the papers carefully aside, began to think what I should do to escape from my captivity.

My first thought was of my crew. The men would seem to

have abandoned the *Mary-Jane*. Everything on board, so far as I could perceive, though rotting away, was untouched. There were no signs of plunder; neither had they taken the ship's last boat, in any attempt to put to sea on their own account.

I looked down into the hold, and saw the great packing-cases lying half under water, apparently undisturbed since the hour when I left the vessel. Surely, then, the men must have landed and gone up the island. In that case, where were they? How long had they been gone? What time had gone by since we parted? Was it possible that they could be all lost—or dead? Was I absolutely and utterly alone in this unknown island: and was it my fate to live and die here, like a dog? Alas! alas! of what use were diamonds and gold to me, if this were the price at which I was to purchase them?

With these bitter reflections pressing on my mind, I roused myself by a great effort, and resolved that my first step should be to institute a thorough search for my men along the coast. In order to do this, it was necessary that I should find myself some place of temporary habitation, either in the wreck or on the shore, to which I could retire at night. Also that I should lay up a store of provisions for my daily use. I likewise determined to set up some kind of signals, here and there, along the cliffs, to guide the men to me, if they were yet wandering about the island.

My bundle of jewels, too, needed to be placed in a secure spot, lest any strange ship should find its way into the bay, and other treasure-seekers lay hands upon it. I looked round about me at the rotting timbers and the leaky cabin, and shuddered at the notion of passing a night on board the *Mary-Jane*. The ship looked as if it must be phantom haunted. It was, at all events, too remarkable an object to be a secure storehouse for my treasures, in case of the arrival of strangers.

It was the first place they would ransack. Altogether, I felt it would be safer and pleasanter to stow myself and my jewels in some cavern along the cliffs. I had seen plenty on my way, and I determined to set off at once in search of what I wanted. So I went down again into the cabin to look for some weapon to carry with me, and having found a rusty marling-spike and cut-lass still hanging where I had left them behind the door, thrust them into my belt, slung my bundle over my shoulder, let my-self down over the ship's side, and started for a walk under the cliffs.

I had not gone far before I found just the spot I wanted. It was a deep cavern, about three feet above the level of the beach, the mouth of which was almost hidden by an angle of rock, and was quite invisible from some little distance. The inside of the cave was smooth, and carpeted with soft white sand. The walls were dry, and tapestried here and there with velvety lichens. In short, it was precisely such a retreat as best accorded with my present purposes. I took possession of it at once, by stow-ing away my bundle of jewels on a sort of natural shelf at the remotest end of the cave. I then traced a great cross in the sand before the entrance, that I might find my lodging again without difficulty, and went out to seek something in the shape of food and firewood.

The first easy path up the face of the cliffs brought me to the outskirts of the palm forests. I climbed the nearest tree, and flung down about twenty nuts. They were by no means such fine nuts as those farther in amid the woods; but I had taken a kind of superstitious horror of the interior of the island, and had no mind now to venture one step farther than was necessary. I then carried my nuts to the edge of the cliff, and rolled them over. By these means, I saved myself the labour of carrying them down, and had only to pick them up from the beach, and store them in the cave, close under the shelf where I had hidden my jewels. By this time, in spite of my trouble, I was very hungry; but the sun was bending westward, and I was anxious to make another excursion to the ship before nightfall; so I promised myself that I would dine and sup together by-and-by, and so proceeded once more in the direction of the *Mary-Jane*.

What I wanted now was, if it were possible to find them, a couple of blankets, a hatchet to break up my cocoanuts, a bottle of some kind of spirits, and a piece of tarpaulin to hang at night before the entrance to my cavern. I hauled myself up again by the cable-chain, and went down into the cabin. I found my bed a mere shelf full of rotten rags. If I hoped to find blankets anywhere, it must be among the ship's stores, in some place more protected from the damp.

I forced open the locker in which I used to keep spirits. Here I was fortunate enough to discover two unopened cases of fine French brandy, apparently quite unspoiled. These I at once carried upon deck, and then let myself down into the hold. There I found several pieces of tolerably sound tarpaulin, and some packing-cases on the top, which seemed comparatively dry. One of these, which I knew, by the marks yet visible on the cover, ought to contain many valuable necessaries, I prized open with my marline-spike, and found filled with blankets, rugs, and other woollen goods.

They were damp, and spotted with mildew, but not rotten. I made two great bundles of the best that I could find, and laid them beside the spirit-cases, on the deck. Searching still farther, I came upon a box of carpenter's tools, an old horn-lantern with about an inch of candle left in it, a small chopper, and a bag of rusty nails. There were plenty of barrels of ship's biscuits, pork, gunpowder, and flour in sight; but as they were all more or less immersed in water, I. knew it would be mere waste of time to inspect their contents. Besides, the sun was now declining fast, and I was anxious to carry all that I could to my cavern before the sudden tropical night should come.

I then made three loads of my blankets, tarpaulins, spirit-cases, tools, and so forth; lowered them over the ship's side one by one; and in three journeys conveyed them all to my cave before sunset. I had, even then, time to transport thither some large pieces of timber, the fragments probably of former wrecks, which were lying strewn about the beach. With these I made a good fire, which lighted up the inside of my dwelling, and enabled me to make myself quite comfortable for the night. To spread a warm bed of rugs and blankets, to nail up a large tarpaulin before my door, and to make an excellent supper of cocoa-nuts, cocoa-milk, and a little brandy, were the occupations of my evening. As my fire began to burn low, I wrapped myself in my blankets, murmured a short prayer for safety and forgiveness, and fell sound asleep.

I woke next morning with the sunrise, and started directly after breakfast upon my first expedition in search of the crew of the *Mary-Jane*, All that day I travelled along the margin of the bay in a north-west and westerly direction, stopping every now and then to pile up a little cairn of loose stones that might serve as a signal. I returned to my cavern at dusk, having seen no sign of human footsteps or human habitation in any direction, and having walked, first and last, a good twenty miles at the least. This time I brought home some more firewood, and about half a bushel of mussels, which I had found clustered on the low rocks by the sea. I ate the mussels uncooked for my supper, and, having a famous appetite, thought them the most delicious dish I had ever tasted.

The next day, and the next again, and for many days after that, I persevered in my search, trying first north, and then east and south, and finding no trace of my crew. Wherever I went, I raised cairns along the beach and on the edges of the cliffs; and once or twice even laboured to carry up a piece of broken mast and a scrap of ragged canvas to some little headland, and so raised a kind of humble flagstaff where I thought it might be seen conspicuously from either sea or shore. I often stopped in these voluntary tasks, to sit down and shed a torrent of bitter tears.

At night I amused myself by shaping my cocoa shells into drinking-cups and basins, and fitting up my cave with shelves and other little conveniences. I contrived, too, to vary my diet with cockles, mussels, and occasionally a young turtle, when I was so fortunate as to find one on the beach. These I ate sometimes boiled and sometimes roasted; and as I grew very weary of so much cocoa-milk, I brought a leathern bucket from the wreck, and used to fetch myself fresh water from a spring about half a mile from home.

I likewise searched out a kettle, a couple of hatchets, a pea-jacket but little the worse for damp, two or three pair of shoes, a chest containing some uninjured stores of sugar and spices, some more cases of wine and spirits, and various other articles, all of which contributed essentially to my comfort. I also found one or two Bibles; but these were so much spoiled that no more than twenty or thirty leaves were legible in each.

As these were not, however, the same in each book, I found I had between seventy and eighty readable leaves—in all, about one hundred and fifty-five pages printed in double columns; the perusal and possession of which proved a great blessing to me in my lonely situation, and gave me strength, many and many a time, to bear my trial with fortitude, when I should otherwise have sunk into utter despair.

Thus a long time passed. I took no regular account of the weeks; but perhaps as many as fourteen or fifteen may have gone by in this manner. I devoted at first every day, then about four days, and at last not more than one or two days in each week, to the prosecution of my apparently hopeless search.

At last I found that I had explored all that part of the island which lay immediately round about my cavern for a distance of at least twelve miles in all directions. I could now do no more, unless I shifted the centre of my observations, or undertook a regular tour of the coast. After some deliberation I decided upon the latter course, and, having furnished myself with a flask of brandy, a blanket tightly strapped up like a soldier's knapsack, a hatchet, cutlass, compass, telescope, tinderbox, and staff, started one morning upon my journey.

It was now, as nearly as I could judge, about the first week in April, and the weather was enchantingly beautiful. My route, for the first day, lay along the same path that I had already trodden once or twice, up the north side of the great bay. When I wanted food, I gathered some cocoanuts from the adjacent woods, and at night I slept in a cavern very much like the one which I now called my "home." The next day I pursued the same direction, and provided myself with food and shelter after the same fashion. On the third day, I came to a point where the cliffs receded from the seaboard, and a broad tract of grassland came down almost to the verge of the beach.

I was now obliged to have recourse to shell-fish and such berries as I could find, for my daily food. This made me somewhat anxious for the future; for I foresaw that, if the palm forests were to fail me for many days together, I should be obliged to give up my design, and return home with my doubts yet unresolved. However, I made up my mind to persevere as long as possible; and, having walked till nearly nightfall, supped on such fare as I could pick up from the beach and the bushes, and slept in the open air, with only the deep grass for my couch and the stars for my canopy.

On the fourth day I pursued the same course, with the savannah still bordering the shore, and on the fifth had the satisfaction of finding the palms, and some other trees, again fringing the beach; sometimes in clumps or plantations; sometimes scattered here and there on rising knolls, like the trees in a well-arranged English park. Among these, to my great joy and refreshment, I found several fine bread-trees and some wild sugar-canes; and, towards afternoon, came upon a delicious spring of fresh water, which bubbled up from the midst of a natural reservoir, and flowed away among the deep grasses in a little channel almost hidden by flowers and wild plants.

In this charming spot I determined to stay for the remainder of the day; for I was weary, and in need of repose. So I lay down beside the spring; feasted on bread fruit and sugar-cane juice; bathed my face and hands in the cool spring; and enjoyed some hours of delicious rest. At nightfall I crept into a little nook amid a clump of spreading trees, and slept profoundly.

The next morning I awoke, as usual, with the sunrise. I had been thinking the evening before that this would be the pleasantest spot in which to pitch my tent for the summer, should nothing more hopeful turn up; and I now resolved, before resuming my journey, to reconnoitre the little oasis, and fix upon some site where I might command a good view of the sea, and yet enjoy the benefits of the trees and the grass. A green hill, surmounted by a crown of palms and other trees, and lying about half a mile from the water-line, looked as if it might exactly present the advantages I sought. I went up to it, in the clear, cool air of the early morning, brushing the dew from the grass as I strode along, and feeling quite reinvigorated by my night's rest.

As I mounted the little hill, a new prospect began opening before me, and I saw, what I had not suspected while on the level below, that the savannah was surrounded on three sides by the sea, and that by crossing it in a direct line I should save some miles of coasting. A little reflection led me, consequently, to the conclusion that I had now reached the most northerly part of the island, according to the chart, and that from the summit of the hill I should probably come in sight of the smaller island.

Absorbed In these thoughts, I reached the top almost before I was aware of it, and was proceeding to make my way through the trees in search of the view on the other side, when something close by, reared against the stems of three palms which grew near together in a little angle, attracted my attention. I advanced—hesitated—rushed forward. My eyes had not deceived me—it was a hut!

At first, I was so agitated that I had to lean against a tree for support. When I had somewhat recovered my composure, and came to examine the outside of the hut with attention, I saw that it was utterly dilapidated, and bore every mark of having been deserted for a long time. The sides were made of wattled twigs and clay, and the roof, which had partly fallen in, of canes, palm-leaves, and interwoven branches.

On the turf outside were the remains of a blackened circle, as if large fires had been kindled there; and in the midst of the circle lay some smooth stones, which might have once served the purposes of an oven. Close by, at the foot of a large bread-tree, about half-way between the hut and the spot where I was standing, rose two grassy mounds of about six feet each in length and two feet in width—just such mounds as may be seen in the corner appropriated to the poor in any English country church-yard.

At the sight of these graves—for graves I felt they were—my heart sank within me. I went up to the low arch which served as an entrance to the hut. It was partially closed from the inside by a couple of rotten planks. I removed the planks with a trembling hand, and looked within. All was dark and damp, save where a portion of the roof had fallen in, and hidden the ground beneath. Feverishly, desperately, I began to tear away the wattled walls. I felt that I must penetrate the secret of the place. I knew, as surely as if the hand of God himself had written it on the earth and sky, that my poor sailors had here found their last resting-places.

Oh, heavens! how shall I describe the scene that met my eyes when I had torn the frail fence from its foundations, and lifted away the roof, that had fallen as if on purpose to hide that melancholy scene from the very stars and sun! A bed of dead leaves and mosses—a human skeleton yet clothed in a few blackened rags—three rusty muskets—a few tin cups, and knives, and such poor necessaries, all thickly coated with red dust—some cocoa shells—a couple of hatchets—a bottle corked and tied over at the mouth, as sailors prepare records for committal to the sea—these were the relics that I found, and the sight of them smote me with a terrible, unutterable conviction of misfortune.

I seized the bottle, staggered away to a distance of some yards from the fatal spot, broke it against the bark of the nearest tree, and found, as I had expected, a written paper inside. For some minutes I had not courage to read it. When, at last, my eyes were less dim, and my hand steadier, I deciphered the following words:—

August 30th 1761.

I, Aaron Taylor, mate of the schooner *Mary-Jane*, write these words:—Our captain, William Barlow, left the vessel in the small boat, accompanied by Joshua Dunn, seaman, two hours after daybreak on the 24th of December last, a.d. 1760. The weather was foggy, and the ship lay to within hearing of breakers. The captain left me in charge of the vessel, with directions to anchor in the bay off which we then lay, and left orders that we were to send an exploring party ashore in case he did not return by the evening of the fourth day. In the course of the 25th (Christmas Day), the fog cleared off, and we found ourselves lying just off the curve of the bay, as our captain had stated.

We then anchored according to instructions. The four days went by, and neither the captain nor Joshua Dunn returned. Neither did we see any signs of the boat along that part of the shore against which we lay at anchor. The two seamen who yet remained on board were then despatched by me in the long-boat, to search along the east coast of the island; but they returned at the end of three days without having seen any traces of the captain, the sailor, or the small boat.

One of these men, named James Grey, and myself, started again at the end of a few more days of waiting. I left John Cartwright in charge of the vessel, with orders to keep a strict lookout along shore for the captain or Dunn. We landed, hauled our boat up high and dry, and made for the interior of the country, which consisted apparently of nothing but dense forest, in which we wandered for five days without success. Returning in a south-east direction from the northward part of the forest-land, James Grey fell ill with fever, and was unable to get back so far as the boat. I left him on a high spot of ground sheltered by trees, made him a bed of leaves and moss, and went back to the ship for help.

When I reached the *Mary-Jane*, I found John Cartwright also sick with fever, though less ill than Grey. He was able to help in bringing along blankets and other necessaries, and he and I built up this hut together, and laid our dying messmate in it. On the second day from this, Cartwright, who had over-exerted himself while he was already ailing of the same disease, became so much worse that he, too, was unable to get back to the ship, or to do anything but lie down in the hut beside Grey.

I did all I could for them, and tried to do my duty by the ship as well as by the men. I went down to the shore every evening to look after the schooner, and went on board every morning; and I nursed the poor fellows as well as I could, by keeping up fires just outside the hut, and supplying them with warm food, warm drinks, and well aired blankets. It was not for me to save them, however. They both died before a fortnight was gone by—James Grey first, and Cartwright a few hours after.

I buried them both close against the hut, and returned to the ship, not knowing what better to do, but having very little hope left of ever seeing Captain Barlow or Joshua Dunn in this world again. I was now quite alone, and, as I believed, the last survivor of all the crew. I felt it my duty to remain by the ship, and at anchor in the same spot, till every chance of the captain's return should have gone by. I made up my mind, in short, to stay till the 25th of March, namely, three months from the time when Captain Barlow left the vessel; and then to navigate her into the nearest port. Long before that, however, I began to feel myself ailing. I doctored myself from the captain's medicine-chest; but the drugs only seemed to make me worse instead of better.

I was not taken, however, exactly as Grey and Cartwright were. They fell ill and broke down suddenly—I ailed, and lingered, got better and worse, and dragged on a weary, sickly life from week to week, and from month to month, till not only the three months had gone, but three more to the back of them; and yet I had no strength or power to stir from the spot. I was so weak that I could not have weighed anchor to save my life; and so thin that I could count every bone under my skin.

At length, on the night of the 18th of June, there came a tremendous hurricane, which tore the schooner from her moorings, and drove her upon the shore, high and dry— about a hundred yards above the usual high-water mark.

I thought she would have been dashed to pieces, and was almost glad to think I should now be rid of my miserable life, and die in the sea at last. But it was God's will that I should not end so.

The ship was stranded, and I with her. I now saw my fate before me. I was doomed, anyhow, to live or die on the island. If I recovered, I could never get the *Mary-Jane* to sea again, but must spend all my years alone on the cursed island. This was my bitterest grief. I think it has broken my heart.

Since I have been cast ashore, I have grown more and more sickly, and now that I feel I have not many more days to live, I write this narrative of all that has happened since Captain Barlow left the ship, in the hope that it may someday fall into the hands of some Christian seaman who will communicate its contents to my mother and sisters at Bristol. I have been living up at the hut of late, since the heat set in; and have written this in sight of my mess-mates' graves.

When I have sealed it in a bottle, I shall try to carry it down to the shore, and either leave it on board the *Mary-Jane*, or trust it to the waves. I should like my mother to have my gold watch, and I give my dog Peter, whom I left at home, to my cousin Ellen. If any kind Christian finds this paper, I pray him to bury my bones. God forgive me all my sins. Amen.

Aaron Taylor.

August 30th, 1761.

I will not try to describe what I felt on reading this simple and straightforward narrative; or with what bitter remorse and helpless wonder I looked back upon the evil my obstinacy had wrought. But for me, and my insatiate thirst for wealth, these men would now have been living and happy. I felt as if I had been their murderer, and raved and wept miserably as I dug a third trench, and laid in it the remains of my brave and honest mate.

Besides all this, there was a heavy mystery hanging upon me, which I tried to fathom, and could not comprehend. Taylor's narrative was dated just eight months after I left the ship, and to me it seemed that scarcely three had gone by. Nor was that all. His body had had time to decay to a mere skeleton—the ship had had time to become a mere wreck—my own head had had time to grow grey! What had happened to me? I asked myself that weary question again, and again, and again, till my head and my heart ached, and I could only kneel down and pray to God that my wits were not taken from me.

I found the watch with difficulty, and, taking it and the paper with me, went back, sadly and wearily, to my cavern by the sea. I had now no hope or object left but to escape from the island if I could, and this thought haunted me all the way home, and possessed me day and night. For more than a week I deliberated as to what means were best for my purpose, and hesitated whether to build me a raft of the ship's timbers, or try to fit the long-boat for sea. I decided at last upon the latter. I spent many weeks in piecing, calking and trimming her to the best of my ability, and thought myself quite a skilful ship's carpenter when I had fitted her with a mast, and a sail, and a new rudder, and got her ready for the voyage.

This done, I hauled her down, with infinite labour and difficulty, as far as the tide mark on the beach, ballasted her with provisions and fresh water, shoved her off at high tide, and put to sea. So eager was I to escape, that I had all but forgotten my bundle of jewels, and had to run for them at the last moment, at the risk of seeing my boat floated off before I could get back. As to venturing once again to the city of treasures, it had never crossed my mind for an instant since the morning when I came down through the palm-forests and found the *Mary-Jane* a ruin on the beach.

Nothing would now have induced me to return there. I believed the place to be accursed, and could not think of it without a shudder. As for the captain of the *Adventure*, I believed him to be the Evil One in person, and his store of gold an infernal bait to lure men to destruction! I believed it then, and I believe it now, solemnly.

The rest of my story may be told very briefly. After running before the wind for eleven days and nights, in a north-easterly direction, I was picked up by a Plymouth merchantman, about forty-five miles west of Marignana. The captain and crew treated me with kindness, but evidently looked upon me as a harmless madman.

No one believed my story. When I described the islands, they laughed; when I opened my store of jewels, they shook their heads, and gravely assured me that they were only lumps of spar and sandstone; when I described the condition of my ship, and related the misfortunes of my crew, they told me the schooner *Mary-Jane* had been lost at sea twenty years ago, with every hand on board.

Unfortunately, I found that I had left my mate's narrative behind me in the cavern, or perhaps my story would have found more credit. When I swore that to me it seemed less than six months since I had put off in the small boat with Joshua Dunn, and was capsized among the breakers, they brought the ship's log to prove that instead of its being the 20th of December a.d. 1760, when I came back to the beach, and saw the *Mary-Jane* lying high and dry between the rocks, it must have been nearer the 25th of December, 1780, the twentieth Christmas, namely, of the glorious and happy reign of our most gracious sovereign. King George the Third.

Was this true? I know not. Everyone says so; but I cannot bring myself to believe that twenty years could have passed over my head like one long summer day. Yet the world is strangely changed, and I with it, and the mystery is still unexplained as ever to my bewildered brain.

I went back to England with the merchantman, and to my native place among the Mendip Hills. My mother had been dead twelve years. Bessie Robinson was married, and the mother of four children. My youngest brother was gone to America; and my old friends had all forgotten me. I came among them like a ghost, and for a long time they could hardly believe that I was indeed the same William Barlow who had sailed away in the *Mary-Jane*, young and full of hope twenty years before.

Since my return home, I have tried to sell my jewels again and again; but in vain. No merchant will buy them. I have sent charts of the Treasure Isles over and over again to the Board of Admiralty, but receive no replies to my letters. My dream of wealth has faded year by year, with my strength and my hopes. I am poor, and I am declining into old age. Everyone is kind to me, but their kindness is mixed with pity; and I feel strange and bewildered at times, not knowing what to think of the past, and seeing nothing to live for in the future. Kind people who read this true statement, pray for me.

    (Signed)   William Barlow,

Discoverer of the Treasure Isles, and formerly Captain of the Schooner *Mary-Jane*.

The Eleventh of March

(From a Pocket-book of Forty Years ago)

An old pocket-book lies before me, bound in scarlet morocco, and fastened with a silver clasp. The leather is mildewed; the
silver tarnished; the paper yellow; the ink faded. It has been bidden away at the back of an antique oaken bureau since the last
day of the year during which I had it in use; and that was forty
years ago. Aye, here is a page turned down —turned down at
Wednesday, March the eleventh, eighteen hundred and twenty-
six. The entry against that date is brief and obscure enough.

Wednesday, March 11th.—Walked from Frascati to Palazzuola,
the ancient site of Alba Longa, on the Alban lake. Lodged at
Franciscan convent. Brother Geronimo. Dare one rely on the
testimony of the senses? *Dieu sait tout*

Brief as it is, however, that memorandum fires a train of long-
dormant memories, and brings back with painful vividness all
the circumstances to which it bears reference. I will endeavour
to relate them as calmly and succinctly as possible.

I started on foot from Frascati immediately after breakfast,
and rested midway in the shade of a wooded ravine between
Marino and the heights of Alba Longa. I seem to remember
every trivial incident of that morning walk. I remember how
the last year's leaves crackled under my feet, and how the green
lizards darted to and fro in the sunlight. I fancy I still hear the
slow drip of the waters that trickled down the cavernous rocks
on either hand. I fancy I still smell the heavy perfume of the

262

violets among the ferns.

It was not yet noon when I emerged upon the upper ridge, and took the path that leads to Monte Cavo. The woodcutters were busy among the chestnut slopes of Palazzuola. They paused in their work, and stared at me sullenly as I passed by. Presently a little turn in the footway brought the whole lake of Albano before my eyes. Blue, silent, solitary, set round with overhanging woods, it lay in the sunshine, four hundred feet below, like a sapphire at the bottom of a malachite vase.

Now and then, a soft breath from the west ruffled the placid mirror, and blurred the pictured landscape on its surface. Now and then, a file of mules, passing unseen among the forest-paths, sent a faint sound of tinkling bells across the lake. I sat down in the shade of a clump of cork-trees, and contemplated the panorama. To my left, on a precipitous platform at the verge of the basin, with Monte Cavo towering up behind, stretched the long white facade of the Convent of Palazzuola; on the opposite height, standing clear against the sky, rose the domes and pines of Castel Gondolfo; to the far right, in the blinding sunshine of the Campagna, lay Rome and the Etruscan hills.

In this spot I established myself for the day's sketching. Of so vast a scene, I could, necessarily, only select a portion. I chose the Convent, with its background of mountain, and its foreground of precipice and lake; and proceeded patiently to work out, first the leading features, and next the minuter details of the subject. Thus occupied (with an occasional pause to watch the passing of a cloud-shadow, or listen to the chiming of a distant chapel-bell), I lingered on, hour after hour, till the sun hung low in the west, and the woodcutters were all gone to their homes.

I was now at least three miles from either the town of Albano or the village of Castel Gondolfo, and was, moreover, a stranger to the neighbourhood. I looked at my watch. There remained but one half hour of good daylight, and it was important that I should find my way before the dusk closed in. I rose reluctantly, and, promising myself to return to the same spot on the morrow, packed away my sketch, and prepared for the road.

At this moment, I saw a monk standing in an attitude of meditation upon a little knoll of rising ground some fifty yards ahead. His back was turned towards me; his cowl was up, his arms were folded across his breast. Neither the splendour of the heavens, nor the tender beauty of the earth, was anything to him. He seemed unconscious even of the sunset.

I hurried forward, eager to inquire my nearest path along the woods that skirt the lake; and my shadow lengthened out fantastically before me as I ran. The monk turned abruptly. His cowl fell. He looked at me. face to face. There were not more than eighteen yards between us. I saw him as plainly as I now see the page on which I write. Our eyes met . . . My God ! shall I ever forget those eyes?

He was still young, still handsome, but so lividly pale, so emaciated, so worn with passion, and penance, and remorse, that I stopped involuntarily, like one who finds himself on the brink of a chasm. We stood thus for a few seconds—both silent, both motionless. I could not have uttered a syllable, had my life depended on it. Then, as abruptly as he had turned towards me, he turned away, and disappeared among the trees. I remained for some minutes gazing after him. My heart throbbed painfully. I shuddered, I knew not why. The very air seemed to have grown thick and oppressive; the very sunset, so golden a moment since, had turned suddenly to blood.

I went on my way, disturbed and thoughtful. The livid face and lurid eyes of the monk haunted me. I dreaded every turn of the path, lest I should again encounter them. I started when a twig fell, or a dead leaf fluttered down beside me. I was almost ashamed of the sense of relief with which I heard the sound of voices some few yards in advance, and, emerging upon an open space close against the convent, saw some half dozen friars strolling to and fro in the sun- set. I inquired my way to Albano, and learned that I was still more than two miles distant.

"It will be quite dark before the *Signore* arrives," said one, courteously. "The *Signore* would do well to accept a cell at Palazzuola for the night."

I remembered the monk, and hesitated.

"There is no moon now," suggested another; "and the paths are unsafe for those who do not know them."

While I was yet undecided, a bell rang, and three or four of the loiterers went in.

"It is our supper hour," said the first speaker. "The *Signore* will at least condescend to share our simple fare; and afterwards, if he still decides to sleep at Albano, one of our younger brethren shall accompany him as far as the Cappucini, at the entrance to the town."

I accepted this proposition gratefully, followed my entertainers through the convent gates, and was ushered into a stone hall, furnished with a long dining table, a pulpit, a clock, a double row of deal benches, and an indifferent copy of the Last Supper of Leonardo da Vinci. The Superior advanced to welcome me.

"You have come among us, *Signore*," he said, "on an evening when our table is but poorly provided. Although this is not one of the appointed fast-days of the Church, we have been abstaining at Palazzuola in memory of certain circumstances connected with our own brotherhood. I hope, however, that our larder may be found to contain something better suited to a traveller's appetite than the fare you now see before you."

Saying thus, he placed me at his right hand at the upper end of the board, and there stood till the monks were all in their places. He then repeated a Latin grace; after which each brother took his seat and began. They were twenty-three in number, twelve on one side, and eleven on the other; but I observed that a place was left vacant near the foot of the table, as if the twelfth man were yet to come. The twelfth, I felt sure, was he whom I had encountered on the way. Once possessed with this conviction, I could not keep from watching the door. Strange ! I so dreaded and loathed his coming, that I almost felt as if his presence would be less intolerable than the suspense in which I awaited it!

In the meantime the monks ate in silence; and even the Superior, whose language and address were those of a well-informed man, seemed constrained and thoughtful. Their supper was of the most frugal description, and consisted of only bread, salad, grapes, and macaroni. Mine was before long reinforced with a broiled pigeon and a flask of excellent Orvieto. I enjoyed my fare, however, as little as they seemed to enjoy theirs. Fasting as I was, I had no appetite. Weary as I was, I only longed to push my plate aside, and resume my journey.

"The *Signore* will not think of going farther tonight," said the Superior, after an interval of prolonged silence.

I muttered something about being expected at Albano.

"Nay, but it is already dusk, and the sky hath clouded over suddenly within the last fifteen minutes," urged he. "I fear much that we have a storm approaching. What sayest thou, Brother Antonio?"

"It will be a wild night," replied the brother with whom I had first spoken.

"Ay, a wild night," repeated an old monk, lower down the table; "like this night last year—like this night two years ago!"

The Superior struck the table angrily with his open hand.

"Silence!" he exclaimed authoritatively. "Silence there; and let Brother Anselmo bring lights."

It was now so dark that I could scarcely distinguish the features of the last speaker, or those of the monk who rose and left the room. Again the profoundest silence fell upon all present. I could hear the footsteps of Brother Anselmo echo down the passage, till they died away; and I remember listening vaguely to the ticking of the clock at the farther end the refectory, and comparing it in my own mind to the horrible beating of an iron heart. Just at that moment a sharp gust of wind moaned past the windows, bearing with it a prolonged reverberation of distant thunder.

"Our storms up here in the mountain are severe and sudden," said the Prior, resuming our conversation at the point where it had been interrupted; "and even the waters of yonder placid lake are sometimes so tempestuous that no boat dare venture across. I fear, *Signore*, that you will find it impossible to proceed

266

to Albano."

"Should the tempest come up, reverend father," I replied, "I will undoubtedly accept your hospitality, and be grateful for it; but if . . . ."

I broke off abruptly. The words failed on my lips, and I pushed away the flask from which I was about to fill my glass.

Brother Anselmo had brought in the lamps, and there, in the twelfth seat at the opposite side of the table, sat the monk. I had not seen him take his place. I had not heard him enter. Yet there he sat, pale and death-like, with his burning eyes fixed full upon me! No one noticed him. No one spoke to him. No one helped him to the dishes on the table. He neither ate, nor drank, nor held companionship with any of his fellows; but sat among them like an excommunicated wretch, whose penance was silence and fasting.

"You do not eat, *Signore*," said the prior.

"I—I thank you, reverend father," I faltered. "I have dined."

"I fear, indifferently. Would you like some other wine ? Our cellar is not so ill-furnished as our larder."

I declined by a gesture.

"Then we will retire to my room, and take coffee."

And the Superior rose, repeated a brief Latin thanksgiving, and ushered me into a small well-lighted parlour, opening off a passage at the upper end of the hall, where there were some half-dozen shelves of books, a couple of easy chairs, a bright wood fire, and a little table laden with coffee and cakes. We had scarcely seated ourselves when a tremendous peal of thunder seemed to break immediately over the convent, and was followed by a cataract of rain.

"The *Signore* is safer here than on the paths between Palazzuola and Albano," said the Superior, sipping his coffee.

"I am, indeed," I replied. "Do I understand that you had a storm here on the same night last year, and the year before?"

The Prior's face darkened.

"I cannot deny the coincidence," he said, reluctantly; "but it is a mere coincidence, after all. The—the fact is that a very grievous and terrible catastrophe happened to our community on this day two years ago; and the brethren believe that heaven sends the tempest in memory of that event. Monks, *Signore*, are superstitious; and if we consider their isolated lives, it is not surprising that they should be so."

I bowed assent. The Prior was evidently a man of the world.

"Now, with regard to Palazzuola," continued he, disregarding the storm, and chatting on quite leisurely, "here are twenty-three brethren, most of them natives of the small towns among the mountains hereabout; and of that twenty-three, not ten have even been so far as Rome in their lives."

"Twenty-three," I repeated. "Twenty-four, surely, *mio padre!*"

"I did not include myself," said the Prior, stiffly.

"Neither did I include you," I replied; "but I counted twenty-four of the order at table just now."

The Prior shook his head.

"No, no, *Signore*," said he. "Twenty-three only."

"But I am positive," said I.

"And so am I," rejoined he, politely but firmly.

I paused. I was certain. I could not be mistaken.

"Nay, *mio padre*," I said; "they were twenty-three at first; but the brother who came in afterwards made the twenty-fourth."

"Afterwards!" echoed the Prior. "I am not aware that any brother came in afterwards."

"A sickly, haggard-looking monk," pursued I, "with singularly bright eyes—eyes which, I confess, produced on me a very unpleasant impression. He came in just before the lights were brought."

The Prior moved uneasily in his chair, and poured out another cup of coffee.

"Where did you say he sat, *Signore*?" said he.

"In the vacant seat at the lower end of the table, on the opposite side to myself."

The Prior set down his coffee untasted, and rose in great agitation.

"For God's sake, Signore," stammered he, "be careful what

you say! Did you—did you see this? Is this true?"

"True" I repeated, trembling I knew not why, and turning cold from head to foot. "As true as that I live and breathe! Why do you ask?"

"Sickly and haggard-looking, with singularly bright eyes," said the Prior, looking very pale himself. "Had it—had it the appearance of a young man?"

"Of a young man worn with suffering and remorse," I replied. "But—but it was not the first time, *mio padre*! I saw him before—this afternoon—down near the chestnut-woods, on a knoll of rising ground, overlooking the lake. He was standing with his back to the sunset."

The Prior fell on his knees before a little carved crucifix that hung beside the fireplace.

"*Requiem æternam dona eis, Domine; et lux perpetua luceat eis,*" said he, brokenly.

The rest of his prayer was inaudible, and he remained for some minutes with his face buried in his hands.

"I implore you to tell me the meaning of this," I said, when he at length rose, and sank, still pale and agitated, into his chair.

"I will tell what I may, *Signore*," he replied; "but I must not tell you all. It is a secret that belongs to our community, and none of us are at liberty to repeat it. Two years ago, one of our brethren was detected in the commission of a great crime. He had suffered, struggled against it, and at last, urged by a terrible opportunity, committed it. His life paid for the offence. One who was deeply wronged by the deed, met him as he was flying from the spot, and slew him as he fled. *Signore*, the name of that monk was the Fra Geronimo. We buried him where he fell, on a knoll of rising ground close against the chestnut woods that border the path to Marino. We had no right to lay his remains in consecrated ground; but we fast, and say masses for his soul, on each anniversary of that fearful day."

The Prior paused and wiped his brow.

"But, *mio padre* . . ." I began.

"This day last year," interrupted he, "one of the woodcutters yonder took a solemn oath that he met the Fra Geronimo on that very knoll at sunset. Our brethren believed the man—but I, heaven forgive me! was incredulous. Now, however . . ."

"Then—then you believe," faltered I, "you believe that I have seen . . ."

"Brother Geronimo," said the Prior, solemnly.

And I believe it too. I am told, perhaps, that it was an illusion of the senses. Granted; but is not such an illusion, in itself, a phenomenon as appalling as the veriest legend that superstition evokes from the world beyond the grave ? How shall we explain the nature of the impression? Whence comes it ? By what material agency is it impressed upon the brain?

These are questions leading to abysses of speculation before which the sceptic and the philosopher alike recoil—questions which I am unable to answer. I only know that these things came within the narrow radius of my own experience; that I saw them with my own eyes; and that they happened just forty years ago, on the eleventh of March, *anno Domini* eighteen hundred and twenty-six.

The Four-Fifteen Express
Aka: The Engineer's Story

The events which I am about to relate took place between nine and ten years ago. Sebastopol had fallen in the early spring, the peace of Paris had been concluded since March, our commercial relations with the Russian empire were but recently renewed; and I, returning home after my first northward journey since the war, was well pleased with the prospect of spending the month of December under the hospitable and thoroughly English roof of my excellent friend, Jonathan Jelf, Esq., of Dumbleton Manor, Clayborough, East Anglia.

Travelling in the interests of the well-known firm in which it is my lot to be a junior partner, I had been called upon to visit not only the capitals of Russia and Poland, but had found it also necessary to pass some weeks among the trading ports of the Baltic; whence it came that the year was already far spent before I again set foot on English soil, and that, instead of shooting pheasants with him, as I had hoped, in October, I came to be my friend's guest during the more genial Christmas-tide.

My voyage over, and a few days given up to business in Liverpool and London, I hastened down to Clayborough with all the delight of a schoolboy whose holidays are at hand. My way lay by the Great East Anglian line as far as Clayborough station, where I was to be met by one of the Dumbleton carriages and conveyed across the remaining nine miles of country. It was a foggy afternoon, singularly warm for the 4th of December, and I had arranged to leave London by the 4.15 express.

The early darkness of winter had already closed in; the lamps were lighted in the carriages; a clinging damp dimmed the windows, adhered to the door-handles, and pervaded all the atmosphere; while the gas-jets at the neighbouring book-stand diffused a luminous haze that only served to make the gloom of the terminus more visible. Having arrived some seven minutes before the starting of the train, and, by the connivance of the guard, taken sole possession of an empty compartment, I lighted my travelling-lamp, made myself particularly snug, and settled down to the undisturbed enjoyment of a book and a cigar. Great, therefore, was my disappointment when, at the last moment, a gentleman came hurrying along the platform, glanced into my carriage, opened the locked door with a private key, and stepped in.

It struck me at the first glance that I had seen him before—a tall, spare man, thin-lipped, light-eyed, with an ungraceful stoop in the shoulders, and scant grey hair worn somewhat long upon the collar. He carried a light waterproof coat, an umbrella, and a large brown japanned deed-box, which last he placed under the seat. This done, he felt carefully in his breast-pocket, as if to make certain of the safety of his purse or pocket-book, laid his umbrella in the netting overhead, spread the waterproof across his knees, and exchanged his hat for a travelling-cap of some Scotch material. By this time the train was moving out of the station and into the faint grey of the wintry twilight beyond.

I now recognized my companion. I recognized him from the moment when he removed his hat and uncovered the lofty, furrowed, and somewhat narrow brow beneath. I had met him, as I distinctly remembered, some three years before, at the very house for which, in all probability, he was now bound, like myself. His name was Dwerrihouse, he was a lawyer by profession, and, if I was not greatly mistaken, was first cousin to the wife of my host. I knew also that he was a man eminently "well-to-do", both as regarded his professional and private means. The Jelfs entertained him with that sort of observant courtesy which falls to the lot of the rich relation, the children made much of him, and the old butler, albeit somewhat surly "to the general", treated him with deference.

I thought, observing him by the vague mixture of lamplight and twilight, that Mrs. Jelf's cousin looked all the worse for the three years' wear and tear which had gone over his head since our last meeting. He was very pale, and had a restless light in his eye that I did not remember to have observed before. The anxious lines, too, about his mouth were deepened, and there was a cavernous, hollow look about his cheeks and temples which seemed to speak of sickness or sorrow. He had glanced at me as he came in, but without any gleam of recognition in his face. Now he glanced again, as I fancied, somewhat doubtfully. When he did so for the third or fourth time I ventured to address him.

"Mr. John Dwerrihouse, I think?"

"That is my name," he replied.

"I had the pleasure of meeting you at Dumbleton about three years ago."

"I thought I knew your face," he said; "but your name, I regret to say——"

"Langford—William Langford. I have known Jonathan Jelf since we were boys together at Merchant Taylors', and I generally spend a few weeks at Dumbleton in the shooting season. I suppose we are bound for the same destination."

"Not if you are on your way to the manor," he replied. "I am travelling upon business—rather troublesome business, too—while you, doubtless, have only pleasure in view."

"Just so. I am in the habit of looking forward to this visit as to the brightest three weeks in all the year."

"It is a pleasant house," said Mr. Dwerrihouse.

"The pleasantest I know."

"And Jelf is thoroughly hospitable."

"The best and kindest fellow in the world.

"They have invited me to spend Christmas week with them," pursued Mr. Dwerrihouse, after a moment's pause.

"And you are coming?"

"I cannot tell. It must depend on the issue of this business which I have in hand. You have heard perhaps that we are about to construct a branch line from Blackwater to Stockbridge."

I explained that I had been for some months away from England, and had therefore heard nothing of the contemplated improvement. Mr. Dwerrihouse smiled complacently.

"It *will* be an improvement," he said, "a great improvement. Stockbridge is a flourishing town, and needs but a more direct railway communication with the metropolis to become an important centre of commerce. This branch was my own idea. I brought the project before the board, and have myself superintended the execution of it up to the present time."

"You are an East Anglian director, I presume?"

"My interest in the company," replied Mr. Dwerrihouse, "is threefold. I am a director, I am a considerable shareholder, and, as head of the firm of Dwerrihouse, Dwerrihouse and Craik, I am the company's principal solicitor."

Loquacious, self-important, full of his pet project, and apparently unable to talk on any other subject, Mr. Dwerrihouse then went on to tell of the opposition he had encountered and the obstacles he had overcome in the cause of the Stockbridge branch. I was entertained with a multitude of local details and local grievances. The rapacity of one squire, the impracticability of another, the indignation of the rector whose glebe was threatened, the culpable indifference of the Stockbridge townspeople, who could *not* be brought to see that their most vital interests hinged upon a junction with the Great East Anglian line; the spite of the local newspaper, and the unheard-of difficulties attending the Common question, were each and all laid before me with a circumstantiality that possessed the deepest interest for my excellent fellow-traveller, but none whatever for myself.

From these, to my despair, he went on to more intricate matters: to the approximate expenses of construction per mile; to the estimates sent in by different contractors; to the probable traffic returns of the new line; to the provisional clauses of the new act as enumerated in Schedule D of the company's last half-yearly report; and so on and on and on, till my head ached and my attention flagged and my eyes kept closing in spite of every effort that I made to keep them open. At length I was roused by these words:

"Seventy-five thousand pounds, cash down."

"Seventy-five thousand pounds, cash down," I repeated, in the liveliest tone I could assume. "That is a heavy sum."

"A heavy sum to carry here," replied Mr. Dwerrihouse, pointing significantly to his breast-pocket, "but a mere fraction of what we shall ultimately have to pay."

"You do not mean to say that you have seventy-five thousand pounds at this moment upon your person?" I exclaimed.

"My good sir, have I not been telling you so for the last half-hour?" said Mr. Dwerrihouse, testily. "That money has to be paid over at half-past eight o'clock this evening, at the office of Sir Thomas's solicitors, on completion of the deed of sale."

"But how will you get across by night from Blackwater to Stockbridge with seventy-five thousand pounds in your pocket?"

"To Stockbridge!" echoed the lawyer. "I find I have made myself very imperfectly understood. I thought I had explained how this sum only carries us as far as Mallingford—the first stage, as it were, of our journey—and how our route from Blackwater to Mallingford lies entirely through Sir Thomas Liddell's property."

"I beg your pardon," I stammered. I fear my thoughts were wandering. So you only go as far as Mallingford tonight?"

"Precisely. I shall get a conveyance from the Blackwater Arms. And you?"

"Oh, Jelf sends a trap to meet me at Clayborough! Can I be the bearer of any message from you?"

"You may say, if you please, Mr. Langford, that I wished I could have been your companion all the way, and that I will come over, if possible, before Christmas."

"Nothing more?"

Mr. Dwerrihouse smiled grimly. "Well," he said, "you may tell my cousin that she need not burn the hall down in my honour this time, and that I shall be obliged if she will order the blue-room chimney to be swept before I arrive."

"That sounds tragic. Had you a conflagration on the occasion of your last visit to Dumbleton?"

"Something like it. There had been no fire lighted in my bedroom since the spring, the flue was foul, and the rooks had built in it; so when I went up to dress for dinner I found the room full of smoke and the chimney on fire. Are we already at Blackwater?"

The train had gradually come to a pause while Mr. Dwerrihouse was speaking, and, on putting my head out of the window, I could see the station some few hundred yards ahead. There was another train before us blocking the way, and the guard was making use of the delay to collect the Blackwater tickets. I had scarcely ascertained our position when the ruddy-faced official appeared at our carriage door.

"Tickets, sir!" said he.

"I am for Clayborough," I replied, holding out the tiny pink card.

He took it, glanced at it by the light of his little lantern, gave it back, looked, as I fancied, somewhat sharply at my fellow-traveller, and disappeared.

"He did not ask for yours," I said, with some surprise.

"They never do," replied Mr. Dwerrihouse; "they all know me, and of course I travel free."

"Blackwater! Blackwater!" cried the porter, running along the platform beside us as we glided into the station.

Mr. Dwerrihouse pulled out his deed-box, put his travelling-cap in his pocket, resumed his hat, took down his umbrella, and prepared to be gone.

"Many thanks, Mr. Langford, for your society," he said, with old-fashioned courtesy. "I wish you a good-evening."

"Good-evening," I replied, putting out my hand.

But he either did not see it or did not choose to see it, and, slightly lifting his hat, stepped out upon the platform. Having done this, he moved slowly away and mingled with the departing crowd.

Leaning forward to watch him out of sight, I trod upon something which proved to be a cigar-case. It had fallen, no doubt, from the pocket of his waterproof coat, and was made of dark morocco leather, with a silver monogram upon the side. I sprang out of the carriage just as the guard came up to lock me in.

"Is there one minute to spare?" I asked, eagerly. "The gentleman who travelled down with me from town has dropped his cigar-case; he is not yet out of the station."

"Just a minute and a half, sir," replied the guard. "You must be quick."

I dashed along the platform as fast as my feet could carry me. It was a large station, and Mr. Dwerrihouse had by this time got more than half-way to the farther end.

I, however, saw him distinctly, moving slowly with the stream. Then, as I drew nearer, I saw that he had met some friend, that they were talking as they walked, that they presently fell back somewhat from the crowd and stood aside in earnest conversation. I made straight for the spot where they were waiting. There was a vivid gas-jet just above their heads, and the light fell upon their faces. I saw both distinctly—the face of Mr. Dwerrihouse and the face of his companion.

Running, breathless, eager as I was, getting in the way of porters and passengers, and fearful every instant lest I should see the train going on without me, I yet observed that the newcomer was considerably younger and shorter than the director, that he was sandy-haired, *moustachioed*, small-featured, and dressed in a close-cut suit of Scotch tweed. I was now within a few yards of them. I ran against a stout gentleman, I was nearly knocked down by a luggage-truck, I stumbled over a carpet-bag; I gained the spot just as the driver's whistle warned me to return.

To my utter stupefaction, they were no longer there. I had seen them but two seconds before—and they were gone! I stood still; I looked to right and left; I saw no sign of them in any direction. It was as if the platform had gaped and swallowed them.

"There were two gentlemen standing here a moment ago," I said to a porter at my elbow; "which way can they have gone?"

"I saw no gentlemen, sir," replied the man.

The whistle shrilled out again. The guard, far up the platform, held up his arm, and shouted to me to "come on!"

"If you're going on by this train, sir," said the porter, "you must run for it."

I did run for it, just gained the carriage as the train began to move, was shoved in by the guard, and left, breathless and bewildered, with Mr. Dwerrihouse's cigar-case still in my hand.

It was the strangest disappearance in the world; it was like a transformation trick in a pantomime. They were there one moment—palpably there, talking, with the gaslight full upon their faces—and the next moment they were gone. There was no door near, no window, no staircase; it was a mere slip of barren platform, tapestried with big advertisements. Could anything be more mysterious?

It was not worth thinking about, and yet, for my life, I could not help pondering upon it—pondering, wondering, conjecturing, turning it over and over in my mind, and beating my brains for a solution of the enigma. I thought of it all the way from Blackwater to Clayborough. I thought of it all the way from Clayborough to Dumbleton, as I rattled along the smooth highway in a trim dog-cart, drawn by a splendid black mare and driven by the silentest and dapperest of East Anglian grooms.

We did the nine miles in something less than an hour, and pulled up before the lodge-gates just as the church clock was striking half-past seven. A couple of minutes more, and the warm glow of the lighted hall was flooding out upon the gravel, a hearty grasp was on my hand, and a clear jovial voice was bidding me "welcome to Dumbleton."

"And now, my dear fellow," said my host, when the first greeting was over, "you have no time to spare. We dine at eight, and there are people coming to meet you, so you must just get the dressing business over as quickly as may be. By the way, you will meet some acquaintances; the Biddulphs are coming, and Prendergast (Prendergast of the Skirmishers) is staying in the house. *Adieu!* Mrs. Jelf will be expecting you in the drawing-room."

I was ushered to my room—not the blue room, of which Mr. Dwerrihouse had made disagreeable experience, but a pretty little bachelor's chamber, hung with a delicate chintz and made cheerful by a blazing fire. I unlocked my portmanteau. I tried to be expeditious, but the memory of my railway adventure haunted me. I could not get free of it; I could not shake it off. It impeded me, it worried me, it tripped me up, it caused me to mislay my studs, to mistie my cravat, to wrench the buttons off my gloves. Worst of all, it made me so late that the party had all assembled before I reached the drawing-room. I had scarcely paid my respects to Mrs. Jelf when dinner was announced, and we paired off, some eight or ten couples strong, into the dining-room.

I am not going to describe either the guests or the dinner. All provincial parties bear the strictest family resemblance, and I am not aware that an East Anglian banquet offers any exception to the rule. There was the usual country baronet and his wife; there were the usual country parsons and their wives; there was the sempiternal turkey and haunch of venison. *Vanitas vanitatum.* There is nothing new under the sun.

I was placed about midway down the table. I had taken one rector's wife down to dinner, and I had another at my left hand. They talked across me, and their talk was about babies; it was dreadfully dull. At length there came a pause. The *entrées* had just been removed, and the turkey had come upon the scene. The conversation had all along been of the languidest, but at this moment it happened to have stagnated altogether. Jelf was carving the turkey; Mrs. Jelf looked as if she was trying to think of something to say; everybody else was silent. Moved by an unlucky impulse, I thought I would relate my adventure.

"By the way, Jelf," I began, "I came down part of the way today with a friend of yours."

"Indeed!" said the master of the feast, slicing scientifically into the breast of the turkey. "With whom, pray?"

"With one who bade me tell you that he should, if possible, pay you a visit before Christmas."

"I cannot think who that could be," said my friend, smiling.

"It must be Major Thorp," suggested Mrs. Jelf.

I shook my head.

"It was not Major Thorp," I replied; "it was a near relation of your own, Mrs. Jelf."

"Then I am more puzzled than ever," replied my hostess. "Pray tell me who it was."

"It was no less a person than your cousin, Mr. John Dwerrihouse."

Jonathan Jelf laid down his knife and fork. Mrs. Jelf looked at me in a strange, startled way, and said never a word.

"And he desired me to tell you, my dear madam, that you need not take the trouble to burn the hall down in his honour this time, but only to have the chimney of the blue room swept before his arrival."

Before I had reached the end of my sentence I became aware of something ominous in the faces of the guests. I felt I had said something which I had better have left unsaid, and that for some unexplained reason my words had evoked a general consternation. I sat confounded, not daring to utter another syllable, and for at least two whole minutes there was dead silence round the table. Then Captain Prendergast came to the rescue.

"You have been abroad for some months, have you not, Mr. Langford?" he said, with the desperation of one who flings himself into the breach. "I heard you had been to Russia. Surely you have something to tell us of the state and temper of the country after the war?"

I was heartily grateful to the gallant Skirmisher for this diversion in my favour. I answered him, I fear, somewhat lamely; but he kept the conversation up, and presently one or two others joined in, and so the difficulty, whatever it might have been, was bridged over—bridged over, but not repaired. A something, an awkwardness, a visible constraint remained. The guests hitherto had been simply dull, but now they were evidently uncomfortable and embarrassed.

The dessert had scarcely been placed upon the table when the ladies left the room. I seized the opportunity to select a vacant chair next Captain Prendergast.

"In Heaven's name," I whispered, "what was the matter just now? What had I said?"

"You mentioned the name of John Dwerrihouse."

"What of that? I had seen him not two hours before."

"It is a most astounding circumstance that you should have seen him," said Captain Prendergast. "Are you sure it was he?"

"As sure as of my own identity. We were talking all the way between London and Blackwater. But why does that surprise you?"

"*Because,*"replied Captain Prendergast, dropping his voice to the lowest whisper—"*because John Dwerrihouse absconded three months ago with seventy-five thousand pounds of the company's money, and has never been heard of since.*"

John Dwerrihouse had absconded three months ago—and I had seen him only a few hours back! John Dwerrihouse had embezzled seventy-five thousand pounds of the company's money, yet told me that he carried that sum upon his person! Were ever facts so strangely incongruous, so difficult to reconcile? How should he have ventured again into the light of day? How dared he show himself along the line? Above all, what had he been doing throughout those mysterious three months of disappearance?

Perplexing questions these—questions which at once suggested themselves to the minds of all concerned, but which admitted of no easy solution. I could find no reply to them. Captain Prendergast had not even a suggestion to offer. Jonathan Jelf, who seized the first opportunity of drawing me aside and learning all that I had to tell, was more amazed and bewildered than either of us. He came to my room that night, when all the guests were gone, and we talked the thing over from every point of view; without, it must be confessed, arriving at any kind of conclusion.

"I do not ask you," he said, "whether you can have mistaken your man. That is impossible."

"As impossible as that I should mistake some stranger for yourself."

"It is not a question of looks or voice, but of facts. That he should have alluded to the fire in the blue room is proof enough of John Dwerrihouse's identity. How did he look?"

"Older, I thought; considerably older, paler, and more anxious."

"He has had enough to make him look anxious, anyhow," said my friend, gloomily, "be he innocent or guilty."

"I am inclined to believe that he is innocent," I replied. "He showed no embarrassment when I addressed him, and no uneasiness when the guard came round. His conversation was open to a fault. I might almost say that he talked too freely of the business which he had in hand."

"That again is strange, for I know no one more reticent on such subjects. He actually told you that he had the seventy-five thousand pounds in his pocket?"

"He did."

"Humph! My wife has an idea about it, and she may be right——"

"What idea?"

"Well, she fancies—women are so clever, you know, at putting themselves inside people's motives—she fancies that he was tempted, that he did actually take the money, and that he has been concealing himself these three months in some wild part of the country, struggling possibly with his conscience all the time, and daring neither to abscond with his booty nor to come back and restore it."

"But now that he has come back?"

"That is the point. She conceives that he has probably thrown himself upon the company's mercy, made restitution of the money, and, being forgiven, is permitted to carry the business through as if nothing whatever I had happened."

"The last," I replied, "is an impossible case. Mrs. Jelf thinks like a generous and delicate-minded woman, but not in the least like a board of railway directors. They would never carry forgiveness so far."

"I fear not; and yet it is the only conjecture that bears a semblance of likelihood. However, we can run over to Clayborough tomorrow and see if anything is to be learned. By the way, Prendergast tells me you picked up his cigar-case."

"I did so, and here it is."

Jelf took the cigar-case, examined it by the light of the lamp, and said at once that it was beyond doubt Mr. Dwerrihouse's property, and that he remembered to have seen him use it.

"Here, too, is his monogram on the side," he added—"a big J transfixing a capital D. He used to carry the same on his notepaper."

"It offers, at all events, a proof that I was not dreaming."

"Ay, but it is time you were asleep and dreaming now. I am ashamed to have kept you up so long. Goodnight."

"Goodnight, and remember that I am more than ready to go with you to Clayborough or Blackwater or London or anywhere, if I can be of the least service."

"Thanks! I know you mean it, old friend, and it may be that I shall put you to the test. Once more, goodnight."

So we parted for that night, and met again in the breakfast-room at half-past eight next morning. It was a hurried, silent, uncomfortable meal; none of us had slept well, and all were thinking of the same subject. Mrs. Jelf had evidently been crying, Jelf was impatient to be off, and both Captain Prendergast and myself felt ourselves to be in the painful position of outsiders who are involuntarily brought into a domestic trouble. Within twenty minutes after we had left the breakfast-table the dog-cart was brought round, and my friend and I were on the road to Clayborough.

"Tell you what it is, Langford," he said, as we sped along between the wintry hedges, "I do not much fancy to bring up Dwerrihouse's name at Clayborough. All the officials know that he is my wife's relation, and the subject just now is hardly a pleasant one. If you don't much mind, we will take the 11.10 to Blackwater. It's an important station, and we shall stand a far better chance of picking up information there than at Clayborough."

So we took the 11.10, which happened to be an express, and, arriving at Blackwater about a quarter before twelve, proceeded at once to prosecute our inquiry.

We began by asking for the station-master, a big, blunt, businesslike person, who at once averred that he knew Mr. John Dwerrihouse perfectly well, and that there was no director on the line whom he had seen and spoken to so frequently. "He used to be down here two or three times a week about three months ago," said he, "when the new line was first set afoot; but since then, you know, gentlemen——"

He paused significantly.

Jelf flushed scarlet.

"Yes, yes," he said, hurriedly; "we know all about that. The point now to be ascertained is whether anything has been seen or heard of him lately."

"Not to my knowledge," replied the station-master.

"He is not known to have been down the line any time yesterday, for instance?"

The station-master shook his head.

"The East Anglian, sir," said he, "is about the last place where he would dare to show himself. Why, there isn't a station-master, there isn't a guard, there isn't a porter, who doesn't know Mr. Dwerrihouse by sight as well as he knows his own face in the looking-glass, or who wouldn't telegraph for the police as soon as he had set eyes on him at any point along the line. Bless you, sir! there's been a standing order out against him ever since the 25th of September last."

"And yet," pursued my friend, "a gentleman who travelled down yesterday from London to Clayborough by the afternoon express testifies that he saw Mr. Dwerrihouse in the train, and that Mr. Dwerrihouse alighted at Blackwater station."

"Quite impossible, sir," replied the station-master, promptly.

"Why impossible?"

"Because there is no station along the line where he is so well known or where he would run so great a risk. It would be just running his head into the lion's mouth; he would have been mad to come nigh Blackwater station; and if he had come he would have been arrested before he left the platform."

"Can you tell me who took the Blackwater tickets of that train?"

"I can, sir. It was the guard, Benjamin Somers."

"And where can I find him?"

"You can find him, sir, by staying here, if you please, till one o'clock. He will be coming through with the up express from Crampton, which stays at Blackwater for ten minutes."

We waited for the up express, beguiling the time as best we could by strolling along the Blackwater road till we came almost to the outskirts of the town, from which the station was distant nearly a couple of miles. By one o'clock we were back again upon the platform and waiting for the train. It came punctually, and I at once recognized the ruddy-faced guard who had gone down with my train the evening before.

"The gentlemen want to ask you something about Mr. Dwerrihouse Somers," said the station-master, by way of introduction.

The guard flashed a keen glance from my face to Jelf's and back again to mine.

"Mr. John Dwerrihouse, the late director?" said he, interrogatively.

"The same," replied my friend. "Should you know him if you saw him?"

"Anywhere, sir."

"Do you know if he was in the 4.15 express yesterday afternoon?"

"He was not, sir."

"How can you answer so positively?"

"Because I looked into every carriage and saw every face in that train, and I could take my oath that Mr. Dwerrihouse was not in it. This gentleman was," he added, turning sharply upon me. "I don't know that I ever saw him before in my life, but I remember his face perfectly. You nearly missed taking your seat in time at this station, sir, and you got out at Clayborough."

"Quite true, guard," I replied; "but do you not also remember the face of the gentleman who travelled down in the same carriage with me as far as here?"

"It was my impression, sir, that you travelled down alone," said Somers, with a look of some surprise.

"By no means. I had a fellow-traveller as far as Blackwater, and it was in trying to restore him the cigar-case which he had dropped in the carriage that I so nearly let you go on without me."

"I remember your saying something about a cigar-case, certainly," replied the guard; "but——"

"You asked for my ticket just before we entered the station."

"I did, sir."

"Then you must have seen him. He sat in the corner next the very door to which you came."

"No, indeed; I saw no one."

I looked at Jelf I began to think the guard was in the ex-director's confidence, and paid for his silence.

"If I had seen another traveller I should have asked for his ticket," added Somers. "Did you see me ask for his ticket, sir?"

"I observed that you did not ask for it, but he explained that by saying——" I hesitated. I feared. I might be telling too much, and so broke off abruptly.

The guard and the station-master exchanged glances. The former looked impatiently at his watch.

"I am obliged to go on in four minutes more, sir," he said.

"One last question, then," interposed Jelf, with a sort of desperation. "If this gentleman's fellow-traveller had been Mr. John Dwerrihouse, and he had been sitting in the corner next the door by which you took the tickets, could you have failed to see and recognize him?"

"No, sir; it would have been quite impossible."

"And you are certain you did *not* see him?"

"As I said before, sir, I could take my oath I did not see him. And if it wasn't that I don't like to contradict a gentleman, I would say I could also take my oath that this gentleman was quite alone in the carriage the whole way from London to Clayborough. Why, sir," he added, dropping his voice so as to be inaudible to the station-master, who had been called away to speak to some person close by, "you expressly asked me to give you a compartment to yourself, and I did so. I locked you in, and you were so good as to give me something for myself."

"Yes; but Mr. Dwerrihouse had a key of his own."

"I never saw him, sir; I saw no one in that compartment but yourself. Beg pardon, sir; my time's up."

And with this the ruddy guard touched his cap and was gone. In another minute the heavy panting of the engine began afresh, and the train glided slowly out of the station.

We looked at each other for some moments in silence. I was the first to speak.

"Mr. Benjamin Somers knows more than he chooses to tell," I said.

"Humph! do you think so?"

"It must be. He could not have come to the door without seeing him; it's impossible."

"There is one thing not impossible, my dear fellow."

"What is that?"

"That you may have fallen asleep and dreamed the whole thing."

"Could I dream of a branch line that I had never heard of? Could I dream of a hundred and one business details that had no kind of interest for me? Could I dream of the seventy-five thousand pounds?"

"Perhaps you might have seen or heard some vague account of the affair while you were abroad. It might have made no impression upon you at the time, and might have come back to you in your dreams, recalled perhaps by the mere names of the stations on the line."

"What about the fire in the chimney of the blue room–should I have heard of that during my journey?"

"Well, no; I admit there is a difficulty about that point."

"And what about the cigar-case?"

"Ay, by jove! there is the cigar-case. That is a stubborn fact. Well, it's a mysterious affair, and it will need a better detective than myself, I fancy, to clear it up. I suppose we may as well go home."

A week had not gone by when I received a letter from the secretary of the East Anglian Railway Company, requesting the favour of my attendance at a special board meeting not then many days distant. No reasons were alleged and no apologies offered for this demand upon my time, but they had heard, it was clear, of my inquiries anent the missing director, and had a mind to put me through some sort Of official examination upon the subject. Being still a guest at Dumbleton Hall, I had to go up to London for the purpose, and Jonathanjelf accompanied me. I found the direction of the Great East Anglian line represented by a party of some twelve or fourteen gentlemen seated in solemn conclave round a huge green baize table, in a gloomy boardroom adjoining the London terminus.

Being courteously received by the chairman (who at once began by saying that certain statements of mine respecting Mr. John Dwerrihouse had come to the knowledge ofthe direction, and that they in consequence desired to confer with me on those points), we were placed at the table, and the inquiry proceeded in due form.

I was first asked if I knew Mr. John Dwerrihouse, how long I had been acquainted with him, and whether I could identify him at sight. I was then asked when I had seen him last. To which I replied, "On the 4th of this present month, December, 1856." Then came the inquiry of where I had seen him on that fourth day of December; to which I replied that I met him in a first-class compartment of the 4.15 down express, that he got in just as the train was leaving the London terminus, and that he alighted at Blackwater station. The chairman then inquired whether I had held any communication with my fellow-traveller; whereupon I related, as nearly as I could remember it, the whole bulk and substance of Mr. John Dwerrihouse's diffuse information respecting the new branch line.

To all this the board listened with profound attention, while the chairman presided and the secretary took notes. I then produced the cigar-case. It was passed from hand to hand, and recognized by all. There was not a man present who did not remember that plain cigar-case with its silver monogram, or to whom it seemed anything less than entirely corroborative of my evidence. When at length I had told all that I had to tell, the chairman whispered something to the secretary; the secretary touched a silver hand-bell, and the guard, Benjamin Somers, was ushered into the room.

He was then examined as carefully as myself. He declared that he knew Mr. John Dwerrihouse perfectly well, that he could not be mistaken in him, that he remembered going down with the 4.15 express on the afternoon in question, that he remembered me, and that, there being one or two empty first-class compartments on that especial afternoon, he had, in compliance with my request, placed me in a carriage by myself. He was positive that I remained alone in that compartment all the way from London to Clayborough.

He was ready to take his oath that Mr. Dwerrihouse was neither in that carriage with me, nor in any compartment of that train. He remembered distinctly to have examined my ticket at Blackwater; was certain that there was no one else at that time in the carriage; could not have failed to observe a second person, if there had been one; had that second person been Mr. John Dwerrihouse, should have quietly double-locked the door of the carriage and have at once given information to the Blackwater station-master. So clear, so decisive, so ready, was Somers with this testimony, that the board looked fairly puzzled.

"You hear this person's statement, Mr. Langford," said the chairman. "It contradicts yours in every particular. What have you to say in reply?"

"I can only repeat what I said before. I am quite as positive of the truth of my own assertions as Mr. Somers can be of the truth of his."

"You say that Mr. Dwerrihouse alighted at Blackwater, and that he was in possession of a private key. Are you sure that he had not alighted by means of that key before the guard came round for the tickets?"

"I am quite positive that he did not leave the carriage till the train had fairly entered the station, and the other Blackwater passengers alighted. I even saw that he was met there by a friend."

"Indeed! Did you see that person distinctly?"

"Quite distinctly."

"Can you describe his appearance?"

"I think so. He was short and very slight, sandy-haired, with a bushy moustache and beard, and he wore a closely fitting suit of grey tweed. His age I should take to be about thirty-eight or forty."

"Did Mr. Dwerrihouse leave the station in this person's company?"

"I cannot tell. I saw them walking together down the platform, and then I saw them standing aside under a gas-jet, talking earnestly. After that I lost sight of them quite suddenly, and just then my train went on, and I with it."

The chairman and secretary conferred together in an undertone. The directors whispered to one another. One or two looked suspiciously at the guard. I could see that my evidence remained unshaken, and that, like myself, they suspected some complicity between the guard and the defaulter.

"How far did you conduct that 4.15 express on the day in question, Somers?" asked the chairman.

"All through, sir," replied the guard, "from London to Crampton."

"How was it that you were not relieved at Clayborough? I thought there was always a change of guards at Clayborough."

"There used to be, sir, till the new regulations came in force last midsummer, since when the guards in charge of express trains go the whole way through."

The chairman turned to the secretary.

"I think it would be as well," he said, "if we had the day-book to refer to upon this point."

Again the secretary touched the silver hand-bell, and desired the porter in attendance to summon Mr. Raikes. From a word or two dropped by another of the directors I gathered that Mr. Raikes was one of the under-secretaries.

He came, a small, slight, sandy-haired, keen-eyed man, with an eager, nervous manner, and a forest of light beard and moustache. He just showed himself at the door of the board-room, and, being requested to bring a certain day-book from a certain shelf in a certain room, bowed and vanished.

He was there such a moment, and the surprise of seeing him was so great and sudden, that it was not till the door had closed upon him that I found voice to speak. He was no sooner gone, however, than I sprang to my feet.

"That person," I said, "is the same who met Mr. Dwerrihouse upon the platform at Blackwater!"

There was a general movement of surprise. The chairman looked grave and somewhat agitated.

"Take care, Mr. Langford," he said; "take care what you say."

"I am as positive of his identity as of my own."

"Do you consider the consequences of your words? Do you consider that you are bringing a charge of the gravest character against one of the company's servants?"

"I am willing to be put upon my oath, if necessary. The man who came to that door a minute since is the same whom I saw talking with Mr. Dwerrihouse on the Blackwater platform. Were he twenty times the company's servant, I could say neither more nor less."

The chairman turned again to the guard.

"Did you see Mr. Raikes in the train or on the platform?" he asked. Somers shook his head.

"I am confident Mr. Raikes was not in the train," he said,

291

"and I certainly did not see him on the platform."

The chairman turned next to the secretary.

"Mr. Raikes is in your office, Mr. Hunter," he said. "Can you remember if he was absent on the 4th instant?"

"I do not think he was," replied the secretary, "but I am not prepared to speak positively. I have been away most afternoons myself lately, and Mr. Raikes might easily have absented himself if he had been disposed."

At this moment the under-secretary returned with the day-book under his arm.

"Be pleased to refer, Mr. Raikes," said the chairman, "to the entries of the 4th instant, and see what Benjamin Somers's duties were on that day."

Mr. Raikes threw open the cumbrous volume, and ran a practised eye and finger down some three or four successive columns of entries. Stopping suddenly at the foot of a page, he then read aloud that Benjamin Somers had on that day conducted the 4.15 express from London to Crampton.

The chairman leaned forward in his seat, looked the under-secretary full in the face, and said, quite sharply and suddenly:

"Where were *you*, Mr. Raikes, on the same afternoon?"

"*I*, sir?"

"You, Mr. Raikes. Where were you on the afternoon and evening of the 4th of the present month?"

"Here, sir, in Mr. Hunter's office. Where else should I be?"

There was a dash of trepidation in the under-secretary's voice as he said this, but his look of surprise was natural enough.

"We have some reason for believing, Mr. Raikes, that you were absent that afternoon without leave. Was this the case?"

"Certainly not, sir. I have not had a day's holiday since September. Mr. Hunter will bear me out in this."

Mr. Hunter repeated what he had previously said on the subject, but added that the clerks in the adjoining office would be certain to know. Whereupon the senior clerk, a grave, middle-aged person in green glasses, was summoned and interrogated.

His testimony cleared the under-secretary at once. He declared that Mr. Raikes had in no instance, to his knowledge, been absent during office hours since his return from his annual holiday in September.

I was confounded. The chairman turned to me with a smile, in which a shade of covert annoyance was scarcely apparent.

"You hear, Mr. Langford?" he said.

"I hear, sir; but my conviction remains unshaken."

"I fear, Mr. Langford, that your convictions are very insufficiently based," replied the chairman, with a doubtful cough. "I fear that you 'dream dreams', and mistake them for actual occurrences. It is a dangerous habit of mind, and might lead to dangerous results. Mr. Raikes here would have found himself in an unpleasant position had he not proved so satisfactory an alibi."

I was about to reply, but he gave me no time.

"I think, gentlemen," he went on to say, addressing the board, "that we should be wasting time to push this inquiry further. Mr. Langford's evidence would seem to be of an equal value throughout. The testimony of Benjamin Somers disproves his first statement, and the testimony of the last witness disproves his second. I think we may conclude that Mr. Langford fell asleep in the train on the occasion of his journey to Clayborough, and dreamed an unusually vivid and circumstantial dream, of which, however, we have now heard quite enough."

There are few things more annoying than to find one's positive convictions met with incredulity. I could not help feeling impatience at the turn that affairs had taken. I was not proof against the civil sarcasm of the chairman's manner. Most intolerable of all, however, was the quiet smile lurking about the corners of Benjamin Somers's mouth, and the half-triumphant, half-malicious gleam in the eyes of the under-secretary. The man was evidently puzzled and somewhat alarmed. His looks seemed furtively to interrogate me. Who was I? What did I want? Why had I come here to do him an ill turn with his employers? What was it to me whether or not he was absent without leave?

Seeing all this, and perhaps more irritated by it than the thing deserved, I begged leave to detain the attention of the board for a moment longer. Jelf plucked me impatiently by the sleeve.

"Better let the thing drop," he whispered. "The chairman's right enough; you dreamed it, and the less said now the better."

I was not to be silenced, however, in this fashion. I had yet something to say, and I would say it. It was to this effect: that dreams were not usually productive of tangible results, and that I requested to know in what way the chairman conceived I had evolved from my dream so substantial and well-made a delusion as the cigar-case which I had had the honour to place before him at the commencement of our interview.

"The cigar-case, I admit, Mr. Langford," the chairman replied, "is a very strong point in your evidence. It is your only strong point, however, and there is just a possibility that we may all be misled by a mere accidental resemblance. Will you permit me to see the case again?"

"It is unlikely," I said, as I handed it to him, "that any other should bear precisely this monogram, and yet be in all other particulars exactly similar."

The chairman examined it for a moment in silence, and then passed it to Mr. Hunter. Mr. Hunter turned it over and over, and shook his head.

"This is no mere resemblance," he said. "It is John Dwerrihouse's cigar-case to a certainty. I remember it perfectly; I have seen it a hundred times."

"I believe I may say the same," added the chairman; "yet how account for the way in which Mr. Langford asserts that it came into his possession?"

"I can only repeat," I replied, "that I found it on the floor of the carriage after Mr. Dwerrihouse had alighted. It was in leaning out to look after him that I trod upon it, and it was in running after him for the purpose of restoring it that I saw, or believed I saw, Mr. Raikes standing aside with him in earnest conversation."

Again I felt Jonathan Jelf plucking at my sleeve.

"Look at Raikes," he whispered; "look at Raikes!"

I turned to where the under-secretary had been standing a

294

moment before, and saw him, white as death, with lips trembling and livid, stealing towards the door.

To conceive a sudden, strange, and indefinite suspicion, to fling myself in his way, to take him by the shoulders as if he were a child, and turn his craven face, perforce, towards the board, were with me the work of an instant.

"Look at him!" I exclaimed. "Look at his face! I ask no better witness to the truth of my words."

The chairman's brow darkened.

"Mr. Raikes," he said, sternly, "if you know anything you had better speak."

Vainly trying to wrench himself from my grasp, the under-secretary stammered out an incoherent denial.

"Let me go," he said. "I know nothing—you have no right to detain me—let me go!"

"Did you, or did you not, meet Mr. John Dwerrihouse at Blackwater station? The charge brought against you is either true or false. If true, you will do well to throw yourself upon the mercy of the board and make full confession of all that you know."

The under-secretary wrung his hands in an agony of helpless terror.

"I was away!" he cried. "I was two hundred miles away at the time! I know nothing about it—I have nothing to confess—I am innocent—I call God to witness I am innocent!"

"Two hundred miles away!" echoed the chairman. "What do you mean?"

"I was in Devonshire. I had three weeks" leave of absence—I appeal to Mr. Hunter—Mr. Hunter knows I had three weeks' leave of absence! I was in Devonshire all the time; I can prove I was in Devonshire!"

Seeing him so abject, so incoherent, so wild with apprehension, the directors began to whisper gravely among themselves, while one got quietly up and called the porter to guard the door.

"What has your being in Devonshire to do with the matter?"

said the chairman. "When were you in Devonshire?"

"Mr. Raikes took his leave in September," said the secretary, "about the time when Mr. Dwerrihouse disappeared."

"I never even heard that he had disappeared till I came back!"

"That must remain to be proved," said the chairman. "I shall at once put this matter in the hands of the police. In the meanwhile, Mr. Raikes being myself a magistrate and used to deal with these cases, I advise you to offer no resistance, but to confess while confession may yet do you service. As for your accomplice——"

The frightened wretch fell upon his knees.

"I had no accomplice!" he cried. "Only have mercy upon me—only spare my life, and I will confess all! I didn't mean to harm him! I didn't mean to hurt a hair of his head! Only have mercy upon me, and let me go!"

The chairman rose in his place, pale and agitated. "Good heavens!" he exclaimed, "what horrible mystery is this? What does it mean?"

"As sure as there is a God in heaven "said Jonathan Jelf, "it means that murder has been done."

"No! no! no!" shrieked Raikes, still upon his knees, and cowering like a beaten hound. "Not murder! No jury that ever sat could bring it in murder. I thought I had only stunned him—I never meant to do more than stun him! Manslaughter—manslaughter—not murder!"

Overcome by the horror of this unexpected revelation, the chairman covered his face with his hand and for a moment or two remained silent.

"Miserable man," he said at length, "you have betrayed yourself!"

"You made me confess! You urged me to throw myself upon the mercy of the board!"

"You have confessed to a crime which no one suspected you of having committed," replied the chairman, "and which this board has no power either to punish or forgive. All that I can do for you is to advise you to submit to the law, to plead guilty, and to conceal nothing. When did you do this deed?"

The guilty man rose to his feet, and leaned heavily against the table. His answer came reluctantly, like the speech of one dreaming.

"On the 22nd of September!"

On the 22nd of September! I looked in Jonathan Jelf's face, and he in mine. I felt my own paling with a strange sense of wonder and dread. I saw his blanch suddenly, even to the lips.

"Merciful heaven!" he whispered. "*What was it, then, that you saw in the train?*"

What was it that I saw in the train? That question remains unanswered to this day. I have never been able to reply to it. I only know that it bore the living likeness of the murdered man, whose body had then been lying some ten weeks under a rough pile of branches and brambles and rotting leaves, at the bottom of a deserted chalk-pit about half-way between Blackwater and Mallingford. I know that it spoke and moved and looked as that man spoke and moved and looked in life; that I heard, or seemed to hear, things related which I could never otherwise have learned; that I was guided, as it were, by that vision on the platform to the identification of the murderer; and that, a passive instrument myself, I was destined, by means of these mysterious teachings, to bring about the ends of Justice. For these things I have never been able to account.

As for that matter of the cigar-case, it proved, on inquiry, that the carriage in which I travelled down that afternoon to Clayborough had not been in use for several weeks, and was, in point of fact, the same in which poor John Dwerrihouse had performed his last journey. The case had doubtless been dropped by him, and had lain unnoticed till I found it.

Upon the details of the murder I have no need to dwell. Those who desire more ample particulars may find them, and the written confession of Augustus Raikes, in the files of *The Times* for 1856. Enough that the under-secretary, knowing the history of the new line, and following the negotiation step by step through all its stages, determined to waylay Mr. Dwerri-house, rob him of the seventy-five thousand pounds, and escape to America with his booty.

In order to effect these ends he obtained leave of absence a few days before the time appointed for the payment of the money, secured his passage across the Atlantic in a steamer advertised to start on the 23rd, provided himself with a heavily loaded "life-preserver", and went down to Blackwater to await the arrival of his victim. How he met him on the platform with a pretended message from the board, how he offered to conduct him by a short cut across the fields to Mallingford, how, having brought him to a lonely place, he struck him down with the life-preserver, and so killed him, and how, finding what he had done, he dragged the body to the verge of an out-of-the-way chalk-pit, and there flung it in and piled it over with branches and brambles, are facts still fresh in the memories of those who, like the connoisseurs in De Quincey's famous essay, regard murder as a fine art.

Strangely enough, the murderer, having done his work, was afraid to leave the country. He declared that he had not intended to take the director's life, but only to stun and rob him; and that, finding the blow had killed, he dared not fly for fear of drawing down suspicion upon his own head. As a mere robber he would have been safe in the States, but as a murderer he would inevitably have been pursued and given up to justice. So he forfeited his passage, returned to the office as usual at the end of his leave, and locked up his ill-gotten thousands till a more convenient opportunity. In the meanwhile he had the satisfaction of finding that Mr. Dwerrihouse was universally believed to have absconded with the money, no one knew how or whither.

Whether he meant murder or not, however, Mr. Augustus Raikes paid the full penalty of his crime, and was hanged at the Old Bailey, in the second week in January, 1857. Those who desire to make his further acquaintance may see him any day (admirably done in wax) in the Chamber of Horrors at Madame Tussaud's exhibition, in Baker Street. He is there to be found in the midst of a select society of ladies and gentlemen of atrocious memory, dressed in the close-cut tweed suit which he wore on the evening of the murder, and holding in his hand the identical life-preserver with which he committed it.

The Phantom Coach

A.k.a.:The North Mail,The Death Coach or Another Past Lodger
Relates His Own Ghost Story

The circumstances I am about to relate to you have truth to recommend them. They happened to myself, and my recollection of them is as vivid as if they had taken place only yesterday. Twenty years, however, have gone by since that night. During those twenty years I have told the story to but one other person. I tell it now with a reluctance which I find it difficult to overcome. All I entreat, meanwhile, is that you will abstain from forcing your own conclusions upon me. I want nothing explained away. I desire no arguments. My mind on this subject is quite made up, and, having the testimony of my own senses to rely upon, I prefer to abide by it.

Well! It was just twenty years ago, and within a day or two of the end of the grouse season. I had been out all day with my gun, and had had no sport to speak of. The wind was due east; the month, December; the place, a bleak wide moor in the far north of England. And I had lost my way. It was not a pleasant place in which to lose one's way, with the first feathery flakes of a coming snowstorm just fluttering down upon the heather, and the leaden evening closing in all around.

I shaded my eyes with my hand, and staled anxiously into the gathering darkness, where the purple moorland melted into a range of low hills, some ten or twelve miles distant. Not the faintest smoke-wreath, not the tiniest cultivated patch, or fence, or sheep-track, met my eyes in any direction. There was nothing for it but to walk on, and take my chance of finding what shelter I could, by the way. So I shouldered my gun again, and pushed wearily forward; for I had been on foot since an hour after daybreak, and had eaten nothing since breakfast.

Meanwhile, the snow began to come down with ominous steadiness, and the wind fell. After this, the cold became more intense, and the night came rapidly up. As for me, my prospects darkened with the darkening sky, and my heart grew heavy as I thought how my young wife was already watching for me through the window of our little inn parlour, and thought of all the suffering in store for her throughout this weary night.

We had been married four months, and, having spent our autumn in the Highlands, were now lodging in a remote little village situated just on the verge of the great English moorlands. We were very much in love, and, of course, very happy. This morning, when we parted, she had implored me to return before dusk, and I had promised her that I would. What would I not have given to have kept my word!

Even now, weary as I was, I felt that with a supper, an hour's rest, and a guide, I might still get back to her before midnight, if only guide and shelter could be found.

And all this time, the snow fell and the night thickened. I stopped and shouted every now and then, but my shouts seemed only to make the silence deeper. Then a vague sense of uneasiness came upon me, and I began to remember stories of travellers who had walked on and on in the falling snow until, wearied out, they were fain to lie down and sleep their lives away. Would it be possible, I asked myself, to keep on thus through all the long dark night? Would there not come a time when my limbs must fail, and my resolution give way? When I, too, must sleep the sleep of death.

Death! I shuddered. How hard to die just now, when life lay all so bright before me! How hard for my darling, whose whole loving heart but that thought was not to be borne! To banish it, I shouted again, louder and longer, and then listened eagerly. Was my shout answered, or did I only fancy that I heard a far-off cry? I halloed again, and again the echo followed. Then a wavering speck of light came suddenly out of the dark, shifting, disappearing, growing momentarily nearer and brighter. Running towards it at full speed, I found myself, to my great joy, face to face with an old man and a lantern.

"Thank God!" was the exclamation that burst involuntarily from my lips.

Blinking and frowning, he lifted his lantern and peered into my face.

"What for?" growled he, sulkily.

"Well—for you. I began to fear I should be lost in the snow."

"Eh, then, folks do get cast away hereabouts fra' time to time, an' what's to hinder you from bein' cast away likewise, if the Lord's so minded?"

"If the Lord is so minded that you and I shall be lost together, friend, we must submit," I replied; "but I don't mean to be lost without you. How far am I now from Dwolding?"

"A gude twenty mile, more or less."

"And the nearest village?"

"The nearest village is Wyke, an' that's twelve mile t'other side."

"Where do you live, then?"

"Out yonder," said he, with a vague jerk of the lantern.

"You're going home, I presume?"

"Maybe I am."

"Then I'm going with you."

The old man shook his head, and rubbed his nose reflectively with the handle of the lantern.

"It ain't o' no use," growled he. "He 'ont let you in—not he."

"We'll see about that," I replied, briskly. "Who is He?"

"The master."

"Who is the master?"

"That's nowt to you," was the unceremonious reply.

"Well, well; you lead the way, and I'll engage that the master

302

shall give me shelter and a supper tonight."

"Eh, you can try him!" muttered my reluctant guide; and, still shaking his head, he hobbled, gnome-like, away through the falling snow. A large mass loomed up presently out of the darkness, and a huge dog rushed out, barking furiously.

"Is this the house?" I asked.

"Ay, it's the house. Down, Bey!" And he fumbled in his pocket for the key.

I drew up close behind him, prepared to lose no chance of entrance, and saw in the little circle of light shed by the lantern that the door was heavily studded with iron nails, like the door of a prison. In another minute he had turned the key and I had pushed past him into the house.

Once inside, I looked round with curiosity, and found myself in a great raftered hall, which served, apparently, a variety of uses. One end was piled to the roof with corn, like a barn. The other was stored with flour-sacks, agricultural implements, casks, and all kinds of miscellaneous lumber; while from the beams overhead hung rows of hams, flitches, and bunches of dried herbs for winter use.

In the centre of the floor stood some huge object gauntly dressed in a dingy wrapping-cloth, and reaching half way to the rafters. Lifting a corner of this cloth, I saw, to my surprise, a telescope of very considerable size, mounted on a rude movable platform, with four small wheels. The tube was made of painted wood, bound round with bands of metal rudely fashioned; the speculum, so far as I could estimate its size in the dim light, measured at least fifteen inches in diameter. While I was yet examining the instrument, and asking myself whether it was not the work of some self-taught optician, a bell rang sharply.

"That's for you," said my guide, with a malicious grin. "Yonder's his room."

He pointed to a low black door at the opposite side of the hall. I crossed over, rapped somewhat loudly, and went in, without waiting for an invitation. A huge, white-haired old man rose from a table covered with books and papers, and confronted me sternly.

"Who are you?" said he. "How came you here? What do you want?"

"James Murray, barrister-at-law. On foot across the moor. Meat, drink, and sleep."

He bent his bushy brows into a portentous frown.

"Mine is not a house of entertainment," he said, haughtily. "Jacob, how dared you admit this stranger?"

"I didn't admit him," grumbled the old man. "He followed me over the muir, and shouldered his way in before me. I'm no match for six foot two."

"And pray, sir, by what right have you forced an entrance into my house?"

"The same by which I should have clung to your boat, if I were drowning. The right of self-preservation."

"Self-preservation?"

"There's an inch of snow on the ground already," I replied, briefly; "and it would be deep enough to cover my body before daybreak."

He strode to the window, pulled aside a heavy black curtain, and looked out.

"It is true," he said. "You can stay, if you choose, till morning. Jacob, serve the supper."

With this he waved me to a seat, resumed his own, and became at once absorbed in the studies from which I had disturbed him.

I placed my gun in a corner, drew a chair to the hearth, and examined my quarters at leisure. Smaller and less incongruous in its arrangements than the hall, this room contained, nevertheless, much to awaken my curiosity. The floor was carpetless. The whitewashed walls were in parts scrawled over with strange diagrams, and in others covered with shelves crowded with philosophical instruments, the uses of many of which were unknown to me.

On one side of the fireplace, stood a bookcase filled with dingy folios; on the other, a small organ, fantastically decorated with painted carvings of medieval saints and devils. Through the half-opened door of a cupboard at the further end of the room, I saw a long array of geological specimens, surgical preparations, crucibles, retorts, and jars of chemicals; while on the mantelshelf beside me, amid a number of small objects, stood a model of the solar system, a small galvanic battery, and a microscope. Every chair had its burden. Every corner was heaped high with books. The very floor was littered over with maps, casts, papers, tracings, and learned lumber of all conceivable kinds.

I stared about me with an amazement increased by every fresh object upon which my eyes chanced to rest. So strange a room I had never seen; yet seemed it stranger still, to find such a room in a lone farmhouse amid those wild and solitary moors! Over and over again, I looked from my host to his surroundings, and from his surroundings back to my host, asking myself who and what he could be? His head was singularly fine; but it was more the head of a poet than of a philosopher.

Broad in the temples, prominent over the eyes, and clothed with a rough profusion of perfectly white hair, it had all the ideality and much of the ruggedness that characterises the head of Louis von Beethoven. There were the same deep lines about the mouth, and the same stern furrows in the brow. There was the same concentration of expression. While I was yet observing him, the door opened, and Jacob brought in the supper. His master then closed his book, rose, and with more courtesy of manner than he had yet shown, invited me to the table.

A dish of ham and eggs, a loaf of brown bread, and a bottle of admirable sherry, were placed before me.

"I have but the homeliest farmhouse fare to offer you, sir," said my entertainer. "Your appetite, I trust, will make up for the deficiencies of our larder."

I had already fallen upon the viands, and now protested, with the enthusiasm of a starving sportsman, that I had never eaten anything so delicious.

He bowed stiffly, and sat down to his own supper, which consisted, primitively, of a jug of milk and a basin of porridge. We ate in silence, and, when we had done, Jacob removed the tray. I then drew my chair back to the fireside. My host, somewhat to my surprise, did the same, and turning abruptly towards me, said:

"Sir, I have lived here in strict retirement for three-and-twenty years. During that time, I have not seen as many strange faces, and I have not read a single newspaper. You are the first stranger who has crossed my threshold for more than four years. Will you favour me with a few words of information respecting that outer world from which I have parted company so long?"

"Pray interrogate me," I replied. "I am heartily at your service."

He bent his head in acknowledgment; leaned forward, with his elbows resting on his knees and his chin supported in the palms of his hands; stared fixedly into the fire; and proceeded to question me.

His inquiries related chiefly to scientific matters, with the later progress of which, as applied to the practical purposes of life, he was almost wholly unacquainted. No student of science myself, I replied as well as my slight information permitted; but the task was far from easy, and I was much relieved when, passing from interrogation to discussion, he began pouring forth his own conclusions upon the facts which I had been attempting to place before him. He talked, and I listened spellbound. He talked till I believe he almost forgot my presence, and only thought aloud.

I had never heard anything like it then; I have never heard anything like it since. Familiar with all systems of all philosophies, subtle in analysis, bold in generalisation, he poured forth his thoughts in an uninterrupted stream, and, still leaning forward in the same moody attitude with his eyes fixed upon the fire, wandered from topic to topic, from speculation to speculation, like an inspired dreamer. From practical science to mental philosophy; from electricity in the wire to electricity in the nerve; from Watts to Mesmer, from Mesmer to Reichenbach, from Reichenbach to Swedenborg, Spinoza, Condillac, Descartes, Berkeley, Aristotle, Plato, and the Magi and mystics of the East, were transitions which, however bewildering in their variety and scope, seemed easy and harmonious upon his lips as sequences in music.

By-and-by—I forget now by what link of conjecture or illustration—he passed on to that field which lies beyond the boundary line of even conjectural philosophy, and reaches no man knows whither. He spoke of the soul and its aspirations; of the spirit and its powers; of second sight; of prophecy; of those phenomena which, under the names of ghosts, spectres, and supernatural appearances, have been denied by the sceptics and attested by the credulous, of all ages.

"The world," he said, "grows hourly more and more sceptical of all that lies beyond its own narrow radius; and our men of science foster the fatal tendency. They condemn as fable all that resists experiment. They reject as false all that cannot be brought to the test of the laboratory or the dissecting-room. Against what superstition have they waged so long and obstinate a war, as against the belief in apparitions?

"And yet what superstition has maintained its hold upon the minds of men so long and so firmly? Show me any fact in physics, in history, in archæology, which is supported by testimony so wide and so various. Attested by all races of men, in all ages, and in all climates, by the soberest sages of antiquity, by the rudest savage of today, by the Christian, the Pagan, the Pantheist, the Materialist, this phenomenon is treated as a nursery tale by the philosophers of our century. Circumstantial evidence weighs with them as a feather in the balance. The comparison of causes with effects, however valuable in physical science, is put aside as worthless and unreliable. The evidence of competent witnesses, however conclusive in a court of justice, counts for nothing. He who pauses before he pronounces, is condemned as a trifler. He who believes, is a dreamer or a fool."

He spoke with bitterness, and, having said thus, relapsed for some minutes into silence. Presently he raised his head from his hands, and added, with an altered voice and manner, "I, sir, paused, investigated, believed, and was not ashamed to state my convictions to the world. I, too, was branded as a visionary, held up to ridicule by my contemporaries, and hooted from that field of science in which I had laboured with honour during all the best years of my life. These things happened just three-and-twenty years ago. Since then, I have lived as you see me living now, and the world has forgotten me, as I have forgotten the world. You have my history."

"It is a very sad one," I murmured, scarcely knowing what to answer.

"It is a very common one," he replied. "I have only suffered for the truth, as many a better and wiser man has suffered before me."

He rose, as if desirous of ending the conversation, and went over to the window.

"It has ceased snowing," he observed, as he dropped the curtain, and came back to the fireside.

"Ceased!" I exclaimed, starting eagerly to my feet. "Oh, if it were only possible—but no! it is hopeless. Even if I could find my way across the moor, I could not walk twenty miles tonight."

"Walk twenty miles tonight!" repeated my host. "What are you thinking of?"

"Of my wife," I replied, impatiently. "Of my young wife, who does not know that I have lost my way, and who is at this moment breaking her heart with suspense and terror."

"Where is she?"

"At Dwolding, twenty miles away."

"At Dwolding," he echoed, thoughtfully. "Yes, the distance, it is true, is twenty miles; but—are you so very anxious to save the next six or eight hours?"

"So very, very anxious, that I would give ten guineas at this moment for a guide and a horse."

"Your wish can be gratified at a less costly rate," said he, smiling. "The night mail from the north, which changes horses at Dwolding, passes within five miles of this spot, and will be due at a certain cross-road in about an hour and a quarter. If Jacob were to go with you across the moor, and put you into the old coach-road, you could find your way, I suppose, to where it joins the new one?"

"Easily—gladly."

He smiled again, rang the bell, gave the old servant his directions, and, taking a bottle of whisky and a wineglass from the cupboard in which he kept his chemicals, said:

"The snow lies deep, and it will be difficult walking tonight on the moor. A glass of usquebaugh before you start?"

I would have declined the spirit, but he pressed it on me, and I drank it. It went down my throat like liquid flame, and almost took my breath away.

"It is strong," he said; "but it will help to keep out the cold. And now you have no moments to spare. Good night!"

I thanked him for his hospitality, and would have shaken hands, but that he had turned away before I could finish my sentence. In another minute I had traversed the hall, Jacob had locked the outer door behind me, and we were out on the wide white moor.

Although the wind had fallen, it was still bitterly cold. Not a star glimmered in the black vault overhead. Not a sound, save the rapid crunching of the snow beneath our feet, disturbed the heavy stillness of the night. Jacob, not too well pleased with his mission, shambled on before in sullen silence, his lantern in his hand, and his shadow at his feet. I followed, with my gun over my shoulder, as little inclined for conversation as himself.

My thoughts were full of my late host. His voice yet rang in my ears. His eloquence yet held my imagination captive. I remember to this day, with surprise, how my over-excited brain retained whole sentences and parts of sentences, troops of brilliant images, and fragments of splendid reasoning, in the very words in which he had uttered them.

Musing thus over what I had heard, and striving to recall a lost link here and there, I strode on at the heels of my guide, absorbed and unobservant. Presently—at the end, as it seemed to me, of only a few minutes—he came to a sudden halt, and said:

"Yon's your road. Keep the stone fence to your right hand, and you can't fail of the way."

"This, then, is the old coach-road?"

"Ay, 'tis the old coach-road."

"And how far do I go, before I reach the cross-roads?"

"Nigh upon three mile."

I pulled out my purse, and he became more communicative.

"The road's a fair road enough," said he, "for foot passengers; but 'twas over steep and narrow for the northern traffic. You'll mind where the parapet's broken away, close again the sign-post. It's never been mended since the accident."

"What accident?"

"Eh, the night mail pitched right over into the valley below—a gude fifty feet an' more—just at the worst bit o' road in the whole county."

"Horrible! Were many lives lost?"

"All. Four were found dead, and t'other two died next morning."

"How long is it since this happened?"

"Just nine year."

"Near the sign-post, you say? I will bear it in mind. Good night."

"Gude night, sir, and thankee." Jacob pocketed his half-crown, made a faint pretence of touching his hat, and trudged back by the way he had come.

I watched the light of his lantern till it quite disappeared, and then turned to pursue my way alone. This was no longer matter of the slightest difficulty, for, despite the dead darkness overhead, the line of stone fence showed distinctly enough against the pale gleam of the snow. How silent it seemed now, with only my footsteps to listen to; how silent and how solitary!

A strange disagreeable sense of loneliness stole over me. I walked faster. I hummed a fragment of a tune. I cast up enormous sums in my head, and accumulated them at compound interest. I did my best, in short, to forget the startling speculations to which I had but just been listening, and, to some extent, I succeeded.

Meanwhile the night air seemed to become colder and colder, and though I walked fast I found it impossible to keep myself warm. My feet were like ice. I lost sensation in my hands, and grasped my gun mechanically. I even breathed with difficulty, as though, instead of traversing a quiet north country highway, I were scaling the uppermost heights of some gigantic Alp. This last symptom became presently so distressing, that I was forced to stop for a few minutes, and lean against the stone fence.

As I did so, I chanced to look back up the road, and there, to my infinite relief, I saw a distant point of light, like the gleam of an approaching lantern. I at first concluded that Jacob had retraced his steps and followed me; but even as the conjecture presented itself, a second light flashed into sight—a light evidently parallel with the first, and approaching at the same rate of motion. It needed no second thought to show me that these must be the carriage-lamps of some private vehicle, though it seemed strange that any private vehicle should take a road professedly disused and dangerous

There could be no doubt, however, of the fact, for the lamps grew larger and brighter every moment, and I even fancied I could already see the dark outline of the carriage between them. It was coming up very fast, and quite noiselessly, the snow being nearly a foot deep under the wheels.

And now the body of the vehicle became distinctly visible behind the lamps. It looked strangely lofty. A sudden suspicion flashed upon me. Was it possible that I had passed the cross-roads in the dark without observing the sign-post, and could this be the very coach which I had come to meet?

No need to ask myself that question a second time, for here it came round the bend of the road, guard and driver, one outside passenger, and four steaming greys, all wrapped in a soft haze of light, through which the lamps blazed out, like a pair of fiery meteors.

I jumped forward, waved my hat, and shouted. The mail came

311

down at full speed, and passed me. For a moment I feared that I had not been seen or heard, but it was only for a moment. The coachman pulled up; the guard, muffled to the eyes in capes and comforters, and apparently sound asleep in the rumble, neither answered my hail nor made the slightest effort to dismount; the outside passenger did not even turn his head. I opened the door for myself, and looked in. There were but three travellers inside, so I stepped in, shut the door, slipped into the vacant corner, and congratulated myself on my good fortune.

The atmosphere of the coach seemed, if possible, colder than that of the outer air, and was pervaded by a singularly damp and disagreeable smell. I looked round at my fellow-passengers. They were all three, men, and all silent. They did not seem to be asleep, but each leaned back in his corner of the vehicle, as if absorbed in his own reflections. I attempted to open a conversation.

"How intensely cold it is tonight," I said, addressing my opposite neighbour.

He lifted his head, looked at me, but made no reply.

"The winter," I added, "seems to have begun in earnest."

Although the corner in which he sat was so dim that I could distinguish none of his features very clearly, I saw that his eyes were still turned full upon me. And yet he answered never a word.

At any other time I should have felt, and perhaps expressed, some annoyance, but at the moment I felt too ill to do either. The icy coldness of the night air had struck a chill to my very marrow, and the strange smell inside the coach was affecting me with an intolerable nausea. I shivered from head to foot, and, turning to my left-hand neighbour, asked if he had any objection to an open window?

He neither spoke nor stirred.

I repeated the question somewhat more loudly, but with the same result. Then I lost patience, and let the sash down. As I did so, the leather strap broke in my hand, and I observed that the glass was covered with a thick coat of mildew, the accumulation, apparently, of years. My attention being thus drawn to the condition of the coach, I examined it more narrowly, and saw by the uncertain light of the outer lamps that it was in the last stage of dilapidation.

Every part of it was not only out of repair, but in a condition of decay. The sashes splintered at a touch. The leather fittings were crusted over with mould, and literally rotting from the woodwork. The floor was almost breaking away beneath my feet. The whole machine, in short, was foul with damp, and had evidently been dragged from some outhouse in which it had been mouldering away for years, to do another day or two of duty on the road.

I turned to the third passenger, whom I had not yet addressed, and hazarded one more remark.

"This coach," I said, "is in a deplorable condition. The regular mail, I suppose, is under repair?"

He moved his head slowly, and looked me in the face, without speaking a word. I shall never forget that look while I live. I turned cold at heart under it. I turn cold at heart even now when I recall it. His eyes glowed with a fiery unnatural lustre. His face was livid as the face of a corpse. His bloodless lips were drawn back as if in the agony of death, and showed the gleaming teeth between.

The words that I was about to utter died upon my lips, and a strange horror—a dreadful horror—came upon me. My sight had by this time become used to the gloom of the coach, and I could see with tolerable distinctness. I turned to my opposite neighbour. He, too, was looking at me, with the same startling pallor in his face, and the same stony glitter in his eyes. I passed my hand across my brow. I turned to the passenger on the seat beside my own, and saw—oh Heaven! how shall I describe what I saw?

I saw that he was no living man—that none of them were living men, like myself! A pale phosphorescent light—the light of putrefaction—played upon their awful faces; upon their hair, dank with the dews of the grave; upon their clothes, earth-stained and dropping to pieces; upon their hands, which were as the hands of corpses long buried. Only their eyes, their terrible eyes, were living; and those eyes were all turned menacingly upon me!

A shriek of terror, a wild unintelligible cry for help and mercy; burst from my lips as I flung myself against the door, and strove in vain to open it.

In that single instant, brief and vivid as a landscape beheld in the flash of summer lightning, I saw the moon shining down through a rift of stormy cloud—the ghastly sign-post rearing its warning finger by the wayside—the broken parapet—the plunging horses—the black gulf below. Then, the coach reeled like a ship at sea. Then, came a mighty crash—a sense of crushing pain—and then, darkness.

It seemed as if years had gone by when I awoke one morning from a deep sleep, and found my wife watching by my bedside I will pass over the scene that ensued, and give you, in half a dozen words, the tale she told me with tears of thanksgiving. I had fallen over a precipice, close against the junction of the old coach-road and the new, and had only been saved from certain death by lighting upon a deep snowdrift that had accumulated at the foot of the rock beneath.

In this snowdrift I was discovered at daybreak, by a couple of shepherds, who carried me to the nearest shelter, and brought a surgeon to my aid. The surgeon found me in a state of raving delirium, with a broken arm and a compound fracture of the skull. The letters in my pocket-book showed my name and address; my wife was summoned to nurse me; and, thanks to youth and a fine constitution, I came out of danger at last. The place of my fall, I need scarcely say, was precisely that at which a frightful accident had happened to the north mail nine years before.

I never told my wife the fearful events which I have just related to you. I told the surgeon who attended me; but he treated the whole adventure as a mere dream born of the fever in my brain. We discussed the question over and over again, until we found that we could discuss it with temper no longer, and then we dropped it.

Others may form what conclusions they please—I know that twenty years ago I was the fourth inside passenger in that Phantom Coach.

The Recollections of
Professor Henneberg

There are more things in heaven and earth, Horatio,
Than are dreamt of in your philosophy.—Hamlet.

There are remembrances for which no philosophy will account—sensations for which experience can discover no parallel, Few persons will hesitate to confess to you that they have beheld scenes and faces which were new and yet familiar; of which they seemed to have dreamed in time gone by; and which, without any apparent cause, produced a painfully intimate impression upon their minds. I myself have dreamed of a place, and again forgotten that dream. Years have passed away, and the dream has returned to me, unaltered in the minutest particular.

I have at last come suddenly upon the scene in some wild land which I had never visited before, and have recognised it, tree for tree, field for field, as I had beheld it in my dream. Then the dream and the scene became one in my mind, and by that Union I learned to wrest from Nature a portion of one of her obscurest secrets. What are these phenomena? Whence these fragmentary recollections which seem to establish a mysterious link between death and sleep? What is death? What is sleep? It is a law of the philosophy of mind that we can think of nothing which we have not perceived, The induction is, that we have perceived these things; but not, perhaps, in our present State of being."

"You believe, then, in the doctrine of pre-existence!" I exclaimed, pushing back my chair, and looking my guest earnestly in the face.

"I believe in the immortality of the soul," replied the Professor with unmoved solemnity. "I feel that I am, and that I have been. Eternity is a circle—you reduce it to a crescent, if you deny the previous half of its immensity. For the soul there is, properly speaking, neither past nor future. It is *now* and eternal. You profess to believe in the immortality of the soul, and in the same breath advance an opinion which, if submitted to a due investigation, would establish a totally adverse System.

"If this soul of yours be immortal, it must have existed from all time. If not, what guarantee have you that it will continue to be during all time to come? That which shall have no end can have no beginning. It is a part of God, and partakes of his nature. To be born is the same as to die. Both are transitionary; not creative or final. Life is but a restore of the Soul, and as often as we die, we but change one vesture for another."

"But this is the theory of the metempsychosis!" I said, smiling. "You have studied the philosophy of Oriental literature till you have yourself become a believer in the religion of Bramah!"

"All tradition," said the Professor, "is a type of Spiritual truth. The superstitions of the East, and the mythologies of the North—the beautiful Fables of old Greece, and the bold investigations of modern science—all tend to elucidate the same principles; all take their root in those promptings and questionings which are innate in the brain and heart of man. Plato believed that the soul was immortal, and born frequently; that it knew all things; and that what we call learning is but the effort which it makes to recall the wisdom of the Past. 'For to search and to learn,' saith the poet-philosopher, 'is reminiscence all.' At the bottom of every religious theory, however wild and savage, lies a perception—dim perhaps, and distorted, but still a perception—of God and immortality."

"And you think that we have all lived before, and all shall live again?"

"I know it," replied the Professor, "My life has been one long succession of these revelations; and I am persuaded that if we would compel the mind to a severe contemplation of itself—if we would resolutely study the phenomena of psychology as developed within the limits of our own consciousness—we might all arrive at the recognition of this mystery of pre-existence. The 'caverns of the mind' are obscure, but not impenetrable; and all who have courage may follow their labyrinthine windings to the light of truth beyond."

Two days after this conversation I left Leipzig for Frankfort. Just as I was taking my seat in the diligence, a man wearing the livery of a College messenger, made his appearance at the window. He was breathless with running, and held a small parcel in his band.

"What is this?" I asked, as he handed it to me.

"From Professor Henneberg," he replied. He was proceeding to say more, but the diligence gave a lurch, and rolled heavily forward; the messenger sprang back; the postillions cracked their whips; and in a moment we were clattering over the rough pavement of the town.

There were but two passengers in the interior, beside myself. One was a priest, who did nothing but sleep and read his breviary, and who was perfumed, moreover, with a strong scent of garlic. The other was a young German Student, who sat with his head banging outside the window, smoking cigars.

As I did not find either of my companions particularly prepossessing, and as I had forgotten to furnish my pockets with any literature more entertaining than *Murray's Handbook of South Germany*, I was agreeably surprised, on opening the packet, to discover a considerable number of pages in my learned friend's very peculiar handwriting, neatly tied together at the corners, and accompanied by a note. in which he gave me to understand that the MSS. contained a brief sketch of some passages in his life which he thought might interest me, and which were, moreover, illustrative of that doctrine of pre-existence respecting which we had been conversing a few evenings before.

These papers I have taken the liberty of styling—

My parents resided in Dresden, where I was born on the evening of the fourth of May, 1790.

My mother died before I was many hours in being, and I was sent out to nurse at a farmhouse in the immediate neighbourhood of the city. I cannot say that I have any distinct remembrance of the first few years that ushered in this present life with which I am endued. I was kindly treated. I grew in the fields and the sun, like a young plant. My father came regularly every Sunday and Thursday to see me; and I learned to look upon the Frau Schleitz as my mother. When I had reached the age of ten years, I was removed to a large public school in Dresden.

Up to this time I had received no education whatever. I was as ignorant as a babe of two years old. I therefore entered the academy at a period when I was just of an age to be painfully conscious of my inferiority to boys considerably my Juniors. Undoubtedly my father did me a great injustice by thus delaying to furnish my young mind with that intellectual nutriment which is as essential to our mental being as wine and meat to our physical nature; but he was eccentric, arbitrary, and a visionary.

It was one of his favourite theories that early childhood should be sacred from the anxieties of learning, and devoted wholly to the acquisition of bodily health; that youth should be appropriated to study; that manhood should be passed in action; and that old age should enjoy repose. Into these four epochs he would have had the lives of all mankind divided; forgetting that between stages so opposite there could exist no harmony of disposition or unity of purpose. Had he been an absolute monarch, he would have compelled his subjects to conform to these regulations. As he was only a German merchant, and possessed entire control over but one creature in the World, he practised his System at my expense.

For the first month or two I suffered acutely. I found myself pitied by the masters and despised by the boys. The
latter excluded me from their sports and openly derided
my ignorance. When I stood up to repeat my task, I stood
where, five minutes before, boys younger than myself had
been reading aloud from Tacitos and Herodotus. When I
strove to acquire the rudiments of arithmetic, it was in a
room where the least advanced scholar was already occupied upon the problems of Euclid.

To a proud nature such as mine, this State of degradation
was intolerable. Though sometimes almost overborne by
shame and anguish, I made superhuman efforts to regain
the time which had been lost. I was speedily rewarded for
my exertions. My progress was astonishing; and, though
still far behind the rest, the rapidity with which I mastered
all that was given me to learn, and, indeed, the manner in
which I frequently anticipated the Instructions of the tu-
tors, became the marvel of the school.

My father was wealthy and supplied me liberally with
money, This money I devoted wholly to the purchase of
books. When the other boys were playing in the grounds
of the academy, I used to steal away to the deserted bed-
chambers, or to my accustomed corner in the empty
classroom, and there labour earnestly at the acquisition of
some of those branches of learning into which I had been
but lately inducted, or at which, in the regular course of
study, I had not yet arrived.

Thus, too, in the morning, before any of my companions
were awake, I would draw a volume from under my pillow, or tax my memory to recall all the information which
I had gathered during the previous day. By these means I
not only continued to add hourly to my store, but I forgot
nothing that I had once made my own.

And now let me confess something connected with my
progress—something upon which I have often reflected
with sensations approaching to terror—something which

I have since attempted to analyze, and which has guided me to the interpretation of that mystery in which my subsequent life has been enveloped.

Nothing that I learned was entirely new to me.

Yes, strange and awful as it may appear, I never read a book which did not seem as if it had once been familiar to me. All knowledge vibrated in my soul like the echo of a familiar voice. When my teacher was elucidating a problem, or explaining some of the phenomena of science, I invariably outstripped the sense of his argument, and, taking the words from his mouth, would leap at the conclusion before he had well begun. Many times he has started, questioned me, accused me of previously studying the book; and always I have proved to him that it had never been for an instant in my possession.

I thus obtained a character for natural powers of reasoning which I could not refute, and yet which I felt were undeserved. It was by no internal ratiocination that I arrived at the knowledge which so surprised, not only my instructors, but myself. The faculty was spontaneous. I had no control over it. It came with all the sudden clearness of conviction, and illumined the subject at once, like a gleam of lightning. I was sometimes bewildered to find how intimately the workings of this comprehension resembled the unsought promptings of memory.

However, I was at this time too young to enter minutely upon so difficult an investigation as that of the operations of the mind, and my thoughts were already charged with undertakings almost beyond their powers. I was therefore content to accept my good fortune without questioning its sources too curiously.

Five years elapsed. During that time I had passed from the lowest bench to the rank of senior scholar at the academy; I had mastered two of the living languages (English and French) besides my own; I was tolerably well-read in the classics; I had gone through the entire routine of school mathematics; and I was the author of an anonymous volume on Social Philosophy.

At this point of my education, my father, in compliance with my earnest solicitations, transferred me to the University of Leipzig, where I had scarcely entered my name when I received intelligence of his sudden death. My grief was deep and sincere; but it only served to augment my love of knowledge, and to increase the severity of my studies.

I now directed my attention principally towards Oriental languages and Oriental literature. I lived the life of a hermit. I existed only in the past. I avoided the abstractions of the outer world; and I devoted myself entirely to the acquisition of Hebrew, Persian, Hindoo, and Indian learning.

At College, as at school, my efforts were followed by the same rapid and unvarying success. I bore away the prize at every public examination, and finally received the highest university honours. Still I had no inclination to leave Leipzig. I continued to occupy my old apartments, to prosecute my old studies, and to lead precisely the same life as heretofore. Thus six years more were added to my term of existence; and at twenty-one years of age, on the death of one of my own instructors, I was by unanimous election inducted into the vacant professorship of Oriental literature.

This unparalleled progress surprised no one so much as myself , f or I alone knew the extraordinary manner in which it was accomplished. Knowledge came to me more as a revelation than a study—yet the word 'revelation' is inadequate to express my meaning. *Memory*, I repeat—*memory* is the only mental process resembling that to which I owed my success.

I had one friend, by name Frank Ormesby. He was an Englishman, and had entered the university about a year later than myself. Young, brilliantly gifted, and saturated with the spirit of German literature, he had chosen to finish his education at Leipzig. But for this friendship I should scarcely have had a tie of human affection in common with the World around me.

Frank Ormesby was the last male descendant of an old aristocratic family in the West of England. His ancestors had suffered extensive losses during the period of the Commonwealth, and had regained but a small portion of their property at the hands of the graceless and profligate Charles. Two or three farms, with the old manor-house and park, alone remained to that family whose loyal cavaliers had not hesitated to arm their tenantry and melt their hereditary plate in the service of the Stuarts. Small as it was, the estate was rendered still less valuable through the extravagance of some later Ormesbys; and, when Frank succeeded to it, was so encumbered as scarcely to yield him the few annual hundreds which were necessary to supply the expenses of a gentleman.

In this remote and melancholy manor, shut in by dark old trees, and attended only by a governess and one or two old servants, my friend's young sister lived, in deep seclusion. The pair were orphans; and they were all in all to each other. Frank had not a thought in which the happiness of Grace was not considered; Grace looked up to Frank as to a paragon of truth and talent.

During the long walks which we used sometimes to take beyond the confines of the city, Frank delighted to talk to me of his sister's gentleness and beauty; and I delighted to listen to him. It was a topic of which we were never weary, and which no discussion could exhaust.

Secluded as I was from the gentle influences of female society, these conversations produced a profound impression upon my heart. I learned to love without having beheld her. I suffered myself to dream golden dreams. I hung upon his words with the enraptured faith of a devotee before the shrine of a veiled divinity, and yielded up my whole soul to the dangerous fascination.

At length the time came when Frank must return to England. When I must be once more alone— more alone than if I had never possessed his friendship!

One evening we were loitering through the garden of the university, arm in arm, silent and melancholy. Each knew the other's thoughts, and neither spoke of parting. Suddenly Frank turned, and said:—

"Why don't you come with me, Henneberg? The trip to England would do you good."

I smiled, and shook my head.

"Ah! No," I said, "I am a snail, and the college is my shell."

"Nonsense!" he replied. "You must come. I will have it so. Who knows? Perhaps you and Grace may fall in love with each other!"

The hot blood rushed up to my face; but I made no answer. Frank stopped short, and looking earnestly into my eyes.

"Heinrich," he said, "I seem to have spoken lightly, but I have thought deeply. Could this Union be, it would fulfil the wish that lies nearest to my heart."

My pulse throbbed—my eyes became suffused with tears. Still I remained silent.

"Will you come " he asked.

I said, "Yes."

Never before had I travelled beyond the limits of my native Saxony, and so far from feeling any of the anticipative delight of youth, I shrank from the journey with the nervous timidity of a recluse. Frank rallied me upon my apprehensions.

"My good fellow," he exclaimed, "you have shut yourself up in this old German College till you are little better than a dusty moth-eaten folio yourself! You are but twenty-one years of age, and you are pale and wise as a philosopher of eighty. Your clothes hang about you like an old-fashioned binding; your face is as yellow as parchment; you bow as if you were making an Eastern *salaam*; and the very character of your handwriting is distorted into a resemblance of Oriental characters. This will never do! You must become rejuvenescent, and make up your mind to descend for once to the level of other people. Be a martyr, Heinrich, and write to your tailor for a dress-suit!"

Having resolved to travel round by the Rhine, we proceeded first of all to Mayence.

On the morning of the third day, an incident occurred which, to my thinking, was deeply significant. It wanted more than two hours of noon. The carriage was ascending a precipitous hill, and we were walking some fifty yards in advance. The air was deliciously cool and fragrant, and we paused every now and then to look upon the fair level prospect of wood and vineyard which we were leaving behind. The birds were singing in the green shade of the lindens beside the road.

An old man and a young girl passed us with pleasant words of greeting, and we heard the voices of the vintagers down in the valley. Frank was in high spirits, and sprang forward as if he dared the toilsome hill to weary him. "See!" he cried, "we shall soon reach the summit, and then I predict that we shall be rewarded by the sight of a divine landscape! Mayence must be close at hand, and we shall see the broad, bright rushing Rhine below."

And he began singing in a loud, clear voice, that song beloved of German students, "To the Rhine—to the Rhine!" I smiled at his fresh-hearted enthusiasm, and followed him somewhat more slowly. It was, indeed, as he had said; and on a sudden we beheld, close under our feet, the streets—the cathedral of Mayence—the wide rapid river—the long boat-bridge—the lordly façade of the Palace of Biberich—the banks clothed with plants and autumn flowers —the hurrying steamers with their canvas awnings and their clouds of fleecy smoke—and then, far away, the shadowy hills, the vineyards, the riverside villages, and the winding Rhine flashing along for miles and miles into the far distance. It was a glorious prospect; but the effect which it produced upon me was fearful and unexpected. I stood quite still and pale; then, uttering a wild cry, I clasped my hands over my eyes and cast myself upon the ground.

I distinctly remembered to have seen that very prospect—those spires and towers—that bridge—that red-hued palace—that far landscape, in some past stage of being, vague, dark, forgotten as a dream I When they came to lift me from the spot where I had fallen, they found me in a State of insensibility; and when I recovered my consciousness, it was in a bedchamber of the Königlicher Hof, a little roadside tavern just outside the city. I did not tell Frank the real cause of my illness.

I alleged a sudden giddiness as the reason of my cry when falling. He fancied that it might have been a slight sun-stroke, and I allowed him to think so. The next morning I had sufficiently recovered to resume the journey. We now proposed to take a Rhine steamer to Cologne; but as the boat would not start before the afternoon, I yielded to my friend's persuasions, and went with him to visit the Cathedral of Mayence.

All here was so cool and still, that I felt my troubled heart grow calmer. The sunlight coming in through the stained windows flickered in patches of gold and purple on the marble pavement, and cast long lines of light through the dim cloisters beyond. The *sacristan* was putting fresh flowers on the altar; the great organ, with its front of shining pipes, was quite dumb and breathless, like a dead giant.

Some little flaring tapers were burning on a votive stand beside the door; and an old beggar-woman, with her crutches lying beside her on the ground, was devoutly kneeling before the altar. Leaving these, we hurried through the dirty narrow streets of the town, and sat under the shadow of some leafy walnuts on one of the hills looking over the Rhine. Here we watched the women spinning at their doors, and my friend recited Schiller's wondrous ballad, *The Cranes of Ibycus.*

Thus the morning passed away, and in a few hours more we were gliding along the broad current, between vine-yards and rocks, and ruined blank-eyed towers; islands with trees dipping down to the water; quaint old towns, with gothic spires; and sloping forests of the oak and pine.

But there is no need that I should describe the Rhine to you, my friend, for whom I write these brief pages of troubled memories! Since those days of my youth, you, too, have traversed the scenes of which I speak—you, too, have felt the influence of their beauty sink like dew upon the arid sands of your thirsty heart. If I say that we went on and on, past Coblentz and Andernach, and Bonn— that we stayed for a day at Cologne; that we there hired a vehicle to transport us to Cleves; and that from thence we proceeded along the smooth roads of Holland, you will recall sufficient of your own experience to follow in our track, and to imagine the feelings with which I, a hermit-student, must have contemplated such varied and remarkable scenery.

From Rotterdam we took the steamer for England, and in rather more than a fortnight from the date of our departure, arrived one sultry evening in London.

"Shall we stay here for a few days, that I may show you some of the wonders of our great city?" asked Frank, as we sat at supper in a dismal sitting-room at the back of a great gloomy inn in the neighbourhood of St. Paul's Cathedral. But I felt stunned by the roar and hurry of the streets through which we had just passed.

"Ah, no!" I said; "I am not fit for this place. So much life oppresses me. Let us go quickly to your old quiet home. I shall be happier amid the dim alleys of your park, or dreaming over the books in your library. I need peace—

peace and rest!"

It was already evening when we reached the gates of Ormesby Park. They were very rusty old gates, and creaked mournfully upon their hinges as we rolled through them. A white-headed man crept out of the dilapidated lodge to admit us, and stood looking after the chaise in feeble wonder, as it proceeded up the avenue.

"Poor old Williams!" said Frank, leaning back with a sigh. "He has quite forgotten me!"

"What superb trees!" I exclaimed, looking up at the gigantic branches overhead.

"They are beautiful!" replied my friend, more cheerfully. "I have often been tempted, I confess, to cut down the old timber; but now I vow it shall never be desecrated by the axe. See! there you catch a glimpse of the house."

I leaned forward, and just saw it for a moment through a passing gap. It was an antique Elizabethan building, with gable-ends and large bay windows, and a terraced garden in front.

"I think I know at which window Grace is standing!" said Ormesby. "I wonder how she looks! To think of its being five years since we parted!"

I began to get nervous.

"Does she know that I am coming?" I asked, hurriedly.

Frank burst into a hearty laugh.

"Know that you are coming! to be sure she does; and she will be surprised enough when she sees you. Why, man, I told her that I was going to bring the Professor of Oriental Literature with me—a grave old gentleman of eccentric habits, but profound learning, whom I hoped she would try to like for my sake!"

"My dear Frank," I said hastily, "it was unnecessary, I think, to place your friend in so ridiculous a position at his first interview . . ."

"Hush!" said he, grasping me affectionately by the hand; "do not say that. She has long known how I love and value Heinlich Henneberg. And now jump out, for here we are at last!"

We had driven round to the back of the house, where two or three old servants were gathered to receive us. Frank ran past them, and taking a lady in his arms, who was standing near the door, covered her cheeks and brow with kisses.

"Grace, my darling Grace!" he said, bending his proud head fondly down towards her.

"My dear brother!" replied the lady, hiding her face upon his shoulder, and sobbing aloud.

I turned away; for I had no place there, and my own eyes filled with tears.

"So tall too!" I heard him say; "so tall and so beautiful! So changed; and yet the same dear Grace I left five years ago!"

"Five years ago!" echoed the lady in a low voice.

"But here is Professor Henneberg, waiting to be introduced to you," said Frank, drawing her arm through his. "Heinrich, this is my dear and only sister: Grace, welcome this gentleman he is my friend."

It was not because I had heard and thought so much of her already; it was not even for her beauty, rare and winning though it was—No, it was for none of these, but for the earnest soul looking out from her dark eyes, that I succumbed in one moment to that deep and passionate tide of love which has never ceased since then to overflow my heart.

Confused and silent, I could only bow to her; and when she extended her hand—that small white band—what could I do but hold it, tremblingly and irresolutely in mine, and then stoop down and kiss it?

"My friend has saluted you after our German fashion, Grace," said Frank smiling, as he saw her embarrassment and mine.

"Abroad we kiss the hand of a lady, and we only shake that

of a gentleman. If he be a heart-friend, or a brother, we rub our rough beards together in a fraternal embrace."

A little while afterwards, when we were sitting in a window overlooking the old park, the lady, after glancing doubtfully towards me twice or thrice, laid her hand gently on her brother's arm, and said—

"But where, my dear Frank, is the other gentleman—the Oriental scholar—whom you prepared me to receive?"

A malicious smile hovered over his lips, and danced in his dark eyes.

"This is the learned Professor in person," he replied, laughingly. "Speak for yourself, friend; and if Grace continues to doubt your identity, reply with a spirited harangue in Syriac or Sanskrit! By the way, sister mine, can you discover who it is that Henneberg resembles? From the moment I first saw him, I knew that I had been used to a face strangely like his, *e'en from my boyish days*; yet for my life I cannot tell whose that face may be."

"Nor I," replied Grace Ormesby. "But Professor Henneberg's face seems not unknown to me."

"How beautiful this is!" I exclaimed, stepping out upon the balcony, and looking over the wide, wooded country, the distant hills, the park, and the quaint, formal garden. The moon was just rising on one side, and the red sun sinking slowly on the other.

"It is a truly English scene," replied the lady; "but I suppose it will not bear comparison with your German forests and vineyards. We have, however, many charming drives around, and some points of view that might delight even a poet."

"*Even* a poet!" repeated Frank, smiling. "Why, I think poets are more easily delighted than other people. There is no scene so dull, and no subject so dry, but they will contrive to throw a grace and glory upon it. We must take you round tomorrow, Henneberg, to the grotto which we, when children, used to call our Hermitage. And there is the old chapel for you to see; it lies down in that hollow, within the park boundaries. It is a picturesque old place enough. The tombs of our predecessors are ranged all down the side-aisles, and their rusty armour hangs above them—

The knights' bones are dust,
And their good swords rust;
Their souls are with the saints I trust!

"Then your library of old folios!" I exclaimed; "I must see that before anything. flow delightful to stroll out with some quaint black-letter pamphlet redolent of the dust of centuries, and lie reading in the shade of yonder trees!"
The lady smiled, and added:—
"Where you will moralize, like 'the melancholy Jaques'—

Under an oak, whose antique roots peep out
Upon the brook that brawls along this wood.'

But I ask your pardon; I should not quote Shakespeare to a foreigner."
"Miss Ormesby is mistaken, if she supposes that we Germans are ignorant of the works of her great poet!" I said, earnestly, "Shakespeare—to use the words of a great German critic—was naturalised in Germany the moment that he was known. The same critic—Augustus Wilhelm von Schlegel—enjoys the distinction of having first directed the attention of Europe to the philosophical significance of his dramas.. Before Schlegel, Lessing wrote upon Shakespeare; Herder has studied him; Tieck began a series of letters upon his plays; and Goethe, in his *Wilhelm Meister,* has spoken of him with reverence and enthusiasm."
"This is indeed a pleasant tale for English ears!" exclaimed the lady, with a flush upon her pale cheek; "and we should be proud to hear it. I wish I spoke your language as well as you speak ours."
And so the conversation changed, and flowed on into oth-

er Channels, like a mountain-stream, now winding past a little quiet isle, now dashing over the steep rocks, now murmuring softly through the rushes near a cottage-door, and anon wandering out and losing itself in the deep sea. Thus the hours glided away unnoticed, and it was nearly midnight when I withdrew.

Mine was a large dark room, with an enormous bed, like a hearse, in the centre of the floor. Two ebony cabinets, richly inlaid, stood on either side of the fireplace. An antique Venetian mirror was suspended above the toilette-table, and some high-backed chairs and *moyen age fauteuils* were scattered about in various directions.

Glancing round at these details, I walked over to one of the casements, threw it open, and, leaning forward into the moonlight, thought of the lady whom I already dared to love. It was long past midnight when I returned into the chamber, and dropped upon a chair:

Benedetto sia 'l giorno, el mese, e l'anno,
E la stagione, e'l tempo, e l'ora, e '1 punto,
E'l bei paese, e'l loco, ov' io fui giunto
Da due begli occhi che legato m'hanno!"[1]

I exclaimed, in the impassioned words of Petrarch, as I bent my head down upon my hands, and whispered one name softly to myself.

After a time I looked up again; my eyes wandered listlessly round the room, and encountered a picture which I had not before observed. I rose; I advanced towards it; I raised the candle . . . a freezing sensation came upon me; my eyes grew dim; my heart stood still in that portrait I recognized—*myself*!

Suddenly I turned and rushed to the door; but, as my fingers closed upon the handle, I paused.

---

1. *Blessed be the day, the month, the year, the season, the weather, the hour, and point of time, and the beautiful country, and the place where I was taken captive by those two beautiful eyes which have enchanted me!*

"What folly!" I said. "It can be nothing but a mirror!"
So I nerved myself to return.

Once more I stood before it, and surveyed it steadily. It was no mirror, but a picture—an old oil-painting, cracked in many places, and mellow with the deepened tones of age. The Portrait represented a young man in the costume of the reign of James the first, with raff and doublet. But the face—the face! I sickened as I gazed upon it; for every feature was mine! The long light hair, descending almost to the Shoulders; the pallid hue and anxious brow, the compressed lips and fair moustache, the very form and expression of the eye—all, all my own, as though reflected from the surface of a mirror!

I stood fascinated, spellbound: my eyes were riveted upon the picture, and its eyes, glance for glance, on mine. At length the tide of horror seemed to burst its bounds; a groan broke from my Ups, and, dashing my lamp upon the ground that I might behold the face no more, I flew to the window, and leaped out into the garden.

All that night, hour after hour, I wandered through the avenues and glades of the park, startling the red-deer in their midnight covers, and scattering the dewdrops from the ferns as I passed by.

The morning dawned ere long; the sun shone; the lark rose singing; and the dayflowers opened in the grass. At seven o'clock I bent my steps towards the house, weary, haggard, and depressed. Frank met me in the garden.

"You are early this morning, Heinrich," he said, gaily. Then, observing something strange in my expression, "Good heavens!" he exclaimed, "what is the matter?"

"I have not slept at all," I replied, in a hollow tone; "and I have suffered the torture of a hundred sleepless nights in one. Come with me to my bedchamber, and I will tell you."

We went, and I told him. He heard me out in silence, and looked frequently from the portrait to my face. When I had done, he laughed aloud and shook his head.

"I acknowledge," he said, "that the resemblance is striking; and not only the resemblance, but the coincidence; for, to tell you the truth, this is actually the portrait of one of your countrymen—a Baron von Ravensberg, of Suabia, who married a daughter of our house in the year 1614. At the same time, my dear Heinrich, I will hear of nothing supernatural in the matter. It is one of those fortuitous circumstances which are of daily occurrence; and, after all, the likeness may be, in a great measure, simply national.

"We know how strongly the peasantry of Scotland and of Ireland are impressed with one physiognomical stamp; and (not to cite the tribes of coloured men, or even the Chinese and Tatars) how remarkably are these facial characteristics imprinted upon the natives of America! The last instance is, indeed, one which admits of wide physiological inquiry. The Americans, gathered together as they are from all the shores of the old world, have, as it were, received a stamp of individuality from the very climate in which they live."

I heard, but scarcely heeded his words. When he had ceased speaking, I looked up as if from a dream.

"It may be all very true, Ormesby," I replied; "but I cannot occupy this room another night."

"Nor is there any occasion that you should," said he, cheerily, "Come down to the breakfast-parlour, and I will order the green bedroom to be prepared for you!"

I felt now as if some destiny were upon me; and many days elapsed before I regained my cheerfulness. By degrees, however, the impression wore away, and as I no longer saw, I ceased to think of the picture.

Oh, thou solitary dream of my life! come back once more, and let me for a brief moment forget the years that have risen up between my soul and thee!

I loved her—shall I say loved? Ah, no! I love her still. I shall love her till I die! Let me tell how deep and passionate that love was; how I lived day after day in the sweet air she breathed; how I sat and watched the inner-light of her dark, earnest eyes; how my heart failed within me, listening to her voice.

Her voice! Ah, that sweet low voice! It vibrates even now upon my ear, and brings the stranger tears back to my eyes! How can I paint the long golden days of that dreamy autumn season, when I went forth by her side through the yellow cornfields, and the pleasant lanes? Sometimes we sat beneath the spreading boughs, while I read aloud to her from Shakespeare, or translated a few pages of Schiller. How my voice rose and trembled as the words gave utterance to the language of my heart!

Then there were happy evenings when we sat by the open windows of the old drawing-room, looking out upon the dusky park and the starry sky; when the harvest-moon shone down upon the stirless trees; when the nightingale shook her wild song from her little throat hard by; and the drowsy air hung enchanted over all!

At such times Grace would touch the keys of the piano, and sing the ballads of my native land.

Why do I linger thus? It was but a dream—let me tell of my awakening.

At the extremity of my friend's garden there stood an old-fashioned summerhouse, shaped like a pagoda, with a gilt ball upon the summit. This point commanded an extensive and beautiful prospect. In front stood the old house, with its carven gable ends and burnished weathercocks; the garden, curiously planted in formal beds, and interspersed with trees of quaintly-cut pyramidal form; the terraced walks; the spreading park; and, beyond the park, the summits of the blue hills far away. In the summerhouse stood a table and two rustic chairs; and just before the entrance a simple pedestal was erected, whereon a dial, worn and rusted by the storms of many years, told the silent hours by the sun.

Here it was that I sat one sunny morning, face to face with her. An open volume lay beside me on the table, I had been reading aloud, and she was busy with some dainty needlework. I could not see her eyes for the dark curls that fell down her cheeks.

The book was *Chaucer*—I remember it well. I had been reading the *Knight's Tale*, and we had broken off at the death of Arcite. After a few words of admiration, there came a pause; and as I turned to resume the poem, my eyes rested upon her, and I could not remove them. Very silently I sat there looking at her, watching the flitting of her fingers, and the Coming and going of her breath; and I asked myself—"Can this be life, or is it nothing but a dream?"

Suddenly, I felt the deep love welling upwards from my heart to my ups; and then—

then I found myself at her feet, clasping her hands in mine, and saying over and over again, in a quick broken voice, between tears and trembling:—

"Grace! dear, dearest Grace, I love you!"

But she made no answer, and only sat quite pale, and still, and downward looking, like a marble saint.

"Not one word, Grace—not one?" Her lips quivered. Slowly she lifted up her face, and fixed her eyes on mine. Oh! how deep they were—how dark—how earnest!

"Heinrich," she said, in a low dear voice, "Heinrich, I loved you long ago—I loved you in imagination, for years before we met."

Surely there was nothing in these words that should not have filled me with delight, and yet they smote upon me with a sensation of indescribable horror.

I had heard them before—ay, and in that very spot!

With the swiftness of lightning it rushed upon me; and in one passing second, as a landscape is seen in the flashes of a storm, I recollected, oh! heavens, not only the place, the hour, the summer-house, the garden; but herself—her words—her eyes! all, all as familiar as they were a portion of my own being!

"Grace! Grace!" I shrieked, springing to my feet, and clasping my hands wildly above my head, "do you not remember?—once before—here, here—centuries ago!—do you not remember?—do you not—do you not remem . . . ."

A choking, dreadful feeling arrested my breath; the ground rocked beneath my feet; a red mist swam before my eyes—I staggered—I fell!

I remember nothing of what followed.

Even now it seems to me as if years passed away between that moment and the period when my consciousness returned. Long passionless years—without a thought, without a hope, without a fear; dark as night, and blank as dreamless sleep!

But it was not so. Scarcely three weeks had elapsed since I was seized with the fever; and so far from having lain there in a passive trance, I had all the time been racked by the burning visions of delirium.

Brought to the very confines of the grave, weak, emaciated, and heedless of all around me, I permitted two or three days to pass away in this state of listless debility, without asking even a question about the past, or daring to dwell for an instant upon the future. I had no strength to think. Those first days of sanity glided by like waking dreams, and I passed insensibly from drowsy perception to long and frequent slumbers. While awake, I listened idly to the ticking of the clock, and to the passing footsteps on the stairs; watched the sunlight creeping slowly round the walls with the advancing day; followed, like a child, the quiet movements of my nurse: and accepted, without question, the medicines and aliments which she brought me. I was feebly conscious, too, of the frequent visits of the doctor; and when he felt my pulse, and enjoined me not to speak, I was too weak and weary even to reply.

On the morning of the third (or it might have been the fourth) day, I woke from a long sleep which seemed to have lasted all the night, and I felt the springs of life and thought renewed within me. I looked round the room, and, for the first time, wondered where I was.

The nurse was soundly sleeping in an armchair at my bedside. The room was large and airy. The window was shadowed by a tree, the leaves of which rustled in the wind. Some bookshelves, laden with bright new volumes, were suspended against the wall; and a small table, covered with phials and wine-glasses, was placed at the foot of the bed. I asked myself where I had been before this illness, and in one moment I remembered all, even to the last broken words!

I must have given utterance to some exclamation, for my attendant woke, and turned a startled face upon me.

"Nurse," I said eagerly, "where am I?—whose house is this?"

"Hush, sir! this is Dr. Howard's; but you are to keep quiet. Here is the doctor himself!"

The door opened, and a gentlemanly-looking man entered. Seeing me awake, he smiled pleasantly, and took a seat beside my bed.

"I see by your face, my young friend, that you are better," he said. "Did I hear you asking where you are? You are my guest and patient."

"How came I here?"

"You have had a brain fever, and were removed to my dwelling at my request. By that Arrangement I have been enabled to give your case more attention. I live in the village of Torringhurst, two miles from Ormesby Park."

"And Frank, and—and Miss Ormesby?" I began hesitatingly.

"Your friends have been very anxious for you," he said, with some irresolution, as if scarce knowing how to reply, "Mr, Ormesby watched many nights at your bedside.

They—they waited till they knew you to be out of danger."

"And then?" I cried eagerly,

"And then they left Ormesby Park for the Continent."

"For the Continent!" I repeated, "Then I must follow them!"

The doctor laid his hand gently on my shoulder. I sank back upon the pillows, utterly powerless; and he resumed:—

"I have promised not to say where they are gone; and—and they do not wish that you should follow."

"But I *will* go! Why should I not? What have I done that I should be treated thus? Oh! cruel, cruel!"

I was so weak and wretched that I burst into tears, and sobbed like a child.

He looked at me gravely and compassionately.

"Herr Professor," he said, taking my band in his, and looking into my eyes, "you are a man of education and intellect. I well know that to leave you in doubt would be not only the unkindest, but the unwisest thing that I could do. Now listen to me, and prepare yourself for a great disappointment. Shortly before your seizure, you made some observations (owing probably to the approach of fever) which much shocked and alarmed your friend's sister. It appears, likewise, that a few weeks before, you expressed yourself very strangely with respect to a picture.

"These two circumstances, I regret to say, have impressed your friends with the idea that you are the victim, I will not say of unsound mind, but of a delusive theory, highly injurious to your own mental and physical wellbeing, as well as to the happiness of those connected with you. Such being the case, Mr. Ormesby is of opinion that your intimacy with his sister must unavoidably cease; and the better to effect this, he has taken her abroad for a time. Mr. Ormesby entrusted me with this letter for you."

Here is a transcript of the letter:—

Deeply painful as it is to me thus to address you after so

severe an illness, my dear Heinrich, I must write a few lines, entreating your forgiveness for the apparent unkindness of which I am guilty in thus quitting England before you are sufficiently recovered to wish me farewell. I will leave to my kind friend Dr. Howard the ungrateful task of explaining my motives for this departure; bat I can trust only my own pen to describe to you the deep grief which that determination has cost me. Nothing but the sense of a duty still more imperative than that of friendship could have forced me to inflict upon you a disappointment in which I entreat you to believe I have an equal share. My dear old College friend, forgive and still love me, for my attachment to you must and will ever be the same. Perhaps in time to come, when all that has lately passed shall be, if not forgotten, at least unregretted, you will suffer me to resume my old place in your confidence, and will welcome to your hearth and heart

Your friend,

Frank Ormesby.

There are times when this beautiful world seems to put on a mourning garb, as if in sympathy with the grief that consumes us; 'when the trees shake their arms in mute sorrow, and scatter their withered leaves like ashes on our heads; when the slow rains weep down around us, and the very clouds look old above'. Then, like Hamlet the Dane:

This goodly frame, the earth, seems to us a sterile promontory; this most excellent canopy, the air, this brave o'er hanging firmament, this majestical roof, fretted with golden fire, appears no other thing than a foul and pestilent congregation of vapours.

And so it was with me, Walking solitary and sad beneath the sighing trees in one of the public gardens of Paris. The dead leaves rustled as I trod, and the bare branches clashed together in the wind. A little to the right flowed the tide of pleasure-seekers. Overhead the clouds hung low and dark, now and then shedding brief showers.

I was still weak and suffering; but I could not stay in the country she had left. I came hither, seeking change and distraction—perhaps, too, with a vague hope that I might find her. Could I but see her once more; could I but hear the sweet sound of her voice, bidding me (if it must be so) an eternal farewell, I felt I should be more at peace with the world and myself.

But in Paris I had found her not—neither had I found peace, nor hope, nor rest. The clouds had rolled between me and the sun, and every land alike was darkened.

I then felt that I could say with Sir Thomas Brown—*For the world, I count it not an inn, but an hospital; and a place not to live, but to die in.*

Yet I never reproached her with my sorrow! Nay, I blessed her for the love that had once beamed on me from her eyes, and for the happy, happy times that must return no more.

Think you, my friend, that I have changed since then? No, I love her still, with a love and reverence inexpressible. She believed me mad. It is a hard word— perhaps it was a hard thought—but was it hers?

I cannot tell; yet I think not. At all events, I feel the sweet assurance that she once loved, and that she always pitied me.

Sometimes I feared it might be as she thought. Might not these flashes of strange memory be the fitful precursors of insanity? I reasoned. I examined myself; but I found no inward corroboration. And all this time, even when my heart was breaking, I loved her, and was thankful that I loved. Even then, I would not have changed the memory of that dream for the blank that went before.

I hold it true, whate'er befall;

I feel it when I sorrow most;
'Tis better to have loved and lost,
Than never to have loved at all.

Fare thee well, sweet Grace Ormesby—fare thee well, dear lady of my love! Go from these pages as from my life, and therein be no more seen. Thy pale face and earnest eyes are still present to me through the mists of many years. Yet doth Time with every season steal somewhat from the distinctness of the Vision; and as mine eyes grow dim, so doth thine image recede farther and farther into the dusky Chambers of the Past. Peace be with thee, lady, wheresoe'er thou art—peace be with thee!

The life of a great city accords ill with a great grief; and yet we do well to mingle with our fellow-creatures, though it be only in the streets of a city where we have no friends. Not the most misanthropic can thread that varying tide without feeling that he is a portion of the many, and that it is his duty to be a worker among men. He has a part to play, and he there knows that he is called upon to play it. Walking in that deserted alley of the Luxembourg Gardens, within hearing, though not within sight of the living stream beyond, this truth became clear to me, and I said—"I have been idle and a dreamer. Books have been my world. From this present suffering I must be free or die; and in activity alone can I ever find forgetfulness. Now I, too, will work."

And I made up my mind to do the work for which I was fitted. I resolved to write my long-contemplated book on *The Languages and Poetry of the East*.

That night my quiet rooms in the dead, old-fashioned Rue du Mont Parnasse, seemed less dreary. It was now almost winter; it had rained at intervals for many days, and the air was very chill. I found a cheerful fire in my sitting-room. The curtains shut out the dismantled garden. I drew my table to the fireplace, trimmed my lamp, took pen and paper, and sketched the outline of my work.

My evening's occupation was followed by a night of sound refreshing sleep; and from this day I recovered rapidly. The next morning found me, for the first time, before the gloomy entrance to the old Bibliotheque Royale, then lodged in the ancient Palais du Cardinal.

I passed through the solemn courtyard, with its little garden, its mounted statue, and its air of classic stillness. I passed on to the reading-rooms, and chose a remote corner by a window. There I took my place amid a busy company, and began my life of authorship in Paris.

Day after day, week after week, I occupied the same place; followed the same train of thought; and resolutely carried out my plan of work. And work rewarded me with a portion of my lost peace. Amid those venerable archives of old learning; amid the wealth of literature amassed from antique days by Francis I., by the Medici, by the Sforzi, by the Visconti, by Petrarch—I lost for awhile the remembrance of my private sorrows.

Excluded on Sundays from the library, I generally passed those mornings in the Louvre, wandering through the galleries of antiquities; pursuing my studies of ancient history amidst the vases, mosaics, and cameos of the Musée Grec et Egyptien; and sometimes, though rarely, mingling with the throngs who on this day frequent the art-galleries.

As the springtime came, I used to escape on Sundays into the pleasant parks in the neighbourhood of Paris. There, in the sylvan glades of St. Cloud, among the alleys of Vincennes, or in the forest-shades of St. Germains, I used to spend long days with a book and my own thoughts. I was resigned, if not happy; and my work progressed as the weeks and months went by.

There was an attendant at the Bibliotheque Royale, in whom I took a considerable interest. He was called M. Benoit. I first remarked him for the respectability of his appearance, and for the courtliness of his address; and I was surprised one day to find that he read the oriental languages with facility.

It happened thus:—I had written the name of a rare Arabic work upon a slip of paper—as is the custom of the place—and requested him to procure it for me. He looked at it, and shook his head.

"It is useless, *monsieur*," he said. "That work is not in the collection. I have been often asked for it, but in vain. If *monsieur* will write for this work instead, I think he will find its contents very similar."

And he wrote the title of another book upon the back of my paper, and wrote it, moreover, in the Arabic characters.

"You write Arabic?" I exclaimed with amazement.

He smiled sadly.

"I was once a rich man, *monsieur*," he said, with a sigh, "and my education is all that I have not lost."

After this I had many conversations with M. Benoit, and he frequently visited me at my apartments in the Faubourg St. Germain. I learned that he was the son of a wealthy builder; that he had received a learned and expensive education; that his property had been swept away in the Reign of Terror; and that during the Consulate he had obtained this subordinate Situation through the interest of an early college-friend. I compared this poor old man's condition with my own, and learned a lesson from his patient cheerfulness. I found his conversation learned— often profound; and I gradually unfolded to him the plan and purpose of my book and of my opinions.

One evening I had read a chapter aloud to him, and we were arguing upon certain inductions which I had therein made from the System of Zoroaster.

"It is very strange," said M. Benoit; "but it strikes me that we have a manuscript in which the author has anticipated you."

"Indeed!" I said, with some disappointment. "I had hoped that my views were original."

"They may be original, Monsieur Henneberg, without being new," replied the old gentleman; "and I know that they are original; for the manuscript in question has never been copied, and indeed I think has never been read, excepting by myself and the writer."

"Perhaps you are the writer !" I exclaimed, hastily.

"Indeed I am not," he said; "but I knew him well—very well. He was a Professor in the College Royale de France, and from him I received the greater part of my education in the Oriental tongues. He was a great sufferer, and he loved me dearly. I was his favourite pupil—I attended his deathbed. Just before he died he gave the manuscript into my care, and bade me present it to the Bibliotheque Royale. I did so, and read it. It is utterly unknown—it lies amid thousands of others; and I believe no person has ever perused it before or since."

"I should like to see this work," I said.

"*Très bien*" he replied, "I will show it to you tomorrow."

I could not rest that night for thinking of what the old librarian had told me. I felt disquieted that another should have been before me in this path, which I had hitherto believed a virgin solitude. My self-love was wounded; and I rose in the morning feverish and unrefreshed.

Precisely as the hour of admittance arrived, I entered the reading-rooms of the library. I looked around in every direction; but M. Benoit was nowhere to be seen. I tried to read—to work; but in vain. I could not keep my attention fixed for five minutes together, and I turned my head every instant towards the door.

More than an hour elapsed before he came; but at last he entered the room and advanced to the corner where I was sitting.

"Where is the manuscript, M. Benoit ?" I said, eagerly— "the manuscript on Oriental literature which you named to me last evening?"

"It is here, M. Henneberg," he replied, pointing to a packet beneath his arm. "I had some difficulty in finding it, for it has lain there untouched these twenty years, or more!"

Slowly, with the tremulous fingers of age, he untied the

papers in which it was wrapped, and placed the manuscript before me.

I opened the leaves at random; I started back; I rubbed my eyes to make sure I was not dreaming.

The handwriting upon those pages was my own!

I think I have already said that mine was a very peculiar hand. There was no mistaking it; and here it was reproduced before my eyes, in a manuscript written, probably, years before I was born!

By a powerful effort, I mastered my emotion, and said hoarsely:—

"So it was a countryman of yours who wrote this, M. Benoit?"

"A kind friend and master of mine, M. Henneberg," replied the librarian. "Not a countryman."

"indeed !" I said. "Was he not French?"

"*Ah, mon Dieu!* no; he was a German."

Again I started. I turned to the beginning of the manuscript; my eyes fell upon the first few sentences .... I had half expected it. Their import, though not their phraseology, corresponded precisely with the first lines of my own work!

"And pray from what part of Germany did your friend come, M. Benoit?" I asked, with forced composure.

"From the confines of Bohemia."

"And his name?"

"Karl Schmidt."

"May I ask the date of his decease?"

The old gentleman removed his glasses, and brushed a tear from his eyes.

"*Hélas, mon pauvre ami!* He died on the evening of the 4th of May, 1790."

The very date and moment of my birth.

I rose suddenly, I gasped for breath, I felt as if the ground were sinking from beneath my feet ....

"Help, my friend!" I gasped—"help! I—I am dying!"

In another moment I had fainted. I was very ill for some days after this; but as soon as I had sufficiently recovered to bear the fatigue of so long a journey, I left Paris for Leipzig. I have never since passed the boundaries of the city walls. Here, in the apartments which I occupied as a youth, I live an aged and an austere man. Here I shall soon end my "strange eventful history." Such is the story of my life—a life cursed and withered by glimpses of a past, which is known only to God.

I have remembered scenes and people; I have beheld palpable evidences and traces of myself in former stages of my being, Whereunto do these things tend? Will death bring me to a full knowledge of these mysteries? or is this Spiritual particle, which men call the soul, destined to migrate eternally from shape to shape, never rising to a higher and diviner immortality? Alas! I know not; neither, friend, canst thou reply to me. Life is a problem; Death, perchance, a word! Will no hand lift the curtain of eternity?

It was nearly dusk by the time I had arrived at the end of the Professor's MSS., and the castle and church-spires of Gotha were already in sight. Presently the diligence stopped at an inn in the town; a party of young men surrounded the novel-reading student, and bore him off with tumultuous congratulations. The priest alighted, and wished me a civil good evening; and I went to the nearest inn and dined execrably.

When I returned to the vehicle to resume my night journey, I found the three vacant places already occupied by three new passengers, and so went on towards Frankfort. About a fortnight after, I went to Baden-Baden, and liked the place so well that I stayed there for some weeks.

One day, sitting idly in the *salle à manger* of the Hotel Suisse, I happened to take up a copy of *Galignani's Messenger*. One of the first things that caught my eye was the following announcement—

347

May, 1854

Died suddenly, on the evening of the 4th inst., in his Chambers, at the College of —— in Leipzig, Heinrich Henneberg, Professor of Oriental literature, in the 65th year of his age; greatly beloved and regretted.

And so this was the end. Dead! and on the anniversary of his birth! Some people to whom I have read the foregoing memoir, say that these things are coincidences, and that too much learning touched my poor friend's brain. It may be so; but there was a strange method in his madness after all; and who can tell what revelations in psychology may yet be in store for future generations?

The Story of Salome

A few years ago, no matter how many, I, Harcourt Blunt, was travelling with my friend Coventry Turnour, and it was on the steps of our hotel that I received from him the announcement that he was again in love.

"I tell you, Blunt," said my fellow-traveller, "she's the loveliest creature I ever beheld in my life."

I laughed outright.

"My dear fellow," I replied, "you've so often seen the loveliest creature you ever beheld in your life."

"Ay, but I am in earnest now for the first time."

"And you have so often been in earnest for the first time! Remember the inn-keeper's daughter at Cologne."

"A pretty housemaid, whom no training could have made presentable."

"Then there was the beautiful American at Interlaken."

"Yes; but—"

"And the *bella Marchesa* at Prince Torlonia's ball."

"Not one of them worthy to be named in the same breath with my imperial Venetian. Come with me to the Merceria and be convinced. By taking a gondola to St. Mark's Place we shall be there in a quarter of an hour."

I went, and he raved of his new flame all the way. She was a Jewess—he would convert her. Her father kept a shop in the Merceria—what of that? He dealt only in costliest Oriental merchandise, and was as rich as a Rothschild. As for any probable injury to his own prospects, why need he hesitate on that

349

account? What were "prospects" when weighed against the happiness of one's whole life? Besides, he was not ambitious. He didn't care to go into Parliament. If his uncle, Sir Geoffrey, cut him off with a shilling, what then? He had a moderate independence of which no one living could deprive him, and what more could any reasonable man desire?

I listened, smiled, and was silent. I knew Coventry Turnour too well to attach the smallest degree of importance to anything that he might say or do in a matter of this kind. To be distractedly in love was his normal condition. We had been friends from boyhood; and since the time when he used to cherish a hopeless attachment to the young lady behind the counter of the tart-shop at Harrow, I had never known him "fancy-free" for more than a few weeks at a time. He had gone through every phase of no less than three *grandes passions* during the five months that we had now been travelling together; and having left Rome about eleven weeks before with every hope laid waste, and a heart so broken that it could never by any possibility be put together again, he was now, according to the natural course of events, just ready to fall in love again.

We landed at the *traghetto* San Marco. It was a cloudless morning towards the middle of April, just ten years ago. The Ducal Palace glowed in the hot sunshine; the boatmen were clustered, gossiping, about the quay; the orange-vendors were busy under the arches of the *piazzetta*; the *flâneurs* were already eating ices and smoking cigarettes outside the cafes. There was an Austrian military band, strapped, buckled, moustachioed, and white-coated, playing just in front of St. Mark's; and the shadow of the great bell-tower slept all across the square.

Passing under the low round archway leading to the Merceria, we plunged at once into that cool labyrinth of narrow, intricate, and picturesque streets, where the sun never penetrates—where no wheels are heard, and no beast of burden is seen—where every house is a shop, and every shop-front is open to the ground, as in an Oriental bazaar—where the upper balconies seem almost to meet overhead, and are separated by only a strip of burning sky—and where more than three people cannot march abreast in any part.

Pushing our way as best we might through the motley crowd that here chatters, cheapens, buys, sells, and perpetually jostles to and fro, we came presently to a shop for the sale of Eastern goods. A few glass jars, filled with spices and some pieces of stuff, untidily strewed the counter next the street; but within, dark and narrow though it seemed, the place was crammed with costliest merchandise.

Cases of gorgeous Oriental jewellery; embroideries and fringes of massive gold and silver bullion; precious drugs and spices; exquisite toys in filigree; miracles of carving in ivory, sandalwood, and amber; jewelled *yataghans*; *scimitars* of state, rich with "barbaric pearl and gold;" bales of Cashmere shawls, China silks, India muslins, gauzes, and the like, filled every inch of available space from floor to ceiling, leaving only a narrow lane from the door to the counter, and a still narrower passage to the rooms beyond the shop.

We went in. A young woman who was sitting reading on a low seat behind the counter, laid aside her book, and rose slowly. She was dressed wholly in black. I cannot describe the fashion of her garments. I only know that they fell about her in long, soft, trailing folds, leaving a narrow band of fine cambric visible at the throat and wrists; and that, however graceful and unusual this dress may have been, I scarcely observed it, so entirely was I taken up with admiration of her beauty.

For she was indeed very beautiful—beautiful in a way I had not anticipated Coventry Turnour, with all his enthusiasm, had failed to do her justice. He had raved of her eyes—her large, lustrous, melancholy eyes,—of the transparent paleness of her complexion, of the faultless delicacy of her features; but he had not prepared me for the unconscious dignity, the perfect nobleness and refinement, that informed her every look and gesture.

My friend requested to see a bracelet at which he had been looking the day before. Proud, stately, silent, she unlocked the case in which it was kept, and laid it before him on the counter.

He asked permission to take it over to the light. She bent her head, but answered not a word. It was like being waited upon by a young Empress.

Tumour took the bracelet to the door and affected to examine it. It consisted of a double row of gold coins linked together at intervals by a bean-shaped ornament studded with pink coral and diamonds. Coming back into the shop he asked me if I thought it would please his sister, to whom he had promised a remembrance of Venice.

"It is a pretty trifle," I replied; "but surely a remembrance of Venice should be of Venetian manufacture. This, I suppose, is Turkish."

The beautiful Jewess looked up. We spoke in English; but she understood, and replied.

"*E Greco, signore*" she said coldly.

At this moment an old man came suddenly forward from some dark counting-house at the back—a grizzled, bearded, eager-eyed Shylock, with a pen behind his ear.

"Go in, Salome—go in, my daughter," he said hurriedly. "I will serve these gentlemen."

She lifted her eyes to his for one moment—then moved silently away, and vanished in the gloom of the room beyond.

We saw her no more. We lingered awhile looking over the contents of the jewel-cases; but in vain. Then Tumour bought his bracelet, and we went out again into the narrow streets, and back to the open daylight of the Gran' Piazza.

"Well," he said breathlessly, "what do you think of her?"

"She is very lovely."

"Lovelier than you expected?"

"Much lovelier. But—"

"But what?"

"The sooner you succeed in forgetting her the better."

He vowed, of course, that he never would and never could forget her. He would hear of no incompatibilities, listen to no objections, believe in no obstacles. That the beautiful Salome was herself not only unconscious of his passion and indifferent to his person, but ignorant of his very name and station, were facts not even to be admitted on the list of difficulties. Finding him thus deaf to reason, I said no more.

It was all over, however, before the week was out.

"Look here, Blunt," he said, coming up to me one morning in the coffee-room of our hotel just as I was sitting down to answer a pile of home-letters; "would you like to go on to Trieste tomorrow? There, don't look at me like that—you can guess how it is with me. I was a fool ever to suppose she would care for me—a stranger, a foreigner, a Christian. Well, I'm horribly out of sorts, anyhow—and—and I wish I was a thousand miles off at this moment!"

We travelled on together to Athens, and there parted, Tumour being bound for England, and I for the East. My own tour lasted many months longer. I went first to Egypt and the Holy Land; then joined an exploring party on the Euphrates; and at length, after just twelve months of Oriental life, found myself back again at Trieste about the middle of April in the year following that during which occurred the events I have just narrated. There I found that batch of letters and papers to which I had been looking forward for many weeks past; and amongst the former, one from Coventry Tumour. This time he was not only irrecoverably in love, but on the eve of matrimony. The letter was rapturous and extravagant enough. The writer was the happiest of men; his destined bride the loveliest and most amiable of her sex; the future a paradise; the past a melancholy series of mistakes. As for love, he had never, of course, known what it was till now.

And what of the beautiful Salome?

Not one word of her from beginning to end. He had forgotten her as utterly as if she had never existed. And yet how desperately in love and how desperately in despair he *was* "one little year ago!" Ah, yes; but then it was "one little year ago;" and who that had ever known Coventry Tumour would expect him to remember *la plus grande des grandes passions* for even half that time?

I slept that night at Trieste and went on next day to Venice.

Somehow I could not get Tumour and his love-affairs out of my head. I remembered our visit to the Merceria. I was haunted by the image of the beautiful Jewess. Was she still so lovely? Did she still sit reading in her wonted seat by the open counter, with the gloomy shop reaching away behind, and the cases of rich robes and jewels all around?

An irresistible impulse prompted me to go to the Merceria and see her once again. I went. It had been a busy morning with me, and I did not get there till between three and four o'clock in the afternoon. The place was crowded. I passed up the well-remembered street, looking out on both sides for the gloomy little shop with its unattractive counter; but in vain. When I had gone so far that I thought I must have passed it, I turned back. House by house I retraced my steps to the very entrance, and still could not find it. Then, concluding I had not gone far enough at first, I turned back again till I reached a spot where several streets diverged. Here I came to a stand-still, for beyond this point I knew I had not passed before.

It was now evident that the Jew no longer occupied his former shop in the Merceria, and that my chance of discovering his whereabouts was exceedingly slender. I could not inquire of his successor, because I could not identify the house. I found it impossible even to remember what trades were carried on by his neighbours on either side. I was ignorant of his very name. Convinced, therefore, of the inutility of making any further effort, I gave up the search, and comforted myself by reflecting that my own heart was not made of adamant, and that it was, perhaps, better for my peace not to see the beautiful Salome again. I was destined to see her again, however, and that ere many days had passed over my head.

A year of more than ordinarily fatiguing Eastern travel had left me in need of rest, and I had resolved to allow myself a month's sketching in Venice and its neighbourhood before turning my face homeward.

As, therefore, it is manifestly the first object of a sketcher to select his points of view, and as no more luxurious machine than a Venetian *gondola* was ever invented for the use of man, I proceeded to employ the first days of my stay in endless boatings to and fro; now exploring all manner of canals and *canaletti*; now rowing out in the direction of Murano; now making for the islands beyond San Pietro Castello, and in the course of these pilgrimages noting down an infinite number of picturesque sites, and smoking an infinite number of cigarettes.

It was, I think, about the fourth or fifth day of this pleasant work, when my *gondolier* proposed to take me as far as the Lido. It wanted about two hours to sunset, and the great sand-bank lay not more than three or four miles away; so I gave the word, and in another moment we had changed our route and were gliding farther and farther from Venice at each dip of the oar.

Then the long, dull, distant ridge that had all day bounded the shallow horizon rose gradually above the placid level of the Lagune; assumed a more broken outline; resolved itself into hillocks and hollows of tawny sand; showed here and there a patch of parched grass and tangled brake; and looked like the coasts of some inhospitable desert beyond which no traveller might penetrate. My boatman made straight for a spot where some stakes at the water's edge gave token of a landing-place; and here, though with some difficulty, for the tide was low, ran the gondola aground. I landed. My first step was among graves.

"*E'l Cimiterio Giudaico, signore*" said my *gondolier*, with a touch of his cap.

The Jewish cemetery! The *ghetto* of the dead! I remembered now to have read or heard long since how the Venetian Jews, cut off in death as in life from the neighbourhood of their Christian rulers, had been buried from immemorial time upon this desolate waste. I stooped to examine the headstone at my feet. It was but a shattered fragment, crusted over with yellow lichens, and eaten away by the salt sea air. I passed on to the next, and the next.

Some were completely matted over with weeds and brambles; some were half-buried in the drifting sand; of some only a corner remained above the surface. Here and there a name, a date, a fragment of emblematic carving or part of a Hebrew inscription, was yet legible; but all were more or less broken and effaced.

Wandering on thus among graves and hillocks, ascending at every step, and passing some three or four glassy pools overgrown with gaunt-looking reeds, I presently found that I had reached the central and most elevated part of the Lido, and that I commanded an uninterrupted view on every side. On the one hand lay the broad, silent Lagune bounded by Venice and the Euganean hills—on the other, stealing up in long, lazy folds, and breaking noiselessly against the endless shore, the blue Adriatic. An old man gathering shells on the seaward side, a distant gondola on the Lagune, were the only signs of life for miles around.

Standing on the upper ridge of this narrow barrier, looking upon both waters, and watching the gradual approach of what promised to be a gorgeous sunset, I fell into one of those wandering trains of thought in which the real and unreal succeed each other as capriciously as in a dream.

I remembered how Goethe here conceived his vertebral theory of the skull—how Byron , too lame to walk, kept his horse on the Lido, and here rode daily to and fro—how Shelley loved the wild solitude of the place, wrote of it in *Julian and Maddalo*, and listened perhaps from this very spot, to the mad-house bell on the island of San Giorgio. Then I wondered if Titian used sometimes to come hither from his gloomy house on the other side of Venice, to study the gold and purple of these western skies—if Othello had walked here with Desdemona—if Shylock was buried yonder, and Leah whom he loved "when he was a bachelor."

And then in the midst of my reverie, I came suddenly upon another Jewish cemetery.

Was it indeed another, or but an outlying portion of the first? It was evidently another, and a more modern one. The ground was better kept. The monuments were newer. Such dates as I had succeeded in deciphering on the broken sepulchres lower down were all of the fourteenth and fifteenth centuries; but the inscriptions upon these bore reference to quite recent interments.

I went on a few steps farther. I stopped to copy a quaint Italian couplet on one tomb—to gather a wild forget-me-not from the foot of another—to put aside a bramble that trailed across a third—and then I became aware for the first time of a lady sitting beside a grave not a dozen yards from the spot on which I stood.

I had believed myself so utterly alone, and was so taken by surprise, that for the first moment I could almost have persuaded myself that she also was "of the stuff that dreams are made of." She was dressed from head to foot in deepest mourning; her face turned from me, looking towards the sunset; her cheek resting in the palm of her hand. The grave by which she sat was obviously recent. The scant herbage round about had been lately disturbed, and the marble headstone looked as if it had not yet undergone a week's exposure to wind and weather.

Persuaded that she had not observed me, I lingered for an instant looking at her. Something in the grace and sorrow of her attitude, something in the turn of her head and the flow of her sable draperies, arrested my attention. Was she young? I fancied so. Did she mourn a husband?—a lover?—a parent? I glanced towards the headstone. It was covered with Hebrew characters; so that, had I even been nearer, it could have told me nothing.

But I felt that I had no right to stand there, a spectator of her sorrow, an intruder on her privacy. I proceeded to move noiselessly away. At that moment she turned and looked at me.

It was Salome.

Salome, pale and worn as from some deep and wasting grief, but more beautiful, if that could be, than ever. Beautiful, with a still more spiritual beauty than of old; with cheeks so wan, and eyes so unutterably bright and solemn, that my very heart seemed to stand still as I looked upon them. For one second I paused, half fancying, half hoping that there was recognition in her glance; then, not daring to look or linger longer, turned away. When I had gone far enough to do so without discourtesy, I stopped and looked back. She had resumed her former attitude, and was gazing over towards Venice and the setting sun. The stone by which she watched was not more motionless.

The sun went down in glory. The last flush faded from the domes and bell-towers of Venice; the northward peaks changed from rose to purple, from gold to grey; a scarcely perceptible film of mist became all at once visible upon the surface of the Lagune; and overhead, the first star trembled into light. I waited and watched till the shadows had so deepened that I could no longer distinguish one distant object from another. Was that the spot? Was she still there? Was she moving? Was she gone? I could not tell. The more I looked, the more uncertain I became. Then, fearing to miss my way in the fast-gathering twilight, I struck down towards the water's edge and made for the point at which I had landed.

I found my gondolier fast asleep, with his head on a cushion and his bit of gondola-carpet thrown over him for a counterpane. I asked if he had seen any other boat put off from the Lido since I left? He rubbed his eyes, started up, and was awake in a moment.

"*Per Bacco, signore,* I have been asleep," he said apologetically; "I have seen nothing."

"Did you observe any other boat moored hereabouts when we landed?"

"None, *signore.*"

"And you have seen nothing of a lady in black?"

He laughed and shook his head.

"*Consolatevi, signore,*" he said, archly; "she will come tomorrow."

Then, seeing me look grave, he touched his cap, and with a gentle "*Scusate, signore,*" took his place at the stern, and there waited. I bade him row to my hotel; and then, leaning dreamily back, folded my arms, closed my eyes, and thought of Salome.

How lovely she was! How infinitely more lovely than even my first remembrance of her! How was it that I had not admired her more that day in the Merceria? Was I blind, or had she become indeed more beautiful? It was a sad and strange place in which to meet her again. By whose grave was she watching? By her father's? Yes, surely by her father's. He was an old man when I saw him, and in the course of nature had not long to live. He was dead: hence my unavailing search in the Merceria. He was dead. His shop was let to another occupant. His stock-in-trade was sold and dispersed.

And Salome—was she left alone? Had she no mother?—no brother?—no lover? Would her eyes have had that look of speechless woe in them if she had any very near or dear tie left on earth? Then I thought of Coventry Turnour, and his approaching marriage. Had he ever really loved her? I doubted it. *True love*, saith an old song, *can ne'er forget*; but he had forgotten, as though the past had been a dream. And yet he was in earnest while it lasted—would have risked all for her sake, if she would have listened to him. Ah, if she *had* listened to him!

And then I remembered that he had never told me the particulars of that affair. Did she herself reject him, or did he lay his suit before her father? And was he rejected only because he was a Christian? I had never cared to ask these things while we were together; but now I would have given the best hunter in my stables to know every minute detail connected with the matter.

Pondering thus, travelling over the same ground again and again, wondering whether she remembered me, whether she was poor, whether she was, indeed, alone in the world, how long the old man had been dead, and a hundred other things of the same kind,—I scarcely noticed how the watery miles glided past, or how the night closed in. One question, however, recurred oftener than any other: How was I to see her again?

I arrived at my hotel; I dined at the *table d'hôte*; I strolled out after dinner to my favourite cafe in the piazza; I dropped in for half an hour at the Fenice, and heard one act of an extremely poor opera; I came home restless, uneasy, wakeful; and sitting for hours before my bedroom fire, asked myself the same perpetual question—How was I to see her again ?

Fairly tired out at last, I fell asleep in my chair, and when I awoke the sun was shining upon my window.

I started to my feet. I had it now. It flashed upon me, as if it came with the sunlight. I had but to go again to the cemetery, copy the inscription upon the old man's tomb, ask my learned friend, Professor Nicolai of Padua, to translate it for me, and then, once in possession of names and dates, the rest would be easy.

In less than an hour, I was once more on my way to the Lido.

I took a rubbing of the stone. It was the quickest way, and the surest; for I knew that in Hebrew everything depended on the pointing of the characters, and I feared to trust my own untutored skill.

This done, I hastened back, wrote my letter to the professor, and despatched both letter and rubbing by the midday train.

The professor was not a prompt man. On the contrary, he was a pre-eminently slow man; dreamy, indolent, buried in Oriental lore. From any other correspondent one might have looked for a reply in the course of the morrow; but from Nicolai of Padua it would have been folly to expect one under two or three days. And in the meanwhile? Well, in the meanwhile there were churches and palaces to be seen, sketches to be made, letters of introduction to be delivered. It was, at all events, of no use to be impatient.

And yet I was impatient—so impatient that I could neither sketch, nor read, nor sit still for ten minutes together. Possessed by an uncontrollable restlessness, I wandered from gallery to gallery, from palace to palace, from church to church. The imprisonment of even a gondola was irksome to me. I was, as it were, impelled to be moving and doing; and even so, the day seemed endless.

The next was even worse. There was just the possibility of a reply from Padua, and the knowledge of that possibility unsettled me for the day. Having watched and waited for every post from eight to four, I went down to the *traghetto* of St. Mark's, and was there hailed by my accustomed *gondolier*.

He touched his cap and waited for orders.

"Where to, *signore*?" he asked, finding that I remained silent.

"To the Lido."

It was an irresistible temptation, and I yielded to it; but I yielded in opposition to my judgment. I knew that I ought not to haunt the place. I had resolved that I would not. And yet I went.

Going along, I told myself that I had only come to reconnoitre. It was not unlikely that she might be going to the same spot about the same hour as before; and in that case I might overtake her *gondola* by the way, or find it moored somewhere along the shore. At all events, I was determined not to land. But we met no gondola beyond San Pietro Castello; saw no sign of one along the shore. The afternoon was far advanced; the sun was near going down; we had the Lagune and the Lido to ourselves.

My boatman made for the same landing-place, and moored his *gondola* to the same stake as before. He took it for granted that I meant to land; and I landed. After all, however, it was evident that Salome could not be there, in which case I was guilty of no intrusion. I might stroll in the direction of the cemetery, taking care to avoid her, if she were anywhere about, and keeping well away from that part where I had last seen her.

So I broke another resolve, and went up towards the top of the Lido. Again I came to the salt pools and the reeds; again stood with the sea upon my left hand and the Lagune upon my right, and the endless sandbank reaching on for miles between the two. Yonder lay the new cemetery. Standing thus I overlooked every foot of the ground. I could even distinguish the headstone of which I had taken a rubbing the morning before. There was no living thing in sight. I was, to all appearance, as utterly alone as Enoch Arden on his desert island.

Then I strolled on a little nearer and a little nearer still; and then, contrary to all my determinations, I found myself standing upon the very spot, beside the very grave, which I had made up my mind on no account to approach.

The sun was now just going down—had gone down, indeed, behind a bank of golden-edged *cumuli*—and was flooding earth, sea, and sky with crimson. It was at this hour that I saw her. It was upon this spot that she was sitting. A few scant blades of grass had sprung up here and there upon the grave. Her dress must have touched them as she sat there—her dress—perhaps her hand. I gathered one, and laid it carefully between the leaves of my note-book.

At last I turned to go, and, turning, met her face to face!

She was distant about six yards, and advancing slowly towards the spot on which I was standing. Her head drooped slightly forward; her hands were clasped together; her eyes were fixed upon the ground. It was the attitude of a nun. Startled, confused, scarcely knowing what I did, I took off my hat, and drew aside to let her pass.

She looked up—hesitated—stood still—gazed at me with a strange, steadfast, mournful expression—then dropped her eyes again, passed me without another glance, and resumed her former place and attitude beside her father's grave.

I turned away. I would have given worlds to speak to her; but I had not dared, and the opportunity was gone. Yet I might have spoken. She looked at me—looked at me with so strange and piteous an expression in her eyes—continued looking at me as long as one might have counted five. . . . I might have spoken. I surely might have spoken! And now—ah! now it was impossible. She had fallen into the old thoughtful attitude, with her cheek resting on her hand. Her thoughts were far away. She had forgotten my very presence.

I went back to the shore, more disturbed and uneasy than ever. I spent all the remaining daylight in rowing up and down the margin of the Lido, looking for her *gondola*—hoping, at all events, to see her put off—to follow her, perhaps, across the waste of waters. But the dusk came quickly on, and then darkness; and I left at last without having seen any farther sign or token of her presence.

Lying awake that night, tossing uneasily upon my bed, and

thinking over the incidents of the last few days, I found myself perpetually recurring to that long, steady, sorrowful gaze which she fixed upon me in the cemetery. The more I thought of it, the more I seemed to feel that there was in it some deeper meaning than I, in my confusion, had observed at the time.

It was such a strange look—a look almost of entreaty, of asking for help or sympathy; like the dumb appeal in the eyes of a sick animal. Could this really be? What, after all, more possible than that, left alone in the world—with, perhaps, not a single male relation to advise her—she found herself in some position of present difficulty, and knew not where to turn for help? All this might well be. She had even, perhaps, some instinctive feeling that she might trust me. Ah! if she would indeed trust me

I had hoped to receive my Paduan letter by the morning delivery; but morning and afternoon went by as before, and still no letter came. As the day began to decline, I was again on my way to the Lido; this time for the purpose, and with the intention, of speaking to her. I landed, and went direct to the cemetery. It had been a dull day. Lagune and sky were both one uniform leaden grey, and a mist hung over Venice.

I saw her from the moment I reached the upper ridge. She was walking to and fro among the graves, like a stately shadow. I had felt confident, somehow, that she would be there; and now, for some reason that I could not have defined for my life, I felt equally confident that she expected me.

Trembling and eager, yet half dreading the moment when she should discover my presence, I hastened on, printing the loose sand at every noiseless step. A few moments more, and I should overtake her, speak to her, hear the music of her voice—that music which I remembered so well, though a year had gone by since I last heard it. But how should I address her? What had I to say? I knew not. I had no time to think. I could only hurry on till within some ten feet of her trailing garments; stand still when she turned, and uncover before her as if she were a queen.

She paused and looked at me, just as she had paused and looked at me the evening before. With the same sorrowful meaning in her eyes; with even more than the same entreating expression. But she waited for me to speak.

I did speak. I cannot recall what I said; I only know that I faltered something of an apology—mentioned that I had had the honour of meeting her before, many months ago; and, trying to say more—trying to express how thankfully and proudly I would devote myself to any service however humble, however laborious, I failed both in voice and words, and broke down utterly.

Having come to a stop, I looked up and found her eyes still fixed upon me.

"You are a Christian?" she said.

A trembling came upon me at the first sound of her voice. It was the same voice; distinct, melodious, scarce louder than a whisper—and yet it was not quite the same. There was a melancholy in the music, and if I may use a word which, after all, fails to express my meaning, a *remoteness*, that fell upon my ear like the plaintive cadence in an autumnal wind.

I bent my head, and answered that I was.

She pointed to the headstone of which I had taken a rubbing a day or two before.

"A Christian soul lies there," she said, "laid in earth without one Christian prayer—with Hebrew rites—in a Hebrew sanctuary. Will you, stranger, perform an act of piety towards the dead?"

"The *Signora* has but to speak," I said. "All that she wishes shall be done."

"Read one prayer over this grave; and trace a cross upon this stone."

"I will."

She thanked me with a gesture, slightly bowed her head, drew her outer garment more closely round her, and moved away to a rising ground at some little distance. I was dismissed. I had no excuse for lingering—no right to prolong the interview— no business to remain there one moment longer. So I left her there, nor once looked back till I had reached the last point from which I knew I should be able to see her. But when I turned for that last look, she was no longer in sight.

I had resolved to speak to her, and this was the result. A stranger interview never, surely, fell to the lot of man! I had said nothing that I meant to say—had learnt nothing that I sought to know. With regard to her circumstances, her place of residence, her very name, I was no wiser than before. And yet I had, perhaps, no reason to be dissatisfied. She had honoured me with her confidence, and entrusted to me a task of some difficulty and importance. It now only remained for me to execute that task as thoroughly and as quickly as possible. That done, I might fairly hope to win some place in her remembrance—by and by, perhaps, in her esteem.

Meanwhile, the old question rose again—whose grave could it be? I had settled this matter so conclusively in my own mind from the first, that I could scarcely believe even now that it was not her father's. Yet that he should have died a secret convert to Christianity was incredible. Whose grave could it be? A lover's? A Christian lover's? Alas! it might be. Or a sister's? In either of these cases, it was more than probable that Salome was herself a convert. But I had no time to waste in conjecture. I must act, and act promptly.

I hastened back to Venice as fast as my gondolier could row me; and as we went along I promised myself that all her wishes should be carried out before she visited the spot again. To secure at once the services of a clergyman who would go with me to the Lido at early dawn and there read some portion, at least, of the burial service; and at the same time to engage a stonemason to cut the cross;—to have all done before she, or anyone, should have approached the place next day, was my especial object. And that object I was resolved to carry out, though I had to search Venice through before I laid my head upon my pillow.

I found a clergyman without difficulty. He was a young man occupying rooms in the same hotel, and on the same floor as myself. I had met him each day at the *table d'hôte*, and conversed with him once or twice in the reading-room. He was a North-countryman, had not long since taken orders, and was both gentlemanly and obliging. He promised in the readiest manner to do all that I required, and to breakfast with me at six next morning, in order that we might reach the cemetery by eight.

To find my stonemason, however, was not so easy; and yet I went to work methodically enough. I began with the Venetian Directory; then copied a list of stonemasons' names and addresses; then took a *gondola a due remi* and started upon my voyage of discovery.

But a night's voyage of discovery among the intricate back *canaletti* of Venice is no very easy and no very safe enterprise. Narrow, tortuous, densely populated, often blocked by huge hay, wood, and provision barges, almost wholly unlighted, and so perplexingly alike that no mere novice in Venetian topography need ever hope to distinguish one from another, they baffle the very *gondoliers*, and are a *terra incognita* to all but the dwellers therein.

I succeeded, however, in finding three of the places entered on my list. At the first I was told that the workman of whom I was in quest was working by the week somewhere over by Murano, and would not be back again till Saturday night. At the second and third, I found the men at home, supping with their wives and children at the end of the day's work; but neither would consent to undertake my commission. One, after a whispered consultation with his son, declined reluctantly. The other told me plainly that he dared not do it, and that he did not believe I should find a stonemason in Venice who would be bolder than himself.

The Jews, he said, were rich and powerful; no longer an oppressed people; no longer to be insulted even in Venice with impunity. To cut a Christian cross upon a Jewish headstone in the Jewish Cemetery, would be "a sort of sacrilege," and punishable, no doubt, by the law. This sounded like truth; so, finding that my rowers were by no means confident of their way, and that the *canaletti* were dark as the catacombs, I prevailed upon the stonemason to sell me a small mallet and a couple of chisels, and made up my mind to commit the sacrilege myself.

With this single exception, all was done next morning as I had planned to do it. My new acquaintance breakfasted with me, accompanied me to the Lido, read such portions of the burial service as seemed proper to him, and then, having business in Venice, left me to my task. It was by no means an easy one. To a skilled hand it would have been, perhaps, the work of half-an-hour; but it was my first effort, and rude as the thing was—a mere grooved attempt at a Latin cross, about two inches and a half in length, cut close down at the bottom of the stone, where it could be easily concealed by a little piling of the sand—it took me nearly four hours to complete.

While I was at work, the dull grey morning grew duller and greyer; a thick sea-fog drove up from the Adriatic; and a low moaning wind came and went like the echo of a distant requiem. More than once I started, believing that she had surprised me there—fancying I saw the passing of a shadow—heard the rustling of a garment—the breathing of a sigh. But no. The mists and the moaning wind deceived me. I was alone.

When at length I got back to my hotel, it was, just two o'clock. The hall-porter put a letter into my hand as I passed through. One glance at that crabbed superscription was enough. It was from Padua. I hastened to my room, tore open the envelope, and read these words:—

Caro Signore,—The rubbing you send is neither ancient nor curious, as I fear you suppose it to be. It is a thing of yesterday. It merely records that one Salome, the only and beloved child of a certain Isaac Da Costa, died last Autumn on the eighteenth of October, aged twenty-one years, and that by the said Isaac Da Costa this monument is erected to the memory of her virtues and his grief.

I pray you, *caro signore*, to receive the assurance of my sincere esteem.

Nicolo Nicolai.

The letter dropped from my hand. I seemed to have read

without understanding it. I picked it up; went through it again, word by word; sat down; rose up; took a turn across the room; felt confused, bewildered, incredulous, Could there, then, be two Salomes? or was there some radical and extraordinary mistake?

I hesitated; I knew not what to do. Should I go down to the Merceria, and see whether the name of Da Costa was known in the *quartier*? Or find out the registrar of births and deaths for the Jewish district? Or call upon the principal *rabbi*, and learn from him who this second Salome had been, and in what degree of relationship she stood towards the Salome whom I knew? I decided upon the last course. The chief *rabbi's* address was easily obtained. He lived in an ancient house on the Giudecca, and there I found him—a grave, stately old man, with a grizzled beard reaching nearly to his waist.

I introduced myself and stated my business. I came to ask if he could give me any information respecting the late Salome da Costa who died on the 18th of October last, and was buried on the Lido.

The *rabbi* replied that he had no doubt he could give me any information I desired, for he had known the lady personally, and was the intimate friend of her father.

"Can you tell me," I asked, "whether she had any dear friend or female relative of the same name—Salome?"

The *rabbi* shook his head.

"I think not," he said. "I remember no other maiden of that name."

"Pardon me, but I know there was another," I replied. "There was a very beautiful Salome living in the Merceria when I was last in Venice, just this time last year."

"Salome da Costa was very fair," said the *rabbi*; "and she dwelt with her father in the Merceria. Since her death, he hath removed to the neighbourhood of the Rialto."

"This Salome's father was a dealer in Oriental goods," I said, hastily.

"Isaac da Costa is a dealer in Oriental goods," replied the old man very gently. "We are speaking, my son, of the same persons."

"Impossible!"

He shook his head again.

"But she lives!" I exclaimed, becoming greatly agitated. " She lives. I have seen her. I have spoken to her. I saw her only last evening."

"Nay," he said, compassionately, "this is some dream. She of whom you speak is indeed no more."

"I saw her only last evening," I repeated.

"Where did you suppose you beheld her?"

"On the Lido."

"On the Lido?"

"And she spoke to me. I heard her voice—heard it as distinctly as I hear my own at this moment."

The *rabbi* stroked his beard thoughtfully, and looked at me. "You think you heard her voice!" he ejaculated. "That is strange. What said she?"

I was about to answer. I checked myself—a sudden thought flashed upon me—I trembled from head to foot.

"Have you—have you any reason for supposing that she died a Christian?" I faltered.

The old man started and changed colour.

"I—I—that is a strange question," he stammered. "Why do you ask it?"

"Yes or no?" I cried wildly. "Yes or no?"

He frowned, looked down, hesitated.

"I admit," he said, after a moment or two,—"I admit that I may have heard something tending that way. It may be that the maiden cherished some secret doubt. Yet she was no professed Christian."

"*Laid in earth without one Christian prayer; with Hebrew rites; in a Hebrew sanctuary!*" I repeated to myself.

"But I marvel how you come to have heard of this," continued the *rabbi*. "It was known only to her father and myself."

"Sir," I said solemnly, "I know now that Salome da Costa is dead; I have seen her spirit thrice, haunting the spot where . ."

My voice broke. I could not utter the words.

"Last evening at sunset," I resumed, "was the third time. Never doubting that—that I indeed beheld her in the flesh, I spoke to her. She answered me. She—she told me this."

The *rabbi* covered his face with his hands, and so remained for some time, lost in meditation. "Young man," he said at length, "your story is strange, and you bring strange evidence to bear upon it. It may be as you say; it may be that you are the dupe of some waking dream—I know not."

He knew not; but I . . . Ah! I knew only too well. I knew now why she had appeared to me clothed with such unearthly beauty. I understood now that look of dumb entreaty in her eyes—that tone of strange remoteness in her voice. The sweet soul could not rest amid the dust of its kinsfolk, "unhousel'd, unanointed, unanealed," lacking even "one Christian prayer" above its grave. And now—was it all over? Should I never see her more?

Never—ah! never. How I haunted the Lido at sunset for many a month, till Spring had blossomed into Autumn, and Autumn had ripened into Summer; how I wandered back to Venice year after year at the same season, while yet any vestige of that wild hope remained alive; how my heart has never throbbed, my pulse never leaped, for love of mortal woman since that time—are details into which I need not enter here. Enough that I watched and waited; but that her gracious spirit appeared to me no more. I wait still, but I watch no longer. I know now that our place of meeting will not be here.

Was it an Illusion? A Parson's Story

The facts which I am about to relate happened to myself some sixteen or eighteen years ago, at which time I served Her Majesty as an Inspector of Schools. Now, the Provincial Inspector is perpetually on the move; and I was still young enough to enjoy a life of constant travelling.

There are, indeed, many less agreeable ways in which an un-beneficed parson may contrive to scorn delights and live laborious days. In remote places where strangers are scarce, his annual visit is an important event; and though at the close of a long day's work he would sometimes prefer the quiet of a country inn, he generally finds himself the destined guest of the rector or the squire. It rests with himself to turn these opportunities to account. If he makes himself pleasant, he forms agreeable friendships and sees English home-life under one of its most attractive aspects; and sometimes, even in these days of universal commonplaceness, he may have the luck to meet with an adventure.

My first appointment was to a West of England district large-ly peopled with my personal friends and connections. It was, therefore, much to my annoyance that I found myself, after a couple of years of very pleasant work, transferred to what a policeman would call 'a new beat,' up in the North.

Unfortunately for me, my new beat—a rambling, thinly populated area of something under 1,800 square miles—was three times as large as the old one, and more than proportionately unmanageable. Intersected at right angles by two ranges of barren hills and cut off to a large extent from the main lines of railway, it united about every inconvenience that a district could possess. The villages lay wide apart, often separated by long tracts of moorland; and in place of the well-warmed railway compartment and the frequent manor-house, I now spent half my time in hired vehicles and lonely country inns.

I had been in possession of this district for some three months or so, and winter was near at hand, when I paid my first visit of inspection to Pit End, an outlying hamlet in the most northerly corner of my county, just twenty-two miles from the nearest station. Having slept overnight at a place called Drumley, and inspected Drumley schools in the morning, I started for Pit End, with fourteen miles of railway and twenty-two of hilly cross-roads between myself and my journey's end.

I made, of course, all the enquiries I could think of before leaving; but neither the Drumley schoolmaster nor the landlord of the Drumley 'Feathers' knew much more of Pit End than its name. My predecessor, it seemed, had been in the habit of taking Pit End 'from the other side', the roads, though longer, being less hilly that way. That the place boasted some kind of inn was certain; but it was an inn unknown to fame, and to mine host of the 'Feathers'. Be it good or bad, however, I should have to put up at it.

Upon this scant information I started. My fourteen miles of railway journey soon ended at a place called Bramsford Road, whence an omnibus conveyed passengers to a dull little town called Bramsford Market. Here I found a horse and 'trap' to carry me on to my destination; the horse being a rawboned grey with a profile like a camel, and the trap a rickety high gig which had probably done commercial travelling in the days of its youth. From Bramsford Market the way lay over a succession of long hills, rising to a barren, high-level plateau. It was a dull, raw afternoon of mid-November, growing duller and more raw as the day waned and the east wind blew keener.'How much further now, driver?' I asked, as we alighted at the foot of a longer and a stiffer hill than any we had yet passed over.

He turned a straw in his mouth, and grunted something

about 'fewer or foive mile by the rooad'.

And then I learned that by turning off at a point which he described as 't'owld tollus', and taking a certain footpath across the fields, this distance might be considerably shortened. I decided, therefore, to walk the rest of the way; and, setting off at a good pace, I soon left driver and trap behind. At the top of the hill I lost sight of them, and coming presently to a little road-side ruin which I at once recognized as the old toll-house, I found the footpath without difficulty.

It led me across a barren slope divided by stone fences, with here and there a group of shattered sheds, a tall chimney, and a blackened cinder-mound, marking the site of a deserted mine. A light fog, meanwhile, was creeping up from the east, and the dusk was gathering fast.

Now, to lose one's way in such a place and at such an hour would be disagreeable enough, and the footpath—a trodden track already half obliterated—would be indistinguishable in the course of another ten minutes. Looking anxiously ahead, therefore, in the hope of seeing some sign of habitation, I hastened on, scaling one stone stile after another, till I all at once found myself skirting a line of park-palings. following these, with bare boughs branching out overhead and dead leaves rustling underfoot, I came presently to a point where the path divided; here continuing to skirt the enclosure, and striking off yonder across a space of open meadow.

Which should I take?

By following the fence, I should be sure to arrive at a lodge where I could enquire my way to Pit End; but then the park might be of any extent, and I might have a long distance to go before I came to the nearest lodge. Again, the meadow-path, instead of leading to Pit End, might take me in a totally opposite direction. But there was no time to be lost in hesitation; so I chose the meadow, the further end of which was lost to sight in a fleecy bank of fog.

Up to this moment I had not met a living soul of whom to ask my way; it was, therefore, with no little sense of relief that I saw a man emerging from the fog and coming along the path. As we neared each other—I advancing rapidly; he slowly—I observed that he dragged the left foot, limping as he walked. It was, however, so dark and so misty, that not till we were within half a dozen yards of each other could I see that he wore a dark suit and an Anglican felt hat, and looked something like a dissenting minister. As soon as we were within speaking distance, I addressed him.

'Can you tell me', I said, 'if I am right for Pit End, and how far I have to go?'

He came on, looking straight before him; taking no notice of my question; apparently not hearing it.

'I beg your pardon,' I said, raising my voice; 'but will this path take me to Pit End, and if so'—He had passed on without pausing; without looking at me; I could almost have believed, without seeing me!

I stopped, with the words on my lips; then turned to look after—perhaps, to follow—him.

But instead of following, I stood bewildered.

What had become of him? And what lad was that going up the path by which I had just come—that tall lad, half-running, half-walking, with a fishing-rod over his shoulder? I could have taken my oath that I had neither met nor passed him. Where then had he come from? And where was the man to whom I had spoken not three seconds ago, and who, at his limping pace, could not have made more than a couple of yards in the time? My stupefaction was such that I stood quite still, looking after the lad with the fishing-rod till he disappeared in the gloom under the park-palings.

Was I dreaming?

Darkness, meanwhile, had closed in apace, and, dreaming or not dreaming, I must push on, or find myself benighted. So I hurried forward, turning my back on the last gleam of daylight, and plunging deeper into the fog at every step. I was, however, close upon my journey's end. The path ended at a turnstile; the turnstile opened upon a steep lane; and at the bottom of the lane, down which I stumbled among stones and ruts, I came in sight of the welcome glare of a blacksmith's forge.

Here, then, was Pit End. I found my trap standing at the door of the village inn; the rawboned grey stabled for the night; the landlord watching for my arrival.

The 'Greyhound' was a hostelry of modest pretensions, and I shared its little parlour with a couple of small farmers and a young man who informed me that he 'travelled in' Thorley's Food for Cattle. Here I dined, wrote my letters, chatted awhile with the landlord, and picked up such scraps of local news as fell in my way.

There was, it seemed, no resident parson at Pit End; the incumbent being a pluralist with three small livings, the duties of which, by the help of a rotatory curate, he discharged in a somewhat easy fashion. Pit End, as the smallest and furthest off, came in for but one service each Sunday, and was almost wholly relegated to the curate. The squire was a more confirmed absentee than even the vicar. He lived chiefly in Paris, spending abroad the wealth of his Pit End coal-fields.

He happened to be at home just now, the landlord said, after five years' absence; but he would be off again next week, and another five years might probably elapse before they should again see him at Blackwater Chase.

Blackwater Chase!—the name was not new to me; yet I could not remember where I had heard it. When, however, mine host went on to say that, despite his absenteeism, Mr Wolstenholme was 'a pleasant gentleman and a good landlord', and that, after all, Blackwater Chase was 'a lonesome sort of world-end place for a young man to bury himself in', then I at once remembered Phil Wolstenholme of Balliol, who, in his grand way, had once upon a time given me a general invitation to the shooting at Blackwater Chase. That was twelve years ago, when I was reading hard at Wadham, and Wolstenholme-the idol of a clique to which I did not belong-was boating, betting, writing poetry, and giving wine parties at Balliol.

Yes; I remembered all about him—his handsome face, his

luxurious rooms, his boyish prodigality, his utter indolence, and the blind faith of his worshippers, who believed that he had only 'to pull himself together' in order to carry off every honour which the University had to bestow. He did take the Newdigate; but it was his first and last achievement, and he left college with the reputation of having narrowly escaped a plucking.

How vividly it all came back upon my memory—the old college life, the college friendships, the pleasant time that could never come again! It was but twelve years ago; yet it seemed like half a century. And now, after these twelve years, here were Wolstenholme and I as near neighbours as in our Oxford days! I wondered if he was much changed, and whether, if changed, it were for the better or the worse.

Had his generous impulses developed into sterling virtues, or had his follies hardened into vices?

Should I let him know where I was, and so judge for myself? Nothing would be easier than to pencil a line upon a card to-morrow morning, and send it up to the big house. Yet, merely to satisfy a purposeless curiosity, was it worthwhile to reopen the acquaintanceship? Thus musing, I sat late over the fire, and by the time I went to bed, I had well nigh forgotten my adventure with the man who vanished so mysteriously and the boy who seemed to come from nowhere.

Next morning, finding I had abundant time at my disposal, I did pencil that line upon my card—a mere line, saving that I believed we had known each other at Oxford, and that I should be inspecting the National Schools from nine till about eleven. And then, having dispatched it by one of my landlord's sons, I went off to my work. The day was brilliantly fine. The wind had shifted round to the north, the sun shone clear and cold, and the smoke-grimed hamlet, and the gaunt buildings clustered at the mouths of the coal pits round about, looked as bright as they could look at any time of the year.

The village was built up a long hillside; the church and schools being at the top, and the 'Greyhound' at the bottom. Looking vainly for the lane by which I had come the night before, I climbed the one rambling street, followed a path that skirted the churchyard, and found myself at the schools. These, with the teachers' dwellings, formed three sides of a quadrangle; the fourth side consisting of an iron railing and a gate. An inscribed tablet over the main entrance-door recorded how 'These school-houses were rebuilt by Philip Wolstenholme, Esquire: *a.d.* 18—.'

Mr Wolstenholme, sir, is the Lord of the Manor,' said a soft, obsequious voice.

I turned, and found the speaker at my elbow, a square-built, sallow man, all in black, with a bundle of copy-books under his arm.

'You are the—the schoolmaster?' I said; unable to remember his name, and puzzled by a vague recollection of his face.

'Just so, sir. I conclude I have the honour of addressing Mr Frazer?'

It was a singular face, very pallid and anxious looking. The eyes, too, had a watchful, almost a startled, look in them, which struck me as peculiarly unpleasant.

'Yes,' I replied, still wondering where and when I had seen him. 'My name is Frazer. Yours, I believe, is—is—,' and I put my hand into my pocket for my examination papers.

'Skelton-Ebenezer Skelton. Will you please to take the boys first, sir?'

The words were commonplace enough, but the man's manner was studiously, disagreeably deferential; his very name being given, as it were, under protest, as if too insignificant to be mentioned.

I said I would begin with the boys; and so moved on. Then, for we had stood still till now, I saw that the schoolmaster was lame. In that moment I remembered him. He was the man I met in the fog.

'I met you yesterday afternoon, Mr Skelton,' I said, as we went into the school-room.

'Yesterday afternoon, sir?' he repeated.

'You did not seem to observe me,' I said, carelessly. 'I spoke to you, in fact; but you did not reply to me.'

'But—indeed, I beg your pardon, sir—it must have been someone else,' said the schoolmaster, 'I did not go out yesterday afternoon.'

How could this be anything but a falsehood? I might have been mistaken as to the man's face; though it was such a singular face, and I had seen it quite plainly. But how could I be mistaken as to his lameness? Besides, that curious trailing of the right foot, as if the ankle was broken, was not an ordinary lameness.

I suppose I looked incredulous, for he added, hastily: 'Even if I had not been preparing the boys for inspection, sir, I should not have gone out yesterday afternoon. It was too damp and foggy. I am obliged to be careful—I have a very delicate chest.'

My dislike to the man increased with every word he uttered. I did not ask myself with what motive he went on heaping lie upon lie; it was enough that, to serve his own ends, whatever those ends might be, he did lie with unparalleled audacity.

'We will proceed to the examination, Mr Skelton,' I said, contemptuously.

He turned, if possible, a shade paler than before, bent his head silently, and called up the scholars in their order.

I soon found that, whatever his shortcomings as to veracity, Mr Ebenezer Skelton was a capital schoolmaster. His boys were uncommonly well taught, and as regarded attendance, good conduct, and the like, left nothing to be desired. When, therefore, at the end of the examination, he said he hoped I would recommend the Pit End Boys' School for the Government grant, I at once assented. And now I thought I had done with Mr Skelton for, at all events, the space of one year. Not so, however. When I came out from the Girls' School, I found him waiting at the door.

Profusely apologizing, he begged leave to occupy five minutes of my valuable time. He wished, under correction, to suggest a little improvement. The boys, he said, were allowed to play in the quadrangle, which was too small, and in various ways inconvenient; but round at the back there was a piece of waste land, half an acre of which, if enclosed, would admirably answer the purpose. So saying, he led the way to the back of the building, and I followed him.

'To whom does this ground belong?' I asked.

'To Mr Wolstenholme, sir.'

'Then why not apply to Mr Wolstenholme? He gave the schools, and I dare say he would be equally willing to give the ground.'

'I beg your pardon, sir. Mr Wolstenholme has not been over here since his return, and it is quite possible that he may leave Pit End without honouring us with a visit. I could not take the liberty of writing to him, sir.'

'Neither could I in my report suggest that the Government should offer to purchase a portion of Mr Wolstenholme's land for a playground to schools of Mr Wolstenholme's own building.' I replied. 'Under other circumstances'.

I stopped and looked round.

The schoolmaster repeated my last words.

'You were saying, sir—under other circumstances?'

I looked round again.

'It seemed to me that there was someone here,' I said; 'some third person, not a moment ago.'

'I beg your pardon, sir—a third person?'

'I saw his shadow on the ground, between yours and mine.'

The schools faced due north, and we were standing immediately behind the buildings, with our backs to the sun. The place was bare, and open, and high; and our shadows, sharply defined, lay stretched before our feet.

'A—a shadow?' he faltered. 'Impossible.'

There was not a bush or a tree within half a mile. There was not a cloud in the sky. There was nothing, absolutely nothing, that could have cast a shadow.

I admitted that it was impossible, and that I must have fancied it; and so went back to the matter of the playground.' Should you see Mr Wolstenholme,' I said, 'you are at liberty to say that I thought it a desirable improvement.'

'I am much obliged to you, sir. Thank you—thank you very much,' he said, cringing at every word. 'But—but I had hoped that you might perhaps use your influence—'

'Look there!' I interrupted. 'Is that fancy?'

We were now close under the blank wall of the boys' schoolroom. On this wall, lying to the full sunlight, our shadows—mine and the schoolmaster's—were projected. And there, too—no longer between his and mine, but a little way apart, as if the intruder were standing back-there, as sharply defined as if cast by lime-light on a prepared background, I again distinctly saw, though but for a moment, that third shadow. As I spoke, as I looked round, it was gone!

'Did you not see it?' I asked.

He shook his head.

'I—I saw nothing,' he said, faintly. 'What was it?'

His lips were white. He seemed scarcely able to stand.

'But you must have seen it!' I exclaimed. 'It fell just there-where that bit of ivy grows. There must be some boy hiding—it was a boy's shadow, I am confident.'

'A boy's shadow!' he echoed, looking round in a wild, frightened way. 'There is no place—for a boy—to hide.'

'Place or no place,' I said, angrily, 'if I catch him, he shall feel the weight of my cane!'

I searched backwards and forwards in event direction, the schoolmaster, with his scared face, limping at my heels; but, rough and irregular as the ground was, there was not a hole in it big enough to shelter a rabbit.

'But what was it?' I said, impatiently.

'An—an illusion. Begging your pardon, sir—an illusion.'

He looked so like a beaten hound, so frightened, so fawning, that I felt I could with lively satisfaction have transferred the threatened caning to his own shoulders.

'But you saw it?' I said again.

'No, sir. Upon my honour, no, sir. I saw nothing—nothing whatever.'

His looks belied his words. I felt positive that he had not only seen the shadow, but that he knew more about it than he chose to tell. I was by this time really angry. To be made the object of a boyish trick, and to be hoodwinked by the connivance of the schoolmaster, was too much. It was an insult to myself and my office.

I scarcely knew what I said; something short and stern at all events. Then, having said it, I turned my back upon Mr Skelton and the schools, and walked rapidly back to the village.

As I neared the bottom of the hill, a dog-cart drawn by a high-stepping chestnut dashed up to the door of the 'Greyhound', and the next moment I was shaking hands with Wolstenholme, of Balliol. Wolstenholme, of Balliol, as handsome as ever, dressed with the same careless dandyism, looking not a day older than when I last saw him at Oxford! He gripped me by both hands, vowed that I was his guest for the next three days, and insisted on carrying me off at once to Backwater Chase.

In vain I urged that I had two schools to inspect tomorrow ten miles the other side of Drumley; that I had a horse and trap waiting; and that my room was ordered at the 'Feathers'. Wolstenholme laughed away my objections.

'My dear fellow,' he said, 'you will simply send your horse and trap back with a message to the "Feathers", and a couple of telegrams to be dispatched to the two schools from Drumley station.

Unforeseen circumstances compel you to defer those inspections till next week!'. And with this, in his masterful way, he shouted to the landlord to send my portmanteau up to the manor-house, pushed me up before him into the dog-cart, gave the chestnut his head, and rattled me off to Backwater Chase.

It was a gloomy old barrack of a place, standing high in the midst of a sombre deer-park some six or seven miles in circumference. An avenue of oaks, now leafless, led up to the house; and a mournful heron-haunted tarn in the loneliest part of the park gave to the estate its name of Blackwater Chase. The place, in fact, was more like a border fastness than an English north-country mansion. Wolstenholme took me through the picture gallery and reception rooms after luncheon, and then for a canter round the park; and in the evening we dined at the upper end of a great oak hall hung with antlers, and armour, and antiquated weapons of warfare and sport.

'Now, tomorrow,' said my host, as we sat over our claret in front of a blazing log-fire; 'tomorrow, if we have decent weather, you shall have a day's shooting on the moors; and on Friday, if you will but be persuaded to stay a day longer, I will drive you over to Broomhead and give you a run with the Duke's hounds. Not hunt? My dear fellow, what nonsense! All our parsons hunt in this part of the world. By the way, have you ever been down a coal pit? No?

Then a new experience awaits you. I'll take you down Carshalton shaft, and show you the home of the gnomes and trolls.'

'Is Carshalton one of your own mines?' I asked.

'All these pits are mine,' he replied. 'I am king of Hades, and rule the underworld as well as the upper. There is coal everywhere underlying these moors. The whole place is honeycombed with shafts and galleries. One of our richest seams runs under this house, and there are upwards of forty men at work in it a quarter of a mile below our feet here every day. Another leads right away under the park, heaven only knows how far! My father began working it five-and-twenty years ago, and we have gone on working it ever since; yet it shows no sign of failing.'

'You must be as rich as a prince with a fairy godmother!'

He shrugged his shoulders.

'Well,' he said, lightly, 'I am rich enough to commit what follies I please; and that is saying a good deal. But then, to be always squandering money—always rambling about the world—always gratifying the impulse of the moment—is that happiness? I have been trying the experiment for the last ten years; and with what result? Would you like to see?'

He snatched up a lamp and led the way through a long suite of unfurnished rooms, the floors of which were piled high with packing cases of all sizes and shapes, labelled with the names of various foreign ports and the addresses of foreign agents innumerable. What did they contain?

Precious marbles from Italy and Greece and Asia Minor; priceless paintings by old and modern masters; antiquities from the Nile, the Tigris, and the Euphrates; enamels from Persia, porcelain from China, bronzes from Japan, strange sculptures from Peru; arms, mosaics, ivories, wood-carvings, skins, tapestries, old Italian cabinets, painted bride-chests, Etruscan terracottas; treasures of all countries, of all ages, never even unpacked since they crossed that threshold which the master's foot had crossed but twice during the ten years it had taken to buy them!

Should he ever open them, ever arrange them, ever enjoy them? Perhaps—if he became weary of wandering—if he married—if he built a gallery to receive them. If not—well, he might found and endow a museum; or leave the things to the nation. What did it matter? Collecting was like fox-hunting; the pleasure was in the pursuit, and ended with it!

We sat up late that first night, I can hardly say conversing, for Wolstenholme did the talking, while I, willing to be amused, led him on to tell me something of his wanderings by land and sea.

So the time passed in stories of adventure, of perilous peaks ascended, of deserts traversed, of unknown ruins explored, of 'hairbreadth 'scapes' from icebergs and earthquakes and storms; and when at last he flung the end of his cigar into the fire and discovered that it was time to go to bed, the clock on the mantelshelf pointed far on among the small hours of the morning.

Next day, according to the programme made out for my entertainment, we did some seven hours' partridge-shooting on the moors; and the day next following I was to go down Carshalton shaft before breakfast, and after breakfast ride over to a place some fifteen miles distant called Picts' Camp, there to see a stone circle and the ruins of a prehistoric fort.

Unused to field sports, I slept heavily after those seven hours with the guns, and was slow to wake when Wolstenholme's valet came next morning to my bedside with the waterproof suit in which I was to effect my descent into Hades.

'Mr Wolstenholme says, sir, that you had better not take your bath till you come back,' said this gentlemanly vassal, disposing the ungainly garments across the back of a chair as artistically as if he were laying out my best evening suit. 'And you will be pleased to dress warmly underneath the waterproofs, for it is very chilly in the mine.'

I surveyed the garments with reluctance. The morning was frosty, and the prospect of being lowered into the bowels of the earth, cold, tasting, and unwashed, was anything but attractive.

Should I send word that I would rather not go? I hesitated; but while I was hesitating, the gentlemanly valet vanished, and my opportunity was lost. Grumbling and shivering, I got up, donned the cold and shiny suit, and went downstairs.

A murmur of voices met my ear as I drew near the breakfast-room. Going in, I found some ten or a dozen stalwart colliers grouped near the door, and Wolstenholme, looking somewhat serious, standing with his back to the fire.

'Look here, Frazer,' he said, with a short laugh, 'here's a pleasant piece of news. A fissure has opened in the bed of Blackwater tarn; the lake has disappeared in the night; and the mine is flooded! No Carshalton shaft for you today!'

'Seven foot o' wayter in Jukes's seam, an' eight in th' owd north and south galleries,' growled a huge red-headed fellow, who seemed to be the spokesman.

'An' it's the Lord's own marcy a' happened o' noight-time, or we'd be dead men all,' added another.

'That's true, my man,' said Wolstenholme, answering the last speaker. 'It might have drowned you like rats in a trap; so we may thank our stars it's no worse. And now, to work with the pumps! Lucky for us that we know what to do, and how to do it.'

So saying, he dismissed the men with a good-humoured nod, and an order for unlimited ale.

I listened in blank amazement. The tarn vanished! I could not believe it. Wolstenholme assured me, however, that it was by no means a solitary phenomenon. Rivers had been known to disappear before now, in mining districts; and sometimes, instead of merely cracking, the ground would cave in, burying not merely houses, but whole hamlets in one common ruin. The foundations of such houses were, however, generally known to be insecure long enough before the crash came; and these accidents were not therefore often followed by loss of life.

'And now,' he said, lightly, 'you may doff your fancy costume; for I shall have time this morning for nothing but business. It is not every day that one loses a lake, and has to pump it up again!'

Breakfast over, we went round to the mouth of the pit, and saw the men fixing the pumps.

Later on, when the work was fairly in train, we started off across the park to view the scene of the catastrophe. Our way lay far from the house across a wooded upland, beyond which we followed a broad glade leading to the tarn. Just as we entered this glade—Wolstenholme rattling on and turning the whole affair into jest—a tall, slender lad, with a fishing-rod across his shoulder, came out from one of the side paths to the right, crossed the open at a long slant, and disappeared among the tree-trunks on the opposite side. I recognized him instantly. It was the boy whom I saw the other day, just after meeting the schoolmaster in the meadow.

'If that boy thinks he is going to fish in your tarn,' I said, 'he will find out his mistake.'

'What boy?' asked Wolstenholme, looking back.

'That boy who crossed over yonder, a minute ago.'

'Yonder!—in front of us?'

'Certainly. You must have seen him?'

'Not I.'

'You did not see him?—a tall, thin boy, in a grey suit, with a fishing-rod over his shoulder. He disappeared behind those Scotch firs.'

Wolstenholme looked at me with surprise.

'You are dreaming!' he said. 'No living thing—not even a rabbit—has crossed our path since we entered the park gates.'

'I am not in the habit of dreaming with my eyes open,' I replied, quickly.

He laughed, and put his arm through mine.

'Eyes or no eyes,' he said, 'you are under an illusion this time!'

An illusion—the very word made use of by the schoolmaster! What did it mean? Could I, in truth, no longer rely upon the testimony of my senses? A thousand half-formed apprehensions flashed across me in a moment. I remembered the illusions of Nicolini, the bookseller, and other similar cases of visual hallucination, and I asked myself if I had suddenly become afflicted in like manner.

'By Jove! this is a queer sight!' exclaimed Wolstenholme. And then I found that we had emerged from the glade, and were looking down upon the bed of what yesterday was Blackwater Tarn.

It was indeed a queer sight—an oblong, irregular basin of blackest slime, with here and there a sullen pool, and round the margin an irregular fringe of bulrushes. At some little distance along the bank—less than a quarter of a mile from where we were standing—a gaping crowd had gathered. All Pit End, except the men at the pumps, seemed to have turned out to stare at the bed of the vanished tarn.

Hats were pulled off and curtsies dropped at Wolstenholme's approach. He, meanwhile, came up smiling, with a pleasant word for everyone.

'Well,' he said, 'are you looking for the lake, my friends? You'll have in go down Carshalton shaft to find it! It's an ugly sight you've come to see, anyhow!'

"Tes an ugly soight, squoire,' replied a stalwart blacksmith in a leathern apron; 'but thar's summat uglier, mebbe, than the mud, ow'r yonder.'

'Something uglier than the mud?' Wolstenholme repeated.

'Wull yo be pleased to stan' this way, squoire, an' look strite across at yon little tump o' bulrashes—doan't yo see nothin'?'

I see a log of rotten timber sticking half in and half out of the mud,' said Wolstenholme; 'and something—a long reed, apparently... by love! I believe it's a fishing rod!'

'It is a fishin' rod, squoire,' said the blacksmith with rough carnesmess; 'an' if yon rotten timber bayn't an unburied corpse, mun I never stroike hammer on anvil agin!'

There was a buzz of acquiescence from the bystanders. 'Twas an unburied corpse, sure enough. Nobody doubted it. Wolstenholme made a funnel with his hands, and looked through it long and steadfastly.

'It must come out, whatever it is,' he said presently. 'Five feet of mud, do you say? Then here's a sovereign apiece for the first two fellows who wade through it and bring that object to land!'

The blacksmith and another pulled off their shoes and stockings, turned up their trousers, and went in at once.

They were over their ankles at the first plunge, and, sounding their way with sticks, went deeper at every tread. As they sank, our excitement rose. Presently they were visible from only the waist upwards. We could see their chests heaving, and the muscular efforts by which each step was gained. They were yet full twenty yards from the goal when the mud mounted to their armpits... a few feet more, and only their heads would remain above the surface!

An uneasy movement ran through the crowd.

'Call 'em back, for God's sake!' cried a woman's voice.

But at this moment—having reached a point where the ground gradually sloped upwards—they began to rise above the mud as rapidly as they had sunk into it. And now, black with clotted slime, they emerge waist-high ... now they are within three or four yards of the spot... and now... now they are there!

They part the reeds—they stoop low above the shapeless object on which all eyes are turned—they half-lift it from its bed of mud—they hesitate—lay it down again—decide, apparently, to leave it there; and turn their faces shorewards. Having come a few paces, the blacksmith remembers the fishing-rod; turns back; disengages the tangled line with some difficulty, and brings it over his shoulder.

They had not much to tell—standing, all mud from head to heel, on dry land again—but that little was conclusive. It was, in truth, an unburied corpse; part of the trunk only above the surface. They tried to lift it; but it had been so long under water, and was in so advanced a stage of decomposition, that to bring it to shore without a shutter was impossible. Being cross-questioned, they thought, from the slenderness of the form, that it must be the body of a boy.

'Thar's the poor chap's rod, anyhow,' said the blacksmith, laying it gently down upon the turf.

I have thus far related events as I witnessed them. Here, however, my responsibility ceases. I give the rest of my story at second-hand, briefly, as I received it some weeks later, in the following letter from Philip Wolstenholme:

Blackwater Chase, Dec. 20th, 18—.

Dear Frazer, My promised letter has been a long time on the road, but I did not see the use of writing till I had something definite to tell you. I think, however, we have now found out all that we are ever likely to know about the tragedy in the tarn; and it seems that—but, no; I will begin at the beginning. That is to say, with the day you left the Chase, which was the day following the discovery of the body.

You were but just gone when a police inspector arrived from Drumley (you will remember that I had immediately sent a man over to the sitting magistrate); but neither the inspector nor anyone else could do anything till the remains were brought to shore, and it took us the best part of a week to accomplish this difficult operation. We had to sink no end of big stones in order to make a rough and ready causeway across the mud. This done, the body was brought over decently upon a shutter. It proved to be the corpse of a boy of perhaps fourteen or fifteen years of age.

There was a fracture three inches long at the back of the skull, evidently fatal. This might, of course, have been an accidental injury; but when the body came to be raised from where it lay, it was found to be pinned down by a pitchfork, the handle of which had been afterwards whittled off, so as not to show above the water, a discovery tantamount to evidence of murder.

The features of the victim were decomposed beyond recognition; but enough of the hair remained to show that it had been short and sandy As for the clothing, it was a mere mass of rotten shreds; but on being subjected to some chemical process, proved to have once been a suit of lightish grey cloth.

A crowd of witnesses came forward at this stage of the inquiry—for I am now giving you the main facts as they came out at the coroner's inquest—to prove that about a year or thirteen months ago, Skelton the schoolmaster had staying with him a lad whom he called his nephew, and to whom it was supposed that he was not particularly kind. This lad was described as tall, thin, mud sandy-haired. He habitually wore a suit corresponding in colour and texture to the shreds of clothing discovered on the body in the tarn; and he was much addicted to angling about the pools and streams, wherever he might have the chance of a nibble.

And now one thing led quickly on to another. Our Pit End shoemaker identified the boy's boots as being a pair of his own making and selling. Other witnesses testified to angry scenes between the uncle and nephew. Finally, Skelton gave himself up to justice, confessed the deed, and was duly committed to Drumley gaol for wilful murder.

And the motive? Well, the motive is the strangest part of my story. The wretched lad was, after all, not Skelton's nephew, but Skelton's own illegitimate son. The mother was dead, and the boy lived with his maternal grandmother in a remote part of Cumberland. The old woman was poor, and the schoolmaster made her an annual allowance for his son's keep and clothing. He had not seen the boy for some years, when he sent for him to come over on a visit to Pit End. Perhaps he was weary of the tax upon his purse. Perhaps, as he himself puts it in his confession, he was disappointed to find the boy, if not actually half-witted, stupid, wilful, and ill brought-up. He at all events took a dislike to the poor brute, which dislike by and by developed into positive hatred.

Some amount of provocation there would seem to have been. The boy was as backward as a child of five years old. That Skelton put him into the Boys' School, and could do nothing with him; that he defied discipline, had a passion for fishing, and was continually wandering about the country with his rod and line, are facts borne out by the independent testimony of various witnesses. Having hidden his fishing-tackle, he was in the habit of slipping away at school-hours, and showed himself the more cunning and obstinate the more he was punished.

At last there came a day when Skelton tracked him to the place where his rod was concealed, and thence across the meadows into the park, and as far as the tarn. His (Skelton's) account of what followed is wandering and confused. He owns to having beaten the miserable lad about the head and arms with a heavy stick that he had brought with him for the purpose; but denies that he intended to murder him.

When his son fell insensible and ceased to breathe, he for the first time realized the force of the blows he had dealt. He admits that his first impulse was one, not of remorse for the deed, but of fear for his own safety. He dragged the body in among the bulrushes by the water's edge, and there concealed it as well as he could. At night, when the neighbours were in bed and asleep, he stole out by starlight, taking with him a pitchfork, a coil of rope, a couple of old iron-bars, and a knife.

Thus laden, he struck out across the moor, and entered the park by a stile and footpath on the Stoneleigh side; so making a circuit of between three and four miles. A rotten old punt used at that time to be kept on the tarn. He loosed this punt from its moorings, brought it round, hauled in the body, and paddled his ghastly burden out into the middle of the lake as far as a certain clump of reeds which he had noted as a likely spot for his purpose. Here he weighted and sunk the corpse, and pinned it down by the neck with his pitchfork. He then cut away the handle of the fork; hid the fishing-rod among the reeds; and believed, as murderers always believe, that discovery was impossible. As regarded the Pit End folk, he simply gave out that his nephew had gone back to Cumberland; and no one doubted it.

Now, however, he says that accident has only anticipated him; and that he was on the point of voluntarily confessing his crime. His dreadful secret had of late become intolerable. He was haunted by an invisible Presence. That Presence sat with him at table, followed him in his walks stood behind him in the school-room, and watched by his bedside. He never saw it; but he felt that it was always there. Sometimes he raves of a shadow on the wall of his cell. The gaol authorities are of opinion that he is of unsound mind.

I have now told you all that there is at present to tell. The trial will not take place till the spring assizes. In the meanwhile I am off tomorrow to Paris, and thence, in about ten days, on to Nice, where letters will find me at the Hotel des Empereurs.

Always, dear Frazer,

Yours, e.t.c.,

P. W.

P.S-Since writing the above, I have received a telegram from Drumley to say that Skelton has committed suicide. No particulars given. So ends this strange eventful history.

By the way, that was a curious illusion of yours the other day when we were crossing the park; and I have thought of it many times. Was it an illusion?—that is the question.'

Ay, indeed! that is the question; and it is a question which I have never yet been able to answer.

Certain things I undoubtedly saw—with my mind's eye, perhaps—and as I saw them, I have described them; withholding nothing, adding nothing, explaining nothing. Let those solve the mystery who can. For myself, I but echo Wolstenholme's question: Was it an illusion?

A Legend of Boisguilbert

Beside this tarn, in ages gone,
As antique legends darkly tell,
A false, false Abbot and forty monks
Did once in sinful plenty dwell.

Accursed of Christ and all the saints,
They robb'd the rich; they robb'd the poor;
They quaff'd the best of Malvoisie;
They turn'd the hungry from their door.

And though the nations groan'd aloud,
And famine stalk'd across the land
And though the noblest Christian blood
Redden'd the thirsty Eastern sand

These monks kept up their ancient state,
Nor cared how long the troubles lasted;
But fed their deer, and stock'd their pond,
And feasted when they should have fasted.

And so it fell one Christmas Eve,
When it was dark, and cold, and late,
A pious knight from Palestine
Came knocking at the convent gate.

He rode a steed of Arab blood;
His helm was up; his mien was bold;
And round about his neck he wore
A chain of Saracenic gold.

"What ho! good monks of Boisguilbert,
Your guest am I tonight!" quoth he.
"Have you a stable for my steed?
A supper, and a cell for me?"

The Abbot laugh'd; the friars scoff'd;
They fell upon that knight renown'd,
And bore him down, and tied his hands,
And threw him captive on the ground.

"Sir guest!" they cried, "your steed shall be
Into our convent stable led;
And, since we have no cell to spare,
Yourself must sleep among the dead!"

He mark'd them with a steadfast eye;
He heard them with a dauntless face;
He was too brave to fear to die;
He was too proud to sue for grace.

They tore the chain from round his neck,
The trophy of a gallant fight,
Whilst o'er the black and silent tarn
Their torches flash'd a sullen light.

And the great pike that dwelt therein,
All startled by the sudden glare,
Dived down among the water-weeds,
And darted blindly here and there.

And one white owl that made her nest
Up in the belfry tow'r hard by,
Flew round and round on swirling wings
And vanished with a ghostly cry.

The Abbot stood upon the brink;
He laugh'd aloud in wicked glee;
He waved his torch: "Quick! fling him in—
Our fish shall feast tonight!" said he.

They flung him in. "Farewell!" they cried,

And crowded round the reedy shore.
He gasping rose "Till Christmas next!"
He said then sank to rise no more.

"Till Christmas next!" They stood and stared
Into each other's guilty eyes;
Then fled within the convent gates,
Lest they should see their victim rise.

The fragile bubbles rose and broke;
The wid'ning circles died away;
The white owl shriek'd again; the pike
Were left to silence and their prey.

A year went by. The stealthy fogs
Crept up the hill, all dense and slow,
And all the woods of Boisguilbert
Lay hush'd and heavy in the snow.

The sullen sun was red by day;
The nights were black; the winds were keen;
And all across the frozen tarn
The footprints of the wolf were seen.

And vague foreshadowings of woe
Beset the monks with mortal fear
Strange shadows through the cloister pac'd
Strange whispers threaten'd every ear.

Strange writings started forth at dusk
In fiery lines along the walls;
Strange spectres round the chapel sat,
At midnight, in the sculptural stalls.

"Oh, father Abbot!" cried the monks,
"We must repent! Our sins are great!
Tomorrow will be Christmas Eve
Tomorrow night may be too late!

"And should the drowned dead arise" . . .
"The Abbot laugh'd with might and main.

"The ice," said he, "is three feet deep.
He'd find it hard to rise again!

"But when tomorrow night is come,
We'll say a mass to rest his soul!"
Tomorrow came, and all day long
The chapel bell was heard to toll.

At eve they met to read the mass.
Bent low was ev'ry shaven crown;
One trembling monk the tapers lit;
One held his missal upside down;

And when their quav'ring voices in
The Dies Irce all united,
Even the Abbot told his beads
And fragments of the Creed recited.

And when but hark! what sounds are those?
Is it the splitting of the ice?
Is it a steel-clad hand that smites
Against the outer portal thrice?

Is that the tread of an armed heel?
The frighten'd monks forget to pray;
The Abbot drops the holy book;
The Dies Irce dies away;

And in the shadow of the door
They see their year-gone victim stand!
His rusty mail drips on the floor;
He beckons with uplifted hand!

The Abbot rose. He could not choose;
He had no voice or strength to pray;
For when the mighty dead command,
The living must perforce obey.

The spectre-knight then gazed around
With stony eye, and hand uprear'd.
"Farewell," said he; "till Christmas next!"—

Then knight and Abbot disappear'd.

And thus it is the place is cursed,
And long since fallen to decay;
For ev'ry Christmas Eve the knight
Came back, and took a monk away.

Came back, while yet a blood-stain'd wretch
The holy convent-garb profaned;
Came back while yet a guilty soul
Of all those forty monks remain'd;

And still comes back to earth, if we
The peasants' story may believe
And rises from the murky tarn
At midnight every Christmas Eve!

Four Ghost Stories

1

Some few years ago a well-known English artist received commission from Lady F. to paint a portrait of her husband It was settled that he should execute the commission at F. Hall, in the country, because his engagements were too many to permit his entering upon a fresh work till the London season should be over. As he happened to be on terms of intimate acquaintance with his employers, the arrangement was satisfactory to all concerned, and on the 13th of September he set out in good heart to perform his engagement.

He took the train for the station nearest to F. Hall, and found himself, when first starting, alone in a carriage. His solitude did not, however, continue long. At the first station out of London, a young lady entered the carriage, and took the corner opposite to him. She was very delicate-looking, with a remarkable blending of sweetness and sadness in her countenance, which did not fail to attract the notice of a man of observation and sensibility. For some time neither uttered a syllable. But at length the gentleman made the remarks usual under such circumstances, on the weather and the country, and, the ice being broken, they entered into conversation.

They spoke of painting. The artist was much surprised by the intimate knowledge the young lady seemed to have of himself and his doings. He was quite certain that he had never seen her before. His surprise was by no means lessened when she suddenly inquired whether he could make, from recollection, the likeness of a person whom he had seen only once, or at most twice? He was hesitating what to reply, when she added, 'Do you think, for example, that you could paint me from recollection?'

He replied that he was not quite sure, but that perhaps he could.

'Well,' she said, 'look at me again. You may have to take a likeness of me.'

He complied with this odd request, and she asked, rather eagerly, 'Now, do you think you could?'

'I think so,' he replied; 'but I cannot say for certain.'

At this moment the train stopped. The young lady rose from her seat, smiled in a friendly manner on the painter, and bade him goodbye; adding, as she quitted the carriage, 'We shall meet again soon.' The train rattled off, and Mr H. (the artist) was left to his own reflections.

The station was reached in due time, and Lady F.'s carriage was there, to meet the expected guest. It carried him to the place of his destination, one of 'the stately homes of England', after a pleasant drive, and deposited him at the hall door, where his host and hostess were standing to receive him. A kind greeting passed, and he was shown to his room: for the dinner-hour was close at hand.

Having completed his toilet, and descended to the drawing-room, Mr H. was much surprised, and much pleased, to see, seated on one of the ottomans, his young companion of the railway carriage. She greeted him with a smile and a bow of recognition. She sat by his side at dinner, spoke to him two or three times, mixed in the general conversation, and seemed perfectly at home. Mr H. had no doubt of her being an intimate friend of his hostess. The evening passed away pleasantly. The conversation turned a good deal upon the fine arts in general, and on painting in particular, and Mr H. was entreated to show some of the sketches he had brought down with him from London. He readily produced them, and the young lady was much interested in them.

At a late hour the party broke up, and retired to their several apartments.

Next morning, early, Mr H. was tempted by the bright sunshine to leave his room, and stroll out into the park. The drawing-room opened into the garden; passing through it, he inquired of a servant who was busy arranging the furniture, whether the young lady had come down yet?

'What young lady, sir?' asked the man, with an appearance of surprise.

The young lady who dined here last night.'

'No young lady dined here last night, sir,' replied the man, looking fixedly at him.

The painter said no more: thinking within himself that the servant was either very stupid or had a very bad memory. So, leaving the room, he sauntered out into the park.

He was returning to the house, when his host met him, and the usual morning salutations passed between them.

'Your fair young friend has left you?' observed the artist.

'What young friend?' inquired the lord of the manor.

'The young lady who dined here last night,' returned Mr H.

'I cannot imagine to whom you refer,' replied the gentleman, very greatly surprised.

'Did not a young lady dine and spend the evening here yesterday?' persisted Mr H., who in his turn was beginning to wonder.

'No,' replied his host; 'most certainly not. There was no one at table but yourself, my lady, and I.'

The subject was never reverted to after this occasion, yet our artist could not bring himself to believe that he was labouring under a delusion. If the whole were a dream, it was a dream in two parts. As surely as the young lady had been his companion in the railway carriage, so surely she had sat beside him at the dinner-table. Yet she did not come again; and everybody in the house, except himself, appeared to be ignorant of her existence.

He finished the portrait on which he was engaged, and returned to London.

For two whole years he followed up his profession: growing in reputation, and working hard. Yet he never all the while forgot a single lineament in the fair young face of his fellow-traveller. He had no clue by which to discover where she had come from, or who she was. He often thought of her, but spoke to no one about her. There was a mystery about the matter which imposed silence on him. It was wild, strange, utterly unaccountable.

Mr H. was called by business to Canterbury. An old friend of his—whom I will call Mr Wylde—resided there. Mr H., being anxious to see him, and having only a few hours at his disposal, wrote as soon as he reached the hotel, begging Mr Wylde to call upon him there. At the time appointed the door of his room opened, and Mr Wylde was announced. He was a complete stranger to the artist; and the meeting between the two was a little awkward.

It appeared, on explanation, that Mr H.'s friend had left Canterbury some time; that the gentleman now face to face with the artist was another Mr Wylde; that the note intended for the absentee had been given to him; and that he had obeyed the summons, supposing some business matter to be the cause of it.

The first coldness and surprise dispelled, the two gentlemen entered into a more friendly conversation; for Mr H. had mentioned his name, and it was not a strange one to his visitor. When they had conversed a little while, Mr Wylde asked Mr H. whether he had ever painted, or could undertake to paint, a portrait from mere description? Mr H. replied, never.

'I ask you this strange question,' said Mr Wylde, 'because, about two years ago, I lost a dear daughter. She was my only child, and I loved her dearly. Her loss was a heavy affliction to me, and my regrets are the deeper that I have no likeness of her. You are a man of unusual genius. If you could paint me a portrait of my child, I should be very grateful.'

Mr Wylde then described the features and appearance of his daughter, and the colour of her eyes and hair, and tried to give an idea of the expression of her face. Mr H. listened attentively, and, feeling great sympathy with his grief, made a sketch. He had no thought of its being like, but hoped the bereaved father might possibly think it so. But the father shook his head on seeing the sketch, and said, 'No, it was not at all like.' Again the artist tried, and again he failed. The features were pretty well, but the expression was not hers; and the father turned away from it, thanking Mr H. For his kind endeavours, but quite hopeless of any successful result.

Suddenly a thought struck the painter; he took another sheet of paper, made a rapid and vigorous sketch, and handed it to his companion. Instantly, a bright look of recognition and pleasure lighted up the father's face, and he exclaimed, 'That is she! Surely you must have seen my child, or you never could have made so perfect a likeness!'

'When did your daughter die?' inquired the painter, with agitation.

'Two years ago; on the 13th of September. She died in the afternoon, after a few days' illness.'

Mr H. pondered, but said nothing. The image of that fair young face was engraven on his memory as with a diamond's point, and her strangely prophetic words were now fulfilled.

A few weeks after, having completed a beautiful full-length portrait of the young lady, he sent it to her father, and the likeness was declared, by all who had ever seen her, to be perfect.

2

Among the friends of my family was a young Swiss lady, who, with an only brother, had been left an orphan in her childhood. She was brought up, as well as her brother, by an aunt; and the children, thus thrown very much upon each other, became very strongly attached. At the age of twenty-two the youth got some appointment in India, and the terrible day drew near when they must part. I need not describe the agony of persons so circumstanced. But the mode in which these two sought to mitigate the anguish of separation was singular. They agreed that if either should die before the young man's return, the dead should appear to the living.

The youth departed. The young lady by-and-by married a Scotch gentleman, and quitted her home, to be the light and ornament of his. She was a devoted wife, but she never forgot her brother. She corresponded with him regularly, and her brightest days in all the year were those which brought letters from India.

One cold winter's day, two or three years after her marriage, she was seated at work near a large bright fire, in her own bedroom upstairs. It was about midday, and the room was full of light. She was very busy, when some strange impulse caused her to raise her head and look round. The door was slightly open, and, near the large antique bed, stood a figure, which she, at a glance, recognised as that of her brother.

With a cry of delight she started up, and ran forward to meet him, exclaiming, 'Oh, Henry! How could you surprise me so! You never told me you were coming!' But he waved his hand sadly, in a way that forbade approach, and she remained rooted to the spot. He advanced a step towards her, and said, in a low soft voice, 'Do you remember our agreement? I have come to fulfil it'; and approaching nearer he laid his hand on her wrist. It was icy cold, and the touch made her shiver. Her brother smiled, a faint sad smile, and, again waving his hand, turned and left the room.

When the lady recovered from a long swoon there was a mark on her wrist, which never left it to her dying day. The next mail from India brought a letter, informing her that her brother had died on the very day, and at the very hour, when he presented himself to her in her room.

3

Overhanging the waters of the Firth of Forth there lived, a good many years ago, a family of old standing in the kingdom of Fife: frank, hospitable, and hereditary Jacobites. It consisted of the squire, or laird—a man well advanced in years—his wife, three sons, and four daughters. The sons were sent out into the world, but not into the service of the reigning family. The daughters were all young and unmarried, and the eldest and the youngest were much attached to each other. They slept in the same room, shared the same bed, and had no secrets one from the other.

It chanced that among the visitors to the old house there came a young naval officer, whose gun-brig often put in to the neighbouring harbours. He was well received, and between him and the elder of the two sisters a tender attachment sprang up.

But the prospect of such an alliance did not quite please the lady's mother, and, without being absolutely told that it should never take place, the lovers were advised to separate. The plea urged, was, that they could not then afford to marry, and that they must wait for better times. Those were times when parental authority—at all events in Scotland— was like the decree of fate, and the lady felt that she had nothing left to do, but to say farewell to her lover. Not so he. He was a fine gallant fellow, and, taking the old lady at her word, he determined to do his utmost to push his worldly fortunes.

There was war at that time with some northern power—I think with Prussia—and the lover, who had interest at the Admiralty, applied to be sent to the Baltic. He obtained his wish. Nobody interfered to prevent the young people from taking a tender farewell of each other, and, he full of hope, and she desponding, they parted. It was settled that he should write by every opportunity; and twice a week—on the post days at the neighbouring village—the younger sister would mount her pony and ride in for letters.

There was much hidden joy over every letter that arrived. And often and often the sisters would sit at the window a whole winter's night listening to the roar of the sea among the rocks, and hoping and praying that each light, as it shone far away, might be the signal-lamp hung at the mast-head to apprise them that the gun-brig was coming. So weeks stole on in hope deferred, and there came a lull in the correspondence. Post-day after post-day brought no letters from the Baltic, and the agony of the sisters, especially of the betrothed, became almost unbearable.

They slept, as I have said, in the same room, and their window looked down well-nigh into the waters of the Firth. One night, the younger sister was awakened by the heavy moanings of the elder. They had taken to burning a candle in their room, and placing it in the window: thinking, poor girls, that it would serve as a beacon to the brig. She saw by its light that her sister was tossing about, and was greatly disturbed in her sleep. After some hesitation she determined to awaken the sleeper, who sprang up with a wild cry, and, pushing back her long hair with her hands, exclaimed, 'What have you done, what have you done!' Her sister tried to soothe her, and asked tenderly if anything had alarmed her. 'Alarmed!' she answered, still very wildly, 'no! But I saw him! He entered at that door, and came near the foot of the bed. He looked very pale, and his hair was wet. He was just going to speak to me, when you drove him away. O what have you done, what have you done!'

I do not believe that her lover's ghost really appeared, but the fact is certain that the next mail from the Baltic brought intelligence that the gun-brig had gone down in a gale of wind, with all on board.

4

When my mother was a girl about eight or nine years old, and living in Switzerland, the Count R. of Holstein, coming to Switzerland for his health, took a house at Vevay, with the intention of remaining there for two or three years. He soon became acquainted with my mother's parents, and between him and them acquaintance ripened into friendship. They met constantly, and liked each other more and more.

Knowing the count's intentions respecting his stay in Switzerland, my grandmother was much surprised by receiving from him one morning a short hurried note, informing her that urgent and unexpected business obliged him to return that very day to Germany. He added, that he was very sorry to go, but that he must go; and he ended by bidding her farewell, and hoping they might meet again someday. He quitted Vevay that evening, and nothing more was heard of him or his mysterious business.

A few years after this departure, my grandmother and one of her sons went to spend some time at Hamburg. Count R., hearing that they were there, went to see them, and brought them to his castle at Breitenburg, where they were to stay a few days. It was a wild but beautiful district, and the castle, a huge pile, was a relic of the feudal times, which, like most old places of the sort, was said to be haunted. Never having heard the story upon which this belief was founded, my grandmother entreated the count to tell it.

After some little hesitation and demur, he consented: 'There is a room in this house,' he began, 'in which no one is ever able to sleep. Noises are heard in it continually, which have never been accounted for, and which sound like the ceaseless turning over and upsetting of furniture. I have had the room emptied, I have had the old floor taken up and a new one laid down, but nothing would stop the noises. At last, in despair, I had it walled up. The story attached to the room is this.'

Some hundreds of years ago, there lived in this castle a countess, whose charity to the poor and kindness to all people were unbounded. She was known far and wide as 'the good Countess R.' and everybody loved her. The room in question was her room. One night, she was awakened from her sleep by a voice near her; and looking out of bed, she saw, by the faint light of her lamp, a little tiny man, about a foot in height, standing near her bedside. She was greatly surprised, but he spoke, and said, 'Good Countess of R., I have come to ask you to be godmother to my child. Will you consent?' She said she would, and he told her that he would come and fetch her in a few days, to attend the christening; with those words he vanished out of the room.

Next morning, recollecting the incidents of the night, the countess came to the conclusion that she had had an odd dream, and thought no more of the matter. But, about a fortnight afterwards, when she had well-nigh forgotten the dream, she was again roused at the same hour and by the same small individual, who said he had come to claim the fulfilment of her promise. She rose, dressed herself, and followed her tiny guide down the stairs of the castle. In the centre of the courtyard there was, and still is, a large square well, very deep, and stretching underneath the building nobody knew how far.

Having reached the side of this well, the little man blindfolded the countess, and bidding her not fear, but follow him, descended some unknown stairs. This was for the countess a strange and novel position, and she felt uncomfortable; but she determined at all hazards to see the adventure to the end, and descended bravely. They reached the bottom, and when her guide removed the bandage from her eyes, she found herself in a room full of small people like himself. The christening was performed, the countess stood godmother, and at the conclusion of the ceremony, as the lady was about to say goodbye, the mother of the baby took a handful of wood shavings which lay in a corner, and put them into her visitor's apron.

'You have been very kind, good Countess of R.,' she said, 'in coming to be godmother to my child, and your kindness shall not go unrewarded. When you rise tomorrow, these shavings will have turned into metal, and out of them you must immediately get made, two fishes and thirty *silberlingen* (a German coin). When you get them back, take great care of them, for so long as they all remain in your family everything will prosper with you; but, if one of them ever gets lost, then you will have troubles without end.'

The countess thanked her, and bade them all farewell. Having again covered her eyes, the little man led her out of the well, and landed her safe in her own courtyard, where he removed the bandage, and she never saw him more.

Next morning the countess awoke with a confused notion of some extraordinary dream. While at her toilet, she recollected all the incidents quite plainly, and racked her brain for some cause which might account for it. She was so employed when, stretching out her hand for her apron, she was astounded to find it tied up, and, within the folds, a number of metal shavings. How came they there? Was it a reality? Had she not dreamed of the little man and the christening? She told the story to the members of her family at breakfast, who all agreed that whatever the token might mean, it should not be disregarded.

It was therefore settled that the fishes and the *silberlingen* should be made, and carefully kept among the archives of the family. Time passed; everything prospered with the house of R. The King of Denmark loaded them with honours and benefits, and gave the count high office in his household. For many years all went well with them.

Suddenly, to the consternation of the family, one of the fishes disappeared, and, though strenuous efforts were made to discover what had become of it, they all failed. From this time everything went wrong. The count then living, had two sons; while out hunting together, one killed the other; whether accidentally or not, is uncertain, but, as the youths were known to be perpetually disagreeing, the case seemed doubtful. This was the beginning of sorrows.

The king, hearing what had occurred, thought it necessary to deprive the count of the office he held. Other misfortunes followed. The family fell into discredit. Their lands were sold, or forfeited to the crown; till little was left but the old castle of Breitenburg and the narrow domain which surrounded it. This deteriorating process went on through two or three generations, and, to add to all other misfortunes, there was always in the family one mad member.

'And now,' continued the count, 'comes the strange part of the mystery. I had never placed much faith in these mysterious little relics, and I regarded the story in connexion with them as a fable. I should have continued in this belief, but for a very extraordinary circumstance. You remember my sojourn in Switzerland a few years ago, and how abruptly it terminated? Well. Just before leaving Holstein, I had received a curious wild letter from some knight in Norway, saying that he was very ill, but that he could not die without first seeing and conversing with me. I thought the man mad, because I had never heard of him before, and he could have no possible business to transact with me. So, throwing the letter aside, I did not give it another thought.

'My correspondent, however, was not satisfied. He wrote again. My agent, who in my absence opened and answered my letters, told him that I was in Switzerland for my health, and that, if he had anything to say, he had better say it in writing, as I could not possibly travel so far as Norway.

'This, however, did not satisfy the knight. He wrote a third time, beseeching me to come to him, and declaring that what he had to tell me was of the utmost importance to us both. My agent was so struck by the earnest tone of the letter, that he forwarded it to me: at the same time advising me not to refuse the entreaty. This was the cause of my sudden departure from Vevay, and I shall never cease to rejoice that I did not persist in my refusal.

'I had a long and weary journey, and once or twice I felt sorely tempted to stop short, but some strange impulse kept me going. I had to traverse well-nigh the whole of Norway; often for days on horseback, riding over wild moorland, heathery bogs, mountains and crags and lonely places, and ever at my left the rocky coast, lashed and torn by the surging waters.

'At last, after some fatigue and hardship, I reached the village named in the letter, on the northern coast of Norway. The knight's castle—a large round tower—was built on a small island off the coast, and communicated with the land by a drawbridge. I arrived there, late at night, and must admit that I felt misgivings when I crossed the bridge by the lurid glare of torchlight, and heard the dark waters surging under me.

'The gate was opened by a man, who, as soon as I entered, closed it behind me. My horse was taken from me, and I was led up to the knight's room. It was a small circular apartment, nearly at the top of the tower, and scantily furnished. There, on a bed, lay the old knight, evidently at the point of death. He tried to rise as I entered, and gave me such a look of gratitude and relief that it repaid me for my pains.

'"I cannot thank you sufficiently, Count of R.," said he, "for granting my request. Had I been in a state to travel I should have gone to you; but that was impossible, and I could not die without first seeing you. My business is short, though important. Do you know this?" And he drew from under his pillow, my long-lost fish. Of course I knew it; and he went on. "How long it has been in this house, I do not know, nor by what means it came here, nor, till quite lately, was I at all aware to whom it rightfully belonged. It did not come here in my time, nor in my father's time, and who brought it is a mystery. When I fell ill, and my recovery was pronounced to be impossible, I heard one night, a voice telling me that I should not die till I had restored the fish to the Count R. of Breitenburg. I did not know you; I had never heard of you; and at first I took no heed of the voice. But it came again, every night, until at length in despair I wrote to you. Then the voice stopped. Your answer came, and again I heard the warning, that I must not die till you arrived. At last I heard that you were coming, and I have no language in which to thank you for your kindness. I feel sure I could not have died without seeing you."

'That night the old man died. I waited to bury him, and then returned home, bringing my recovered treasure with me. It was carefully restored to its place. That same year, my eldest brother, whom you know to have been the inmate of a lunatic asylum for years, died, and I became the owner of this place. Last year, to my great surprise, I received a kind letter from the King of Denmark, restoring to me the office which my fathers once held. This year, I have been named governor to his eldest son, and the king has returned a great part of the confiscated property; so that the sun of prosperity seems to shine once more upon the house of Breitenburg.

Not long ago, I sent one of the *silberlingen* to Paris, and another to Vienna, in order that they might be analysed, and the metal of which they are composed made known to me; but no one is able to decide that point.'

Thus ended the Count of R.'s story, after which he led his eager listener to the place where these precious articles were kept, and showed them to her.

The Portrait-Painter's Story

By Charles Dickens

There was lately published in these pages a paper entitled 'Four Ghost Stories'. The first of those stories related the strange experience of 'a well-known English artist, Mr H.' On the publication of that account, Mr H. himself addressed the Editor of this journal—to his great surprise—and forwarded to him his own narrative of the occurrences in question. As Mr H. wrote, without any concealment, in his own name in full, and from his own studio in London, and as there was no possible doubt of his being a real existing person and a responsible gentleman, it became a duty to read his communication attentively. And great injustice having been unconsciously done to it, in the version published as the first of the Four Ghost Stories, it follows here exactly as received. It is, of course, published with the sanction and authority of Mr H., and Mr H. has himself corrected the proofs. Entering on no theory of our own towards the explanation of any part of this remarkable narrative, we have prevailed on Mr H. to present it without any introductory remarks whatever. It only remains to add, that no one has for a moment stood between us and Mr H. in this matter. The whole communication is at first hand. On seeing the article, Four Ghost Stories, Mr H. frankly and good humouredly wrote, I am the Mr H., the living man, of whom mention is made; how my story has been picked up, I do not know; but it is correctly told. I have it by me, written by myself, and here it is.'

I am a painter. One morning in May, 1858, I was seated in my studio at my usual occupation. At an earlier hour than that at which visits are usually made, I received one from a friend whose acquaintance I had made some year or two previously in Richmond Barracks, Dublin. My acquaintance was a captain in the 3rd West York Militia, and from the hospitable manner in which I had been received while a guest with that regiment, as well as from the intimacy that existed between us personally, it was incumbent on me to offer my visitor suitable refreshments; consequently, two o'clock found us well occupied in conversation, cigars, and a decanter of sherry.

About that hour a ring at the bell reminded me of an engagement I had made with a model, or a young person who, having a pretty face and neck, earned a livelihood by sitting for artists. Not being in the humour for work, I arranged with her to come on the following day, promising, of course, to remunerate her for her loss of time, and she went away. In about five minutes she returned, and, speaking to me privately, stated that she had looked forward to the money for the day's sitting, and would be inconvenienced by the want of it; would I let her have a part? There being no difficulty on this point, she again went.

Close to the street in which I live there is another of a very similar name, and persons who are not familiar with my address often go to it by mistake. The model's way lay directly through it, and, on arriving there, she was accosted by a lady and gentleman, who asked if she could inform them where I lived? They had forgotten my right address, and were endeavouring to find me by inquiring of persons whom they met; in a few more minutes they were shown into my room.

My new visitors were strangers to me. They had seen a portrait I had painted, and wished for likenesses of themselves and their children. The price I named did not deter them, and they asked to look round the studio to select the style and size they should prefer. My friend of the 3rd West York, with infinite address and humour, took upon himself the office of showman, dilating on the merits of the respective works in a manner that the diffidence that is expected in a professional man when speaking of his own productions would not have allowed me to adopt. The inspection proving satisfactory, they asked whether I could paint the pictures at their house in the country, and there being no difficulty on this point, an engagement was made for the following autumn, subject to my writing to fix the time when I might be able to leave town for the purpose. This being adjusted, the gentleman gave me his card, and they left. Shortly afterwards my friend went also, and on looking for the first time at the card left by the strangers, I was somewhat disappointed to find that though it contained the name of Mr and Mrs Kirkbeck, there was no address. I tried to find it by looking at the Court Guide, but it contained no such name, so I put the card in my writing-desk, and forgot for a time the entire transaction.

Autumn came, and with it a series of engagements I had made in the north of England. Towards the end of September, 1858, I was one of a dinner-party at a country-house on the confines of Yorkshire and Lincolnshire. Being a stranger to the family, it was by a mere accident that I was at the house at all. I had arranged to pass a day and a night with a friend in the neighbourhood who was intimate at the house, and had received an invitation, and the dinner occurring on the evening in question, I had been asked to accompany him.

The party was a numerous one, and as the meal approached its termination, and was about to subside into the dessert, the conversation became general. I should here mention that my hearing is defective; at some times more so than at others, and on this particular evening I was extra deaf—so much so, that the conversation only reached me in the form of a continued din. At one instant, however, I heard a word distinctly pronounced, though it was uttered by a person at a considerable distance from me, and that word was Kirkbeck. In the business of the London season I had forgotten all about the visitors of the spring, who had left their card without the address. The word reaching me under such circumstances, arrested my attention, and immediately recalled the transaction to my remembrance. On the first opportunity that offered, I asked a person whom I was conversing with if a family of the name in question was resident in the neighbourhood. I was told in reply, that a Mr Kirkbeck lived at A——, at the farther end of the county.

The next morning I wrote to this person, saying that I believed he called at my studio in the spring, and had made an arrangement with me, which I was prevented fulfilling by there being no address on his card; furthermore, that I should shortly be in his neighbourhood on my return from the north, but should

I be mistaken in addressing him, I begged he would not trouble himself to reply to my note. I gave as my address, The Post Office, York.

On applying there three days afterwards, I received a note from Mr Kirkbeck, stating that he was very glad he had heard from me, and that if I would call on my return, he would arrange about the pictures; he also told me to write a day before I proposed coming, that he might not otherwise engage himself. It was ultimately arranged that I should go to his house the succeeding Saturday, stay till Monday morning, transact afterwards what matters I had to attend to in London, and return in a fortnight to execute the commissions.

The day having arrived for my visit, directly after breakfast I took my place in the morning train from York to London. The train would stop at Doncaster, and after that at Retford junction, where I should have to get out in order to take the line through Lincoln to A———. The day was cold, wet, foggy, and in every way as disagreeable as I have ever known a day to be in an English October. The carriage in which I was seated had no other occupant than myself, but at Doncaster a lady got in.

My place was back to the engine and next to the door. As that is considered the ladies' seat, I offered it to her; she, however, very graciously declined it, and took the corner opposite, saying, in a very agreeable voice, that she liked to feel the breeze on her cheek. The next few minutes were occupied in locating herself. There was the cloak to be spread under her, the skirts of the dress to be arranged, the gloves to be tightened, and such other trifling arrangements of plumage as ladies are wont to make before settling themselves comfortably at church or elsewhere, the last and most important being the placing back over her hat the veil that concealed her features. I could then see that the lady was young, certainly not more than two- or three-and-twenty; but being moderately tall, rather robust in make, and decided in expression, she might have been two or three years younger.

I suppose that her complexion would be termed a medium one; her hair being of a bright brown, or auburn, while her eyes and rather decidedly marked eyebrows were nearly black. The colour of her cheek was of that pale transparent hue that sets off to such advantage large expressive eyes, and an equable firm expression of mouth. On the whole, the ensemble was rather handsome than beautiful, her expression having that agreeable depth and harmony about it that rendered her face and features, though not strictly regular, infinitely more attractive than if they had been modelled upon the strictest rules of symmetry.

It is no small advantage on a wet day and a dull long journey to have an agreeable companion, one who can converse, and whose conversation has sufficient substance in it to make one forget the length and the dreariness of the journey. In this respect I had no deficiency to complain of, the lady being decidedly and agreeably conversational. When she had settled herself to her satisfaction, she asked to be allowed to look at my Bradshaw, and not being a proficient in that difficult work, she requested my aid in ascertaining at what time the train passed through Ret ford again on its way back from London to York.

The conversation turned afterwards on general topics, and, somewhat to my surprise, she led it into such particular subjects as I might be supposed to be more especially familiar with; in- deed, I could not avoid remarking that her entire manner, while it was anything but forward, was that of one who had either known me personally or by report. There was in her manner a kind of confidential reliance when she listened to me that is not usually accorded to a stranger, and sometimes she actually seemed to refer to different circumstances with which I had been con- nected in times past.

After about three-quarters of an hour's conversation the train arrived at Retford, where I was to change carriages. On my alighting and wishing her good morning, she made a slight move- ment of the hand as if she meant me to shake it, and on my do- ing so she said, by way of *adieu*, 'I dare say we shall meet again;' to which I replied, 'I hope that we shall all meet again,' and so parted, she going on the line towards London, and I through Lincolnshire to A——. The remainder of the journey was cold, wet, and dreary.

I missed the agreeable conversation, and tried to supply its place with a book I had brought with me from York, and the *Times* newspaper, which I had procured at Retford. But the most disagreeable journey comes to an end at last, and half-past five in the evening found me at the termination of mine. A carriage was waiting for me at the station, where Mr Kirkbeck was also expected by the same train, but as he did not appear it was concluded he would come by the next—half an hour later; accordingly, the carriage drove away with myself only.

The family being from home at the moment, and the dinner hour being seven, I went at once to my room to unpack and to dress; having completed these operations, I descended to the drawing-room. It probably wanted some time to the dinner hour, as the lamps were not lighted, but in their place a large blazing fire threw a flood of light into every corner of the room, and more especially over a lady who, dressed in deep black, was standing by the chimney-piece warming a very handsome foot on the edge of the fender.

Her face being turned away from the door by which I had entered, I did not at first see her features; on my advancing into the middle of the room, however, the foot was immediately withdrawn, and she turned round to accost me, when, to my profound astonishment, I perceived that it was none other than my companion in the railway carriage. She betrayed no surprise at seeing me; on the contrary, with one of those agreeable joyous expressions that make the plainest woman appear beautiful, she accosted me with, I said we should meet again.'

My bewilderment at the moment almost deprived me of utterance. I knew of no railway or other means by which she could have come. I had certainly left her in a London train, and had seen it start, and the only conceivable way in which she could have come was by going on to Peterborough and then returning by a branch to A——, a circuit of about ninety miles. As soon as my surprise enabled me to speak, I said that I wished I had come by the same conveyance as herself.

'That would have been rather difficult,' she rejoined.

At this moment the servant came with the lamps, and informed me that his master had just arrived and would be down in a few minutes.

The lady took up a book containing some engravings, and having singled one out (a portrait of Lady ——), asked me to look at it well and tell her whether I thought it like her.

I was engaged trying to get up an opinion, when Mr and Mrs Kirkbeck entered, and shaking me heartily by the hand, apologised for not being at home to receive me; the gentleman ending by requesting me to take Mrs Kirkbeck in to dinner.

The lady of the house having taken my arm, we marched on. I certainly hesitated a moment to allow Mr Kirkbeck to pass on first with the mysterious lady in black, but Mrs Kirkbeck not seeming to understand it, we passed on at once. The dinner-party consisting of us four only, we fell into our respective places at the table without difficulty, the mistress and master of the house at the top and bottom, the lady in black and myself on each side.

The dinner passed much as is usual on such occasions. I, having to play the guest, directed my conversation principally, if not exclusively, to my host and hostess, and I cannot call to mind that I or anyone else once addressed the lady opposite. Seeing this, and remembering something that looked like a slight want of attention to her on coming into the dining-room, I at once concluded that she was the governess. I observed, however, that she made an excellent dinner; she seemed to appreciate both the beef and the tart as well as a glass of claret afterwards; probably she had had no luncheon, or the journey had given her an appetite.

The dinner ended, the ladies retired, and after the usual port, Mr Kirkbeck and I joined them in the drawing-room. By this time, however, a much larger party had assembled. Brothers and sisters-in-laws had come in from their residences in the neighbourhood, and several children, with Miss Hardwick, their governess, were also introduced to me. I saw at once that my supposition as to the lady in black being the governess was incorrect.

After passing the time necessarily occupied in complimenting the children, and saying something to the different persons to whom I was introduced, I found myself again engaged in conversation with the lady of the railway carriage, and as the topic of the evening had referred principally to portrait-painting, she continued the subject.

'Do you think you could paint my portrait?' the lady inquired.

'Yes, I think I could, if I had the opportunity.'

'Now, look at my face well; do you think you should recollect my features?'

'Yes, I am sure I should never forget your features.'

'Of course I might have expected you to say that; but do you think you could do me from recollection?'

'Well, if it be necessary, I will try; but can't you give me any sittings?'

'No, quite impossible; it could not be. It is said that the print I showed to you before dinner is like me; do you think so?'

'Not much,' I replied; 'it has not your expression. If you can give me only one sitting, it would be better than none.'

'No; I don't see how it could be.'

The evening being by this time rather far advanced, and the chamber candles being brought in, on the plea of being rather tired, she shook me heartily by the hand, and wished me good night. My mysterious acquaintance caused me no small pondering during the night. I had never been introduced to her, I had not seen her speak to any one during the entire evening, not even to wish them good night—how she got across the country was an inexplicable mystery. Then, why did she wish me to paint her from memory, and why could she not give me even one sitting? Finding the difficulties of a solution to these questions rather increase upon me, I made up my mind to defer further consideration of them till breakfast-time, when I supposed the matter would receive some elucidation.

The breakfast now came, but with it no lady in black. The breakfast over, we went to church, came home to luncheon, and so on through the day, but still no lady, neither any reference to her. I then concluded that she must be some relative, who had gone away early in the morning to visit another member of the family living close by. I was much puzzled, however, by no reference whatever being made to her, and finding no opportunity of leading any part of my conversation with the family towards the subject, I went to bed the second night more puzzled than ever. On the servant coming in in the morning, I ventured to ask him the name of the lady who dined at the table on the Saturday evening, to which he answered: 'A lady, sir? No lady, only Mrs Kirkbeck, sir.'

'Yes, the lady that sat opposite me dressed in black?'

'Perhaps, Miss Hardwick, the governess, sir?'

'No, not Miss Hardwick; she came down afterwards.'

'No lady as I see, sir.'

'Oh dear me, yes, the lady dressed in black that was in the drawing-room when I arrived, before Mr Kirkbeck came home?'

The man looked at me with surprise as if he doubted my sanity, and only answered, 'I never see any lady, sir,' and then left.

The mystery now appeared more impenetrable than ever—I thought it over in every possible aspect, but could come to no conclusion upon it. Breakfast was early that morning, in order to allow of my catching the morning train to London. The same cause also slightly hurried us, and allowed no time for conversation beyond that having direct reference to the business that brought me there; so, after arranging to return to paint the portraits on that day three weeks, I made my *adieus*, and took my departure for town.

It is only necessary for me to refer to my second visit to that house, in order to state that I was assured most positively, both by Mr and Mrs Kirkbeck, that no fourth person dined at the table on the Saturday evening in question. Their recollection was clear on the subject, as they had debated whether they should ask Miss Hardwick, the governess, to take the vacant seat, but had decided not to do so; neither could they recall to mind any such person as I described in the whole circle of their acquaintance.

Some weeks passed. It was close upon Christmas. The light of a short winter day was drawing to a close, and I was seated at my table, writing letters for the evening post. My back was towards the folding-doors leading into the room in which my visitors usually waited. I had been engaged some minutes in writing, when, without hearing or seeing anything, I became aware that a person had come through the folding-doors, and was then standing beside me. I turned, and beheld the lady of the railway carriage. I suppose that my manner indicated that I was somewhat startled, as the lady, after the usual salutation, said, 'Pardon me for disturbing you. You did not hear me come in.'

Her manner, though it was more quiet and subdued than I had known it before, was hardly to be termed grave, still less sorrowful. There was a change, but it was that kind of change only which may often be observed from the frank impulsiveness of an intelligent young lady, to the composure of self-possession of that same young lady when she is either betrothed or has recently become a matron. She asked me whether I had made any attempt at a likeness of her. I was obliged to confess that I had not. She regretted it much, as she wished one for her father.

She had brought an engraving (a portrait of Lady M. A.) with her that she thought would assist me. It was like the one she had asked my opinion upon at the house in Lincolnshire. It had always been considered very like her, and she would leave it with me. Then (putting her hand impressively on my arm) she added, 'She really would be most thankful and grateful to me if I would do it' (and, if I recollect rightly, she added), *'as much depended on it.'*

Seeing she was so much in earnest, I took up my sketch-book, and by the dim light that was still remaining began to make a rapid pencil sketch of her. On observing my doing so, however, instead of giving me what assistance she was able, she turned away under pretence of looking at the pictures around the room, occasionally passing from one to another so as to enable me to catch a momentary glimpse of her features.

In this manner I made two hurried but rather expressive sketches of her, which being all that the declining light would allow me to do, I shut my book, and she prepared to leave. This time, instead of the usual 'Good morning,' she wished me an impressively pronounced 'Goodbye,' firmly holding rather than shaking my hand while she said it. I accompanied her to the door, outside of which she seemed rather to fade into the darkness than to pass through it. But I refer this impression to my own fancy.

I immediately inquired of the servant why she had not announced the visitor to me. She stated that she was not aware there had been one, and that anyone who had entered must have done so when she had left the street door open about half an hour previously, while she went across the road for a moment.

Soon after this occurred I had to fulfil an engagement at a house near Bosworth Field, in Leicestershire. I left town on a Friday, having sent some pictures, that were too large to take with me, by the luggage train a week previously, in order that they might be at the house on my arrival, and occasion me no loss of time in waiting for them.

On getting to the house, however, I found that they had not been heard of, and on inquiring at the station, it was stated that a case similar to the one I described had passed through and gone on to Leicester, where it probably still was. It being Friday, and past the hour for the post, there was no possibility of getting a letter to Leicester before Monday morning, as the luggage office would be closed there on the Sunday; consequently, I could in no case expect the arrival of the pictures before the succeeding Tuesday or Wednesday.

The loss of three days would be a serious one; therefore, to avoid it, I suggested to my host that I should leave immediately to transact some business in South Staffordshire, as I should be obliged to attend to it before my return to town, and if I could see about it in the vacant interval thus thrown upon my hands, it would be saving me the same amount of time after my visit to his house was concluded. This arrangement meeting with his ready assent, I hastened to the Atherstone station on the Trent Valley Railway. By reference to Bradshaw, I found that my route lay through L——, where I was to change carriages, to S——, in Staffordshire.

I was just in time for the train that would put me down at L—— at eight in the evening, and a train was announced to start from L—— for S—— at ten minutes after eight, answering, as I concluded, to the train in which I was about to travel. I therefore saw no reason to doubt but that I should get to my journey's end the same night; but on my arriving at L—— I found my plans entirely frustrated. The train arrived punctually, and I got out intending to wait on the platform for the arrival of the carriages for the other line.

I found, however, that though the two lines crossed at L——, they did not communicate with each other, the L—— station on the Trent Valley line being on one side of the town, and the L—— station on the South Staffordshire line on the other. I also found that there was not time to get to the other station so as to catch the train the same evening; indeed, the train had just that moment passed on a lower level beneath my feet, and to get to the other side of the town, where it would stop for two minutes only, was out of the question.

There was, therefore, nothing for it but to put up at the Swan Hotel for the night. I have an especial dislike to passing an evening at an hotel in a country town. Dinner at such places I never take, as I had rather go without than have such as I am likely to get. Books are never to be had, the country newspapers do not interest me. *The Times* I have spelt through on my journey. The society I am likely to meet have few ideas in common with myself. Under such circumstances, I usually resort to a meat tea to while away the time, and when that is over, occupy myself in writing letters.

This was the first time I had been in L——, and while waiting for the tea, it occurred to me how, on two occasions within the past six months, I had been on the point of coming to that very place, at one time to execute a small commission for an old acquaintance, resident there, and another, to get the materials for a picture I proposed painting of an incident in the early life of

Dr Johnson. I should have come on each of these occasions had not other arrangements diverted my purpose and caused me to postpone the journey indefinitely.

The thought, however, would occur to me, 'How strange! Here I am at L——, by no intention of my own, though I have twice tried to get here and been balked.' When I had done tea, I thought I might as well write to an acquaintance I had known some years previously, and who lived in the cathedral close, asking him to come and pass an hour or two with me. Accordingly, I rang for the waitress and asked, 'Does Mr Lute live in Lichfield?'

'Yes, sir.'

'Cathedral close?'

'Yes, sir.'

'Can I send a note to him?'

'Yes, sir.'

I wrote the note, saying where I was, and asking if he would come for an hour or two and talk over old matters. The note was taken; in about twenty minutes a person of gentlemanly appearance, and what might be termed the advanced middle age, entered the room with my note in his hand, saying that I had sent him a letter, he presumed, by mistake, as he did not know my name. Seeing instantly that he was not the person I intended to write to, I apologised, and asked whether there was not another Mr Lute living in L——?

'No, there was none other.'

'Certainly,' I rejoined, 'my friend must have given me his right address, for I had written him on other occasions here. He was a fair young man, he succeeded to an estate in consequence of his uncle having been killed while hunting with the Quorn hounds, and he married about two years since a lady of the name of Fairbairn.'

The stranger very composedly replied, 'You are speaking of Mr Clyne; he did live in the cathedral close, but he has now gone away.'

The stranger was right, and in my surprise I exclaimed, 'Oh

dear, to be sure, that is the name; what could have made me address you instead? I really beg your pardon; my writing to you, and unconsciously guessing your name, is one of the most extraordinary and unaccountable things I ever did. Pray pardon me.'

He continued very quietly, "There is no need of apology; it happens that you are the very person I most wished to see. You are a painter, and I want you to paint a portrait of my daughter; can you come to my house immediately for the purpose?'

I was rather surprised at finding myself known by him, and the turn matters had taken being so entirely unexpected, I did not at the moment feel inclined to undertake the business; I therefore explained how I was situate, stating that I had only the next day and Monday at my disposal. He, however, pressed me so earnestly, that I arranged to do what I could for him in those two days, and having put up my baggage, and arranged other matters, I accompanied him to his house.

During the walk home he scarcely spoke a word, but his taciturnity seemed only a continuance of his quiet composure at the inn. On our arrival he introduced me to his daughter Maria, and then left the room. Maria Lute was a fair and a decidedly handsome girl of about fifteen; her manner was, however, in advance of her years, and evinced that self-possession, and, in the favourable sense of the term, that womanliness, that is only seen at such an early age in girls that have been left motherless, or from other causes thrown much on their own resources.

She had evidently not been informed of the purpose of my coming, and only knew that I was to stay there for the night; she therefore excused herself for a few moments, that she might give the requisite directions to the servants as to preparing my room. When she returned, she told me that I should not see her father again that evening, the state of his health having obliged him to retire for the night; but she hoped I should be able to see him some time on the morrow.

In the meantime, she hoped I would make myself quite at home, and call for anything I wanted. She, herself, was sitting in the drawing-room, but perhaps I should like to smoke and take something; if so, there was a fire in the housekeeper's room, and she would come and sit with me, as she expected the medical attendant every minute, and he would probably stay to smoke, and take something.

As the little lady seemed to recommend this course, I readily complied. I did not smoke, or take anything, but sat down by the fire, when she immediately joined me. She conversed well and readily, and with a command of language singular in a person so young. Without being disagreeably inquisitive, or putting any question to me, she seemed desirous of learning the business that had brought me to the house. I told her that her father wished me to paint either her portrait or that of a sister of hers, if she had one.

She remained silent and thoughtful for a moment, and then seemed to comprehend it at once. She told me that a sister of hers, an only one, to whom her father was devotedly attached, died near four months previously; that her father had never yet recovered from the shock of her death. He had often expressed the most earnest wish for a portrait of her; indeed, it was his one thought, and she hoped, if something of the kind could be done, it would improve his health. Here she hesitated, stammered, and burst into tears.

After a while she continued, 'It is no use hiding from you what you must very soon be aware of. Papa is insane—he has been so ever since dear Caroline was buried. He says he is always seeing dear Caroline, and he is subject to fearful delusions. The doctor says he cannot tell how much worse he may be, and that everything dangerous, like knives or razors, are to be kept out of his reach. It was necessary you should not see him again this evening, as he was unable to converse properly, and I fear the same may be the case tomorrow; but perhaps you can stay over Sunday, and I may be able to assist you in doing what he wishes.'

I asked whether they had any materials for making a likeness—a photograph, a sketch, or anything else for me to go from. No, they had nothing. 'Could she describe her clearly?' She thought she could; and there was a print that was very much like her, but she had mislaid it. I mentioned that with such disadvantages, and in such an absence of materials, I did not anticipate a satisfactory result. I had painted portraits under such circumstances, but their success much depended upon the powers of description of the persons who were to assist me by their recollection; in some instances I had attained a certain amount of success, but in most the result was quite a failure.

The medical attendant came, but I did not see him. I learnt, however, that he ordered a strict watch to be kept on his patient till he came again the next morning. Seeing the state of things, and how much the little lady had to attend to, I retired early to bed. The next morning I heard that her father was decidedly better; he had inquired earnestly on waking whether I was really in the house, and at breakfast-time he sent down to say that he hoped nothing would prevent my making an attempt at the portrait immediately, and he expected to be able to see me in the course of the day.

Directly after breakfast I set to work, aided by such description as the sister could give me. I tried again and again, but without success, or, indeed, the least prospect of it. The features, I was told, were separately like, but the expression was not. I toiled on the greater part of the day with no better result. The different studies I made were taken up to the invalid, but the same answer was always returned—no resemblance. I had exerted myself to the utmost, and, in fact, was not a little fatigued by so doing—a circumstance that the little lady evidently noticed, as she expressed herself most grateful for the interest she could see I took in the matter, and referred the unsuccessful result entirely to her want of powers of description.

She also said it was so provoking. She had a print—a portrait of a lady—that was so like, but it had gone—she had missed it from her book for three weeks past. It was the more disappointing, as she was sure it would have been of such great assistance. I asked if she could tell me who the print was of, as if I knew, I could easily procure one in London. She answered, Lady M. A. Immediately the name was uttered the whole scene of the lady of the railway carriage presented itself to me. I had my sketch-book in my portmanteau upstairs, and, by a fortunate chance, fixed in it was the print in question, with the two pencil sketches.

I instantly brought them down, and showed them to Maria Lute. She looked at them for a moment, turned her eyes full upon me, and said slowly, and with something like fear in her manner, 'Where did you get these?' Then quicker, and without waiting for my answer, 'Let me take them instantly to papa.' She was away ten minutes, or more; when she returned, her father came with her. He did not wait for salutations, but said, in a tone and manner I had not observed in him before, 'I was right all the time; it was you that I saw with her, and these sketches are from her, and from no one else.

I value them more than all my possessions, except this dear child.' The daughter also assured me that the print I had brought to the house must be the one taken from the book about three weeks before, in proof of which she pointed out to me the gum marks at the back, which exactly corresponded with those left on the blank leaf. From the moment the father saw these sketches his mental health returned.

I was not allowed to touch either of the pencil drawings in the sketch-book, as it was feared I might injure them; but an oil picture from them was commenced immediately, the father sitting by me hour after hour, directing my touches, conversing rationally, and indeed cheerfully, while he did so. He avoided direct reference to his delusions, but from time to time led the conversation to the manner in which I had originally obtained the sketches. The doctor came in the evening, and, after extolling the particular treatment he had adopted, pronounced his patient decidedly, and he believed permanently, improved.

The next day being Sunday, we all went to church. The father, for the first time since his bereavement. During a walk which he took with me after luncheon, he again approached the subject of the sketches, and after some seeming hesitation as to whether he should confide in me or not, said, 'Your writing to me by name, from the inn at L——, was one of those inexplicable circumstances that I suppose it is impossible to clear up. I knew you, however, directly I saw you; when those about me considered that my intellect was disordered, and that I spoke incoherently, it was only because I saw things that they did not.

Since her death, I know, with a certainty that nothing will ever disturb, that at different times I have been in the actual and visible presence of my dear daughter that is gone—oftener, indeed, just after her death than latterly. Of the many times that this has occurred, I distinctly remember once seeing her in a railway carriage, speaking to a person seated opposite; who that person was I could not ascertain, as my position seemed to be immediately behind him. I next saw her at a dinner-table, with others, and amongst those others unquestionably I saw yourself.

I afterwards learnt that at that time I was considered to be in one of my longest and most violent paroxysms, as I continued to see her speaking to you, in the midst of a large assembly, for some hours. Again I saw her, standing by your side, while you were engaged in either writing or drawing. I saw her once again afterwards, but the next time I saw yourself was in the inn parlour.'

The picture was proceeded with the next day, and on the day after the face was completed, and I afterwards brought it with me to London to finish.

I have often seen Mr L. since that period; his health is perfectly re-established, and his manner and conversation are as cheerful as can be expected within a few years of so great a bereavement.

The portrait now hangs in his bedroom, with the print and the two sketches by the side, and written beneath is: 'C. L., 13th September, 1858, aged 22.'

LEONAUR

ALSO FROM LEONAUR

AVAILABLE IN SOFTCOVER OR HARDCOVER WITH DUST JACKET

THE LONG PATROL *by George Berrie*—A Novel of Light Horsemen from Gallipoli to the Palestine campaign of the First World War.

NAPOLEONIC WAR STORIES *by Arthur Quiller-Couch*—Tales of soldiers, spies, battles & sieges from the Peninsular & Waterloo campaingns.

THE FIRST DETECTIVE *by Edgar Allan Poe*—The Complete Auguste Dupin Stories—The Murders in the Rue Morgue, The Mystery of Marie Rogêt & The Purloined Letter.

THE COMPLETE DR NIKOLA—MAN OF MYSTERY: 1 *by Guy Boothby*—*A Bid for Fortune* & *Dr Nikola Returns*—Guy Boothby's Dr.Nikola adventures continue to fascinate readers and enthusiasts of crime and mystery fiction because—in the manner of Raffles, the gentleman cracksman—here is character far removed from the uncompromising goodness of Holmes and Watson or the uncompromising evil of Professor Moriarty.

THE COMPLETE DR NIKOLA—MAN OF MYSTERY: 2 *by Guy Boothby*—*The Lust of Hate, Dr Nikola's Experiment* & *Farewell, Nikola*—Guy Boothby's Dr.Nikola adventures continue to fascinate readers and enthusiasts of crime and mystery fiction because—in the manner of Raffles, the gentleman cracksman—here is character far removed from the uncompromising goodness of Holmes and Watson or the uncompromising evil of Professor Moriarty.

THE CASEBOOKS OF MR J. G. REEDER: BOOK 1 *by Edgar Wallace*—*Room 13, The Mind of Mr J. G. Reeder* and *Terror Keep*—Edgar Wallace's sleuth—whose territory is the London of the 1920s—is an unlikely figure, more bank clerk than detective in appearance, ever wearing his square topped bowler, frock coat, cravat and muffler, Mr Reeder is usually inseparable from his umbrella.

THE CASEBOOKS OF MR J. G. REEDER: BOOK 2 *by Edgar Wallace*—*Red Aces, Mr J. G. Reeder Returns, The Guv'nor* and *The Man Who Passed*—Edgar Wallace's sleuth—whose territory is the London of the 1920s—is an unlikely figure, more bank clerk than detective in appearance, ever wearing his square topped bowler, frock coat, cravat and muffler, Mr Reeder is usually inseparable from his umbrella.

THE COMPLETE FOUR JUST MEN: VOLUME 1 *by Edgar Wallace*—*The Four Just Men, The Council of Justice* & *The Just Men of Cordova*—disillusioned with a world where the wicked and the abusers of power perpetually go unpunished, the Just Men set about to rectify matters according to their own standards, and retribution is dispensed on swift and deadly wings.

LEONAUR

ALSO FROM LEONAUR

AVAILABLE IN SOFTCOVER OR HARDCOVER WITH DUST JACKET

THE COMPLETE FOUR JUST MEN: VOLUME 2 *by Edgar Wallace*—*The Law of the Four Just Men & The Three Just Men*—disillusioned with a world where the wicked and the abusers of power perpetually go unpunished, the Just Men set about to rectify matters according to their own standards, and retribution is dispensed on swift and deadly wings.

THE COMPLETE RAFFLES: 1 *by E. W. Hornung*—*The Amateur Cracksman & The Black Mask*—By turns urbane gentleman about town and accomplished cricketer, life is just too ordinary for Raffles and that sets him on a series of adventures that have long been treasured as a real antidote to the 'white knights' who are the usual heroes of the crime fiction of this period.

THE COMPLETE RAFFLES: 2 *by E. W. Hornung*—*A Thief in the Night & Mr Justice Raffles*—By turns urbane gentleman about town and accomplished cricketer, life is just too ordinary for Raffles and that sets him on a series of adventures that have long been treasured as a real antidote to the 'white knights' who are the usual heroes of the crime fiction of this period.

THE COLLECTED SUPERNATURAL AND WEIRD FICTION OF WILKIE COLLINS: VOLUME 1 *by Wilkie Collins*—Contains one novel 'The Haunted Hotel', one novella 'Mad Monkton', three novelettes 'Mr Percy and the Prophet', 'The Biter Bit' and 'The Dead Alive' and eight short stories to chill the blood.

THE COLLECTED SUPERNATURAL AND WEIRD FICTION OF WILKIE COLLINS: VOLUME 2 *by Wilkie Collins*—Contains one novel 'The Two Destinies', three novellas 'The Frozen deep', 'Sister Rose' and 'The Yellow Mask' and two short stories to chill the blood.

THE COLLECTED SUPERNATURAL AND WEIRD FICTION OF WILKIE COLLINS: VOLUME 3 *by Wilkie Collins*—Contains one novel 'Dead Secret,' two novelettes 'Mrs Zant and the Ghost' and 'The Nun's Story of Gabriel's Marriage' and five short stories to chill the blood.

FUNNY BONES *selected by Dorothy Scarborough*—An Anthology of Humorous Ghost Stories.

MONTEZUMA'S CASTLE AND OTHER WEIRD TALES *by Charles B. Cory*—Cory has written a superb collection of eighteen ghostly and weird stories to chill and thrill the avid enthusiast of supernatural fiction.

SUPERNATURAL BUCHAN *by John Buchan*—Stories of Ancient Spirits, Uncanny Places & Strange Creatures.